"When I heard that Barbara Ann Wright was starting a new fantasy series about three sisters…I knew I wanted to read these books. *The Noble and the Nightingale* is a very intriguing beginning to this series… This novel has something for everyone…The tale is well-written. The setting and world building is superb. The characters are well developed and easy to connect with. The story kept my interest from the first page to the last."—*Rainbow Reflections*

"This book was a ton of fun…I think it is very approachable for all types of readers…I ended up reading this book until 3 [a.m.] because I had to know how everything would unfold and what would happen to all the characters…This is the kind of story to take you on an adventure and just have fun with. Not only could I not stop reading this book, but it put a big smile on my face. I'm a happy reader."—*Lez Review Books*

Lady of Stone

"Yet another stellar read from Barbara Ann Wright, *Lady of Stone* is a wonderful blend of magical fantasy and lesbian romance that had me eager to find out how it all ends, and yet reluctant to have it end."
—*Beauty in Ruins*

Not Your Average Love Spell

"[A] solid little fantasy tale with a lot of really cool elements…Wright plays to all the tropes…in a way that keeps the story fresh while preserving the surprises…As for the romance, that was surprisingly sweet and amusing, with four women at the heart of the story who are entirely likable…the spark of attraction and the emotional connections are undeniable."—*Fem Led Fantasy*

"[A] great story filled with magic, wondrous creatures and adventure but what I really enjoyed about the book was the way that the characters grew…It is a great thing to read in these trying times and I took hope from it. The story pulls with enough magic to feel like a fully fleshed out fantasy world while keeping our heroes relatable and engaging…I give it a full hearted thumbs up and you should definitely check it out."—*Paper Phoenix Ink*

"The adventures, as mentioned above, were plentiful. There are pirates and warriors, a yeti, giant spiders, a possible dragon, lizard people, and in general, a lot of tough-headed knights. The plot was definitely interesting, with a lot of twists and turns. The writing was seasoned with beautiful writing and truths. I highly recommend this book to lovers of fantasy and to those that want characters to be challenged to deconstruct what they know and learn how to live together. It's a beautiful book!"—*The Lesbrary*

Not Your Average Love Spell "is an entertaining…romantic fantasy adventure comedy? (I'm not sure how to categorise its Venn diagram of subgenres, either.) Starring an agoraphobic witch; a bright, curious, talkative homunculus; an archivist/scholar with a revolutionary bent; a knight who—at least initially—believes wholeheartedly in her order's mission to stamp out magic; and an invasion of genocidal warriors, *Not Your Average Love Spell* takes its characters on an entertaining ride and delivers all of them a happy ending. (Except for the genocidal warriors. Their happy ending would be terrible for everyone else.)"—*Tor.com*

The Tattered Lands

"Wright's postapocalyptic romance is a fast-paced journey through devastation…Plenty of action, surprises, and magic will keep readers turning the pages."—*Publishers Weekly*

House of Fate

"[F]ast, fun…entertaining…*House of Fate* delivers on adventure." —*Tor.com*

Lambda Literary Award Finalist *Coils*

"Greek myths, gods and monsters and a trip to the Underworld. Sign me up…This one springs straight into action…a good start, great Greek myth action and a late blooming romance that flowers in the end." —*Dear Author*

"A unique take on the Greek gods and the afterlife make this a memorable book. The story is fun with just the right amount of camp. Medusa is a hot, if unexpected, love interest…A truly unexpected ending has us hoping for more stories from this world."—*RT Book Reviews*

"The gods and monsters of ancient Greek mythology are living, breathing entities, something Cressida didn't expect and is amazed as well as terrified to discover…Cressida soon realizes being in the underworld is no different than being among the living. The heart still feels and love can bloom, even in the world of Myth…The characters are well developed and their wit will elicit more than a few chuckles. A joy to read."—*Lunar Rainbow Reviewz*

Paladins of the Storm Lord

"This was a truly enjoyable read...I would definitely pick up the next book...the mad dash at the end kept me riveted. I would definitely recommend this book for anyone who has a love of sci-fi...An intricate... novel one that can be appreciated at many levels, adventurous sci fi or one that is politically motivated with a very astute look at present day human behavior...There are many levels to this extraordinary and well written book...overall a fascinating and intriguing book."—*Inked Rainbow Reads*

"I loved this...The world that the Paladins inhabited was fascinating... didn't want to put this down until I knew what happened. I'll be looking for more of Barbara Ann Wright's books."—*Lesbian Romance Reviews*

Thrall: Beyond Gold and Glory

"Once more Barbara has outdone herself in her penmanship. I cannot sing enough praises. A little *Vikings*, a dash of *The Witcher*, peppered with *A Game of Thrones*, and a pinch of *Lord of The Rings*. Mesmerizing...I was ecstatic to read this book. It did not disappoint. Barbara pours life into her characters with sarcasm, wit and surreal imagery, they leap from the page and stand before you in all their glory. I am left satisfied and starving for more, the clashing of swords, whistling of arrows still ringing in my ears."—*Lunar Rainbow Reviews*

"In their adventures, the women must wrestle with issues of freedom, loyalty, and justice. The characters were likable, the issues complex, and the battles were exciting. I really enjoyed this book and I highly recommend it."—*All Our Worlds: Diverse Fantastic Fiction*

"This was the first Barbara Ann Wright novel I've read, and I doubt it will be the last. Her dialogue was concise and natural, and she built a fantastical world that I easily imagined from one scene to the next. Lovers of Vikings, monsters and magic won't be disappointed by this one."—*Curve*

The Pyramid Waltz

"[A] healthy dose of a very creative, yet believable, world into which the reader will step to find enjoyment and heart-thumping action. It's a fiendishly delightful tale."—*Lambda Literary*

"Barbara Ann Wright is a master when it comes to crafting a solid and entertaining fantasy novel...The world of lesbian literature has a small handful of high-quality fantasy authors, and Barbara Ann Wright is well on her way to joining the likes of Jane Fletcher, Cate Culpepper, and Andi Marquette…Lovers of the fantasy and futuristic genre will likely adore this novel, and adventurous romance fans should find plenty to sink their teeth into."—*Rainbow Reader*

"Chock full of familiar elements that avid fantasy readers will adore… [*The Pyramid Waltz*] adds in a compelling and slowly evolving romance…Set against a backdrop of political intrigue with the possibility of monsters and mystery at every turn, the two women slowly learn each other, sharing secrets and longing, until a fragile love blossoms between them."—*USA Today Happily Ever After*

For Want of a Fiend

"This book will keep you turning the page to find out the answers… Fans of the fantasy genre will really enjoy this installment of the story. We can't wait for the next book."—*Curve*

"If you enjoyed *The Pyramid Waltz*, *For Want of a Fiend* is the perfect next step. If you haven't read either, know that you'd be embarking on a joyous, funny, sweet and madcap ride around very dark things lovingly told, with characters who will stay with you for months after. The plot still moves at a fast clip. Characterisation continues to deepen—and I love that. I love seeing a passionate, adoring romantic relationship flanked by friendships."—*The Lesbrary*

A Kingdom Lost

"There is only one other time in my life I have uncontrollably shouted out in cheer while reading a book. [*A Kingdom Lost*] made the second… Over the course of these three books all the characters have blossomed and developed so eloquently…I simply just thought this whole novel was brilliant."—*Lesbian Review*

The Fiend Queen

"After reading this series, Barbara Ann Wright has made my favorite author list. Her writing always seems to sweep me away to another world. The pacing, characters, and language were all perfect…Read it! I am obsessed and I don't know how I will ever want to read a non-fantasy Lesfic ever again. I literally felt drunk off the series. Even after I was done with this book I thought about it constantly for at least two days."—*Lesbian Review*

By the Author

Visit us at www.boldstrokesbooks.com

THE MAGE
AND THE MONSTER

by

Barbara Ann Wright

2022

ISBN 13: 978-1-63679-190-6

This Trade Paperback Original Is Published By
Bold Strokes Books, Inc.
P.O. Box 249
Valley Falls, NY 12185

First Edition: October 2022

CREDITS
Editor: Cindy Cresap
Production Design: Stacia Seaman
Cover Design by Tammy Seidick

Acknowledgments

Thanks again to everyone at BSB. Cindy, you remain the best editor forever.

Thanks to my fabulous writing groups. You're my people.

And thanks as always to my mom, Linda Dunn, who never runs out of hope.

This is for everyone who's ever dealt with chronic pain.
Keep breathin'.

PROLOGUE

Vale's mother had once said that the universe never gave someone more strife than they could bear. But when she'd died the following winter, all her strife had passed to Vale. No one had mentioned that part.

Still, she could bear it, even with her stomach currently in knots. Crammed together in the crowded hold, all the mages' stomachs would be growling, but their next meal was still hours in the future. The pain in her joints hadn't subsided to a dull roar yet, and that was more accurate than any clock. The Firellians only fed them once a day, at dusk. Shuddering, blind in the dark, Vale forced her breaths to be slow and even. She had to fight through the fear, the hunger, the pain. She would do it for the others, feeling their suffering like a strike against her body. The universe didn't contain enough strife to bring her low.

Even so, she prayed the gods wouldn't test that theory.

"It's okay," she muttered to whoever crowded next to her, Audrey perhaps, or Cristobal. She couldn't tell if they heard over the creak of the ship or the water splashing against the hull or the groans and whimpering of their fellow captive mages. Still, she said, "It's okay, it's all right," over and over. She clasped random hands or patted limbs. It wasn't a lot, but it was something. While imprisoned in the hold of a Firellian ship, forced to use the precious gift of magic to kill every night, everyone needed *something*.

"It's okay. This won't last forever."

"I'm cold," someone on her left muttered in Firellian. Cristobal's voice. Vale drew him closer, wincing as she felt his ribs through his thin linen shirt. She thanked the gods that she'd picked up a great deal of his language. She could speak to his countrymen and to the Sarrasian mages. Even though their countries were at war, no one's alliances mattered down here.

Cristobal shifted, his arm bumping her hand. Pain spiked in her fingers at even that soft contact, the price of magic still sitting heavily in every joint. She'd cast too many spells the night before and hadn't gotten enough sleep yet to replenish herself. All the others were likely in the same state. Pain alone might have kept them from trying to escape during the day, but the Firellians didn't seem to trust that. No, they employed a deeper strife.

The Scourge. Even the thought of its cold metal eyes made Vale shiver. She could almost feel it waiting above, just beyond the hatch that led into the hold. The vile automaton allowed the Firellians to control the mages, to dictate how they used their magic and when, draining them until they were in agony, with hardly the energy left to feel warm inside. Somehow worse, it could take control of their bodies, too, allowing its wielder to move the mages about like puppets.

Gods and devils, she longed to break its hold, either with her magic or by prying it apart with her bare hands.

"It's okay," she said a little louder, repeating herself in both languages. "It's all right."

"Fucking isn't," a gruff voice said in Firellian. Franka. She followed that with a smattering of Othlan, a language Vale knew nothing of. She could picture Franka beating back the cold and pain with a scowl so deep, it would frighten a horde of devils.

"How did they ever get you, Franka?" Vale asked, her voice hitching as a shard of pain wandered through her spine when she chuckled. "How did they catch someone like you?"

The same way they'd all been caught. The Firellians had brought the Scourge through their towns and villages, and its wielder had commanded any potential mages nearby to come forward. She could still see the cart in her mind's eye. What should have been the greatest day of her life, the day she'd discovered she was a mage at heart, had become the worst.

No, she wouldn't think about that right now. She pushed down pain and despair and did what she could for those around her. "It's going to be okay."

Franka muttered again, her native tongue peppered with Sarrasian and Firellian swears. No doubt she'd learned those when the Scourge had first let her body go, just keeping her magic in check. Vale bet Franka had sunk her teeth into those who'd captured her. No pain in the world could stop those iron jaws. If Vale could just free her from the Scourge, she would fight the Firellians. Vale could free the others, and if she had to remain behind to cover their escape, so be it.

Thoughts of escape led her to the memory of the Sarrasian soldier she'd helped, the one with the metal bird. Zara del Amanecer. Had that only been a few days ago? Perhaps a week? Vale sighed. How could one point in time feel like both yesterday and years ago? She supposed it didn't matter. What mattered was that in the midst of a fire on Vale's old ship, Zara had pledged to help the mages if she found them again. She'd wanted Vale to escape, but…

"Gods, I'm hungry," Cristobal said, snuggling against her. "And cold. I hate it here."

He sounded young. She'd only caught glimpses of him in the light but thought he might be fourteen or fifteen, just six or seven years younger than her. "It's okay," she whispered against his hair, hugging him closer. She couldn't leave, not without the others. It would gnaw at her soul more fiercely than Franka's bite.

Vale shifted, bringing those who huddled against her closer still. Her pain clock said they had a few more hours to sleep, so she changed her litany to, "Hush, sleep now." Their captors wanted them to be tired, less able to struggle. Maybe someone well-rested could break the Scourge's hold.

Vale let her mind drift, and it landed on Zara's metal bird, another automaton but not one of control. Another kind of energy had suffused it, and Zara had seemed as worried for it as she would be for a friend.

No one would call the Scourge a friend.

Vale's thoughts grew hazier, the sounds and smells of the mages meshing with snatches of dreams until she couldn't tell what was real. Even her nightmares weren't wholly hers anymore. Her tired mind splintered, wondering if all the captives now shared the same dreams, nightmares, thoughts, all suffering together, bound in distress and agony.

A few loud *thunks* came from her right. Real or dream? When the huddled mass next to her shivered, she realized it was both, a nightmare come to life. Only the Scourge's metal feet clunked so loudly on the stairs.

The glow from a lamp spread over the hold. Vale put up a hand against the sudden glare, foggy with exhaustion and pain, but she knew what was coming down the narrow stairs. Three feet tall and barely double that length from snout to tail, the Scourge's metal body still seemed to loom. It looked vaguely like a dog: four legs, a muzzle, tail, ears, a barrel chest. Its wedge-shaped head sat atop a thick neck, and the back sloped sharply down toward its hind legs. It gleamed like a golden devil as it fixed them all with unfeeling eyes.

"Up, my lovelies," Warrane called from the bottom of the steps. It was hard not to hate him. He was a mage, too, had to be in order to power the Scourge. Vale had sensed the connection between him and the Scourge, a vague feeling, like an invisible rope tied them together. How could he do this to people just like him?

He held a lantern high, and a golden bangle gleamed from his wrist, a dark red gem sitting atop his pulse, his lifeforce powering the Scourge. His gray uniform was unbuttoned at the neck, and his cheeks and throat were covered in dark blond stubble. The redness around his sky-blue eyes said he'd spent another day in a liquor bottle, but he seemed as cruelly cheerful as ever. "Get up, up, up." He delivered a kick to Audrey's ankle, and she hissed. Vale tried to drag Audrey up, wincing at the pain in her shoulders.

"Night has fallen once again," Warrane sang, a mockery of cheer. Everyone huddled away from him as if a flaming brand had been flung into their midst.

But not for long.

Vale tried to brace herself. She'd had just enough sleep to ease the pain in her limbs. She wanted nothing more than to use her magic to break through these walls and spill everyone into the river to escape, but the Scourge kept her from her magic until Warrane wanted to use it.

"Time to rise," Warrane said.

Vale tried to keep her breathing even as a lead fog settled over her body. She stood straighter, watching the mages across the hold do the same. She could move her eyes, and her thoughts were her own, but her body became Warrane's to play with, his commands made real through the Scourge's power.

He shook his head, his face like a ghoul's as he seemed torn between pity and disgust. "Column, march," he said, though he needed no words at all. Vale turned with the others, everyone moving in sync, lining up for the stairs and following Warrane above.

If Vale could get her hands on that gem…

How? The Scourge controlled her magic by day and both her magic and body at night.

At least they were getting out of the hold. On the deck, under a dark sky full of stars, they were given bowls of watery porridge and hunks of bread. It tasted like nothing, and Vale supposed that was a blessing. She wanted to breathe deep, to stretch and look over the dark river, but she was forced to eat in sync with the others, Warrane's will compelling them using the Scourge's power.

This ship was slightly smaller than the first one Vale had been on, the one that Zara's firebird had destroyed. All the other mages had been evacuated, but Vale had gotten left behind, stuck behind a fallen beam, and when the Scourge had been far enough away, she'd regained control of her body. And her magic. She'd hurled a ball of lightning at the firebird, not even thinking about what its true purpose was or who it might belong to. She'd just wanted the fire to stop.

Then she'd found the metal bird in its smaller form, found Zara, sensed the kindness in them both. If only she'd had the others with her at the time. They could have escaped together. But the Scourge had caught her up in its power again as soon as she'd emerged from the burning ship.

The Firellians had not been happy about their plans for invasion crashing around their ears. The lieutenant in charge of this ship had taken on the mages and their mission. She commanded Warrane to keep a trio of mages awake during the day to keep this ship invisible. The ship had waited for a few days after the firebird had struck, watching the Sarrasians crawl over the shore, looking for traces of Firellian troops trespassing on the Sarrasian side of the river.

Vale wanted to look toward the shore now and maybe see Sarrasian torches bobbing in the dark or mages disarming the remaining traps or a squad of rescuers, but she couldn't even do that until Warrane turned them as one.

He marched them to the railing at last, and Vale finally got to look along the shore. No one seemed about, and her heart leaped at the thought that they might finally be able to get off this cursed ship. Maybe Zara had come back and was hiding in the bushes with reinforcements to rescue them. Non-mages had nothing to fear from the Scourge.

But Warrane would command the mages to attack before anyone could get close.

Gods, she could bear strife, but why did the universe have to give her so much of it?

"What is it tonight?" Warrane asked from somewhere behind her. "Are we resetting traps?"

"What good would it do?" Lieutenant Bijou's voice. She always barked at him instead of speaking normally. None of the Firellians trusted magic, and quite a few abhorred it, though Vale didn't know why. They heaped their disgust onto Warrane, too, but it didn't seem to anger him enough to turn on them.

Maybe he downed too much booze to care.

"We'll keep heading slowly downriver," Bijou said. "Where the cliffs are short enough to climb and from there to the flatlands closer to the capital. The Sarrasian patrols have thinned over three days, enough to limit the danger to us if we use your monsters to attack from the ship."

Warrane snorted a laugh. "Don't call them monsters. They're my obedient little puppies." He passed Vale and slung an arm around Cristobal's thin shoulders. "Aren't you, my sweet? You all obey the big dog." He knocked a knuckle against the Scourge's metal head.

Bijou stepped close to him. Her mouth turned down, and she smoothed a hand over her short black hair. She spared a glare for Cristobal, then Vale behind him and Franka at her side. In the dim lantern light, her dark eyes gleamed like oil. "Rabid puppies."

Warrane shrugged. "Who doesn't go a little wild when let off the leash?"

Their magic had gotten out of hand sometimes, especially when thrown around without regard for the casters or who might be in the vicinity. Vale wanted to say that, wanted to caution them, wanted to plead to be let go, whatever it took, but she could do nothing but chatter in her own head.

"Well," Bijou said with a sigh, "until we have to put them down, it's best to make use of them. Maybe when we get far enough downriver, they can burn a village or two."

Vale's stomach went cold. She wanted to plead, to scream, but all her fear got her nothing.

Franka made a soft noise. Vale would have held her breath if she could. How did Franka do that? Even something as small as a noise of protest had to take effort and concentration. Vale made a note in her mind to ask about it later, to fight past fatigue and pain and everything else to make herself known. Strife wasn't the only thing the universe handed out. There was hope. She would try harder, listen and learn and keep picking away at the Scourge's power. It might not amount to anything, but she would try, and that was something.

CHAPTER ONE

Gisele rolled over as the dim light of dawn filtered through the gauzy curtains in Henrietta's room. At least, she hoped it was dawn and not any later. Her sisters expected her at the breakfast table every morning, and she hated to disappoint them.

Or that was what she told them, anyway.

Really, she hated their endless questions about where she'd been and what she'd been up to and who she was seeing until they backed her into a corner, and she had to admit that she'd spent many nights out of the house lately.

She sighed. It wasn't her fault. Orgasms were to blame; they were even more wonderful when she didn't have to provide them for herself.

Henrietta mumbled in her sleep and shifted. Gisele smiled at her pretty profile in the dim light. Her buzzcut highlighted the sharpness of her cheekbones and the sensuousness of her lips. Her dark skin shone against the light-colored sheets and pillows. And the muscle she'd acquired since joining the constabulary had not gone unappreciated.

But Gisele still slipped out of bed and quietly into her clothes. The nights where she didn't spell herself into agony during the day were rare, and she had to take advantage of every opportunity. That was one of the lessons of pain: seize every moment. And there were many lovely people in Sarras to fool around with who shared her desire for no-strings fun.

Henrietta wouldn't care. She didn't have time for relationships and endless talking, either. And she wouldn't act like some of Gisele's other one-nighters, those poor lonely souls who sent notes or flowers or came around the guild looking for her.

Thank the gods.

It was still barely after dawn when she arrived home. She'd been fortunate enough to snag a late-night cabbie who hadn't minded a side trip to the Oligarch's Ward, a section of the city that saw little traffic late at night. A pity. It would have been much easier to sneak in and out of the house if she lived somewhere with more nightlife.

Still, she smiled at the grand old house, the del Amanecer noble seat. Even as a child, she hadn't resented that every penny her sisters had earned had gone to the house's upkeep. It was an old friend. As Gisele entered the gate, she picked up speed. The oldest sister, Adella, had inherited quite a bit of money more than a month ago, but their middle sister, Zara, still sneered at every "extravagant" expense. She would look as kindly on Gisele using a coach as she did about Gisele staying out all night.

Not that either was anyone's business.

Gisele ducked around the side, headed for the back instead of using the ponderous front door, which weighed a ton and creaked like a devil's coffin. She eased the mud room door open, stepped in, and paused beside the pantry in the kitchen. Quiet. Good. She rubbed her arms to warm them. Spring had come, but winter seemed to be dragging its feet on its way out. She paused again before going into the hall that led to the foyer and the stairs.

A *thump* came from overhead. Someone was awake.

Damn.

Gisele hurried for the stairs but heard a door open above. Why the hell was anyone up this early? She considered making a dash into one of the two front sitting rooms, but the repair people and decorators had left them awash with flotsam to trip over.

She darted back into the kitchen and pulled her cloak tighter around her. She should have kept a dressing gown down here for these sorts of emergencies. At least she wasn't wearing her mage's robes and headdress. No one would believe she'd be ready for work this early, but maybe they'd believe that she'd been unable to sleep and had dressed in the simple clothes she wore now.

And the cloak?

Double damn. She should have jammed it into the closet while she'd been in the hall.

Feeling like a complete novice at sneaking, she started the fire in the stove with a snap of magic, wincing at the twinge of pain it caused in her joints. Then she filled a kettle and began making coffee, still with her cloak around her. It would garner more attention if it was just lying around. She was still chilly, after all.

When Roni came into the kitchen, Gisele sagged in relief. If anyone knew how to keep her mouth shut and mind her own business, it was Zara's former-thief girlfriend.

Roni ran a hand up the back of her head, through her dark red hair, revealing the shaved lower half. "Oh, I'm not the first one up," she said with a smile, not a question in sight.

Gisele could have kissed her. "Just started some coffee. Feel free to help yourself when it's done." She skirted past. She'd be able to dash upstairs and change into her pajamas and dressing gown before the others got up, and hopefully, Roni wouldn't mention seeing her in anything else. That was perfect. She could just say—

"You'll trip if you don't watch where you're going."

Gisele nearly stepped back. She'd been so engrossed, she hadn't heard Zara coming down the stairs.

Fuck.

Zara frowned, looked her up and down, and probably deduced everything, including what she'd done all night and with whom and how long each activity had taken. Her dark eyes bored into Gisele's. "Why are you dressed and in your cloak?"

Gisele made herself stand straight. She wasn't *afraid* of Zara, but that stare still sent worms squirming through her middle. "Maybe I'm going out."

Zara pointed behind her. "The door is that way."

"I woke early. I was cold." Gisele lifted her chin.

"So you came down here to get your cloak instead of donning your warm dressing gown?" Zara said with a frown.

Gisele crossed her arms and debated what to do. The white of the sling holding Zara's arm stood out against her dark blue robe. It had been about two weeks since she'd returned from her mission to the Firellian border with a broken arm. Gisele couldn't shove someone who was wounded. Or light her clothes on fire. "It was upstairs and handy, all right? Can we continue this interrogation some other time?" Her plan to dress for bed and head back down wouldn't work now. The gods-damned question queen would be all over that. "I started some coffee." She pointed toward the kitchen. "But I think I've warmed up enough to go back to sleep now, so you and Roni can enjoy." She put on a leer, knowing that would irritate and unnerve Zara, who looked away right on cue.

Gisele stepped around her, resisting the urge to throw her arms up in victory.

"You've been outside," Zara said.

Gisele tried to make herself keep walking, but that wouldn't make Zara's curiosity go away. She'd only save it for later, when Adella would be awake, and though Gisele tried often enough, she couldn't quite lie to the person who'd raised her after their parents had died when she was four.

But if she just kept walking, she could figure out a way—

"Are you in trouble again? Gisele, I've told you before—"

Nope, that did it. Gods, Zara could get under her skin better than a host of devils with flaming pitchforks. Gisele turned, ready with fire, broken arm be damned.

Zara had the decency to look concerned rather than offended, at least. "We shouldn't give Adella more to worry about."

True enough. Gisele lowered her hand. "I am not in trouble," she said slowly, trying not to speak through her teeth. "I do not get into trouble. I am not a child with a curfew, Z."

"So you were out?" Zara lifted an eyebrow.

Gisele's temper spiked. "Don't raise that brow at me. I know you practice that in the mirror." What that was supposed to prove, she wasn't sure, but it ruffled Zara enough that her cheeks went a little pink under her tan. "What I've been doing and where and with whom are none of your business."

"So there's a whom to worry about as well?"

Fuck, fuck, *fuck*. She took a deep breath, tempted to shove Zara down the stairs and run, maybe break her other arm. "I'm not saying anything else." She put up a hand before Zara could speak again. "If you don't want Adella to be bothered by my forays into *trouble*, just don't mention me to her."

"It is my duty as your sister—"

"I don't need your protection."

"...and as a member of this family—"

"Of my person or my reputation."

"...to safeguard—"

"I swear to all the gods and devils, Z, I will light you on fire!"

Zara drew back, eyes wide. "Gisele," she said. She took a deep breath, obviously calming herself down.

"Zara." Gisele knew what was coming next, managed to get the words out in time with Zara's: "If you weren't my sister..."

Zara's mouth slapped shut before she got to the part about dueling.

Victory. Gisele made herself breathe again. "Just let it alone. I was outside, and it's none of your business. I wasn't doing anything to endanger myself or our house." Reputation was an outdated concept, but Zara and Adella seemed to still care about it. Gods knew why. No one else who mattered did. Some stuffy old noble might like to gossip about who she was screwing, but they couldn't really do anything else.

Zara watched her calmly for a moment. "Why didn't you just say that from the beginning?"

A thousand responses went through Gisele's head, but most of them involved swearing, and that would just stir things up again. Gods, she must have been tired if she couldn't work up the energy to keep pissing Zara off. "I don't know. Can I go to bed now?"

Zara stared as if Gisele had just announced she was a pomegranate in disguise. Not examining one's own motives was probably as strange to Zara as breathing underwater.

But Gisele would get no closer to bed without picking this burr from her collar. "I'm young and foolish?" she tried.

Zara frowned as if she knew that was a lie, but that didn't stop her from gesturing up the stairs. Gisele thanked all the gods as she turned, hesitating when Zara said, "Do you want cocoa or something to eat?"

Gisele sighed, cursing Zara for saying something so hug-worthy right after Gisele had considered killing her. "No, but thank you for worrying about me." A lot of people didn't have anyone to worry about them at all and would welcome a Zara in their lives.

If only she didn't make it so easy to want to give her to them.

CHAPTER TWO

When Gisele woke again, she rolled out of bed and paused in the hall outside her room. Everything was quiet. She sighed in relief, hoping everyone had gone about their business for the day. She wasn't due at the guild today. Good thing, too, because by the way the light came through the window at the end of the hall, it was around midday.

Fantastic. She had time for a leisurely meal without Zara's penetrating glances. She took the stairs quickly, enjoying a day free from pain so far, but hesitated at the doorway when she saw Adella seated alone at the high kitchen table.

It seemed a bit odd to find her there without her girlfriend, Bridget, but Gisele gave her a quick smile before grabbing a mug from the counter. Adella offered a warm smile in return as she sipped her coffee. The kitchen felt wonderfully cozy from the stove and was filled with the scent of whatever pastry Zara had made. The sunlight streaming through the window picked out copper highlights in Adella's blond hair, and it made her bright blue eyes gleam like jewels. She no doubt thought she was hiding her mischievous glint well, but Gisele spotted it as she sat and knew Zara had told on her.

Gisele dipped a pastry in her coffee, wondering if she should make Adella drag the truth out of her, but what the hell? She didn't need games on so fine a morning. "Yes, I got home at dawn."

"I didn't ask." Adella set her mug down.

"Did you banish the others so we can talk?"

Adella lifted one shoulder. She wore the dark blue sweater that she only wore with her fancy black trousers. She must have gotten up feeling confident. "Everyone's at work. Even with the arm, Zara still had to go to the base, which I think is stupid, but..." She shrugged again.

Gisele nodded. After being fired from her ambassadorial job, Adella had taken a dim view of all government bodies, the army included. Though she seemed to give the intelligence agency that employed Bridget and Roni some slack, at least for now. "So you don't want to talk to me about—"

"What's their name?" Adella beamed, giving up all pretext of coyness. She rested her chin on her fists like a giddy child.

Maybe Gisele did have time for a bit of a game. "Who?"

Adella didn't shift, still grinning like an idiot, eyes shining like a magpie's.

Trying to fight a grin and failing, Gisele rolled her eyes. "I'm not sure you're supposed to be this interested in your sister's love life."

"Mmm, so I should show the restraint you did when quizzing me about Bridget?"

Gisele barked a laugh. "There's really nothing to tell. It was a... one-time deal."

Still, Adella *oohed* like someone with a first crush. "And they don't have a name?"

"Names aren't important." Gisele hoped the arch tone she'd mastered conveyed how Adella, at thirty-four, was completely ignorant of the lives of those who were twenty-two.

Adella arched her brows. "They're not invited to dinner, then?"

Gisele rolled her eyes. "No one has their one-nighters over for dinner, Del."

"I do beg your pardon, O Wise Youth." She took a sip, still twinkling. "I can find out, you know. Bridget's taught me a lot about gathering information. And I can always enlist Zara's help in asking around."

"Are you trying to guarantee that no one in the city will ever talk to me again?" Gisele asked, irritation waving through her. Why was it that when she decided to play it cool, her sisters knew just how to chuck her in the oven?

"We only have your best interests at heart."

"You are both nosy troublemakers!"

"Ah." Adella put a hand to her chest and smiled like a cat in the cream. "How I've longed to have those words thrown back at me after launching them at you so often."

Gisele had to laugh. They threw her in the oven but took her out before it became too uncomfortable. It had to be the reason she hadn't killed them yet. "Henrietta is her name. Satisfied?"

"A fellow mage?"

"End of announcement."

"So unfair." Adella shook her head. "After the way you badgered me about Bridget."

"You were in love with Bridget."

Adella paused, some of the twinkle going out. "No love for poor Henrietta?"

After a long sip of coffee and a bite of pastry, which she enjoyed in the face of Adella's impatience, Gisele said, "What part of one-nighter do you not understand?"

"All of it," Adella said, staring at nothing. "I was never very good at loving and leaving."

Gisele wanted to make another crack about the gulf of years between them, but she really didn't fancy having a mug thrown at her head. "To each their own. Now, can we drop it?" Before Adella had a chance to respond, Gisele lifted a hand. "And I say that while knowing I will never stop prying into your love life, and it's not fair, and I don't care."

Adella sighed from the depths of her toes, but she also shrugged again and sipped. "No work today?" she asked after a few moments.

"Not unless I'm sent for. The head of the mages' guild is meeting with field marshals or generals or something to make a plan about the Firellian mages Zara told us about. They're worried some might be stuck on this side of the border."

Adella's eyes went wide. "You won't have to go after them, will you?"

Gisele fought down another irritated wave. "What do you think I do when on a job for the government? I have to investigate wherever they send me."

"Yes, but that's here, in Sarras, where you can be home for dinner. I meant…" She waved as if to indicate the whole world.

All the old arguments rose inside Gisele: she wasn't a child, she wasn't helpless, she was powerful and experienced. But Adella would counter them all with the worry in her eyes. Slowing her temper and counting to ten, Gisele reminded herself that Adella had an outsider's perspective when it came to magic, and all she focused on was the aftereffects: someone she cared about in pain. Even with the marvels Gisele could create, Adella would always look at her as...disabled.

She didn't want that to define her. "Like you always say, we can't see the future," she said, knowing Adella had the hardest time arguing with her own proclamations. And that did shut her up for a few moments.

Gisele fought hard to smother her aggravation completely. Adella would always worry, and Zara would always nag her to get another job, as if being a soldier was a pain-free walk down a springtime lane.

And as if being a mage was just a job.

They didn't know, couldn't know. She repeated that again and again. She hoped the guild would send her up against these Firellian mages. She'd rescue the Sarrasian ones if that was what they wanted, but the one Zara had encountered had mentioned being controlled. If that was the case, Gisele would have to pit her power against the mages just to save them.

She couldn't wait.

With her hands around her warm mug, she was tempted to let herself slip into the intra velum, a place both inside and outside herself, the in-between world where magic came from. It existed in all mages, made them feel drawn to other mages, and once someone went there, well, how could they exist without it?

Zara and Adella might as well suggest she give up breathing.

She'd slipped into it the first time by accident. At twelve years old, on a walk with Adella, Gisele had paused by an open gate in an alley to eavesdrop, a bad habit Adella had tried to break her of for years. This particular gate led into an opulent garden behind a grand house in the Oligarch's Ward. Spying on other great houses was difficult because of fences and heavy doors, but this little gate had stood open just enough for her to see a mage of the guild instructing pupils on how to meditate and seek the intra velum.

After listening for a few moments, she'd followed along and slipped right into a world of starlight. Velvety black, dark as pitch, but the stars had sat close enough to touch. They'd surrounded her, flaring and twinkling in every color, some so close together that the hues mixed and danced, pulsing. She'd felt that pulse as she'd floated without weight, outside of time, outside of physical boundaries. And that first time, she'd sensed that she could bring the stars closer, that boundless magics lay within her grasp, and all she had to do was pit her will against them until they heeded her call and then control the gifts they gave her so she wouldn't be consumed by them.

Luckily, she'd let go of the intra velum that day before trying any spells.

When the mage had shaken her, she'd slipped out of the intra velum, and cramps had overtaken her body, all her joints aflame. She'd screamed and writhed on the stones. Adella had come running from the street where she'd been speaking with a friend. The mage had known how to treat her, and he'd demanded she be brought back the following day to be properly trained since she'd slipped into the intra velum so easily.

Adella hadn't wanted to obey, even after the warnings about mages trying to control or teach themselves. Once Gisele had recovered, she'd pleaded with Adella to let her go back. Without the guided meditation, she hadn't been able to go back into the intra velum on her own, but every inch of her had yearned to merge with that place again. As much as it had hurt afterward, it had felt beyond wonderful in the moment, but she didn't have the words to describe it, then. She struggled to do so even now.

Ultimately, the threat that she could hurt herself or others had caused Adella to give in, and Gisele had learned how to draw those little stars and bend them to her will. It didn't matter if those stars were easy to access—like fire and wind and light or the star that let her read auras—or if they were more difficult to master, required a focusing chant, and had a greater cost, like invisibility and the corpse walk, either making things unseen or seeing that which was hidden from everyone else. She'd completed all spells more easily than anyone in her age group or the groups on either side of her. She was born to live among the stars.

"You're not listening to me," Adella said.

Gisele blinked. Even memories of the intra velum drew her in. But Adella wouldn't understand that. "Sorry, most of me is still asleep."

Adella nodded slowly, but there was that hint of worry in the tightening around her eyes. Gisele bit back the urge to snap. They didn't know, couldn't know.

"I'm fine," Gisele said, meeting her gaze, trying to will the truth of that statement into Adella the way she willed the magic to do her bidding.

But even the most onerous spells had nothing on Adella, not to mention Zara.

"You can't stop being a mage. I can't stop being a big sister." Adella shrugged yet again, but she seemed a tad more relaxed this time.

Gisele supposed that was the best she could hope for. She also hoped that if she was ordered to hunt enemy mages, Adella and Zara wouldn't insist on going with her. And that they wouldn't try to follow her, either. Gods, if they did that, maybe Bridget, Roni, and the entire intelligence agency would come to keep them from blundering into danger.

That might be the best she could hope for.

"What do you say to a one-nighter if you run into them again?" Adella said, looking at the ceiling thoughtfully.

It took Gisele a moment to remember the beginning of their conversation, and her mind drifted back to the feel of Henrietta's soft skin. She took a gulp of coffee to chase any sex thoughts away while sitting with her sister. Her throat tingled with the surge of heat. "I'm not going to instruct you on how to have a one-night stand."

"No one asked for instruction. I'm only curious about afterward. Is it awkward? Are you going to avoid Henrietta from now on?"

Gisele finished her coffee and stood. "I'm going out."

"Are you saying I'm too old to understand?"

"Yep."

Adella muttered something, but Gisele didn't wait to hear more. She rushed upstairs, made herself presentable in a comfortable, simple green dress with her hair loose except for a small gold comb; the inset emeralds would subtly proclaim she wasn't a nobody.

She grabbed her cloak and was out the front door at speed, yelling "Bye, Del," over her shoulder. Nothing good could come from waiting for a response.

It was too early to go to one of her regular bars, and coffee shops weren't fashionable at the moment. Some of her friends might be lingering near the vendors on Bond Street, at the edge of the Ward, but Henrietta might be there, too.

And Adella had been on the right track. Running into a one-nighter could get awkward.

She'd check in at the guild, then. She wasn't in her robes, so she likely wouldn't be pulled into any jobs, but she might find someone willing to go for a long lunch and keep her away from home until Adella found something else to occupy her time. She was still wondering how long that might take when she reached the guild house and stepped into a scene of chaos.

Mages hurried through the grand foyer, and voices chattered desperately, the words jumbled in the press. One lone cry rose above the rest, and Gisele's chest tightened in fear at the pain in that noise. Everyone slowed, the rush of people opening just enough for Gisele to see the burned, mangled body lying atop a stretcher on the marble floor.

With a hand pressed to her mouth, she stepped closer, fighting the urge to gag at the stench of charred meat. The skin peeking through the stained white bandages was almost black, and she couldn't make out the features, but it had to be a fellow mage.

"Who…who…" She wanted to ask who had done this, who could have possibly come in here and killed a mage before anyone could stop them. "Who—" Her words cut off in a gasp as the blackened form shuddered, and one eye fluttered open to lock on her face.

Alive…oh gods…the agony.

Gisele lunged forward, falling into the intra velum, searching through her magic. She couldn't help, but, gods, she had to do something.

CHAPTER THREE

While in the intra velum, Vale could almost pretend she was living a normal life somewhere nice, surrounded by fellow mages working magic for the betterment of their society, safe and warm and valued.

Almost.

But even surrounded by the intra velum, which appeared to her as a field of bright yellow sunflowers under an endless blue sky, she felt the presence of the Scourge. Though she didn't have a body here, she felt as if she was turning constantly, trying to catch something at the edge of her vision, but it was always out of reach, just pulling, pulling, pulling. It reminded her that neither her body nor her magic was her own; her power belonged to someone else. Even in this place of wonders, she was not free, none of her fellow mages were.

She should be angry, but she'd never been good at holding on to even righteous ire. Not when her siblings had cried from lack of food or when her father had turned his hand to her. It had been easier to look to the future than focus on her feelings in those moments.

And when he'd sold her?

No, she would not think about that.

At least on the ship, she was fed every day, and that was something.

Warrane and the Scourge had showed her the intra velum, a heady freedom in her head, all her own, and no one could take it from her. Every trial she'd faced had seemed worth it for such an award. Then, they'd clapped a shackle around it, the Scourge limiting what she could do here, how long she could stay. And everyone around her was suffering the same. That lit her anger, but what could she do to help any of them?

She thought of Franka's noises of protest when the Scourge had them in its grip. She shouldn't have been able to make any noise, to fight at all, but maybe sheer spitefulness had seen it done. Was it simply a question of wills? Well, Vale could bend magic to her will, pull the right flowers to her and use their powers.

Was the Scourge that much more powerful?

While waiting on the deck of the ship for a command, Vale let her mind wander around the problem, thinking about how she manipulated the intra velum. She pulled the flowers to her to use the magic each one represented. She'd never thought about it in reverse. Struggling directly against the Scourge felt as effective as pummeling stone, but what if she tried to will herself *away* from its power, heading out among the magic instead of drawing it in.

She tried a little wiggle, ignoring the pull of the Scourge instead of focusing on it, and willing herself to drift away. The pull followed, but there was something, a small vibration like the hint of give in a chain.

"Eh, what's this?" Warrane's voice drifted through Vale's pale blue sky. "Don't reach for the power before I tell you, ragbag."

Dull pain made the sunflowers shudder, and the real world and the intra velum doubled in her vision, turning her stomach over and making her head hurt, but the Scourge wouldn't let her fall fully back to the deck of the dark, creaking ship.

Interesting. Warrane had felt her efforts but had mistaken them, too. He was a mage like they all were, only a traitor to their kind, not under the Scourge's power because he wielded it. And he hadn't sounded surprised that she was trying to do something. Also interesting. Maybe the others were trying to rebel in varying ways.

When worked collectively through the Scourge, magic was that much more powerful.

"Now," Warrane said, his voice a sour note in this place of peace. "Fire."

Under the Scourge's direction, Vale reached for the flower of flame. As always, she couldn't choose the size of the magic; the Scourge always went for the most powerful spells. Or rather, Warrane did, the better to kill with.

Vale's vision doubled again as the forest on the shore burst into light, the flames white-hot, rivaling a spear of sunlight, catching trees and animals and people alight. She forced the image away as fast as the

Scourge would let her, retreating into the intra velum where it would be harder to hear the screams.

Pain ran through her, and she leaned into it, immersing herself in the agony of her joints trying to come apart, of the feeling of hot lead under her skin as the magic took its price. She deserved to suffer, no matter if she wanted to hurt people or not. She took strange comfort in the fact that Warrane suffered, too, though she couldn't say what toll the Scourge took on him. A hefty one, she prayed to the gods in that moment. *Let it be monstrous.*

The pain subsided to a dull ache, one that would be compounded with each spell until it forced her and her fellow mages out of the intra velum and into the helpless exhaustion that made up their days. But the night was new, and they weren't finished yet. They'd finally reached the lowlands south of the towering cliffs along the border between the Firellian Empire and Sarras. From what Vale had overheard from Lieutenant Bijou and the others, they'd go ashore soon after destroying a watchtower that could report their presence. Then they'd burn and burn and burn as they moved inland, weakening Sarras as best they could so the Firellian army could march in behind them and take the capital city.

Gods, so much death. It sickened her. What would the Scourge do if the desire to throw up overwhelmed her? The feeling doubled when she thought of her fellow captives and of people like Zara del Amanecer, who'd tried to help her, and all those Sarrasian faces she wouldn't even see before she murdered them.

No, she couldn't despair. She shook it off and tried again to will herself away from the Scourge's power. She'd have to keep experimenting, find out when Warrane wasn't paying attention.

And she needed to talk to Franka, to all of them.

The night wore on, the power grating her insides, and her will became as weak as her body. Near dawn, she fell out of the intra velum, the pain forcing her out, overcoming even the Scourge. Every joint felt as if it was full of wet sand and shards of glass. Her hands and feet were numb and so swollen she barely kept from falling down the stairs as she and the other mages were shepherded into the bowel of the ship again. They were all shuffling, slow with pain and fatigue, wincing and groaning in the pale light filtering downstairs. Warrane didn't follow, no doubt in a bit of agony himself, but Vale and her fellow mages didn't need to be under control in order to trip into corners and collapse, too tired and nauseated to eat. Or to be angry or despair. Vale managed to gulp down some water, and she wanted nothing more than to collapse and wait for the pain to subside enough for her to sleep.

But she needed to speak to Franka.

Later. It could wait.

No. None of them would ever escape if she didn't try, if she didn't push through.

Gods and devils, there was no pushing through this. She told herself to move, and it told her to screw off, refusing to obey. A quiver passed through her, as if her body warned that if she pushed too hard, it would just give up and die.

She almost thought, so be it, escape or death, but that would be running away and leaving her fellow mages in danger as surely as if she'd escaped with Zara. She'd give her life for them if it came to that, but dying now would get them nothing.

After a few deep breaths, Vale managed to flop over so she was facing where Franka was an unmoving lump against the hull. "Franka?"

No answer.

Vale's shoulder screamed a protest as she scooted her arm along the floor, prodding at Franka with swollen fingers bent like claws.

"Uh?" Franka said, barely moving.

"How did you do it? How do you talk, make the noises, with the Scourge?" She couldn't keep her words from slurring with fatigue. Franka didn't answer. Vale nearly wept at the thought that she'd have to repeat herself and use a few more precious drops of energy. She wasn't doing anything but pushing sleep further away, and she couldn't—

Franka mumbled something in her native tongue.

"What?" Vale said. She hadn't managed to pick up Othlan the way she'd learned Firellian. Franka didn't speak enough for that.

"Anger, girl," Franka barked. "Get anger."

That was no doubt as good as Vale would get, and her eyes were slipping closed anyway. Get anger. Great. The emotion that seemed the most pointless.

But if it would help her fight the Scourge...

As she drifted to sleep, she made herself linger on the plight of the others, on the undiscovered mages the Firellians might enslave in the future. What would her life have been like if someone had gotten angry on her behalf?

If she could do it for others, it had to be done.

❖

Gisele couldn't stop staring at the spot where Marco had died. They hadn't been close. He'd been several years older and as dull as could be, much more interested in the philosophy around magic than the idea of embracing and using power, but he'd still been a mage.

And he was dead.

Mages didn't die. They retired. She'd heard that as a joke somewhere, but it hadn't made sense at the time and seemed cruel now.

"What happened?" she asked. It felt just like when she'd been standing over him and practically wringing her hands, skimming the edge of the intra velum, making her joints ping and ache, but not actually touching the magic because there was nothing she could do, that anyone could do. Magic couldn't heal.

It couldn't bring back the dead.

"I don't know," Marcella said. She perched on the arm of Gisele's chair and seemed as unable to look at the spot where Marco had died as Gisele was unable to look away. She kept sucking her lip, her light brown skin seeming nearly green beneath the scattering of freckles across her cheeks. Her pale green eyes were hazy with tears, the whites bloodshot, and the skin around them puffy and swollen. She sniffed and dashed the heel of her hand across her nose.

Adella would have clucked at her and rooted around for a handkerchief. Gisele just put a hand on her knee. Marco's death hadn't been Marcella's fault—or any of their faults—but she was a very empathic friend. Gisele was happy to be her rock, to let Marcella depend on her in a way Adella and Zara never did.

"It's going to be all right," Gisele said softly, not believing that for a moment, but Marcella smiled softly, perhaps gleaning some comfort.

When Serrah Fabiola, current maestro of the mages' guild, cleared her throat from the head of the stairs, Gisele stood. Marcella followed suit, and shuffling echoed through the guild house as everyone came out, no one talking. The air was too still, as if even the walls were holding their breath.

Serrah Fabiola's black hair gleamed nearly blue where it cascaded down her back, a daring scoff at fashion. She wore her robe tight over her voluptuous body and squeezed her be-ringed hands in front of her. "Marco has passed."

Gisele gritted her teeth. He'd passed while still downstairs. It must have been the spirit of Zara that made Gisele want to correct her and say that what she meant was the medics couldn't save him, that they'd done all they could in the field and at home, but he'd been too burned to live.

"He had been on loan to the army, and I am assured that his condition was the work of Firellian mages."

A collective gasp came from every room, the house breathing again. Gisele clenched a fist. She'd heard quite a bit about these Firellian mages, not much from Zara, as a sister might expect, but from other mages, from the odd word from Roni or Bridget, who worked with Sarrasian intelligence.

"Is their army advancing?" someone asked.

Serrah Fabiola waited a moment before sighing and shrugging. "They obviously have some mages left on our shores." When quiet murmurs followed, she raised one hand and squared her shoulders. "And we shall stop them."

The murmurs shifted now as the mages reorganized themselves, those who had magic enough to do battle coming to the front, and the researchers falling back. Gisele stepped forward, not needing the way Serrah Fabiola's eyes fell upon her to tell her she would be going, carrying the honor of the guild and the safety of Sarras on her shoulders.

She'd do it for Marco, for her sisters, for Sarras, but mostly, she'd do it to hand these Firellian mages their asses. If they were victims of kidnapping, she'd free them, but if they weren't...

Just the idea of truly flexing her power made her mouth water. Revenge for Marco and protecting her sisters was just icing on the cake.

But before she went to meet with any generals or whatnot, she had to look the part.

Gisele took one of the guild carriages home, then went up the stairs as quickly as she could, walking sideways to make the climb a little easier on her knees. Once in her room, she breathed deep before she donned the black robes that fit her from chin to ankle, though the lacy fabric had slits on both shoulders. Then she curled her hair before donning the headpiece with its many gems sitting along her forehead, each one a testament to her accomplishments, including the central ornament she'd received for once rooting out a Firellian spy and earning her the title of spy hunter.

The youngest one in history, she avoided saying out loud but thought every time. If Bridget hadn't revealed herself to Adella, Gisele would have sniffed her out at some point.

The long earrings and the jewels that dangled from the sides of her headpiece were further signs of her status to anyone who could read such things. She added some silvery makeup to her eyelids and chose a bold shade of red for her lips. All that was left was her bejeweled gloves and a satisfied look in the mirror.

The Firellians didn't stand a chance.

She forced herself to walk more slowly down the stairs, not wanting to upset any of her careful preparations. A glance at the new clock in the foyer showed she'd gotten ready faster than expected. It wouldn't do to show up at the military base before Serrah Fabiola and have to wait around. The guild carriage would linger outside as long as she wanted.

She wandered into the sitting room, wishing someone was at home to talk to, but it was probably for the best that she was alone. Adella would worry, and Zara would probably insist on accompanying her, and being shepherded by her big sisters was the last thing she needed. Roni or Bridget would have been good. Maybe they would have even shared more tidbits from their jobs. When the door opened, Gisele turned in that direction eagerly but just kept from frowning at finding Zara there instead.

"I thought you had the day off," Zara said, nodding at her robe.

"I've gotten called in."

"News of the Firellian mages?"

Any tall tales of mind-reading magic had nothing on Zara. Gisele was going to say that it was none of her business or something, but she looked worried, and Gisele knew the whole business of kidnapped mages had been wearing on her. Gisele told Marco's story quickly and ended with how she was now being summoned to the army base.

As if reading from a script, Zara said, "I'll come with you."

Gisele took a breath to say it wasn't necessary, but Zara was already thundering up the steps, calling, "I just need a few moments to freshen up."

Oh goodie. Gisele couldn't even slip out without her because Zara would catch up in no time, and then she'd be worried and pissed. Ah well, having a military escort onto a military base wouldn't be that unexpected.

Gods, she only hoped Zara didn't embarrass her.

CHAPTER FOUR

Zara kept asking when they were supposed to arrive at the base. Gisele was tempted to throw her out of the guild carriage. "Mages don't operate with military precision," Gisele said one more time, unable to keep from mocking just a little. "I was told to make ready and proceed to the base."

Zara frowned in her peculiar way that left everyone wondering if she was confused or angry. Maybe constipated. Probably all three. "Why didn't you go to the base straight from the guild house after you discovered your colleague had died?"

Gisele gestured to her outfit. "What do you suppose making myself ready referred to?"

"Do the clothes improve your magic?"

Gisele fought the urge to roll her eyes. "Would you go on duty without your uniform?"

Zara shook her head with a thoughtful expression, then frowned again. "But you were already at work without your uniform."

Gods, Gisele did not want to try to explain fashionable behavior or how one had to change clothing to fit the situation and not just the location. Zara would never get it, had probably never gotten it no matter her age. "Never mind. I wouldn't worry about it if I were you."

"If no one ever states a time—"

"Z, drop it, okay? We're on our way now. We're in the present, not the past, so you don't have to worry about the illogic of stuff that's already happened."

Zara snorted. "You sound like Roni."

"She's a smart person." And what she saw in Zara was a mystery, though Gisele was happy to see both her sisters in relationships. It gave them something else to worry about besides her.

The carriage rumbled through the gates of the base after the coach driver presented their guild credentials, and the guard checked their paperwork. At the large central building that housed the general's office, Zara lingered near the lobby even though the officer manning the reception desk waved them through.

"Commander Zara del Amanecer, requesting permission to attend the meeting," she said after the officer saluted her.

"Just come on," Gisele said quietly.

Zara didn't move while the officer hurriedly shuffled papers. "I wasn't told you were coming, Commander," he said, "but I'm sure it will be all right."

"See?" Gisele tugged on Zara's arm.

"I would prefer it if you asked the general's permission."

"Gods." Gisele's cheeks burned when the officer looked between them. But he saluted and moved down the hall. "I told you not to embarrass me." If they hadn't been in public, she might have lit Zara's trousers on fire again.

Even though she'd promised Adella she wouldn't.

"Why should you be embarrassed by proper protocol?" Zara asked. She wouldn't understand embarrassment either, not if Gisele had a thousand years to explain.

Luckily, they didn't have long to wait before the officer came back and waved them through again. "You're clear to serve as escort, Commander," he said.

Zara nodded and led the way. Gisele followed, swallowing the urge to seethe. She did not need an escort. She could protect herself. But now she was in a land where Zara felt at home. People here might understand Zara before they understood Gisele.

Gods, what a terrifying thought.

Serrah Fabiola and a few other mages waited in the office with General Antonia Garcia, whom Gisele had met once before, when she'd been summoned to this office to give her opinion on Firellian magic. She wished they'd given her a few soldiers to go after these Firellian mages then. All she'd needed was someone to help her find them. Then Marco would be alive.

She tried to put that out of her thoughts as she swept in and took a chair. At least she was the last to arrive, an important distinction, given her rank among the mages.

"I apologize if we're late," Zara said.

Gisele fought down a swear. Gods and devils.

"Not necessary," the general said. "Glad you could join us." She was a stern-looking woman with penetrating eyes and hair pulled back so tightly, it stretched the skin at her temples. Zara wasn't the only soldier who needed to learn how to relax.

"We have reached a crisis point," General Garcia said, eschewing introductions. "I'd hoped the infantry would have been able to sweep aside these mages, as they have the Firellian troops, but we've received disturbing reports from the lowlands along the river."

"Reports and a dead mage," Serrah Fabiola said, her eyes flashing.

"Many have lost their lives," the general said, but she gave a nod. "So we'll be sending strike teams upriver to catch these mages and their ships that have managed to slip past our watchtowers."

"Teams?" Marcella asked from where she practically hid behind Serrah Fabiola. "That doesn't sound like the entire army. We need protection." One of the others grumbled and nodded.

Gisele wanted to shake her head even as she also wanted to comfort her friend. Marcella seemed unable to get that the mages *were* the protection. Too many troops would only get in the way.

General Garcia lifted a hand. "When it comes to fighting magic, I was told that mages are more effective. You'll have plenty of people to guard you from mundane threats." She looked past Gisele and nodded, and Gisele turned in time to see Zara lower her hand.

Devils, she'd raised her hand to speak. How grammar school. Gisele was never going to live her down.

"What of the mages who are imprisoned?" Zara asked. "Freed, they might join our forces."

"The strike teams will rescue these mages if possible," the general said. "But your first priority must be to prevent further incursions into Sarras and to guard the lives of our citizens."

Serrah Fabiola frowned as if disagreeing. No doubt she put the salvation of mages above the other objective.

"Field Marshal Ortiz has ordered our cooperation with…" General Garcia sneered slightly before her normal look returned. "Sarrasian intelligence. A few of their members will be part of each team." Her gaze snapped to the space behind Gisele again. "And before you ask, Commander, those already on medical leave will not be allowed in the field."

Yes! At least Gisele would be spared the ignominy of her older sister trying to boss her around while she was in her element.

"But," General Garcia said, and Gisele's heart sank back into her boots, "if certain, highly specialized units wished to join a team under the command of one of the intelligence operatives, that wish would be approved."

Gisele frowned. So she wouldn't have to suffer Zara but some "specialized unit" of Zara's choice? Great. She imagined the *specialization* was probably the fact that they had been a nursemaid before becoming a soldier.

The general went on to say they'd be assigned teams and given routes and must be ready to depart in three days. She also "strongly suggested" that they opt for muted clothing and no jewels. Gisele supposed that was all right, even if the idea grated on her. But it grated less than if she were to catch her robe or headdress on a tree branch and have to be rescued from her own outfit.

After that, they were dismissed and filed from the building, but Zara held Gisele back from following Serrah Fabiola and the other mages to the waiting coaches. Marcella gave her a worried look, but Gisele waved her on, happy Zara waited for everyone to go before starting whatever lecture she had in mind.

Zara seemed nervous, scanning the ground, quite unlike herself, unless her mind was getting away from her as it sometimes did. Gisele bit back all the hasty words that wanted to charge forth and touched Zara's arm lightly, wishing Adella was there. No one got Zara back on track like her.

"It's okay," Gisele tried. "I know you're upset that they won't let you go, but—"

"It's not that." Zara frowned. "I mean, I am a little, but that's not…" She sighed, then straightened. "It's the…specialized unit."

There it was, nursemaid time. "I don't need some overprotective sergeant or stuffy colonel—"

"You mean corporal. A colonel is too high in rank to—"

"Whatever. I don't need anyone to hold my hand." Gisele glanced around at the people hurrying around the base and lowered her voice. "Look, Zara—"

"Hand-holding is not what I or the general have in mind."

"Would you quit interrupting me?"

"I could ask the same."

"If you weren't my sister," Gisele said before Zara had a chance. "I'd light your whole uniform on fire."

Zara made a hissing noise, like steam escaping, but she, too, gave a quick look around and spoke in a low tone. "The…specialized unit might just save your life. I would not even think of introducing you, save for the grievous nature of your mission and the fact that Roni will surely accompany you."

"Roni?" When Zara marched away, Gisele hurried to keep up with her longer legs. "Wouldn't she rather stay with you?" As spies for Zara went, Roni was preferable to most, but she would still be thinking of Zara first.

"She's the only one I trust with…the unit."

"Ugh. Can you stop with that ominous pause? Who the hell is this person?"

"Language."

Gisele couldn't get another word out of her until they reached a squat, unadorned stone building that looked as if it could stand the largest firebomb Gisele could throw. She was about to let loose a stream of swears guaranteed to make Zara talk, when they went inside, and a man behind a long counter handed Zara a box without her having to ask.

And what a box. Gisele knew ancient craftsmanship when she saw it and recognized the precise pattern Zara used to open it, though she was certain Zara would be unable to remember, not being a mage. When Zara lifted out a chain and jewel and looped them around her hand and wrist in another such pattern, excitement made Gisele go weak in the knees.

Gods, could it be?

"Mind your manners," Zara said before leading the way into a small room where a golden bird sat upon a perch, glinting and sparkling in the sunlight.

Gisele approached with awe, scarcely believing what she was seeing. A little squeal escaped her when the head turned, and a golden eye fixed on her.

"Gisele, this is the Vox Feram."

She barely heard the name. "You have…an automaton." The Vox leaped from the perch, the metal pieces of the body flattening and tinkling until it became a smaller version of itself and landed on Zara's wrist atop the control gem. Gisele had read about automatons, even seen a few old, broken ones, but this was so much better, the most breathtaking, exhilarating…

And it was *Zara's*?

Fury pushed the awe aside. "You have an automaton, and you never told me?"

❖

Zara went on and on about the Vox being "them" and how they had a chorus of voices and preferred this or that shape. She seemed happy to talk, at least, and continued to brag about the Vox's power until afternoon was giving way to evening. Gisele deduced that the Vox had achieved a sort of sentience, which the oldest automatons were rumored to develop, especially if they were the sort that could be operated by non-mages. The operation of any automaton took a toll on the user, but non-mages had no way to keep their consciousness separate from the automaton by putting part of themselves in the intra velum.

"How long can you operate them?" Gisele asked, circling Zara outside the armory.

Zara shifted uncomfortably, as if she didn't want to say.

Gisele fought to keep her voice level. The more emotional she got, the harder Zara was to deal with. She tamped down her temper, recalling all of Adella's lessons in controlling it, even though she'd rolled her eyes heavenward when she'd first been taught. "Come on, Z, you can't show me something so intriguing and not answer my questions."

"I suppose." Zara eased her dark hair over her shoulder. "If the Vox is fairly inactive, I can power them for days. Flying for long periods or doing a great deal of shifting cuts that down to twenty-four hours or less. For one of their mythic shapes, the answer is minutes." She cocked her head for several seconds and glanced off to the side.

A thrill of excitement coursed through Gisele. "They're talking to you right now, aren't they?" She grinned.

Zara smiled back. "I'm glad you're as in awe of them as I am. And while they are glad to meet you, they would like to know the reason for all your questions."

Gisele couldn't wait to speak to them herself. "Just wanting to know what to expect. I've never powered an automaton, let alone one who's gained sentience."

Zara took a step back, face falling. "And you aren't going to now."

Gisele had to have heard wrong. Zara couldn't wave this under her nose, then just... "Wait—"

"Why do you think I mentioned Roni going with you?"

"Roni? What the hell does she know about—" Zara opened her mouth, and Gisele held up a finger. "Don't you dare tell me to watch my language."

Zara's mouth shut with a snap before she said, "Roni is the only one I trust with the Vox." The words were strained, as if coming through her teeth.

Anger and hurt billowed inside Gisele. "I'm your sister and a mage."

"Roni and the Vox know each other." She waved vaguely. "They already have a rapport."

"The Vox is an automaton. Anyone who powers them will have a rapport."

When Zara's face went stony, and the Vox gave what sounded like an indignant squawk, Gisele knew she'd said the wrong thing.

"You're…friends with them," Gisele said, scarcely believing it, but Zara was treating the Vox like a loved one all the same. Extraordinary. She didn't quite know how to react, save that, if she laughed, she sensed she would ruin her chance to ever get her hands on the Vox.

"Yes," Zara said, the word covered in ice.

"I'm sorry." Gisele hung her head. "That's unusual, just so you know. Then again, most automatons are not sentient."

Zara nodded, her expression softening slightly. "If the Vox is an anomaly, I suppose I cannot be angry at your amazement." Her gaze slid to the side again before moving back to Gisele. "However, the Vox does not believe your contrition is wholly genuine and fears that if left in your care, they may be damaged by experimentation."

Gods and devils, the Vox wasn't just sentient. They had learned how to read people better than an actual person.

And they were right.

She bowed to them. "I continue to be amazed. But I am sorry if it seemed like I was disrespectful. I'm eager to learn, that's all." She bit her lip. "If I could just talk to you, to them," she added, glancing at Zara, "I could ease my curiosity and your fears."

"No."

Gisele waited for more, forcing herself to keep a pleasant face. "That's it? Not, 'I'll think about it,' or 'maybe later'?"

"No," Zara said again, smug little smile in place.

Gisele put her hands on her hips, temper boiling over. "Why the hell not?"

Zara rolled her eyes and began to walk back toward the armory.

"What makes Roni so much more trustworthy than me?"

"She has the best intentions for someone other than herself," Zara threw over her shoulder.

There came the hurt to go with the anger, and that just spurred the anger on, her entire history with Zara cycling around again. How the hell could she find someone insufferable *and* want to please them? She marched toward Zara's back, fighting not to fall into the intra velum and fulfill her obviously questionable intentions by throwing magic around.

The Vox watched her over Zara's shoulder with one cold eye, and she swallowed a bit of temper in a dash of fear. They did seem very intelligent; if they cared about Zara as much as she seemed to care about them…

Preposterous. Gisele was a mage, for fuck's sake. She could override the will of any automaton and best direct them. "My intentions," she said quietly as she regained Zara's side, "are to defend Sarras and its citizens, not to mention freeing these mages you're so worried about."

"All of which you can achieve without powering the Vox." She glanced at Gisele out of the corner of her eye. "But since your task may prove difficult, the Vox has agreed to travel as your ally."

A million arguments lined up in Gisele's mind: about Zara's stubbornness, about her own abilities, about the things the Vox could teach her, or hell, what she could teach them, but to badger Zara was to encourage her to dig in her heels.

Maybe Roni would be easier to sway. Gisele would have to work on her.

"Remember, Gisele, the Vox has their own mind. Even if you steal them, they will fight back."

Heat rushed to Gisele's cheeks. Seemed like the fucking Vox was a mind reader as well or near enough. Still, some protest was necessary. "I am not a thief."

Zara didn't respond, not even a twitch, and though the Vox's beak didn't seem like it could smile, they seemed as smug as Zara.

CHAPTER FIVE

Vale awoke slowly, a rarity. The fact that she could stretch and groan and blink fooled her for a moment, and she expected to see any of the places she'd laid her head other than the ship. But the darkness felt the same, along with the soft sounds of movement from her fellow captive mages and the creaks and groans of the ship. How long had it been since she hadn't been startled out of sleep? Since her waking routine did not include shouting and the odd kick?

She still felt exhausted and sore, but this slight freedom brought her fully awake. If their captors had let them sleep later than usual, perhaps…

No, the intra velum eluded her. The Scourge kept her from that, even when it wasn't controlling her body.

Vale looked at the glow outlining the trapdoor above the stairs. No one else seemed to be stirring, no doubt taking advantage of the chance for extra sleep. That was good. The fewer of them moving about, the better. She stood slowly, giving her body some time to unkink, excitement helping dull the pain of waking. She slid a foot forward, feeling for her neighbor before stepping over them in the dark. She picked her way across the floor in the same fashion, nearly grinding her teeth at how slowly she had to travel, but she couldn't risk waking everyone and having their noise bring the guards.

She wiped sweat from her forehead as she reached the steps and headed up. Any moment, Warrane could lift the trapdoor, and the Scourge would come through. Every sound above made her flinch, her heart trying to beat a path from her chest. Gods, the guards couldn't come now, not when she was so close to seeing what this small freedom might grant her.

Franka would no doubt ask, "What if they do come? What is one more beating? They haven't killed us yet."

No, not yet.

So before they could, she owed it to everyone to stretch as far as she could reach.

The bottom of the trapdoor felt rough, some of the boards not fitting as tightly as they could. She paused, listening hard, forcing herself to breathe through her nose. A low hum of voices came from somewhere nearby, but she couldn't make out the words. Damn.

Well, the devils had led her this far. And no one had killed her yet.

Vale lifted the trapdoor an inch, two, enough to bring her ear closer. The voices spoke Firellian, and it was hard to make them out with the background noise above and below. She had to fight to keep from telling her fellow captives to hush. If she lifted the door any higher, someone might see. She closed her eyes and held her breath, fighting to let herself fall into the rhythm of the speech.

"…how many?"

"Several teams…wouldn't say…"

"Bastard thinks he's in charge."

"He gets results." This voice got louder as footsteps *thunked* overhead.

Vale lowered the door a little. The moving voice sounded like Bijou, and she was coming closer.

"One day, Baxter's luck may run out but not today," Bijou said. "And any plan that gets rid of more Sarrasian mages is a good one."

"That's what they're for," someone cried. Warrane. And the stress on the word "they" left no doubt he was talking about Vale and the others.

The rest of the voices talked over him or told him to shut up. Maybe he would eventually become so angry at the other Firellians, he'd let the mages off their leash. Though the idea of being his ally still soured her stomach.

Her conscience pricked her at the thought. In a way, he seemed like a prisoner, too. As such, if he could be saved…

"Let Baxter's assassins do their jobs," Bijou said. "And we'll have fewer mages to fight when the time comes."

So they had a plan to kill Sarrasian mages before they even had a chance to encounter Vale and the others. She was happy at the thought of personally killing fewer people, but this Baxter person might hurt Zara and her family.

How could she warn them?

"…wake them up?" someone asked. When no one answered, there came a *thump*, and the same voice rose in volume. "Hey, asshole, we're finally giving you permission to speak. Shouldn't you wake up your pets?"

"Do you want them standing around like scarecrows until it's time to move?" Warrane asked with a growl.

"Let them sleep a few more hours," Bijou said. "Your metal dog will still keep them from the magic, yes?"

"Yes," he snapped.

"Good." Her footsteps faded across the floor, her next words lost in a clatter of movement. Vale fought to make out more, but it sounded as if the lot of them were moving away. Someone called something like, "where it belongs," and the voices faded completely.

She held her breath, waiting, and heard nothing more. She lifted the door a little higher. Seeing no one, she was determined to scout possible escape routes. She pushed up again, stepping out enough to see the galley surrounding her. She paused again, listening. When she turned to look behind her, she had to close her mouth on a scream.

The Scourge stood there, cold metal eyes fixed on nothing. Vale half expected it to pounce and tear her limbs off. When it didn't move, she relaxed slightly, freezing again when Warrane stepped back inside the galley, muttering, "I'll show them where I belong, the fuckers." When his eyes met Vale's, she realized she had frozen when she should have been ducking.

He stared for a moment before he took another bite of the apple he was carrying and came toward her.

Run, her inner voice shouted. Either at him or away from him, but she could do neither, and it wasn't the Scourge who held her. His bloodshot eyes didn't seem harsh as he loomed over her and took the door from her nerveless fingers.

He glanced past her. "Awake early, are we?" he asked. "And alone. Escaping?"

She couldn't answer, had no idea what to say when he wasn't shouting or striking out.

"Well?" he asked, and she started, one fist balling. "Are you coming out or going back, little mongrel pup?"

She frowned at the familiar slur and condescension. But if this was the chance for more information, she had to take it. She emerged the rest of the way and at his gesture, shut the trapdoor behind her.

❖

After Zara put the Vox away, Gisele had little left to do except brood as they took a guild carriage back home in the gathering dark. Zara would no doubt label Gisele's thoughts as plotting if she could read minds. But since nothing would convince Zara of the unique opportunity the Vox presented for study, Gisele would have to be sneaky.

Zara would forgive her once she saw the sheer amount of info Gisele could glean after just a little bit of experimentation. She was just getting to some serious daydreaming about it when something knocked against the side of the carriage.

"What was that?" Zara asked.

"Probably just a rock or something." But now the horses were slowing and meandering to the left of the road. Gisele stuck her head out the window but couldn't see much in the light from the streetlamps. An unmoving lump in the street behind them could have been a person. Had they hit someone? Why didn't they stop? "What in the gods' names is—"

The horses turned sharply, the carriage jerking toward an alley. Gisele tried to hold on to the door, but the motion tore her grip from the window and threw her into Zara. She struggled to right herself, fear and confusion warring with anger, but Zara grabbed her and pushed them both to the floor.

"Zara—" Gisele's cry of recrimination cut short as Zara clapped a hand over her mouth. Anger won in Gisele's mind as the coach rocked to a halt, and she fell into the intra velum, called the star of wind to her, and snapped back to reality with a spell ready to throw Zara into the seat and blow the door off the carriage.

When it began to open on its own, she swallowed the spell, left with an ache in her throat, as if she'd taken too large a drink, and pain flitted through her fingers. She didn't want to flatten any poor rescuer who—

Zara kicked the door, and someone on the other side grunted. Probably just an innocent bystander. Gisele pushed forward to check on them, but Zara was already sliding out. When Zara drew her saber awkwardly with her left hand, Gisele hurried after before Zara could trap her in the carriage.

The door hit her foot all the same, and she bit back a curse. "Zara, wait!"

Zara didn't spare her a glance before moving to engage a man in leather armor. Light shone from several windows above, but most of the alley stayed a mass of shadows, and Gisele squinted, fighting to keep track of who was whom so she could join the fight.

The man in leather blocked Zara's strike, and another man stood from the shadows of the wall where he'd no doubt fallen from Zara's kick. Oh shit. The armor and weapons said these weren't the helpful bystanders she'd imagined.

Even with a broken arm, Zara managed to hold two attackers at bay by swinging and kicking and staying ahead of their strikes. As impressive as she was, she wouldn't be able to hold off the third leather-clad warrior who scrambled down from the coach seat.

Gisele grinned. Time to remind everyone that she could be impressive, too.

She darted to where Zara stood in a slanting block of light coming from a window before unleashing the spell. She'd kept a lazy hold on the star of wind and unleashed it now. The three attackers flew away amidst a rain of dirt and garbage. They slammed into the wall at the alley's end, weapons falling from their hands. They fell to the ground, wheezing and groaning.

Gisele couldn't help turning to Zara, hoping to see admiration in her gaze.

Zara blinked at her before her eyes shifted to the side. She frowned hard and shoved past. Gisele swore. All she wanted was one damn word of—

Their attackers were fleeing through a door to the side. Zara ran in pursuit.

"Fuck." Gisele followed, but her joints were smarting. It was one devil-ridden spell, but still powerful, and power always took its toll. By the time she pushed through the door into a dimly lit room crowded with crates and boxes, Zara had disappeared. Gisele hurried down a twisting hallway that sported intermittent sconces. When she met someone coming around a corner, she bit back another spell as a small woman in a maid's uniform cried out.

"Go away, go away," the maid shouted as she rushed past. Gisele flattened against the wall, letting the maid continue yelling as she ran down the hall. "Murderers! Robbers!"

What had they gotten into?

More cries came from ahead. Gisele followed the noise to find Zara standing at an intersection of three halls and a staircase, looking all around, saber still drawn. People fled in all directions, dashing into rooms while others poked their heads out like curious groundhogs.

The damask wallpaper in this section and the fine carpets finally clued Gisele in about their location: the hotel at the corner of Bond and Midway. "Zara, come on." Gisele led the way toward the lobby, right where their attackers had no doubt gone if they'd scouted this escape route beforehand.

Amazingly, Zara followed without argument. In the lobby, two members of the constabulary were already coming through the doors, following the pointing fingers of patrons and staff. One hysterical person pointed at Zara and squealed, "There she is."

The constables approached, truncheons at the ready.

Gisele drew herself up, ignoring the ache in her hips. As she hoped, the constables eyed her robe and headdress. "Excuse us, serrah," one said. They gestured vaguely at Zara. "We have to question that—"

"*This* is Zara del Amanecer, a noble of Sarras, a commander in the army, and my sister."

That set them back on their heels. Gisele fought the urge to smile, happy someone finally recognized—

Zara shoved past her. "We're in pursuit of three suspects." She gave them a quick description and sent them into the hotel. Even the staff jumped at her orders once they knew her identity, fanning out or going for reinforcements.

Gisele stood there stunned. Zara didn't even ask her to help. Not that she could, admittedly. She could read the auras in the room, but there would be too many in a hotel, and she wouldn't be able to recognize the auras of the attackers from all the others.

But no one had even *asked*.

CHAPTER SIX

Vale sat at the small table in the galley and breathed hard. Warrane sat across from her, slurping at his apple and staring. What did he want? How long could they sit here before the others caught them and threw her back in the hold?

Most importantly, how could she look for possible escape routes with him watching her?

Without breaking eye contact, he reached above his head to a hanging basket and brought down a plum. "Hungry, pup?" He rolled it across the table.

Franka might have spit in his eye, but Vale had learned long ago that food was too precious to spurn. She bit into it eagerly, delighting in the juice running over her tongue before remembering her earlier thoughts about turning Warrane into an ally. Or at least, a resource. "Thank you," she said, something she'd never heard his compatriots say.

He shrugged but finally looked away as if embarrassed. So he could feel shame. She'd have to push a little further. "My name is Vale."

"I don't care about your name," he said over her. He glared at the wall, but if he was trying to sound indifferent and not more ashamed, he was failing. "Why are you awake, pup? Did I not drive you hard enough last night?"

"I've never been a good sleeper." See, she wanted to say, I'm a person, we all are, and we had lives before you took us.

But she sensed that pleas wouldn't do any good, and he got enough recrimination from the others. She fought down her emotions, determined now to plant "us" versus "them" in his mind if she could.

"I could sleep for weeks," he said, staring at nothing.

"Do they keep you awake?" She nodded at the steps that led to the main deck.

"Hmm, sometimes."

"So leave." She tried to keep her voice and face expressionless as his eyes snapped to hers. She nibbled her plum as nonchalantly as she could, as if they were comrades who could leave whenever they wanted.

He snorted a laugh. "Oh yes? Swim to the other bank and walk away, eh?"

She nodded at his half-buttoned uniform jacket. "Soldiers can't quit?"

"You're ignorant of the real world, pup." He finished eating and stood, and she knew her time was up.

Damn it. She fought the urge to cry, beyond frustrated. She'd accomplished nothing except eating half a stupid plum. Warrane started toward the trapdoor. Vale's mind raced. She had to do or say something that at least planted a seed for escape, but Warrane was right. She was ignorant. What had made her think she could manipulate him? Or stage a mutiny or beat him to a bloody pulp and toss the Scourge in the river?

Franka could have done it. But Vale stood without being prompted, pathetic and defeated as she moved toward her prison cell. It wasn't in her to be violent or turn other people's thoughts against them. She couldn't be Franka, but there had to be something she could do with this hateful man.

She flinched, moving slowly. In spite of all Warrane had done, "hateful" didn't seem fair. His crew was hateful, to him and everyone else. And the way he slouched and muttered and drank said he was suffering on some level. Perhaps to make him an ally, she'd have to actually see him as one, as a creature as pitiable as the rest of them.

She didn't touch him, but she asked, "How do you stand it?"

He looked at her curiously, and she wanted to say something about treating his fellow human beings like animals, but she couldn't shame him. Also, he wasn't a nice person, not yet, at least. Whether he could be was still unknown, but she didn't want to risk it and maybe get *thrown* into the hold.

"The Scourge," she said hurriedly. "How do you stand the pain of it?"

He nodded as if that was a reasonable question, one he understood. "It's just like any other magic, though more irritating than most."

"And how do you stand working with those…assholes?" she asked, harnessing the swear the other Firellians had lobbed at him.

It got her a smile. "The same as working with any other jerks."

"Though more irritating than most?"

He chuckled and opened the trapdoor. "Sleep, pup, or later, you'll wish you had." It wasn't kindness so much as a soft threat, but she'd take it as progress.

Vale took the rest of her plum into the darkness, a little something for whoever needed it most while she had a chance to think, maybe even dream.

❖

Gisele wanted to walk home no matter that Zara tried to forbid it. But Henrietta, her one-nighter from the night before, showed up as a member of the backup team and asked her nicely to stay inside the lobby until they'd searched the surrounding area and could arrange an escort.

Gisele had said yes only because Henrietta looked a little hurt, her eyes a bit sad, and Gisele felt guilty about sneaking out without a word that morning. She'd told herself that they'd both understood that all they had was a casual fling, but if that was true, she should have stayed to say good-bye. Henrietta wouldn't have grabbed her knees and begged her to stay. But the sad eyes said she deserved…something.

So Gisele did as she was told and sat in an uncomfortable chair in the stupid lobby, even though she didn't need a stupid, gods-cursed escort, all because of sad eyes and her stupid, gods-cursed, fucking sister.

Zara, still acting as if she was in charge, and people were listening to her, and Gisele began to feel invisible, just like when she was younger, and she couldn't wait to get back to someplace where people listened to her, and—

She took a deep breath, forced her shoulders to relax, and unclenched her hands. Her knuckles had turned white, and she'd left little pink half circles on her palms from her fingernails. She hoped her face didn't look as frustrated as she felt.

Maybe that was it. She should seem bored, above it. A mage wouldn't run around after…whoever had attacked them.

Right. She should be thinking her way through the attack, not focusing on petty bullshit. Who could have attacked them? And why? Did that have to do with Zara, too? Maybe from her foray to the border with the empire? Well, if Firellians were infiltrating Sarras, they wouldn't just go after some commander in the army. And they'd attacked a mage guild carriage, injuring the coach driver, poor woman. They had to be after mages, after Gisele.

Maybe they were after other mages in the city, too.

Gisele stood, determined to warn the others no matter Zara's commands or Henrietta's sad eyes. One of the constables tried to block her path, and she nearly reached for the intra velum.

The sight of Jean-Carlo walking through the door stopped her halfway across the carpet. What was someone from Sarrasian intelligence doing here? Bridget was on his heels.

"Gisele," Bridget said, "thank the gods you're all right." She frowned, her dark blue eyes concerned. "We heard you'd been attacked."

Her fear was touching, but right now, it only added to Gisele's frustration. "I'm fine, we're fine." She paused at a horrifying thought: "Adella's not with you, right?" The very last thing she needed was someone petting her hair and clutching her hand.

"No, I heard while I was with..." She nodded toward Jean-Carlo.

"You and Zara should come with us," Jean-Carlo said after he gave her a bow, his black braid hanging over one shoulder. His dark eyes didn't cease scanning the lobby. He wasn't that tall, but his bearing made him seem larger, his trim muscular form drawing many eyes. None of which he seemed to notice. "Adella has already been taken to a safe location."

"What location? What's going on?"

"That'll have to wait," Bridget said. She brushed strands of her short dark hair off her forehead as she nodded disarmingly at the small crowd that had gathered in the lobby. "As the most powerful person among us, Gisele, we need you to be on your guard."

Finally! Gisele gave Bridget a smile, more than ready to go now. "Has someone been sent to warn the other mages?" At their curious looks, she added, "Are the other mages in danger, or just..." She'd been about to say "me," but she feared how that would sound. And feared that it was true, at least a little. She felt the weight of everyone's eyes now, wondering where the danger might come from.

She was almost relieved when Zara joined them.

"We'll explain everything when we get to a place of safety," Bridget said.

Zara and Jean-Carlo eyed one another for a moment. He touched his chin before dropping his hand quickly, as if unaware he'd even touched his face. Zara had knocked him out with a hit there once, a feat not many had accomplished, if Adella and Bridget were to be believed.

And she'd only managed it because Gisele had made her invisible at the time.

Zara's expression didn't change to either gloating or embarrassment or even apology. She didn't dwell on the past, even when the tiniest bit of dwelling was called for.

She listened to the same hasty words Gisele had been given and agreed without question, surprising Gisele again. Jean-Carlo and Bridget led the way back down the halls they'd just come from, then turned as if steering for the rear of the hotel instead of the alley to the side.

"Why didn't you ask where we're going?" Gisele whispered to Zara, curious rather than worried.

"Haste seemed prudent," Zara said. When they paused for Bridget to peer around a corner, Zara added, "You and I are more than a match for these two in combat, even if I didn't trust Adella's paramour or Roni's colleague."

Still said without ego, so very Zara, and Gisele couldn't help a flare of pride. It was infuriating the way she could hate and love her sister simultaneously. Part of her wanted to rant and demand to know why Zara often treated her like a baby if she knew Gisele could handle herself, but Zara would no doubt say something dumb like, "You're my sister," which didn't explain and—

Gisele forced herself to stop obsessing and concentrate. If Zara had to save her...gods, she'd never hear the end of it.

When they reached the rear exit, Jean-Carlo went to scout ahead. Bridget drew close. "We've got a cab waiting two streets over. Gisele, it would be best if you removed your mage's raiment."

If the attackers were targeting mages, they could bring it on, but Gisele had the others to consider. At least Bridget didn't make it an order as Zara would have.

Zara frowned. "Can you walk that far at a brisk pace?"

"I'm not an invalid," Gisele reminded her as she removed her headdress and her jeweled gloves. "And I'm keeping my robe on, Bridget, unless you think we'll attract less attention if I'm in my underwear."

Bridget grinned, then coughed, covering her mouth as if hiding her expression. "Definitely not." She shrugged out of her jacket. "But can you wear this over it?"

"If I must." She was certain it made her look incredibly unfashionable, but hopefully, they'd be walking too quickly for anyone to recognize her.

Gods willing.

CHAPTER SEVEN

Gisele was surprised when Bridget finally opened the cab door in an alley behind a bar, a spot she recognized: the Donkey's Rest. She'd been back a few times since she'd come with her sisters to save Bridget from capture. And the proprietor, Serrah Nunez, was a favorite guest at the house.

Well, not everyone's favorite. Zara frowned as she stared at the dingy alley and the back door. She'd seemed as surprised as Gisele when they'd found out Bridget had taken Adella here on their first date. It wasn't exactly a bad part of town, but it was a far cry from the exclusive world of the Oligarch's Ward.

Of course, since then, Adella had become familiar with the many worlds of Sarras through her charity work, helping the homeless find a place to stay and aiding many others in search of employment outside of the underground economy of crime. Gisele was proud of the way Adella had become passionate about both causes through Bridget and Roni, two orphans who'd turned to criminal activity because, as Roni put it, "Morals always lose in a fight with bread."

The lantern-lit street in front of the bar was clogged with people, but no one waited in the alley. Bridget knocked on the back door, and seconds later, it nearly flew open, held by a flustered-looking man who took one look at them and jerked a thumb over his shoulder.

Bridget led the way through a hot, clamoring kitchen and upstairs to a room just under the roof, one sparsely decorated with two beds, two dressers, and two trunks. Gisele paused, overcome with memories from her last time here, when Jean-Carlo and Bridget had caught and killed a Firellian spy. And also where Zara had clobbered Jean-Carlo.

Which she wouldn't have been able to do if Gisele hadn't made them all invisible. She hoped no one ever forgot that point.

Roni, Adella, and Cortez waited inside. Gisele stepped past Roni and Zara kissing hello. She barely had a moment before Adella swallowed her in a hug.

"I'm all right," she tried to say against Adella's shoulder. Gods, why couldn't she have Zara's height so no one could crush her like this?

Adella asked the question despite just getting the answer, then cooed and clucked and looked Gisele up and down after finally releasing her.

"I'm fine, Del, really." She made herself push Adella back softly when she wanted to shove. Caring was one thing, but there were *other people* here, people who would take their cues from her.

And no sooner had Adella let go than Serrah Nunez appeared in the doorway and took her place, catching Gisele up in a whirl of color and glitter and cologne. "My sweet toffee pudding, what have they done to you?" she asked from over a foot above Gisele's head.

"Nothing," she mumbled, spitting flounces out of her mouth. "I'm fine."

"Thank the gods." Serrah Nunez held her at arm's length. She wore a gown of white and silver that bore hundreds of golden stars and shimmered with crystals and opalescent glitter. Her wig was deep black crossed with silver braids, and her eyelids and lips were painted gold. Her cheek bore a beauty mark in the shape of a star.

Gisele swallowed her irritation. She couldn't be angry with anyone whose entire being seemed geared toward generating happiness. When she smiled, Serrah Nunez's expression brightened, too. She steered Gisele to one of the beds with an unarguable grip and made her sit. "I'll fetch you a medicinal brandy."

"She doesn't need brandy," Zara said as she took a seat on the opposite bed.

"I don't," Gisele said, "but I'd love a gin cocktail."

"Coming right up." Serrah Nunez swept from the room.

Zara sighed but said nothing. Everyone except Jean-Carlo sat on the beds, even Cortez, another member of Sarrasian intelligence. And it was pretty clear from the frosty glance that he still hated Jean-Carlo's guts.

Gisele didn't know why; no one seemed to. But it was good to know.

Once Serrah Nunez returned with a tray of drinks and sat on a trunk at the end of one of the beds, Jean-Carlo cleared his throat, one arm cocked across his waist. A signet ring on his forefinger caught the light before he dropped his arm. The movement was too quick for Gisele to study the ring and determine who his family was. Why did he bother with it at all? No one wore signet rings anymore. The nobility either knew who you were, or you were nobody special. And everyone else could deduce one's station by the decorations in their hair.

His was a simple, tidy black braid, no jewels or badges, though he wore a somber, dark blue dalmatica like a noble. And he commanded a room like one, too. Everyone ceased talking, even Cortez, and gave Jean-Carlo their attention. "I'm sure you're all aware of the crisis before us. Firellian mages are still active inside the borders of Sarras."

Gisele saw poor Marco in her mind's eye and shivered.

"The Sarrasian army succeeded in driving out the Firellian soldiers," Zara said, a slight frown in place.

Looking completely unruffled, Jean-Carlo nodded to her. Gisele would have to study him and try to copy how he managed to keep Zara's imperious tone from dancing on his every nerve. "It's clear that these mages are still at large from the military reports we've received and the unfortunate death of a Sarrasian mage." He paused and turned to Gisele.

She nodded and hoped her voice wouldn't catch. "Marco. He was…" Gods damn it. "Burned almost beyond recognizing." And now Adella put a hand on hers, and she should have pulled away and straightened her spine, but she held on like a child.

"Everyone thinks these mages will continue on a path of destruction, their goal being to take or destroy the city." Jean-Carlo paused as a few of them murmured.

Roni swore, and Zara said, "The Firellians can't expect to succeed with only a few mages. Besides, the strike teams that the military has planned will stop them."

Gisele didn't know if she should be annoyed or flattered as Zara sneered at mages one moment and lauded them the next. "There's no telling what *a few mages* can do. I'm powerful enough to light someone on fire." She spared a quick glare for Zara. "I can give a ship a blast of speed or conceal several moving people." Another look for Adella and Jean-Carlo. "If these mages are as powerful as I am"—unlikely as that was—"and they are working together in unprecedented ways, who knows what they might accomplish?" Everyone seemed sufficiently cowed, so she waved at Jean-Carlo to continue.

He gave her a small bow. "Based on intelligence we've gathered and the attack today, we believe the Firellians aren't waiting for our strike teams to attack them in the field." He nodded toward Bridget, and Gisele marveled at how quickly everyone's heads turned from one side of the room to another.

"The empire is likely going to send assassins after mages here in the city," Bridget said.

Zara frowned. "Going to? We encountered them already."

Bridget shook her head. "Those were hired thugs, probably Sarrasian. There were three other attacks on mages today, and they all sounded the same, relatively easy to dispatch or elude."

"Easy?" Gisele asked, her pride grumbling.

"Relatively," Bridget repeated with a smile. "No challenge for a mage."

Ah. Gisele inclined her head, her faith in Bridget's intelligence restored.

"The real assassins are still to come," Bridget said.

Zara crossed her arms. "Why would they put their targets on guard beforehand? Why not just send the assassins?"

"It's a two-pronged attack," Bridget said. "Believe it or not, the original attacks are meant to put you somewhat at ease with how quickly they're dispatched. And if some are successful, that's just a bonus." She seemed to realize who her current audience was and offered a sheepish grin. "A bonus for terrible people. The first attack is also to test the target's strength. The assassins were no doubt watching today." She shrugged. "It's what I would have done in my spying days."

Gisele couldn't contain a little shiver, but she still wished these assassins had shown themselves. Then she could have displayed her strength for real. Adella's tightened grip on her hand made her offer a reassuring smile, but she bet Adella wouldn't have gripped Zara's hand with such worry.

"The first attack also lets the assassin see how you respond to danger, where you go afterward, and who with," Bridget said.

"Hence our roundabout route to somewhere unexpected," Jean-Carlo said, waving at the space around them.

"The other mages might scatter," Cortez added. "Wrongly thinking they'd be safer if they split up outside their guild house, making smaller targets."

Gisele sat up straighter. "You warned them about that, too, right?"

"We did," Roni said. "Don't worry."

"None of you tasty dumplings need worry," Serrah Nunez said. "Any assassin who gets in here is going to regret it." Her heavy-looking rings glinted as she brushed a stray hair off her shoulder.

"And we won't be here long," Jean-Carlo said, looking at Gisele. "Your strike team is leaving in secret tomorrow."

Worry and excitement warred in Gisele's stomach. She slipped her hand from Adella's even stronger grip before any of her fingers could break. "Who's on my team?"

"You're looking at most of them," Roni said. She pointed to herself and Bridget, then Cortez and Jean-Carlo. "Zara will collect our…specialist tomorrow, and Jean-Carlo will fetch one other mage."

"Which one?" Gisele asked. Other teams might need more than one, but she was the most powerful mage in the guild, for the devils' sake.

"Marcella Dumonde," Jean-Carlo said. "I believe she's a friend of yours?" At her nod, he added, "As we go, perhaps you and she might uncover how these Firellian mages combine their powers."

She supposed that made sense. And at least it was Marcella instead of someone annoying. Or weak. Though when it came time to fight, Marcella might hide instead of attack, embarrassing as that was. "She's not the bravest," Gisele said, feeling as if she was betraying a confidence, but they had to know.

"Understood."

Perhaps he already knew. Just how much did he know about their family and friends? His enigmatic smile in response to her stare made it seem like he could read her mind, and the answer to her question was a firm *I'll never tell.*

Just to irk him, Gisele looked at Cortez. "I'm so happy you'll be going with us. Roni says you're the best in the field."

He seemed mildly surprised but smiled, his brown eyes sparkling. Roni pursed her lips and looked away, no doubt knowing exactly what Gisele was up to. Gisele dared not look at Jean-Carlo, or she'd laugh. She'd have to ask someone about his expression later.

"What are we meant to do?" Adella asked, pointing between herself and Zara.

Bridget took her hand. "Be very careful. Anywhere you go, the assassins might think Gisele is with you or meeting you there."

"It might be best for you to stay here, honeybun," Serrah Nunez said. "At least for a few days."

"Your house will definitely be watched," Jean-Carlo said.

Zara nodded. "Or we could stay on the army base."

"Ooh." Serrah Nunez's face lit up. "I've never done that before. Count me in." She shivered delightedly. "All those uniforms."

Zara frowned. "I know I could get Adella a pass as my sister and as someone in as much danger as me, but you—"

"Me?" Serrah Nunez put a hand to her bosom. "You can't leave me behind." She struck a pose. "I'm the entertainment." After a moment, she dropped her arm. "Plus, bartender and fashion consultant." She twisted a few of her rings around. "And bodyguard, if need be."

Zara's frown didn't go anywhere. "Why would we need any of that on an army—"

"Sounds perfect," Adella cut in, smiling at Serrah Nunez. "I simply won't go anywhere without my entertainer-bartender-fashion consultant-bodyguard."

Serrah Nunez blew her a kiss.

"Well," Jean-Carlo said with an amused smile. "Now that we've got that sorted out." He looked at Gisele. "I'll need a list of whatever supplies you might want."

"Won't those assassins recognize you if you go out?" she asked. "You've been to our house often enough."

Cortez cleared his throat. "I'll do all the fetching. No one ever recognizes me."

True. He did blend in with any crowd with his eyes, hair, and skin all nearly the same shade of medium brown. How tragic for his social life. Serrah Nunez could probably give him some tips on how to stand out.

"And I've got plenty of lovely sweeties working here who'd gladly go shopping for the cause," Serrah Nunez said. "And for a generous tip."

Gisele would have to remember to ask for a tip the next time the government came calling. As the meeting broke up, she could barely contain her excitement. She was finally on her way, outside of Adella's and Zara's reach, going somewhere she could test her skills for real, saving her country and family and friends. Life didn't get much sweeter than that.

❖

Serrah Nunez's guest accommodations weren't large. Besides the attic room, she had an even smaller room that mostly served as storage.

Since no one now occupied the attic on a regular basis, Zara, Roni, and Cortez would sleep up there, Adella and Bridget got the closet, and Jean-Carlo offered to stay in the taproom after closing.

"Hanging from the rafters like a bloodsucking bat," Cortez whispered to Gisele before going upstairs.

She grinned. Working with those two was going to be fun.

As for where Gisele was going to sleep, Serrah Nunez offered to put a cot in her own room, and Gisele jumped at the chance if only to see the décor.

As she stepped into a riot of colors and sparkle and scents, she was not disappointed.

The fabric tacked to the ceiling put her in mind of the inside of a fortune teller's tent, with panels made of different colors of sparkling silk. The vanity table in the corner held so many small pots and vials and bottles, it looked like a crowded shelf in a cosmetics shop. Clothes burst from the wardrobe and hung from the open doors as well as inside. More shelves along the walls held wigs, and a large standing mirror stood open, revealing a jewelry cache so large, the mirror door probably couldn't close.

Gisele felt equal parts delighted and overwhelmed.

Then she looked at the bed.

"By the gods."

Massive. A four-poster. With intricately carved head- and footboards. It had a silk canopy *and* curtains, the latter currently open to reveal a patchwork quilt—again, silk—that glittered with beads in the light of two lamps sitting on the bedside tables.

Gisele frowned and took a step toward the closest table. Both were carved but neither had silk or jewels or glitter. They stood out.

Until she noticed that one was carved to look like a naked woman and the other a naked man, both elegantly posed so their genitals weren't on display, but every other inch of lithe, muscled skin gleamed in the light.

"All right, sweetling?" Serrah Nunez called as she came back in through the door to her private bathroom.

Gisele quickly turned away from the tables, stumbled into her cot, and tripped, sitting heavily, embarrassed to be caught ogling naked furniture.

"Oopsie," Serrah Nunez said, regarding her from the vanity mirror. She sat before it in a robe of yellow silk while she smeared some thick blue cream over her face.

Damn. Gisele had missed the no doubt once-in-a-lifetime opportunity of seeing her without makeup. She'd wound a scarf around her head, concealing her hair as well.

"Now, pudding," Serrah Nunez said as she turned, her eyes alight. "Go change into the night attire that was fetched for you, and let's dish."

Gisele rummaged in the bag under the cot and took out the long nightdress and robe Cortez had bought for her. She was sad to not have her own things, but Jean-Carlo didn't want to risk someone following Cortez from the del Amanecer house. And the garments felt comfortable, even if everything in this room put them to shame. "Dish?"

"Yes. You know." She stood and fluttered to the bed before practically leaping upon it and sitting cross-legged in the middle. "Trading tattle, spreading the buzz like busy bees." When Gisele could do nothing but stare, Serrah Nunez sighed. "Either my patter is completely out of date, or you need to get out more, crumpet. Gossip," she said slowly.

"Oh!"

"Yes!" Serrah Nunez made a shooing motion. "Get changed, hurry."

Gisele laughed, feeling like she was sleeping over with childhood friends again. She ran into the bathroom to change before hurrying back to perch at the end of the bed.

CHAPTER EIGHT

When Vale woke again, her fellow captives were already stirring. The occasional cough or groan threaded through the dark, but every voice sounded clear, rested. She thanked the gods.

"Vale?" Cristobal asked. "Are you awake?"

She grunted as she sat up. Her joints felt wonderfully average pain-wise, all her stiffness coming from sleeping on the cold wooden floor of the hold. "Mm-hmm."

"Thanks again for the fruit," he whispered.

She shook her head even as a jolt of affection made her lean against him. "You don't have to keep thanking me." He'd been the only one awake when she'd returned earlier. He'd gobbled the plum, and they'd huddled together for warmth until they'd both fallen asleep again.

The sounds of movement came from nearby, along with grumbling and a call of "Watch it" and "Mind your feet, you great ox."

Vale craned her neck, though she could only see shadows. "What's—"

Cristobal's warmth vanished with a little cry, and a new body replaced his. "You awake?" Franka.

Vale frowned. "You shouldn't go shoving people around."

Franka chuckled. "Yah, you awake. Mama bird." She clucked several times.

"What do you need, Franka?" Vale asked, irritated.

"Where go?"

"What? You're going to make me move now?" She tried to shift away, but Franka caught her arm.

"Where go?" she asked again softly as she gave Vale's arm a little shake. She said a few Othlan words, then, "In time."

"Before," Cristobal said. "She wants to know where you went a few hours ago."

So he hadn't been the only one awake. But more importantly... "You speak Othlan? You never said."

"I'm not fluent, but my papa used to trade across the border." He sounded sheepish—not to mention very young—and she couldn't be angry with him. She'd never asked, after all.

Franka rattled off a few surprised words, one being the name of her language and followed it with a *smack*. Cristobal gave a hiss of pain.

"No, Franka," Vale said as sternly as she could. "Save your anger for the soldiers." She pulled on Franka's muscled arm, then reached for Cristobal, tugging him in, too. "I was above," she whispered, "talking to Warrane."

Best not to let everyone in the hold know what she was up to, not until she had a plan. With her using Firellian and Sarrasian and Cristobal's sparse, hesitant Othlan, Vale hoped they both understood that she'd been trying to win Warrane's sympathy. If he saw Vale as a person, or even as an object of pity, it could help change his view of all the captives.

Franka made a noise of disgust and muttered something.

"I think I know that one," Cristobal said. "Weasel? Maybe stoat... or rat."

Vale patted his arm. "It's all right. I get the idea. And I don't care for him either, but if helping him do something about his own lowly status helps us, what's the harm?" She gasped as Franka took her arm again, felt down to her hand, and forced her fingers into a fist.

"This," Franka said, shaking her. She said a few more words in Othlan.

"She wants to punch him," Cristobal said. "And I think, kick him in the—"

"Again, I get it," Vale said. "Ask her how she plans to hit and kick the Scourge while she's at it."

"Anger," Franka said after the translation. "Break out." Her rough touch followed Vale's arm to her head. "Here."

Vale shook her head. "Yes. Anger and talking, we can use both."

Franka was silent for a few moments. Then she made Vale's hand into a fist again. "Then hit?"

Vale could only hope not, always wanting a nonviolent solution, but things never seemed to go that way.

Not long after their disjointed discussion, Warrane came down the stairs with the Scourge in full use, and the captive mages marched upstairs as one, onto the top deck to eat in the dark. Vale hoped she wasn't imagining Warrane's improved mood; he seemed to berate them less, and if he kicked anyone, she didn't see it.

Still, she tried to get angry at the loss of control of her own body, of her blessed magic. She managed to twitch her fingers and sneak quietly through the intra velum.

When Warrane didn't demand any spells right away, it was easier to flit through her field of sunflowers, even more so when the Firellians busied themselves devising plans for how to get their captives to the shore, leaving everyone a little distracted.

"The power of the Scourge will never reach across this distance," Warrane said, waving from the ship to the shore. The lantern light made his face a mix of shadows, his eyes glittering. "If we move only a few of your precious *monsters* at a time, we risk losing control."

"How far can you push it?" Bijou asked.

"Or should we get someone more competent?" someone else asked, the same person who had taunted him earlier that night.

"You think you can do it, Andre, hmm?" Warrane stomped past Vale, his angry steps rattling the boards underfoot.

"Keep your distance, dog," Andre said.

Vale wished she could turn and watch, using that desire to make a muscle in her neck jump. She could nearly make the fist Franka wanted, and the flower of fire burned bright in the intra velum, but she couldn't quite touch it.

Bijou shouted everyone down before saying, "How close must the Scourge be to maintain control, Warrane?"

"Close, no more than ten meters or so, maybe fifteen at a push. I can be farther from the Scourge than that and still control it. And *I* am in control, Lieutenant. The Scourge is just a tool. If you want the captives on the shore, you must bring the ship closer so they can all depart at once, the Scourge with them."

"Not if we want to get away quickly," Andre said.

"What if the Scourge is on the shore, and you are here?" Bijou asked.

He sighed, and Vale understood his frustration at having to explain magic to those who could never experience it. And they seemed to ignore most of his explanations while they bossed him around and held him in contempt. "They couldn't go far. I control them *through* the Scourge. Without it, I can do nothing."

"So true," Andre said.

Bijou had to shout again to bring them to order, finally commanding Andre to be elsewhere. "Get ahold of yourself," she said to Warrane.

"I'm perfectly calm," he said through his teeth.

Vale wondered if his anger could break through the will of the Scourge if the metal beast was turned on him. Even Franka might be impressed.

"Perhaps you should bring the ship in here and drop us off," Warrane said. "We can walk to the next target."

Bijou was silent for a few moments as she walked to the rail, her back as straight as a board. "No," she said at last. "We need you to go ashore quickly, attack targets inland, then hurry back to reboard before any Sarrasian troops can catch you. We'll practice coming in close, weighing anchor, then getting underway again."

"Shouldn't you have figured this out before now?" Warrane asked as he crossed to stand beside her.

Bijou sneered. "You think I wanted to be in charge of the monsters? If Captain Dupont hadn't gotten his ship burned up with himself aboard..." She took a few deep breaths before her face turned as calm as ever. "You will carry out my orders as I give them."

He bowed as she departed, but his "Your will, Lieutenant" sounded far from heartfelt.

Vale resigned herself to being stuck on the top deck in the cool breeze as the Firellians brought the ship as close to the shore as they dared, then set sail again, all in the dark. By the strained voices, it didn't go well. She didn't know whether to be worried or relieved.

When Bijou suggested that the mages swim for shore, Vale shivered, beyond grateful when someone else pointed out how strong the current was and how cold the water still seemed. Warrane said that his control over the mages was tightest when he made the desired movements and commanded the mages to copy him. "And I am not going to swim through the river with the Scourge on my back," he said.

Bijou snapped, "You'll do as you're told," but she didn't order them to swim, thank the gods.

Warrane returned to his spot in front of where the mages stood, leaned against the rail, and crossed his arms. When he did glance up, the look in his eyes seemed more than angry, murderous maybe.

Vale shivered again, imagining a scenario she hadn't yet thought of: Warrane using the mages to murder the crew. Would he let them go afterward? She didn't want to win her freedom with even more blood on her hands. But even if he could be convinced to help them escape while the crew still lived, some of the mages might linger and take revenge, and then they might be killed.

Gods, she had to figure out a way to keep all the mages alive.

Even Warrane?

If it could be done, she had to try.

The Firellians continued arguing logistics while Vale probed around the Scourge's control, both physically and in the intra velum, watching closely for when Warrane seemed the most distracted. The crew and the soldiers kept asking questions: how many mages could fit in one dinghy with Warrane and the Scourge? Could those left behind be drugged until his return, or was there a way to drag them behind the boat without drowning them?

Vale's anger let her clench her teeth. And they called their captives monsters?

"What about both dinghies?" Bijou said. "One in tow? There would be room for all the mages, plus two soldiers rowing in each, as well as myself. More soldiers can row in after us if we need them."

Warrane rubbed his chin and looked into the dark water. "There are so many ways the river can be unpredictable. Will that really be faster than bringing the ship in and out?"

Bijou walked up beside him. "There's one way to find out."

He snorted without humor. "It's like that old riddle with the fox, the chicken, and the sack of corn." He wiped a hand down his face. "Except if this fox gets too far from the chickens, they'll run away."

Bijou's smile could have frozen a pond. "The Scourge is the fox. The magic could be considered the corn. I guess that makes you the empty sack." She turned away, and the look he gave her back could have frozen a lake.

They loaded the mages into both dinghies, a trip into the dark that had Vale closing her eyes more than once as her body was steered without her. She sat in the first boat, looking backward over both and the ship in the distance. Warrane sat in the rear of the first boat, the Scourge at his side. Vale clenched her seat, compelled to do as Warrane did after he ordered all the mages to copy them, his will put into practice through the Scourge. The river flowed dark and quiet around them, the water sliding like oil through the puddles of lantern light.

Something struck the boat with a *bump*. Vale jerked sideways, leaning as Warrane did, but she couldn't cry out unless he let her. A dark shadow slipped past, and she conjured images of water horses and hags and other creatures from childhood tales.

She closed her eyes again, the only movement she could make on her own. It was just a branch, that was all.

A deeper *thud* sounded from the second boat, sending it off course slightly to the side, the motion dragging the first boat by the rope. Vale's heart eased into her mouth, and when Warrane gave a cry, the mages echoed him a moment later, the sudden noise sending prickles of fear over Vale's scalp.

The rowers pulled hard, trying to get the boats back in line. Vale clenched the seat so tightly, her hands went numb.

But no one had commanded her to do that.

She held in a gasp that was hers alone. She looked at her fellow mages, but the ones closest to her had their eyes shut tight. None seemed to be moving on their own, and she couldn't manage much. She dipped into the intra velum, but the flowers still seemed too far away.

Another loud *thump* came from beside her.

Then a splash.

Vale cried out in her mind, trying to turn her head to look, but she couldn't quite manage it until Warrane did. When he shouted, "There," they all shouted with him, heads whipping to the side.

A shape bobbed in the light from the ship. One of the mages was in the water. Oh gods, no.

"Keep rowing," Bijou called from the second boat. Were they going to break off and rescue the poor mage? No, they kept going toward shore.

Vale managed a whimper when she wanted to sob, to shout. Gods, they couldn't just let someone drown.

"But…he's there," Warrane said. "There!" The mages pointed and shouted along with him like a chorus crying out against Firellian orders.

The light glimmered off someone struggling in the water, far enough away from the Scourge that they had come back to themselves. They shouted, and Vale knew that voice. Cristobal.

And they weren't going to bother to save him. He had to be too terrified to use his own magic. No, no, the devils couldn't be so cruel.

"Keep quiet and keep going," Bijou said. "It's only one."

Only one mage, one monster, one mongrel. Vale's eyes burned as hot as her heart. She saw the flower of wind in her mind's eye and knew exactly how she'd use it were she able. She'd throw it under the water, willing it up beneath Cristobal to toss him back on the ship, the only place of safety. She could see the flower looming in the intra velum, could feel its power as if from behind a glass wall, and she only had to…push…through.

A tinny sound filled Vale's ears as Cristobal launched into the air just as he was passing the prow of the ship. He screamed and wriggled as he soared over the railing and banged onto the deck. Vale's head filled with the sound of angry bees, and pain rippled through her joints and head. Something hot flowed down her lips, and she tasted copper as spots danced before her vision, blocking out the view of the Firellian sailors swarming Cristobal.

"How dare you?" Bijou said as both dinghies finally reached the shore. She launched out of her boat and splashed to the first one where she grabbed Warrane by the collar. "You will only use the monsters on my orders, you shit-eating dog. Are you so desperate to die? Huh? I will wreck your fucking life, do you hear?"

He licked his lips and nodded hurriedly, even though the spell hadn't been his doing. If all the mages had unleashed the winds at once, they might have capsized the ship. When Bijou let him go, he seemed to search the faces around him until he got to Vale. His jaw dropped, but still, he said nothing. He glanced around quickly before pulling a handkerchief from his pocket and pushing through the other mages.

Vale shivered as the Scourge's control rolled over her once more. She could only stare at him while he wiped her face. He didn't meet her eyes as he commanded the mages to go ashore.

CHAPTER NINE

The next day dragged horribly. Gisele had made a list of necessities, but either Cortez or one of Serrah Nunez's employees fetched everything, and there was nothing to do except sit in the empty taproom and be bored.

When Zara came in with the Vox Feram, Gisele nearly leaped to her side, but Zara only gave her a steely glance, not even removing the Vox or their control gem from the bag she'd hidden them in. She locked herself away with Roni, no doubt to discuss Operation Ruin Gisele's Life by Not Letting Her Examine the Vox at All. If the other mages found out her sister had an automaton and she wasn't allowed near it, they'd ridicule her endlessly.

Except Marcella, of course.

And she would find out about the Vox soon because she was part of the mission. At least she wasn't one for dishing, as Serrah Nunez called it. They'd stayed up several hours trading tidbits about Gisele's sisters and the hordes of people Serrah Nunez knew. Gisele had pointed out that Jean-Carlo and Cortez seemed not to like each other. Serrah Nunez's guess was that they'd been lovers at one time, and it had ended badly.

Very interesting. Worth the occasional yawn now.

When Marcella arrived, escorted by Cortez, Gisele practically dragged her to a nook in the taproom that afforded a little privacy and filled her in on the Vox and the mission. She'd keep the gossip to herself for now.

Marcella's light green eyes stayed so wide during the tale, it was hard to know what impressed her more. By the end, she was biting her nails to the quick, and Gisele kept having to pause and forcibly remove her hands from her mouth.

"And we're leaving today?" Marcella asked, attacking her thumbnail.

Gisele grabbed her hand and held it. "Tonight. Jean-Carlo wants to use the cover of darkness."

Marcella nodded, but her gaze was faraway as her other hand lifted toward her waiting jaws.

"Chell," Gisele said, irritatingly grabbing that hand, too. "You don't have to worry. We're mages, we can take care of ourselves."

"Marco was a mage, too."

Sadness wormed through Gisele, and she squeezed Marcella's hands. "He didn't have the backup we do. Everyone going with us is not only good at combat, they're experts at getting out of tricky situations. And even though I've never worked with them myself, my sisters trust them to watch over me, over us, and that's a huge endorsement." She gave Marcella's hands a shake, forcing eye contact. "And there's an automaton, Chell. Aren't you excited about that?"

Her small smile didn't erase the worry from her eyes. "Can I stay here and talk with the Vox while you go off and do the heroic stuff?" After Gisele sighed, Marcella shook her head, pulled her hands back, and frowned. "I'm not like you, Gilly."

"Shh." She'd admitted that childhood nickname in a moment of tipsiness. She did not need it getting out.

But Marcella only crossed her arms. Better her hands tied up that way than in her mouth. "I don't want to use magic against other people, and I don't want them using it against me."

Gisele would never understand her reluctance, especially since she was one of the most talented mages in the guild. But she was also a friend. "Think of it this way, you don't have to kill anyone. There are lots of ways to subdue someone, and since some of the Firellian mages are prisoners, that's the best course of action. You can leave any heavy-duty combat to me." Mostly. "And you can focus on how the Firellian mages are managing to combine their powers. You're good at figuring out that kind of thing."

Marcella's frown slipped a bit. "And I suppose it wouldn't do you much good if I was experimenting here while you're out there." Her arms fell, and she buried her head in her hands. "I'm such a coward."

"*Tsk*, don't say things like that about a friend of mine." Gisele pulled her hands away to see a hint of a smile. "You're cautious, that's all. And pessimistic."

"Only about things that might get me killed." But she chuckled along with Gisele.

"And that statement is pessimism itself. Let's begin our journey with the basic belief that we'll live to see the end, all right?"

"Fine." She glanced around. "Besides the person who escorted me here, where are the other members of our team?"

Roni and Zara were upstairs with the Vox. She wasn't sure about the others, but they began to trickle in as the day went on. Marcella bowed after everyone was introduced, and they returned the gesture. Gisele had thought Serrah Nunez would capture Marcella's attention as the most fascinating person in any room, but she stared the most at Jean-Carlo, her cheeks going pink every time he so much as looked in her direction.

Gisele didn't get it. He was handsome enough, but he was *at least* ten years older, was a bit drab fashion-wise, and he hardly ever said anything. Maybe Marcella had a thing for noblemen, but his house had obviously faded into obscurity. Gisele's house might not have had much money after her parents had died, but Adella had made sure they'd stayed…relevant.

Ah well, whatever made Marcella more eager for the trip ahead could only be a good thing.

"I suggest we try to get some sleep," Jean-Carlo said when they'd assembled. "We won't be leaving until well after dark, when the bar is full, and we'll likely be awake most of the night."

Gisele thought it sounded a fine time to get her hands on the Vox, but Zara still carried the bag that held them. No doubt she'd sleep with them, too. There would be other opportunities.

She hoped.

Gisele didn't think she had a hope in hell of getting to sleep on an uncomfortable cot in the middle of the day while Marcella snored from where she lay at the foot of Serrah Nunez's bed, but when someone put a hand on her arm, she started out of a half dream, her brain fuzzy.

"Easy," a voice said. "Time to get up. We have to move."

She knew the voice but couldn't place it until it woke Marcella up, too. Then she made out Cortez in the light from the hall. She grabbed her bag, pushed through the stiffness that greeted her every morning, and followed Marcella into the hall. It took a moment for her brain to catch up and tell her that something wasn't right.

The sounds from the bar were only dull murmurs. Last night had been a riot of noise. And the kitchen down the hall barely bustled at all.

"What happened to leaving late?" she asked Cortez as he came downstairs with most of the others.

"His Highness isn't as clever as he thinks he is," Cortez said bitterly.

"Who?" Marcella whispered in Gisele's ear.

"He's talking about Jean-Carlo," Gisele whispered back. "They don't get along."

Marcella glared at Cortez, and Gisele rolled her eyes again. Hopefully, this small crush Marcella was developing would fade as soon as she spent more time in Jean-Carlo's company.

Bridget came through the kitchen, all bundled in a coat and scarf, even though the temperature had been improving the last few days. "We found a spy watching the Donkey. We need to go before anyone else comes."

Gisele didn't want to ask what had become of the spy. She bundled up as heavily as the others and tried to calm the butterflies in her stomach. She moved her mind into a state of readiness, reassuring herself that the intra velum was always a thought away.

"What about Zara and me?" Adella asked. "Should we go home or…"

Bridget shook her head. "We can drop you at the army base on the way."

They all clumped together, and Gisele couldn't even complain when they put her in the middle with Marcella. She'd focus on keeping her calm as well as readying her magic.

A slender figure appeared in the kitchen doorway and waved them on. Gisele thought it must be Jean-Carlo until she noticed short brown hair and narrower shoulders under a velvet jacket. They had a cap pulled low over their face, and she thought it must be one of the Donkey's employees, but she noticed a small jewel in the center of the cap, and that their cravat was affixed with a diamond stickpin.

And that cologne…

"Serrah Nunez?" she asked.

With a wink, Serrah Nunez followed Gisele through the back door into the alley. "Thought I'd be a chap tonight, tartelette, just in case." In case of what, he didn't say. Maybe just to be a further surprise in a sea of extraordinary events.

Bridget went to the end of the alley and looked both ways, then waved them forward. They hurried across the street to a smaller throughway and paused again. Gisele didn't see anyone paying them particular attention, but it was only dusk, and the bars along the street weren't yet packed. And there was still no sign of Jean-Carlo.

They twisted and turned through a few streets before Cortez peeled off, too, taking another route when they paused. The buildings were close together here and mostly silent, with a few doors opening and closing and the occasional babble of voices. Gisele held Marcella's hand and tried to determine where they were but had no clue. She made her shoulders relax, but holding herself in readiness for so long sent aches through every muscle. When Marcella tugged on her hand, Gisele nearly fell into the intra velum to grab the first spell that came to mind.

But Marcella nodded toward Roni and Zara, who were powering up the Vox. And Roni was wearing the golden chain as a glove. Gisele forced herself to relax. Not too eager, she told herself. She could enjoy the spectacle of the Vox coming to life instead of planning how to get her hands on them.

"How beautiful," Adella whispered, and she and Serrah Nunez gasped when the Vox took flight.

"The Vox Feram," Gisele whispered to them as the Vox wheeled overhead, the light of nearby lanterns gleaming off their wings. "That's the automaton that Zara's been hiding from us." When Adella glanced at her, Gisele nodded. "Please give her hell about that. For me."

"Language," Adella muttered, making no promises. But Gisele was still satisfied that Zara would answer to their older sister as she never would to Gisele.

With their scouts deployed, they continued to hurry along. Gisele thanked the gods that no one asked her to bend the light around everyone and make them invisible. She didn't know if she could do so many, even with Marcella taking some, and there wasn't a lot of light to use. And they definitely wouldn't be able to hurry. When the streets began to widen, and the buildings looked more like warehouses, Gisele guessed they were nearing the densest part of the Haymarket, a place close to the Tides that contained mostly businesses, both legal and not, the latter starting as soon as the sun went down.

But Roni seemed confident in the lead, and Gisele took comfort in the fact that a group as large as theirs wouldn't look vulnerable and so probably wouldn't be attacked. Not that she wouldn't welcome the distraction. As the smell of livestock intensified, her want of a distraction shifted into hoping they weren't going to sneak out of the city buried in a wagonload of hay or strapped to the undersides of cows.

When the Vox returned swiftly to perch on Roni's hand, she darted down a side street. Gisele went to follow, but Zara grabbed her arm. "Be ready." She drew her saber and moved to the corner.

Gisele stepped between Adella and the street Roni had taken. She fell into the intra velum and caught hold of the star of wind. Everyone knocked prone would be better than risking friend along with foe. "Ready a burst of light," she whispered to Marcella.

Marcella didn't answer, biting her lip, and Gisele could only hope she'd obey.

Bridget kneeled by Zara and peeked around the corner, one hand to the side of her face as if blocking the light from the larger street. After a tense few moments, she waved them forward. "It's all right."

Gisele let go of the intra velum, but even the small effort pained the joints in her fingers. Marcella made a small groan, and Gisele gave her a nod of sympathy. If she'd been holding on to the intra velum, too, then she'd already passed the first test: obeying orders when things got tense.

Cortez and Roni came into sight, her with a hand under his elbow while he limped slightly. Jean-Carlo followed. A pale white bandage showed from a rip in the arm of his dalmatica near his right elbow, and another crossed his hand. He came closer, revealing one bright red cheek, maybe from a hit or a burn. He looked grim, murder in his eyes.

"Are you all right?" Marcella whispered.

He didn't look at her. "Plan A is no longer available," he said to Bridget. Then he looked at Serrah Nunez. "Time for Plan B."

Serrah Nunez nodded. "Good thing I dressed for the occasion." He started back the way they'd come. "Follow me, cupcakes. Fair warning, you might get a bit damp."

"Wonderful," Bridget muttered. "The river."

CHAPTER TEN

Vale was groggy, as if she'd slept too long. Or maybe it was because she'd been plagued by nightmares where she'd been too late to save Cristobal, and her mind had conjured the worst scenarios if the Firellians found out her magic had saved him.

To her amazement, Warrane had said nothing about her the night before, even going so far as to conceal what she'd done by wiping her face with a handkerchief and taking the blame for her actions.

Or was it credit he'd taken? A chance to show the others he was still powerful or capable of rebellion no matter the consequences Bijou had hurled at him?

Answering those questions wasn't Vale's priority. She'd gone round and round in her head, trying to figure out the exact steps she'd taken to break her magic from the Scourge, but her head had been aching as if a devil lived in her skull, making it hard to think. She'd just waited tensely to be found out while worrying about what the Firellians would do to Cristobal.

Luckily, they'd seemed content to knock him unconscious, and he'd slept fitfully at Vale's side once she'd returned to the hold. He'd first come round just as she awoke; she'd eased him back to sleep. She patted his shoulder now. If luck continued to shine on him, he'd wake up with nothing more than a headache.

After last night's fracas, Bijou had kept up a steady murmur, giving Warrane dark looks, though some of the crew had seemed convinced that Cristobal had saved himself rather than admitting the possibility of Warrane being competent in any way. He hadn't seemed to mind their jibes as much. He'd still given them the odd frown and dirty look but hadn't fought back. And as Vale had stood like a statue or moved like a puppet with the others—sinking back into the Scourge's control after her break—she'd often caught Warrane peering into her face as if studying her. She hadn't been able to read his expression. Fear and anger had seemed to war with something else in his furrowed brow, wide-eyes, and pursed lips, as if he was fighting the urge to cry.

Or smile.

She didn't like the thought of that. If he was happy, it had to be because he'd found a way to use her.

Bijou had finally decided that her attack strategy would be to bring the ship in close to the shore, lower the mages into the water, and have them walk the final meters, cold as that would be. The ship would then prepare to push off as fast as they could once the mages were back onboard. That, or the mages would stay ashore and catch up to the ship farther downriver.

Vale stretched in the dark hold, looking forward to dry land at last. By the sounds of snoring, she was again up before anyone else. She thanked the gods she hadn't been chosen to stay up last night and take a shift at turning the ship invisible during the day. Sleep had allowed the pain in her head to subside.

She checked on Cristobal, and after feeling the rise and fall of his chest, she started toward the stairs. If she caught Warrane alone in the galley again, she might be able to figure out how he felt about everything that had happened.

Halfway up the stairs, she paused. Multiple voices came from directly above. Damn. Maybe she should practice breaking free from the Scourge again? But Warrane already knew it had been her the night before. She didn't want him charging down here and giving her away to the other Firellians. He'd shielded her once, but who knew if he'd do it again?

She waited, head close to the door, listening. Footsteps plodded here or there, and she dared not lift the door. The voices sounded agitated, but she couldn't make out what worried them. Best that she tried to get more sleep before—

The voices above faded as if withdrawing from the room.

Vale waited another few moments, her heartbeat echoing in her ears, before she lifted the door softly and slowly.

It flew open, and she stumbled forward, gasping from shock, then holding in a cry as she banged her knee on the stairs.

"I wondered if you'd come eavesdropping again, pup," Warrane said. His smile seemed more natural than before, though he looked even more of a mess. His hair stuck up wildly in all directions, his eyes were more red than white, his stained shirt was unbuttoned halfway down his chest, and his coat hung open.

And she could smell the booze from where she stood, even with the door and the Scourge between them.

She fought to keep her expression neutral and came up slowly when he waved her on. Her brain kept comparing him in this state with memories of her father, making her even warier. He led the way to the table and gave her an orange this time. When she began to eat it peel and all, he hesitated, blinking at her, but she wasn't going to let any food go to waste.

"If you have bananas, I'll eat that peel, too," she said quietly.

He nodded slowly. "For one in your circumstances, it makes sense."

She nearly choked. Was he finally seeing the mages as people in jeopardy? She wanted to continue pushing in that direction but wasn't sure how. "Thank you," she decided on.

"For not turning you in?"

She nodded. That, too.

"Tell me how you did it?" He leaned forward, and Vale had to fight not to lean back from the sour alcohol smell. Why did he want to know? To prevent it from happening again and score points with the others?

Lucky for her, the truth would tell him nothing. "I don't know, truly. I wanted it to happen when I saw Cristobal in the water, and it did."

Warrane nodded, looking at nothing. "I didn't think the lieutenant would decline a rescue."

"Who's the monster now?" It slipped out before she could stop it, anger and disbelief from the night before overtaking her. She hung her head to hide it. "I'm sorry." She stared at the half an orange she had left until she brought her emotions under control and lifted her eyes, again fighting memories of her father. Defiance only made the punishment worse.

But Warrane wasn't even looking at her. He finally blinked back to her as if just recalling her presence. "Finish that," he said, gesturing at the orange. "You can have another to take with you."

She did, counting that as another victory. When he didn't speak again, she had to, praying that he'd simply tell her the truth. "Why did you shield me?"

He looked at the wall for a while before seeming to notice her again, and that gamut of expressions raced across his features, some little war going on behind his eyes. He scratched at the tabletop with dirty fingernails before resting his chin in one hand. "What does the intra velum look like to you?" he asked.

Why? How could he use the knowledge against her? She didn't see a way, but she also didn't use knowledge against people in the world that existed beyond this ship, beyond the river. "A field of sunflowers." When he smiled, she asked, "And you?"

"Have you ever seen stained glass? Colored glass?"

She cocked her head. "I've seen green and brown bottles. But stained? With liquid?"

He shook his head, a little smile still in place. "They're windows made of different colors of glass." He laced his fingers. "Set together to make a picture. Like a mosaic."

She didn't know what that was either, but she'd nod along if he felt like talking. And it sounded beautiful. "That's what you see?"

"With some stained-glass windows, you have to stare a long time before the picture makes sense. The hospital down the street from where I grew up had one with the image of a doctor helping a person who lay on the ground. As a child, I thought there was a river flowing under the injured person, and it wasn't until I grew up that I realized it was blood pouring from a wound. A river of blood right from their heart."

"Frightening," she said softly.

"Hmm." He stared at nothing again. "I can never quite see the picture in the stained glass of the intra velum. I worry sometimes that part of it will turn out to be blood."

That sounded even scarier, a secret river of blood in one's mind, but it wasn't as scary as being on this river. Or being out in the world. "I grew up in a shack in the country, taking beatings from my father so my siblings didn't have to." She didn't resent those truths, not when her siblings had managed to escape that pain. Besides, they weren't as bad as everything that happened on this river, and she could hold in her tears. "Then he sold me to you, and I found out things could be much worse."

His head tilted as if she was another bit of glass he couldn't see the picture in. "Maybe that's why you broke free of the Scourge. You're more used to fighting monsters than being one."

Before Vale could figure out what that meant, Warrane stood. She followed, not knowing if she'd done any good here or not. When he took down the hanging basket of fruit, she smiled. If he was giving her that, she could share it amongst all the captives. When he shoved the basket into her arms, net and all, she bowed slightly. "Thank you."

"Don't thank me," he snapped. He grabbed her collar, bringing her in closer. She closed her eyes, expecting a blow as she leaned her head away, but he said, "Tell me, what did you think of our plans last night?"

"I don't know—"

He shook her lightly. "The boats? Wading to shore? Swimming? Can you even swim, or would you have drowned if we'd tried?"

But she wouldn't have been swimming on her own. She'd have been copying him, and if he could swim, surely—

He shook her again, more roughly this time. "Answer me." He glanced back as voices came from the top deck. "*Answer me.*"

"Yes, yes, I can swim." She gasped as he yanked her around by the collar, marching her toward the short stairs that led to the top deck. She gripped the basket. "What are you doing?" Her heart thundered in her ears. Was he going to turn her in? Then why give her the fruit? To say she'd stolen it?

"Hang the net on your arm," he said in her ear. "Keep your hands free."

Trembling, she did as she was told. They emerged into twilight that hung hazily around the ship, the colors muted and prismatic inside the shield of invisibility that cloaked them. Vale looked for the soldiers or Bijou or whoever Warrane was going to give her to. She tried to ask, but he tightened his grip, cutting off her voice as he marched her across the deck, hurrying toward the rail.

And the river.

"Farewell, Vale," he whispered. Someone shouted behind them, but he ignored them. "I hope you take your sunflowers, find your dear papa, and burn him to ash."

She choked on a sob. He wasn't going to...he couldn't...but he didn't slow. She tried to say she couldn't leave yet, not without the others, that she wanted him to help them all escape, that she was afraid, but she couldn't get the words out. "Wait," she wheezed.

But they were at the rail already, and her struggles did no good as he lifted her, threw her. She screamed as she fell through the haze and into the dark water below.

CHAPTER ELEVEN

The smell of the river hit Gisele in a wave. She'd caught a gust of wet wood earlier, but the stench of fish as her group turned onto a broader street in the Tides was like a slap in the face. Roni coughed beside her and held her gloved hand to her nose. The Vox had been exploring streets ahead, feeding Roni information, no doubt, and Gisele's jealousy ate at her.

Before she had the stench to think about.

Roni glanced at her and gave a sympathetic smile. "Not long now."

Gisele blinked, hopeful that she meant she'd soon share the Vox, then realized she probably meant it wouldn't be long before they reached their transport and got away from the smell.

She'd take whatever good news she could get.

They passed several bars or restaurants that were just gearing up for the evening, and then they were beyond the warm glow spilling from those windows and doors. They reached the docks as the last of the day faded over the horizon.

Gisele glanced behind them at the only light in the lane, then smacked into Roni's back. Roni grunted and pulled her to the side, out of the light. The Vox returned to her arm, glimmering like a falling star. Gisele kept Marcella's hand in hers. She strained to see the larger ships docked at the raised pier, but they remained part of the stygian darkness that covered the river, their location given away by creaking ropes and clattering wood and slaps of water against the hulls. After her eyes adjusted a little more, she could make out the edge of a pier, but everything beyond stayed dark, the ships' lanterns hidden by their tall sides.

Marcella shivered, clutching her tighter. "It's like a walk along the plank into hell."

Gisele chuckled to hear the sound of her own voice more than anything, proof she still existed when she couldn't even see herself.

"What are they doing?" Marcella whispered.

A low conversation was taking place between several members of their party, but Gisele couldn't make it out. She turned more toward Marcella, leaning against the side of the building, recoiling from the odor of wet tin. It felt rough and damp, no doubt pitted with rust after being buffeted every moment by the soggy air off the river.

"You'd think they'd include us in the conversation," Gisele said as she burrowed her chin into her scarf. "You know, as the linchpins of this whole operation."

"Speak for yourself."

Gisele held in a sigh of frustration. At least the darkness meant she could roll her eyes as much as she wanted.

Roni shifted, and Gisele turned toward her. The Vox had to be close, sitting on her arm or shoulder, but Gisele couldn't grope around her to find out. "Serrah Nunez has a ship ready," Roni whispered. "Some friend of hers, but she's not sure where it's berthed. I can find it while looking through the Vox's eyes, but Jean-Carlo and Bridget think someone may be watching the docks for us."

"So you can't go alone," Gisele said, fighting down the many questions that "looking through the Vox's eyes" inspired.

"We can't all fumble after you in the dark," Adella said from Marcella's other side. Gisele imagined Zara was probably pressed close to her, listening.

"No," Roni said. "But risking a light would make us all vulnerable."

"I'll go with you," Gisele said. Both Adella and Zara drew audible breaths, no doubt to argue, so Gisele rushed on. "You, me, and Serrah Nunez. You can guide the two of us easier than leading everyone. We find the boat, leave Serrah Nunez there to get it ready to sail, then we lead the others down in small groups. If we run into trouble, I'll create a bright light, and everyone can come running."

They were silent for a moment, and Gisele was surprised by the lack of "no" or "absolutely not" or "out of the question."

"It could work." Jean-Carlo's voice. Gods, they were *all* listening. About time. "The enemy can't see in the dark any more than we can, and I doubt they have their own Vox. They'll be waiting for a group with lights. Gisele shouldn't have to act unless you run right into them." There came another of those collective inhales, and he added, "And I'm coming with you."

"Right," Gisele said, cutting off any other arguments. "And Marcella can call a spell of light if you need our help."

Marcella sucked in a sharp breath, but she also didn't argue. The gods were finally on Gisele's side.

"I don't suppose you can make us invisible," Roni said as she took Gisele by the hand and led the way. "Just for an extra layer of protection."

Gisele shook her head before she remembered that no one could see her. Her eyes had adjusted enough to make out Roni's basic shape against the soft glow from the large ships and the smaller boats along the lower docks ahead and below, their destination. "I know it doesn't sound logical, but I need some light for invisibility magic."

"Makes sense," Serrah Nunez said. He held on to Gisele's other hand, with Jean-Carlo behind him. "You said before that you bend the light with that one. No light to bend, no invisibility."

"And less chatter," Jean-Carlo said softly.

"Right," Gisele said. Good thing she could still roll her eyes as much as she liked.

"First step," Roni said.

Ah, the very tricky part, the stairs down to the lower docks. Worn and pitted from time and weather, they were also slick, with only a rope along one side for a railing. Roni guided her hand to it. Gisele guided Serrah Nunez, too, but stopped holding his hand so she could take Roni's back and still hold on to the rope. She stepped carefully, listening to those behind her and clenching her jaw, her eyes painfully wide as she focused. Soft footsteps and breathing rattled in her ears. If anyone wanted to strike at them, now would be the time. Thank the gods they had no lights to give away who and where they were.

Roni gasped, jerking forward as if falling. Gisele yanked back on her hand and tried to cry a warning as she pulled sharply on the rope.

Its snap echoed off the high river wall.

Gisele's heart leaped into her mouth as she staggered after Roni and hit a step that felt as slick as ice. Her foot shot out from under her, and she let go of Roni, flailing to stay upright on her other leg. The weight of Serrah Nunez smacked into her, and she cried out. The intra velum waited for her, and she grabbed for the star of light and fell into nothingness.

A flash of light set spots dancing across her vision and showed Roni lying on the floating pier below. And someone hurrying toward her.

Gisele crashed to the planks on her elbows. Sharp agony swallowed her cry, and her forehead bounced off the wood with a dull smack. The light winked out, her connection to the intra velum knocked from her brain just as the air was knocked from her lungs. She wheezed, trying to fight, to push the pain down like always and think beyond it.

Someone smacked atop her legs with a grunt, and she cried out through clenched teeth as the person shifted, no doubt trying to get up. She had to follow, willed the pain to flow away from her body or to the hole she created in her mind, a place the pain could live until she had time to deal with it.

Roni cried out, and other voices echoed her, along with a screech that had to come from the Vox. They needed her, and she'd be damned before she failed her friends and family like the military had failed Marco.

She gave up fighting to move and fell into the intra velum; the stars burned hotter than ever.

Light first.

The boats' lanterns dimmed as their illumination flowed into the air above her. Roni wrestled with someone in dark clothing while the Vox had another figure on their knees. Buffeted by wings and assaulted by beak and claws, that one could do nothing but cover their head and wildly swing a knife.

More shapes were coming down the pier, weapons gleaming in their hands. The power of the star of wind roared through Gisele, and she flung them into the water, one or two smacking against the river wall.

A pair of boots *thumped* into the pier in front of her: Jean-Carlo leaping off the stairs. He delivered a kick to the knee of Roni's attacker. When they buckled to the side, a roundhouse kick to the head sent them flying into the river, and Gisele knew they probably wouldn't get back up again.

But anyone who attacked the people she cared about deserved to die.

Gisele gasped as someone lifted her, and above her head, Serrah Nunez called, "Be careful. The stairs have been sabotaged."

That explained that.

Serrah Nunez stepped past her and grabbed the attacker who still knelt on the wooden planks. He rammed them into the hull of a docked boat, and they fell, motionless. The Vox flew away down the pier.

"Come on," Roni said, waving, but the others were picking their way slowly down the stairs. Footsteps pounded from above, on top of the wall, and Gisele shaded her eyes and looked, spotting a crossbow leveled at them.

With a blink, she reached for the star of fire, and the crossbow blossomed into flame. That particular star was always ready to answer the call of anger. Pain shot through Gisele again, twanging down her spine and limbs like notes through violin strings.

Serrah Nunez grabbed her again. "All right, love?"

"I'm not tapped yet," she said.

He helped her walk, following Roni while Jean-Carlo lifted the others off the stairs and sent them down the pier. "Douse the light," he called.

Gisele released it, and the boats' lanterns flared, one illuminating where Roni waited ahead. And the river that waited on either side. Gisele didn't let herself worry about that, despite the fact that she'd never been a good swimmer. And with her body aching and cramping…

A splash and a gasp came from the side. One of their attackers regaining the pier? She sent another blast of air in their direction, and they cried out, gurgling and choking. The sound filled her with fear, but she pushed it aside with the pain. Later, later.

"There," Serrah Nunez shouted, waving. "That one." When Roni headed toward one boat, he called, "No, the next!"

Gisele's pain flared as she mis-stepped. Later was fast becoming now. And each spell compounded the pain. The feeling got worse every time, making her threshold lower and lower. Fucking annoying. She stumbled again, her knee buckling, threatening that she could only push her body so far before it ceased to work out of protest. It wasn't fair. She'd barely used any spells. She'd just been holding on to the intra velum for too long.

When Serrah Nunez grabbed her behind the knees and shoulders and lifted, she didn't protest. If she didn't have to walk, she could get out a few more small spells and at least one large one.

"Bastards are swimming out to a boat," Serrah Nunez said between labored breaths. "I can see the light."

Gisele could see nothing past him and the darkness of the boats still moored.

"Looks like they'll live to come after us again."

She grabbed his coat and pulled herself straighter. "I can't see. I have to see them to cast." She wouldn't risk throwing random spells around.

His grin seemed to gleam as he paused beside a lantern. He lifted her with a grunt, and she held in a cry as he brought her higher, perching her on his shoulder while he held her steady. "Here's what you get for fucking with a mage," he said breathlessly.

Indeed. She saw the flicker of light and several shadows running along the deck, pulling more shadows from the river. This high, the wind carried bits of their conversation.

In Firellian.

"...you kill the mage?"

No, serrah, they did not.

The fire star leaped to her call, and the Firellian boat ignited from stem to stern.

She barely felt the satisfaction before agony lit her from the inside. Her head snapped back as every joint from her toes to her jaw filled with molten lead. Vertigo took hold of her mind, her consciousness tumbling away.

CHAPTER TWELVE

Darkness. Suffocation. Cold to rival the deepest well. The water pulled at Vale like a living thing, every current the swallow of a water hag's gullet. She thrust her arms out and kicked, fighting rather than swimming, raging while her mind screamed, and concepts like up and down and forward and back switched places over and over.

The wind hit her face, and she gulped in the darkening air before being pitched and towed and swamped again. Large somethings battered her sides, her chest, their strikes like rocks, but she could feel bark grazing her skin. She fought them away while smaller things tugged at her hair like dozens of tiny hands.

Oh, gods, gods, gods, she was going to die.

Air again. Another breath so large her chest ached.

A huge shadow came toward her in the twilight, and she swam away frantically before another current caught her, and the devils in the river pulled her under again. She kicked and pulled and panicked. She couldn't die here, not like this. The surface was a grasp away.

So was the intra velum.

She grabbed for it instead of the surface, and the flower of wind wrapped tenderly around her. She flung its power into the river beneath her and shot from the water like an arrow.

Breathe, breathe, breathe.

She plunged into the water again.

But now she had control. Of a sort.

She used the winds over and over. The shore had been lost to darkness; the river became her whole world, her joints screaming to stop using the magic while her lungs begged her to carry on. At long last, she slammed into dry ground and breathed and wept. Blessed unconsciousness pounced on her.

Her shivers awakened her to near darkness. Gritty soil and cool grass pressed into her cheek. Her chattering teeth made the dirt grate like sandpaper. The light of a nearly full moon danced on the river. She was free of its grasp. She wept anew at a sense of relief more intense than any she'd ever felt. Gods, she was alive. Battered, bruised, aching in ways that defied description but alive all the same.

She tried to move. Couldn't.

Tried again. Failed. She didn't have a body anymore, just a sack of pain and broken pieces. Her next sob came out as a teakettle's hiss, and she begged for the intra velum to come to her again.

Her field of sunflowers lay over her like a lover, comforting her, the one place she'd never had to share. Tempted to stay and let death come for her, she sighed. It wouldn't be so bad to die in this place and see what the gods had in store.

And wait for Cristobal and Franka and the others to join her? Who did they have in the world apart from her?

The flower of fire unfolded its petals, and she unleashed it nearby. The blast of it singed her face, but the heat still felt wonderful. A pile of driftwood and bracken caught alight near the water's edge. Maybe the entire forest would burn with her in it, but her body refused her call to worry. Her eyes drifted shut; her mind slipped away.

When she opened her eyes again, her front was warm, but the cold had seeped through her back, catching her halfway between frozen and thawed. The world was still dark, save for her smaller fire. Sleep beckoned for her to return to their bed, but she was too alive to give in now.

In her mind, she spoke tenderly to her body, promising as little movement as she could get away with. Her fingers obeyed first, running along the dirt and grass and twigs. Her arm followed, and she finally pushed up from her side, not quite enough to sit up but enough to roll in place and lie down again with her back facing the fire.

"See?" she told herself. "Not too much."

Almost in response, her aches abated a little.

The next time she opened her eyes, the sun shone blissfully on her back. She flexed her hands again, then her arms, finding it easier to move. By the time the sun had progressed a few inches into the sky, she'd managed to sit up and strip and lay her soggy clothing on a nearby rock before sitting in the sun beside her small fire, soaking up the heat like a lizard.

Gods, now what? She'd gotten out of the river and warmed herself up, immediate problems with clear solutions, no matter how hard they'd been to accomplish. The rest of the future was as muddy as the river. Vale drew her knees up and wrapped her arms around them, letting herself weep again, if only for a little while. She didn't know how to survive out here, and her friends were still captives.

But weeping wouldn't solve anything, so she breathed deep to stop it like she'd learned as a child. She wasn't defenseless. And she still had needs. As waterlogged as she felt, she was thirsty, too. She crawled slowly to the water's edge and drank. She'd been surprised to find that the basket of fruit had survived the journey, though the basket itself seemed to be held together by the net Vale had looped over her arm. Slowly, she freed the most damaged fruit and ate that. With the skin broken, it wouldn't last long.

Like her?

With a grunt, she moved with the sun. She had food and water. And though the river had been as cold as a mountain peak, the land was finally leaning toward spring. And she wasn't defenseless, had her magic, hers alone for the very first time.

Gods, what bliss.

Her body sang a symphony of pain when she moved, but she couldn't resist calling a flame, the yellow-red tongue curling and snapping at her will, and adding it to her small campfire. She let the intra velum go. She needed to rest her power if she was going to use it to free the others.

And Warrane? Had he freed her for her sake or his? In time, she might have discovered exactly how she'd freed herself from the Scourge and might have taught the others. Even if Warrane didn't care about his mission, he obviously cared what the others thought of him and wanted to seem in control at all times.

Bijou's words from the night before last came back to her, something about messing up Warrane's life. Did Bijou or the other Firellians have hostages to hold over him? No matter his deeds, that would make him a prisoner, too. Well, she wouldn't forget what he'd done quite so quickly. She'd set everyone loose, then whatever came after would have to stand on its own. Vale closed her eyes and focused on breathing deeply.

When she opened them again, the sun had moved on into afternoon. Gods, she'd nodded off again. She had to stay ahead of the shivers, so she put on her dry clothes and stood on shaky legs. Her muscles were sorer than her joints, reminding her of the infinite varieties of pain.

Still, she stood and took a flaming branch from the fire before dousing the rest. She didn't know how long the makeshift torch would last, but she could relight it as needed. She had to keep walking until she found the ship, whether that was after dark or not. The light would keep her from falling while using her magic as little as possible. The fresher she felt when she found the ship, the more easily she could free the others.

It sounded simple in her head. She couldn't help a sigh, praying that the gods made it so.

❖

Gisele opened her eyes to darkness. Had she awakened before dawn again? Was it time to flee another one-nighter's bed?

A bed that was gently rocking?

Now, that was a mystery, but it disappeared as she blinked, and her memory returned. The fight, the race for the boat, the magic. The pain.

Gods, she'd spelled herself into unconsciousness. It had been a while since she'd done that. Moving was going to be a devil.

She felt around and found the edge of a narrow bed. Her back protested when she sat up, but the rest of her felt surprisingly limber. She must have slept quite a while. Had Cortez bought her any pain tincture?

No, she couldn't afford for her brain to be foggy. She'd already missed too much of the day.

Over her shoulder, light surrounded a door. She felt her way over carefully and opened it to blinding sunshine coming down a short set of stairs and a narrow hallway. They'd been on their way out of town at nightfall, but this seemed like midday sun.

Shit.

She walked up the steps to discover she was aboard a one-masted craft upon the river. The shore moved by slowly; sailing up a river was no doubt harder than sailing down. But currents and tides and whatnot were a mystery to her. Her face went hot at the thought that everyone might have needed her while she'd been out cold.

They had Marcella, though. If she hadn't been spelled unconscious, too.

The sound of voices came from behind her. Serrah Nunez was instructing Roni and Cortez on how to move the sails. Cortez clung to the mast, shouting, "If you want it done faster, climb up here and do it yourself."

Roni laughed and cheered him on. Gisele sighed, happy that she wouldn't have been any help there.

"He has no head for heights," a voice behind her said.

She put a hand to her chest to soothe the jolt and schooled her face to calm before she turned to face Jean-Carlo. "One wonders why he climbed up there, then."

Jean-Carlo smiled softly. "To pretend that he does." He watched the others for a moment before looking at her. "I trust you slept well."

"And for a long time, by the looks of things. Sorry. What happened while I was out?"

He leaned on the rail. "After demanding many assurances about your safety, your sisters disembarked near the army base. We had to press Serrah Nunez into service to sail the boat, but luckily, we'll be onshore soon." He gestured toward the stern. "Marcella has been giving us the odd flow of magical wind to speed our progress. With luck, we shouldn't have to use the oars."

Gisele glanced that way and saw Marcella leaning against the rear rail. That left only one person unaccounted for. "What about Bridget?"

He sighed. "Sadly, she was wounded at the dock." He held up a hand as she opened her mouth, her insides clenched in worry. "Not enough to threaten her life, just enough to make it difficult for her to walk. She disembarked with your sisters." His little smile returned. "I thought Adella was going to have to wrestle her off the boat. It was Zara who finally convinced her to stay behind."

Gisele could almost see the scene in her mind. "Let me guess, Z pointed out that if Bridget could go on the mission with a wounded leg, she could go with a wounded arm?"

He nodded. "And Adella said if everyone else was going, she would not be left behind."

Well, Bridget had to learn sooner or later that it was useless to argue with two del Amanecer sisters united in a cause. If Gisele had been awake, she would have joined in, and as they'd proven before, all anyone could do against all three of them was stand clear or be trampled underfoot.

"I hope she recovers all right," Gisele said. "Did you get everything you need from her about the Firellians?"

Jean-Carlo gave her a look that said she shouldn't attempt to teach a cat how to strut. "I think she might better serve Sarras in this war by staying in the city and helping the other mages avoid assassins, along with advising the government alongside Adella. We shouldn't need a spy like Bridget where we're going."

"Except you and Cortez," she said with a snort.

He frowned. "We have more experience in the wilderness. She's more…city streets."

She made a show of looking him up and down. His dalmatica did not scream wilderness. Nor did his signet ring.

"I can *change*," he said.

True. They hadn't left empty-handed. Still, she couldn't resist winding him up now that Zara wasn't around to irk. "I suppose you'll come in handy if we meet a squirrel that needs a good kicking."

His bland look said she wasn't getting to him at all. She sighed. No fun in the slightest.

"How's your hand and arm?" she asked. He'd sewn up his sleeve, and the cut along his hand seemed to have healed into a long, dull-red line.

He flexed the hand gently. "They shouldn't be a problem, thank you. And Cortez's leg seems better after a bit of rest."

"And a climb in the rigging?" she asked.

"Mmm." He looked that way, but his expression betrayed nothing. If they'd had a love affair, it couldn't have been a very good one.

Or an exciting one. She tried to picture it and nearly burst into laughter at the thought of Jean-Carlo's dispassionate expression while in a passionate embrace.

She couldn't think of a way to broach the subject. That was probably best. She went to join Marcella, still happy to have Jean-Carlo and the others around, though she wouldn't admit it unless she had to. She was more "city streets," too, and the thought of being in a forest or hills or wherever they were bound filled her with nerves. She didn't doubt that she could overcome anything or anyone with her magic, but the idea of surviving nature itself left her with question marks that the others would know how to answer.

"How are you?" she asked when she reached Marcella's side.

"Well enough." Her eyes looked a little drawn, but she didn't seem as anxious as she had in town. "Better for some sleep. You? I know I hate it when I magic myself unconscious."

"Better, too. Sorry to leave you with the tedious jobs." She gestured to the sail.

Marcella grinned. "Just the job I like. And it's fun watching them." She nodded ahead.

Jean-Carlo had paused beside Serrah Nunez, watching Roni and Cortez. Gisele nearly asked why Marcella hadn't joined them, but Gisele might have hesitated to join a group of people she didn't know, too. She was about to offer to ease Marcella into the company when another observation leaped to mind.

Roni didn't have the Vox out. And she wasn't wearing the glove.

Gisele made her heart slow. If she tore belowdecks to rummage around, someone might notice. "Do you know where everyone left their luggage?"

"Mostly downstairs, I think. There are several small rooms."

Gisele licked her lips. She could calmly amble that way. Someone had removed her boots the night before, and she hadn't bothered to put them on again. That was a good excuse.

"You're so obvious," Marcella said with a grin.

"Me? Never." But she smiled, knowing they were thinking the same thing. "Do you want to come with me and look for…them, or will you stay here and cover for me?"

Marcella chuckled and raised her hands. "If you're talking about the automaton, you're on your own. They're in a bag near the wheel at Serrah Nunez's feet."

"Shit." No one could ever accuse Roni of being stupid. "But I'm not imagining the fact that you want to study it, too, right?"

"Oh, I'd love to, but I'm not willing to fight your friends for it, especially…" She trailed off, but her blush pointed to Jean-Carlo.

Gisele rolled her eyes. She'd have to think of a way to sneak the Vox out from under everyone's noses. She could convince Marcella to distract Jean-Carlo, maybe. By the look of her, she'd be happy to do it. Roni and Cortez already seemed engaged in what they were doing. But Serrah Nunez hadn't budged. And if he was steering the ship, he should stay put.

Fuck. She'd have to wait a little longer. She stood and cracked her knuckles. If she couldn't examine the Vox, she could at least be impressive. "Let me know when you want another boost of speed," she called.

Roni and Cortez finished their tasks and climbed down from the rigging before Serrah Nunez said, "Hit it, bonbon."

Gisele took hold of the star of wind and harnessed its power, filling the sail with a powerful gust. Everyone staggered, and she laughed, losing herself in power even as the ache in her joints said she'd pay for it later.

CHAPTER THIRTEEN

Flinging the ship slowly up the river turned out to be almost as boring as waiting around the Donkey had been.

Especially since Roni never left the Vox unattended. At Gisele's request, she did wake the Vox to answer some questions. The Vox even consented to sit on Gisele's arm, their inhuman eyes watching her while the cold metal claws clutched her almost delicately. They were heavier than expected, just as their stare was weightier. They had no expression, but she felt judged all the same.

"Why not let me wear the glove?" she asked, trying to sound nonchalant. "Whatever Zara's afraid of, I can't do it while you're watching me."

Roni shook her head. "I promised." When Gisele rolled her eyes, Roni chuckled. "And I wouldn't say Zara is *afraid* of you doing something. Getting to know the Vox…" She paused, looking up as if searching for the right words. "It's a privilege. One I initially took without permission. Luckily, both Zara and the Vox forgave me." She glanced at the Vox before chuckling again.

Gisele burned with envy. And a little worry. Were they talking about her? Laughing at her? She tried to put the thought out of her mind. "You can ask me anything," she said to the Vox.

"They get to know people through observation," Roni said.

If they could read people better than Zara, Gisele would have to guard herself. She was used to not having to curb her expressions around Zara, who couldn't read them most of the time. "I know I came on a bit strong," Gisele said, smoothing one finger over the Vox's metal feathers. "I'm just so damned curious."

Something in the way the Vox tilted their head reminded her so much of Zara, she could almost hear a censuring mutter of "Language."

"But to read about someone like you, then meet you? Something I never thought would happen?" She sighed. "I'm sure you get the allure."

The Vox held her eyes for a few moments longer, then hopped into the air. The small metal pieces that made up their body rippled and shifted, and the hawk that had perched on Gisele's wrist became a falcon on Roni's.

Gisele beamed. "I appreciate the display."

The Vox took wing again. "They're off scouting," Roni said before shrugging at Gisele. "Sorry."

Gisele left Roni to fly with them, envy biting her once again as she imagined what the river or forest might look like from above. Maybe if she experimented with tandem magic with Marcella awhile, the feeling would fade.

Fat chance.

❖

After a long few hours, Gisele and Marcella simply stared at each other, Marcella looking as mystified as Gisele felt. It didn't seem to matter if they were in the intra velum at the same time or not. It didn't matter if they touched the same magic or cast the same spell. They could sense each other's magic slightly—like the scent of lingering perfume—but couldn't join their magic. All they'd come up with as afternoon faded into evening was more questions. And achy joints.

Gisele didn't fancy trying to work on this problem in the dark. She sighed and sat near a pile of rope, her knees creaking, and her back groaning. "What are we doing wrong?"

"That's not the right question," Marcella said. "What aren't we doing right?"

"Same thing." Gisele sighed and crossed her arms, but Marcella's gaze remained faraway.

"It's not strength," Marcella said. "Your connection to the intra velum is so strong, I can feel it even when you're not casting."

Gisele frowned, not knowing what to say. She'd never felt anyone else's connection to the intra velum, wouldn't even know what it might feel like.

"It can't simply be a case of working the same spell at the same time," Marcella said. "Not with invisibility, not even with the spells side by side."

"Right." Neither of them could make the entire boat invisible on their own. They'd tried bending the light around the deck right next to each other, but there was a visible curve where the magic touched, one that rendered invisibility pointless. Zara had described the Firellian ship as being completely undetectable, and Gisele believed her. No one noticed things like Zara. And the watchtowers along the river would have no doubt noticed random slices of ship drifting by on the wind.

"They must be using something extra," Marcella said. "Some spell that can combine with another or a separate spell that joins the magic of multiple mages."

Gisele shook her head. She'd touched every star it was possible to touch in her night sky. Such magic did not exist.

Marcella sighed. "I need the library at the guild."

"You already looked." As soon as Zara's report had found its way to the guild, Marcella had been researching how tandem magic might work. She'd even practiced with some of the others. That Gisele could make it work seemed like her last hope. Because if Gisele couldn't do it…

Well, she couldn't say that aloud.

"I must have missed something," Marcella said.

Gisele smiled. There was another truth in the guild house. "If *you* can't find it, it can't be found."

Marcella gave her a grateful look. "Appreciated but I'm not sure I agree." She slid down the rail to the deck. After a moment of staring at the sails, she frowned. "Perhaps it's not a spell at all. A ship needs more than wind to move. It needs sails to catch the wind."

"Are we the wind, the sails, or the ship in this analogy?" Gisele asked.

Marcella continued to stare upward. "And ropes and a rudder, a keel, a great many parts."

Gisele had no idea what a keel was but sensed Marcella wouldn't hear even if she asked. "I think I'd rather be the wind than the ship parts. The power."

Marcella's eyes snapped to hers. "Power that's harnessed."

Gisele stared at her for a moment, trying to make sense of her excitement. As a vague notion took shape in her mind, her stomach threatened to turn. "A harness for magic? But it's…ephemeral. Until the spell is let loose, and then most of them are the same as any element."

"Except that it's directed by a mage."

"But we can't co-direct. We've been trying." And that worrying feeling was still nagging at her at the turn their conversation was taking.

Marcella's eyes were alight. "What if it isn't the magic that's directed in tandem spells, but the mages?"

Gisele drew back, disgusted by the idea of harnessed mages being told what to cast and when. People *requested* her help, and she chose the best tools for the job. "What mage would go along—"

"The imprisoned kind," Jean-Carlo said behind her.

Marcella leaped to her feet as if the deck had burned her. Gisele looked up at him and wished he'd make some damn noise when he walked. "It's rude to creep about," she said.

Marcella gave her leg a little kick. "Did you say something, serrah?"

Gisele held in a groan and an eye roll. Marcella knew his fucking name. But he, of course, didn't correct her, just smiling his cat's smile as he crossed his arms. He'd changed into snug trousers and an equally tight jacket, both in the dark colors he seemed to favor. And the garments showed off his body. Marcella was probably fighting not to drool.

"A group of mages as prisoners seems a very dangerous thing," he said. "I've been thinking about that since Zara told us about them. What's to stop them incinerating their captors?"

"Zara said the mage Vale wouldn't escape without the others," Gisele said. "Maybe the Firellians are threatening some to control the others? Or they could have family members in danger."

He cocked his head. "Hauling around a hostage for each mage would be tricky. The prisoners would outnumber the crew on a small ship. And that would be a lot of mouths to feed. And if it's only the lives of the other mages that the captives are worried about, the question *why don't they use their magic and allow everyone to escape* still persists. Answer?"

Marcella beamed at him. "They can't escape because their magic is being directed or harnessed somehow."

Gisele really wanted to argue, if only to stamp out any rapport between these two. It was bad enough living with Jean-Carlo's smugness at home sometimes. She was not going to run into him at work, too, while he visited his paramour. But she could think of nothing to say and focused on the question at hand.

Drugging mages or knocking them out when not needed wouldn't work because the mages would have to be alert at some point in order to cast, and then that persistent question continued.

Along with one other. "How?"

"A spell?" Jean-Carlo asked.

Gisele and Marcella shook their heads. "There is no spell for controlling someone," Marcella said.

"My sisters often thank the gods for that," Gisele added.

"What about communicating without speaking aloud?" Jean-Carlo asked.

Marcella leaned forward as if leaping at the chance to answer. "Nope. That's fairy-tale stuff, sorry."

Gisele couldn't help a smirk at her eagerness, and when their eyes met, Marcella turned several shades of pink.

Jean-Carlo didn't seem to notice. He was staring at nothing, much as Marcella had, only he pointed at where Roni rested against the mast holding the bag containing the Vox. "What about the automaton? The Vox communicates in their wielder's mind, do they not?"

Marcella shook her head. "Automaton magic...well, not much is known about it anymore, but the spells that connect one of them to a person are unique." Her eyes widened.

Gisele sucked in a breath, certain they were thinking the same thing. "Like something that can connect one mage to another."

"Or control them," Jean-Carlo said.

Marcella put a hand to her mouth. Bile churned in Gisele's stomach. "Oh gods," she said. "If the Firellians have an automaton..."

Jean-Carlo looked between them, his brow furrowed. "What are we walking into?" When neither answered, his frown deepened.

Marcella looked stricken, no doubt because she didn't have the answers he wanted. Gisele frowned back at him. For all the time Marcella spent in study, she wasn't a walking library. And they had other assets at their disposal.

Gisele put a comforting hand on Marcella's arm. "We need to talk to the Vox."

CHAPTER FOURTEEN

Vale walked for what felt like miles, keeping the river at her side, a companion she longed to get away from and never see again. Night fell, and she kept walking, her thin shoes giving her blisters and her linen shirt not thick enough to keep out the chill. The captive mages might be awake by now. The ship wouldn't be invisible, not when it had night to hide it. If the crew didn't bother to light the lanterns, she might never find them.

She started to watch the river more closely, but it was a hole in a world already made of shadows. Maybe she would hear a change in the river's sound if she was more used to it, but the same stretch of water could be a whisper or a roar, and she had no idea why. She walked with the flow, following the direction the ship had taken and trusting she was on the Sarrasian side because the river was on her right. As it grew later and her steps began to drag, she questioned even that.

She finally came near a curve in the shoreline and stumbled to a halt, blinking at her dim surroundings. Confused as to why her legs had chosen now to stop, she stared at them, wondering if her tired body had finally chosen to rebel, just as it did after a long night of being forced to use her magic. No matter that her mind wanted to stay awake. Her body demanded sleep.

As if to echo that thought, her torch flickered and died.

She was too tired, considered falling over, then heard a sound from ahead. She shivered. After living with her father's temper, her sleeping mind had become alert to the sounds of him stirring and would wake her from a dead sleep. Now, her ears seemed to have heard something without her brain even knowing and brought her to a halt. She fought down memories of the past and listened.

Voices, rare enough to be heard even over the river.

Heart thumping, Vale eased ahead in the dark. The moon gave a little light out over the river, but near the trees, all was darkness. She tried to step carefully, thankful for the sounds of water that hid her footsteps.

One voice called again. Vale froze at the following sounds of laughter just ahead. She squinted and moved forward until a large shadow blocked her view of the moonlight on the river. They'd brought the ship very close to the shore, and it sat without light, though not silent. Maybe the sailors thought the river would swallow their voices. And it might if they were farther out, but here?

Why had the Firellians come closer to the shore? To send the mages out on an attack like they'd practiced? Or were they still aboard, waiting?

"Damn." Frustrated tears gathered in Vale's eyes. She couldn't rescue her fellow mages if they weren't here. And she had no proof either way. She looked into the dark trees. If the mages were ashore, how in the devils' names could she find them? She had no idea how to follow someone through a forest. And if she got close enough to the Scourge...

Paralysis threatened to overtake her while her mind raced, striving to stay ahead of depression that wanted her to give up, run away, and curl up to die. Clutching her hands into fists, she whispered, "Shut up," to herself and continued to ease forward until she'd passed the ship, hoping to see some sign that might tell her whether the mages were aboard.

Nothing. Just more darkness. She had to think, had to—

As if in response to her despair, lights appeared downriver, too close to be on the opposite shore. Another ship. It seemed smaller than the one she'd been on. And if she was right about the direction she'd traveled in, the ship was coming from Sarras.

The Firellian ship had gone quiet, unseen or heard in the darkness. The soldiers had bows and other weapons. Even if the mages weren't aboard, they could take this new ship by surprise. Or the Sarrasian ship might damage the Firellian one and dump the mages in the river.

Vale bit her lip. Cristobal's cries for help echoed through her mind again. She had to warn the Sarrasian ship and take away the Firellians' advantage. And then she had to preserve the Firellian ship and do whatever it took to save as many lives as possible.

❖

Gisele was tired of waiting. Hell, she was just tired. Even when she wasn't tapped of her magic, she was tired sometimes. The pain of casting was cumulative; what if the fatigue between castings was as well? At this rate, she'd have the stamina of an old woman by thirty.

Zara would repeat her advice to give up magic, but Gisele still wouldn't consider it. No one who'd touched the intra velum would do so, surely.

But apparently, that desire to push through fatigue in order to achieve wonders didn't extend to those who powered the Vox Feram. "Can't this wait until morning?" Roni asked from where she leaned against the single mast. "I'm done-in for the day."

Gisele put on a smile that she hoped screamed, I am disarming, with the purest of intentions. "I'm fresh as newly baked bread and would be happy to ask the Vox questions on my own."

Roni gave her a look summed up in her retort, "Don't bullshit a con."

"We do need answers," Marcella said, smiling nervously when everyone turned to her. "If you can't let one of us power the Vox, you'll have to talk to them for us."

"Information for the mission," Jean-Carlo added.

"You don't have to fly them around," Gisele said. "Just…relay."

Roni muttered something about them not knowing how tiring it was, and Gisele almost snapped that she knew all about pain and fatigue, thank you, but as Serrah Fabiola always reminded them, suffering was not a sport to be won, and no one could put on someone else's experiences and pronounce them better or worse.

Besides, Roni was clearly weakening. And it had gotten too dark for much else besides conversation. "Fine." Roni reached for the bag that held the Vox, then straightened, staring at the river ahead. "What in the gods' names is that?"

Gisele turned to see a ball of lightning crackling far above the water, tendrils of it snapping out to scorch something just below. It fell slowly, arcs streaming from it like shooting stars. Gisele grabbed for the intra velum, but the ball of lightning wasn't anywhere near them. As it fell toward the river, its electric fingers touched a pale swath of something over the water, leaving little scorch marks on wood and cloth.

A ship.

"Get down," Jean-Carlo called.

The silvery light revealed people scrambling over the other deck, some of them lifting weapons before the light disappeared in a skitter of electricity across the water.

Gisele lost her balance as Roni jerked her and Marcella down and pulled them close to the mast. Little *thunks* pelted their boat, and Gisele looked over Roni's arm to find an arrow sticking out of the deck near her foot. An ambush?

She looked frantically for the others. Serrah Nunez had taken cover behind the wheel, and Cortez was kneeling by the rail. He doused one of the lanterns there. Jean-Carlo dashed for another as a new rain of arrows fell among them, one shattering the lantern tied to the mast.

"Scatter." Gisele rolled away from it, her heart in her mouth as burning oil dripped across the deck. Roni shoved Marcella after her, then fell upon the flames with a piece of canvas.

"Light up that ship," Jean-Carlo called.

Gisele shook her head. With only one lantern burning on their boat and none on that ship, they didn't have enough light to pull on. Marcella babbled something to that effect, and Gisele added, "And we can't burn the ship down. The captive mages might be on board." And she'd promised she'd try to rescue them.

Even if it seemed they were giving away their position with random balls of lightning. They were lucky they hadn't lit their own ship on fire. Lightning was hard to control.

Gisele blinked into darkness as Roni put the fire out, and Serrah Nunez doused the last lantern. Her heart stayed in her throat as she felt her way to the rail, guided by Cortez's breathing. The moon glimmered on the water, but the ship was lost to shadow on the Sarrasian shore. She might have to light a fire if only to—

A splash off the side of their boat caught her attention.

"Jean-Carlo?" Cortez called, a loud whisper.

No one answered.

"Damn it, JC," Cortez mumbled, "you bastard."

Something else hit the deck with a thump, then Gisele felt the rush of air as Cortez clambered over the rail to splash into the water. What the hell were they going to do? Swim to the ship and board it? And what the hell were the rest of them supposed to do?

"Gisele?" Marcella's voice came toward her. "Where are you?"

"Here." Gisele reached for her and pulled her alongside the rail.

"If those two are going over there, we have to do something. If there are captive mages over there, they'll have to fend for themselves."

Irritation flashed through Gisele, as well as a familiar dread about letting Zara down. But as Marcella said, what else could they do?

"I'll create a burst of flame where I think the sails are," Marcella said. A ball of fire bloomed in the night sky and illuminated the edge of a sail and some ropes.

Gisele expected the whole mess to catch fire, but the flames disappeared as if snuffed like a candle. So the mages were onboard? Why were they shooting arrows instead of spells? "Hold on, I'll rock the ship, and maybe that will keep them stumbling." And out of the intra velum.

She called on the star of wind instead of the star of water. Like lightning, water was too hard to control from a distance. She gathered a pocket of wind over the river, then flung it toward the enemy ship and waited for the sound of impact and the cries of the sailors.

But the *whoosh* of air only grew louder. Gisele peered into the darkness as the sound changed direction, building to a roar, and the moon caught droplets of water swirling in a larger ball of wind coming toward her.

The bastards had doubled her attack and turned it back on her. She gritted her teeth, anger spiking. "Oh really?" She held the star of wind tightly and shoved at the force, adding to it, too. Jean-Carlo and Cortez could always help the mages to shore when their ship capsized.

The globe of air slowed, stopped. Gisele pushed at it again, but it wouldn't move, no doubt held by another mage. Impossible. She steeled herself against the pain building in her joints and curled her fingers into the wood of the rail, hauling herself to her feet. No one could match her power for power. This had to be the might of several mages at once.

Even so.

She pushed harder, calling on the wrath of nature, adding to the howling, silvery mass that sat atop the water like a tornado. Her joints burned, but she wouldn't lose this, dared not fail everyone.

The ball of force built and built while being pressed from both sides. Marcella called something, the words lost in the din. Dimly, Gisele felt hands on her arm, but she couldn't afford to shift her attention.

"Compressed...too small. It's...explode!"

What was that?

Gisele's ears popped as the air burst around her, lifting her off her feet. She whipped in a circle, losing all direction, losing the intra velum. Her arm knocked painfully into something, the rail, the mast, Marcella, who knew? She screamed even as the howl faded, leaving the sounds of rushing water and the creaks and groans of the boat. Panicking, she clawed for something to hold on to but found only empty air. She tried to curl into a ball before she hit the deck but kept falling and cried out again before she plunged into water so cold, it stole her breath and her screams.

CHAPTER FIFTEEN

*D*o *not panic.*
       It was a mantra in the guild house, where loss of control meant a spell might go awry. More than one mage had been consumed by the very elements they sought to master. And all because they hadn't kept their wits about them.

Gisele forced herself not to scream and fight, though the same fear she'd had at the docks washed over her. Never a strong swimmer, Adella always said. But being immersed in water, carried along by it, wasn't as bad as staring at it and waiting for it to devour her. It was only water, and she knew which star to use for that.

The bright blue star of water wasn't as familiar as wind or fire, but it came to her call as naturally. Water was harder to create than fire or lightning, but she didn't need to make any now. It was a matter of control over creation. With the star in her grasp, she set the water spinning around her, holding her still in the eye of the small storm. The current couldn't catch her as the rest of the river flowed around the funnel she'd created, and she hung in a pocket of still water. Problem one, sorted.

Now for problem two. Her lungs had begun to burn. And she couldn't see how far she was from ship or shore, how alone she might be in the wilderness.

Do not panic.

She ordered the lower end of the funnel to contract, forcing her pocket of calm water to rise. She braced herself for that first gulp of air. A sense of lifesaving relief could knock one from the intra velum as easily as a blow to the head.

Nevertheless, her lungs heaved when her head broke the surface, sending her into coughing, sputtering spasms. Inside, she forced calm to overcome panic, used anger to tighten her focus. She would not be beaten as easily as this.

Next problem, getting out of the devils-cursed river.

Opening her eyes revealed moonlight bouncing along the water, turning her small whirlpool into quicksilver. Shadows waited on either side of the wide expanse, but one was closer, hopefully, the Sarrasian one that they'd been sailing close to. That was good news.

But where was that fucking ship?

No, she should get to the shore first. A glimmer of light appeared out of the corner of her eye, a burst of flame that disappeared as quickly as the other had, but now she had a direction. And the effort of holding the water was filling her joints with globs of molten glass.

She raised herself a little higher in the water and commanded the whirlpool to move her along, gaining speed as she neared the shore and leaving a wake around her. Her focus had let her block out the cold, but it was starting to seep in, easing her joint pain but freezing the rest of her. As soon as her feet touched the river bottom, she gave the water a final push that thrust her forward to stand upon the rocky shore.

Before she released the star, she commanded as much water as she could grasp to flee her person. It fell in a splash, leaving her a bit damp but not soaking. She limped upriver toward where the light had been, hearing the sounds of yelling and a few screams as she got closer. Either the Firellians were turning on each other, or Jean-Carlo and Cortez had gotten aboard.

Another flame appeared above the deck. Wherever Marcella was, she wasn't standing idle. Before the fire disappeared, Gisele seized its illumination with the star of light and lit up the shore around her.

Large green eyes stared from a pale face just a few feet in front of her. Wild, tousled hair streamed in the wind, curling all the way to a trim waist. Delicate hands lifted as if warding Gisele away, and a musical feminine voice said, "Please don't use fire. My friends might be aboard."

Gisele couldn't help but obey this beautiful, sprite-like creature. While holding the star of light, she briefly touched the fire star, snatched Marcella's flame from the ship and set it upon a snarl of nearby wood before she released its light.

Firelight bloomed in the little cove, dimly lighting up the ship. People ran about its deck, calling in Firellian. One voice cut off in a cry. Gisele's heart lifted when a glimmer of metal soared through the rigging and knocked a Firellian into the water. The Vox had joined the fight.

"I know that bird," the forest sprite said excitedly. Her step toward Gisele turned into a stumble, and Gisele caught her, though every vertebra complained. She could feel the sprite's ribs through her rough linen shirt. "Are you with Zara?"

A spark of memory raced through Gisele's mind. This could be the mage Zara had met, though Zara hadn't mentioned how lovely she was. "You're Vale, aren't you? I'm Gisele del Amanecer. Zara's my sister."

The smile on Vale's face nearly knocked Gisele's heart sideways. Vale would have to learn to take care when using such an expression of pure joy, or everyone in Sarras would fall in love with her.

"You rose out of the water like a river goddess," Vale said, "clothed in moonlight. And I can feel your connection to the intra velum like the heat from a fire."

Gisele was amazed to feel similar heat in her cheeks. It must have been the goddess part. She was used to people complimenting her power. And unlike with Marcella, Gisele could feel something otherworldly from Vale, as if she could sense her aura without using that spell. "I think I feel yours, too." Another cry brought Gisele out of her rush of admiration. Right. The others still needed her. "Where are the other mages?"

Vale shook her head. "If they're on the ship, they could be in the hold. But…they might not be here at all." She glanced toward the forest.

"They have to be here. Otherwise, who turned my attack?" The answer was staring at her, smile slipping a little. "But…" No, it had to have been at least a few mages working together to overpower her. Or Vale was just that strong.

And only slightly trained. Her connection to the intra velum felt as wild as her appearance. When Marcella tried again to set part of the ship alight, Vale waved her arms with a frustrated cry, snuffing the fire instead of calmly moving it, and no one had taught her that she didn't have to wave her hands about to cast such easy spells.

"It's not me," Gisele said when Vale gave her a pleading gaze. "There's another mage on my boat. Marcella. And she's just trying to help. The sooner the fight ends, the sooner she'll stop." But how best to bring that about?

"Don't destroy it," Vale said. "Please." She curled an ice-cold hand around Gisele's wrist. "I might be wrong about the mages not being there. I get things wrong sometimes. I can be stupid and—"

Gisele's heart broke a little for her. "It's okay. I won't destroy it." She laid a hand over Vale's. "And I doubt very much that you're stupid."

Another of those smiles threatened to knock her silly, and she wanted just five minutes with whoever had implied that Vale might be stupid. "If you can...please don't kill anyone, I mean, if it's possible."

Pleading for the lives of her captors? Or had Zara been wrong about her being a prisoner? Whatever Vale's motivations, Gisele focused on the fight for now. The fire had grown, adding more light. Gisele took a step closer to the ship, and whenever she saw an unfamiliar face, she threw a gust of wind, trying to knock them overboard. In the river, they'd have a better chance than if Cortez stabbed them, the Vox sliced them to ribbons, or Jean-Carlo broke their necks. She decided to save any thoughts about why she was trying so hard to accommodate Vale's tender heart until later.

❖

Vale had thought she knew how magic worked, but watching Gisele cast was like seeing a master potter at their wheel. It proved she knew nothing at all, an experience as bittersweet as it was awe-inspiring.

Not to mention hopeful. Gisele could free the other mages. She might even be a match for the Scourge, and Vale's heart felt fuller than it had in years.

As far as *how* Gisele and her friends were taking the Firellian ship, Vale was truly torn. Moment after moment passed with no appearance from the mages. They had to be somewhere in the forest, and most of the soldiers would be with them. The ship didn't have a large crew, but they might be enough to handle the few friends Gisele mentioned as she cast one spell after another. Vale wanted to help, but her magic seemed so crude next to Gisele's.

But it wasn't embarrassment that stopped her. It was the desire to watch Gisele work. And to simply watch *her*.

Even damp from the river, her dark hair shone in the firelight. She'd tied it back, held with a pearl-inlaid clip, but Vale could tell it was full, with a gentle wave. Her dark eyes radiated confidence and passion, and Vale could feel her connection to the intra velum as if she stood close to a flame. She could almost see it surrounding Gisele like a guiding star. And though she moved with a pained expression Vale recognized, nothing about her was weak. No wonder she commanded the elements so well. She seemed a force of nature herself.

"Look," Gisele said excitedly, pointing.

Vale looked at the river again. A smaller craft pulled alongside the ship, and another person jumped onboard. The tide of the fight had turned…if Gisele's friends had ever really been in danger.

Vale curled her hands into fists. She didn't want to ask again, especially after Gisele had done so much to aid her, but she had to say, "I'm sure they'll surrender if you ask." The lie bit at her, but *I'm sure* sounded so much better than *I hope*.

Gisele gave her a doubting look, but she shouted, "Take prisoners if you can." She even seemed sheepish as she said quietly, "I'm not exactly leading this mission."

Who would if not her? "Is Zara?"

"No." Her tone turned a bit cold.

"I'm sorry. It's none of my business."

"Nothing for you to be sorry about. She's just not here."

Vale couldn't read her expression, but Gisele's anger was the last thing she wanted. And saying sorry sometimes got a person in more trouble. "Oh," she settled on.

The sounds from the ship were dying down. A man with a dark braid came to the rail and peered at the shore as if searching for something. Gisele waved, and Vale was about to copy her, but someone rushed the dark-braided man from behind. Vale grabbed for the intra velum, but before she could decide what to do, the man turned and kicked, and his attacker fell without a sound.

Vale's insides froze, and she dropped her arm, wondering if she would ever get away from violence, if only for a little while.

With the boat and ship at anchor, Gisele's friends came ashore with two of the Firellian crew, both of whom Vale had seen about the ship. Were they the only two left alive out of how many? Ten? Fifteen? Or had all the soldiers really gone ashore with the mages, leaving only sailors aboard?

Vale stood close to Gisele but behind her, too. She was grateful for the assistance and told herself not to doubt people who were trying to help her. She tried to smile through her discomfort as Gisele introduced them. Roni, Serrah Nunez, and Marcella offered smiles. Cortez and

Jean-Carlo seemed more neutral, though the latter thanked her for revealing the Firellian ship in the first place.

And to Vale's delight, the Vox landed delicately on her outstretched hands. She felt the magic pulsing through them just as she'd felt it from Gisele and even from the Scourge, though that cruel thing masked magic instead of serving as a celebration of it like the Vox.

The way they sat on her hands and flapped their wings, she guessed they were happy to see her again. "I'm glad to see you, too," she said.

Gisele took a step toward her, mouth open. Roni looked at the golden chain wrapped around her hand, the control gem that allowed the Vox to function. "You can hear them?" Gisele asked.

Vale tried not to shrink from all the stares. "Not hear. Sense, maybe?"

"How?" Marcella asked, stepping closer.

Vale took a step back, grateful when Gisele gestured for the others to keep their distance. "I...don't know. After experiencing the Scourge, it's easy to look for, I guess."

This produced an avalanche of questions from all corners, and the desire to run rose within her, but Serrah Nunez clapped. "All right, cupcakes, there will be time enough for stories." He smiled at Vale and lowered his voice to a soothing tone. "If I understand it right, this ship was not at full complement, right, sugar cube?"

She smiled, liking the nickname very much. "True."

"Then we should hustle somewhere unexpected so we can ambush the rest when they return. We can talk while we wait."

A good idea. Even with the mages and the Scourge, if the rest of the Firellians were caught between these dangerous people and the river, with no ship, they might surrender.

And maybe she could even talk Gisele and her friends into less shedding of blood.

CHAPTER SIXTEEN

They moved a little way downriver and sat on the shore, mostly in the dark, though a few half-shuttered lanterns from the boat provided a little light, enough to watch Vale's expressions as she told her story.

The tale worked its own spell on Gisele's body, freezing her blood, turning her stomach, and sending rage burning through her skull. No matter what else happened on this mission, she was taking this Scourge thing apart.

Marcella could always study the pieces.

Cortez said the automaton was probably the only way the Firellians would use magic. When asked why they hated magic and mages so much, the Firellian sailors simply spat upon the ground.

Of course, that was their answer to most questions. But anytime someone even hinted that the captives' lives could quickly become very painful, Vale made a little sound of protest.

"You're not Firellian, right," Gisele asked her quietly while the others talked among themselves. "Zara said you're Sarrasian, but I think she just assumed."

"I'm from Sarras."

"Then why do you care what happens to these sailors, to any enemy personnel? Based on what you've said, they haven't exactly treated you kindly."

"No." Vale stared at nothing.

"So?" Gisele asked gently.

Vale's gaze skated over hers. "Haven't you ever just…wanted violence to end?" Her eyes widened. "Not that I'm judging you."

Gisele patted her hand to reassure her. It was still cold, even though they'd loaned her a heavy jacket and draped a blanket over her shoulders. Gisele pressed the hand between hers. "Sometimes, violence is called for, don't you think?"

Vale winced. Clearly, it wasn't to her. Probably because she'd experienced too much. "But you'll be able to free all the mages without hurting any of them, right? Some of them are Firellian, but they don't want to be here. And what of Warrane?"

Gisele rubbed the bridge of her nose, but Vale still clung to her other hand. Gisele didn't believe for one moment that this Warrane person had helped Vale out of kindness. A kind person would never have used the Scourge in the first place. As for the others? "I want to say yes. I hope we can save them all, but I don't want to lie to you. It might not turn out like we hope." That was the gentlest way she could put it. She wouldn't sugarcoat their chances, even to Vale's big, hopeful eyes.

Vale was silent as the breeze rustled the tree limbs overhead. She let go of Gisele's hand and pulled the blanket tighter around her shoulders.

Missing the touch, Gisele rested a hand on her knee, then drew it back quickly. After everything Vale had gone through, she should be the one deciding when and if she'd be touched. "I'm sorry," Gisele said. "And I think you've been very brave. It's not a crime to have a kind heart."

Vale returned her smile. "I don't feel brave."

Here, Gisele felt on much firmer ground. "You could have run away, but you came back to help the others. That's brave, Vale. I don't know if your friend Franka could have managed so much, despite what you told us about how tough she is."

Vale chuckled and wiped at her cheeks as if mopping up tears.

Gisele felt that chorus of emotions again but tried to focus on something other than anger. She thought of the comfort she might want if their positions were reversed and told herself she couldn't take it personally if the answer to her next question was no. "Can I..." Heat gathered in her cheeks again, but she told herself not to be so silly. "Would you like a hug?"

Vale's eyes widened, giving that forest sprite effect again. After a moment, Gisele was about to withdraw the offer and apologize, but Vale said, "No one asks me, um, usually." She laughed breathlessly. "I'm always the one giving them, but..." She smiled in that blinding way, a look she'd only given Gisele so far, and she selfishly liked to think it was hers alone. "Yes, please."

Gisele stood and drew her in. She fit into the crook of Gisele's shoulder, the top of her head reaching just past Gisele's chin. A perfect fit. Gisele started the hug soft, increasing the pressure slightly when Vale didn't seem in a hurry to get away.

"This is very nice," Vale said softly, her breath tickling Gisele's neck. "You're very warm."

That might have had more to do with how chilly it was outside, but Gisele didn't mention it. It was nice to simply stand here and enjoy each other's warmth. She had a feeling there would be plenty of cold nights in their future.

❖

The later it got, the more nervous Vale grew. The mages hadn't appeared. Cortez and Jean-Carlo had taken the Firellian captives farther down the beach, and Vale couldn't keep from glancing at them. So far, no one seemed hurt, but she couldn't hear what they said. And after the all-too-brief embrace, Gisele had gone to speak with Marcella, and Roni and Serrah Nunez were discussing something, heads close together as they motioned up and down the river. The Vox was in a sack at Roni's feet, and Vale wished she could crawl in there and join them. Maybe then, her imagination would leave her alone.

In her head, she saw the mages attacking Gisele and her friends, casting spells at Warrane's command. For all her assurances, Gisele couldn't be certain all the mages would survive such an encounter. She'd even said she could do nothing more than *try* not to kill them, and that didn't feel good enough.

And yet, it could be no better. Warrane would force the mages to act, and Gisele and her friends would have to defend themselves. Warrane might try to keep the mages alive, but Bijou would have no reservations about using them to shield herself or her fellow soldiers. And from what Cortez had said about the Firellians who'd died on the ship, most of the soldiers hadn't been aboard for the attack. They'd no doubt come ashore to keep an eye on the mages.

Vale only felt a little guilty when contemplating the soldiers' possible deaths, especially since Warrane might be quicker to surrender without the threats of Bijou and the others.

As the night wore on and the mages still didn't appear, Vale felt almost relieved, even though she knew a conflict was inevitable. Her relief gave way to nerves again. Gods, maybe she should be wishing to get this whole blasted business over with. She felt as if she was being torn in two. Being free was still better than being trapped on the ship, but neither experience felt good.

Gisele, Roni, Marcella, and Serrah Nunez asked after her from time to time, and she'd only just stopped checking over her shoulders to see who they were talking to. She managed to avoid doing it when Roni asked, "How are you doing, Vale?"

"I'm okay, thanks. Warmer."

"Good." Her kind smile wasn't as lovely as Gisele's, but they shared some of the same confidence. Gisele commanded a space, though. Roni seemed able to fade into it. Still, hers was a comforting presence, even as she stared nervously at the woods. "It looks like we might have to go in after them."

Vale nodded sadly. "Maybe it will be easier to sneak up on them?" A far more hopeful thought. "If you can knock Warrane unconscious or destroy the Scourge from a distance, the mages won't fight you, and the soldiers might surrender."

"Anything's possible." But she didn't sound convinced as she rubbed a pink scar on her palm. "My last foray into the woods didn't exactly go as planned."

No, things rarely did.

"Anyway." Roni gave her another smile. "At least you'll get a nice rest on the boat with Serrah Nunez."

Panic bloomed in Vale's chest. She barely processed the words, couldn't believe them. "You're...we're leaving? To catch the mages farther downriver?" She glanced at the Firellian captives down the shore. Had they given up some information?

Roni gave her a blank look before her expression relaxed. "Oh, I thought Gisele told you. You'll be waiting with Serrah Nunez on the boat while we go after your friends. You'll sail down the river to a rendezvous point and wait for us to come back."

"What?" Vale went cold all over again. Her mind flashed back to being in the hold, crushed among the others, and forced to wait in misery. "I can't." Her mind couldn't even process the idea of not being part of the rescue effort. "I can't just stay behind and wait." She'd done enough of that to last a lifetime. Maybe that was why she was so nervous; no one was letting her get on with her mission.

She stood, her muscles clenching so she couldn't sit still.

Roni stood, too, and waved. "Shh. Keep your voice down."

"Why do you think I remained here when Zara offered to take me with her?"

Serrah Nunez and Gisele stood, staring. Gisele stepped forward. "What's going on?" she asked softly.

Vale turned to her, mage to mage. "I have to help rescue the others. You have to understand." Desperation clawed at her throat as if her emotions had come to life. "Please."

"You are helping, have helped," Gisele said. "With all the information you've given—"

"No, I have to see it through." She looked between them, willing one of them to understand. "They need me." Like her siblings had needed her. Someone always had to be ready to sacrifice themselves, and she couldn't trust anyone else to do that, not when she could never truly know what was in another's heart.

"You've done enough, sweetie," Serrah Nunez said. "You've earned a rest."

The very idea flooded her with panic. How many people would be hurt while she rested? How many more boats would she be held prisoner in? "I can't."

Looks passed between them, difficult to read in the dim light. They were no doubt wondering if they could trust her, if she might get in the way or put them in danger. Even Gisele didn't know what to say.

Vale breathed out slowly, trying to avoid a sob. All right, she was as alone as she'd always imagined herself to be. She believed in Gisele's kindness and in that of her friends, believed they would help the mages. She even believed that Gisele and her friends thought they were doing right by asking Vale to rest. If she argued anymore, they might even try to restrain her. For her own good, of course.

Gods and devils, she'd heard that too often.

She wouldn't force them to take her prisoner. She had to see this through.

She scooped up a lantern and flicked through memories of the spells Warrane had demanded she use. Bending the light around herself to become invisible was almost second nature, even in light as meager as this.

By the time everyone gasped in shock, she was already running.

CHAPTER SEVENTEEN

To her shame, all Gisele could do after Vale disappeared was stare. She finally burst into motion and grabbed a lantern as her brain caught up. Vale had cast the invisibility spell. And she'd done it without even a chant to focus herself, her magic as strong as a horse.

Gisele opened the lantern's shutter, scanning for footprints in the sand along the rocky shore. Would Vale flee upstream or down? Or into the woods? Gisele had to catch her, had to make her understand that they only wanted to help.

"What in the gods' names happened?" Serrah Nunez cried.

Gisele left Marcella to explain. While Roni dug out the Vox and Cortez and Jean-Carlo rushed over, Gisele headed upriver. She spied a footprint and looked up for the telltale shimmer that accompanied many invisibility spells, but Vale seemed as good at it as Gisele.

Maybe even better.

Shit. What could she do? She wasn't a tracker like Zara.

Or was she? She'd tracked spies through Sarras. Why should the tools change just because of her locale?

She fell into the intra velum, her body protesting, but she only needed a little spell, nothing that created or controlled an element, just one that let her see that which went unseen by non-mages: the aura that surrounded every human being and lingered where they'd passed.

She cast that spell, and her vision sharpened before showing her a series of colorful trails left by everyone who'd recently passed this way. Luckily, there weren't many and only one that came downriver, then went back again.

Gisele hurried after it, happy she'd thought of it and embarrassed she hadn't thought to look for any auras earlier. She would have been able to see if a large number of people had come ashore. She'd let this new terrain fool her into a lack of confidence. By the gods, she wouldn't do that again.

Vale's aura was as bright as Gisele had imagined, gold and blue shimmers that stretched along the ground like a glittering pavement. Gisele still needed her lantern to avoid tripping over far more detritus than in the city, but the tracks were as clear as anything Zara might find.

They turned onto a small game trail that led into the woods. Gisele hurried after. She glanced up now and again to avoid overhanging branches just beginning to bud and the grasping nettles of trees that never lost their green. Still no sight of Vale, and Gisele's lantern might give her more light to use for staying invisible.

Gisele paused, but she couldn't see without light. Didn't even know how Vale had managed the spell with so little illumination. Worried as she was, Gisele also felt strangely proud. Vale had been a captive for a long time, but she was still a mage, and no one could fault a mage's ingenuity.

And no one simply told a mage what to do.

A crashing sound came from Gisele's left. She turned that way, lantern high. "Vale?"

A pale face blinked at her, not one she knew. They were stooped as if they'd stumbled, and the look they gave her was almost... embarrassed. Before their expression changed to a snarl as they came for her, a blade in hand.

Gisele fell back with a yell. As she flung the newcomer away, she spotted their gray uniform. A Firellian soldier. Her joints burned with casting fatigue, and she reached again for the star of wind, her body warning her that fire or more complicated magic was now out of reach.

And there were more noises coming from the woods, more than just one soldier fumbling around. Had the enemy been watching? And she'd charged off alone.

She backtracked, spell at the ready. She'd released her aura spell, and Vale's aura might fade before she could find it again. Some did, and mages could hide their own auras with another spell. Did Vale know how? Or Gisele might lose hers among others. Fuck. She couldn't leave Vale out here on her own.

Someone grabbed her from the left. She yanked away, sending a gust in that direction, but it was only a branch snagging her clothing, the spell wasted, and she only had one or two more in her. She couldn't afford to pass out here. Fear clogged her throat. Every shadow now seemed alive. When one moved down the trail, Gisele paused, lifting the light as the shadow charged. Another soldier.

A large metal owl fell from the branches and landed atop them. The soldier screamed as the Vox tore into them. Roni stumbled through the undergrowth to Gisele's side and dragged her off the trail before Cortez and Jean-Carlo tore past. Gisele's lantern dimmed as light bloomed overhead, a light spell borrowing the glow. No doubt Marcella was just behind everyone else.

Gisele used the power she had left to find Vale's aura again. "Come on," she said to Roni before plunging ahead, catching movement and the sounds of combat in the trees.

"Gisele, wait," Roni said, her voice low and strained. "Come back." But it sounded like she was keeping up, and the Vox would follow her.

Gisele squinted, her lantern getting brighter the farther she got from the light spell, but she still tripped and staggered, no doubt making a devils-cursed racket. When Vale's aura veered sharply to the right, Gisele had to grab a tree to slow and turn without falling.

"Gisele," Roni said, catching up. "Stop. I promised Zara I'd keep you safe, damn it." She cursed the forest more colorfully as the sounds of her steps followed Gisele into the denser trees.

Roni would just have to keep up. Gisele didn't know why she needed to find Vale so urgently, but now that she'd begun…

The aura began to flicker.

"No," Gisele whispered, trying to hurry, but her steps were faltering. By all the fucking gods, she wasn't tapped yet. This couldn't be happening. She tried to hold tighter to the intra velum, but it faded from her mind's eye, ignoring her call.

Gisele stumbled to a halt, fear creeping up her limbs. This wasn't fatigue, wasn't merely an aura fading. She was losing her connection to the intra velum. Terror washed over her. How, by all the devils? Nothing in the world could keep her from it.

No, one thing could.

The Scourge had to be close.

Gisele pictured the haunted look in Vale's eyes as she'd spoken of that brutal power. She clenched her fists and tried to summon her anger, but fear had hold of her now, and the intra velum was lost, something inside her dying.

"Gisele." Roni caught up with her, breathing hard. "Let's go—"

"I have to get out of here." She couldn't stop her voice from trembling. She felt the Scourge now, deeper in the forest, opposite the way Vale had gone. It didn't have a person's presence. More like a void in the world, a pit of the damned. She tried to follow in Vale's footsteps, but she'd lost that trail with the intra velum. "Which way?" she asked, grabbing Roni's arm.

"This way." But the path Roni gestured to would take them closer to that...*thing.*

Gisele threw herself in the opposite direction, her insides freezing. She grasped for the intra velum but felt like a rat clawing at an iron box. She couldn't get any purchase. Sobs welled inside her, but she couldn't let them loose, not yet.

"No, Gisele, the other fucking way," Roni said.

Something caught Gisele's foot, and she lurched forward, losing her balance and smacking into a tree. Her wrist ached where she caught herself, but she had no time to cradle it. A devil was coming, and she...

Her feet wouldn't obey her.

Oh gods.

Gisele tried to turn, to ask Roni for help. She couldn't. She tried to reach out. Couldn't. Tried to struggle or shout or sob.

Nothing.

Her body wasn't her own.

She pleaded with the gods as her body moved without her permission, turning and marching toward the devil, that void in the world, the Scourge. Branches scratched across her face, caught at her clothes and limbs, but she couldn't push them away. She could only watch as she obeyed this call and screamed inside her mind.

CHAPTER EIGHTEEN

Vale had dropped her invisibility spell when she'd felt the mental hand of the Scourge seeking to slam shut her connection to the intra velum. As she'd hoped, dropping the spell before it could force her to seemed to shake it off.

Or that could be because she'd run as soon as she'd felt it.

Was this the way back to the beach? That sounded like a wonderful place to be right now. Most of Gisele's friends wouldn't be affected by the Scourge. They could help.

If only they'd let her help, too.

Devils, maybe she never should have run in the first place. She should have tried harder to talk them into letting her help and making them understand, but she'd run like a coward, just like now.

Except this time, she was bringing trouble right to Gisele and the others.

Unless they'd already encountered it. She'd been focused on her spell while running, but now she heard the sounds of people fighting in the forest. She paused, unable to feel the Scourge any longer, but it had been getting closer. What if Gisele's friends found the mages, and Vale wasn't there to help? In all the devils' names, what if the Scourge found Gisele?

"Gods." Vale turned in circles, holding up the lantern she'd managed to grab when she'd first started running. She stood inside a small gap in the trees, but the moon had set too far to tell which direction was which. She'd proven her own ineptitude once again and had gotten herself lost on top of everything.

A snide, ugly voice inside her, mimicking her father, said she knew which way to go, knew where the captured mages were and what she had to do to help them. If she ran whenever the Scourge showed itself, she really was a coward.

And a softer, kinder voice reminded her that if Gisele had followed her out here, Vale couldn't leave her to the Scourge's mercy.

It had none.

Vale took a deep breath and pulled her borrowed jacket tighter around her. The temperature hadn't dropped as much as she'd feared it would come nightfall. No one would be in danger just from staying outside. If she went back toward the Scourge, she could figure out the range of its power and stay beyond it, fleeing when she had to but always coming back. After she had its range, she'd keep a spell ready but would only be able to destroy it when she could see it *and* be far enough away to resist its pull.

All the ugly voices said she couldn't possibly do it. She was too weak, too stupid. She clenched her fists. Even if the voices were right, she was here, and she would try, and that was something.

Vale glanced around the dense forest as she walked. Her plan wouldn't be easy in the midst of all the sounds she heard, the clangs and cries. She imagined catching a glimpse of the Scourge. She'd stab it with a compressed lightning bolt, a ball of energy, the most powerful spell she knew, one that had crippled an automaton once before, bringing down the Vox in their phoenix form.

After she crippled the Scourge, she would run faster than she ever had and put herself between the mages and the Firellians, the mages and Warrane, and she would tell everyone to run. And some would obey, like Cristobal. Hopefully, those who wanted to live peacefully could convince the others to run, and everyone would be alive to go home again.

She didn't even need the ugly voices to tell her she was naive. And she might be, but those voices couldn't predict the future. Nothing could. And she still had to try, no matter what, and that was still something.

❖

Gisele could feel Roni tugging on her arm, hear her urgent questions, and everything within her wanted to explain, to ask for help, but she could no more speak than move.

When Roni's arms came around her, lifting her around the ribs, she grunted as the air escaped, but she still couldn't turn her head, and to her horror, her legs continued to move as if walking. If anyone was like the automatons of old, it was her.

Gods, she had to make this stop.

Roni staggered a few steps before setting her down, and she was off again. "I'm trying," Roni said to no one.

Gisele wanted to yell, "Try harder," but Roni was already lifting her again, muscling her through the forest.

"Where?" Roni asked. "In the backpacks?" Roni was trying to nudge the lantern along with her foot while wrestling Gisele, making the light dance around wildly. Gisele caught the gleam of metal. The Vox. Roni had to be speaking to them. Gisele prayed for them to put together a plan.

"I can't force her all the way back," Roni said, grunting through the words. "You have to go get it." With the last words, she shoved Gisele to the side. Off-balance, Gisele toppled, cursing in her head. Thankfully, Roni grabbed her before she could hurt herself. "Bring the whole damn backpack, then!" When Gisele tried to get up again, Roni threw herself on top of her. "Please, Gisele, fight this."

What the hell did she imagine Gisele was doing? The very insinuation that she might give up pissed her off, driving away some of the fear.

Her hand twitched.

Yes. What had Vale said about Franka? Anger helped her resist.

She hoped the Scourge got a headful of curses if it could hear her. She managed a few twitches but couldn't make her damned body stop trying to walk. This was taking too long. Either Roni's strength would give out, or the Scourge's handlers would find them. Even if they usually relied on the Scourge to bring mages to them, they couldn't fail to see the light or hear the struggle. Maybe Jean-Carlo or someone would find the Scourge first and destroy it.

Or he'd get roasted by a platoon of mages without more magic on his side.

No, she couldn't lose someone else to those bastards. She screamed in her head again. *Fuck you, fuck you, fuck—*

"You," she cried, the sound strangled. By the devils, she'd done it.

Something *thunked* to the ground nearby. "Thank the gods," Roni said before her weight shifted. It sounded like she was fumbling with something.

Gisele's body still fought to get up, but she regained control of one leg and kept it from walking. It still twitched, and she could only manage a growling cry instead of more words. But she was winning, by all the gods.

Something cold and metallic pressed into her palm.

Her body sagged, and she cried out as everything was under her control again. She pressed herself into the dirt as she let out a half sob. All thoughts that she'd freed herself disintegrated when she looked at the long metal spike in her hand, the same one Roni's old syndicate cronies had used to cripple the Vox.

Gisele gripped it tightly. Marcella would be so happy to study it. Gisele almost laughed at the thought, though she felt more like crying. At least one good thing had come out of her being turned into a puppet.

"Come on," Roni whispered as she lifted Gisele, both of them hissing in pain. "There are too many Firellians out here, and the Vox says more are coming."

Gisele didn't need to be told that. "Thanks," she said, not resisting when Roni led her in the last direction Vale had taken.

"Don't mention it. That was fucking terrifying from the outside. I can't imagine what it felt like inside." She held Gisele a little closer as if shielding her.

For once, Gisele didn't feel like pushing someone away who was helping her while she could still function. She was too happy to be free. But after a moment, she straightened. She had to find Vale now more than ever. She fell into the intra velum, not realizing until then that she'd feared it wouldn't come back. She pushed away the terror that thought spawned and found Vale's aura again. Making herself focus, she confirmed that the aura did seem to be fading as it headed off in a different direction.

"What are you doing?" Roni asked softly. "The beach is this way."

"I still have to find Vale."

"Are you fucking kidding me? Gisele, you were almost captured and forced to work for the enemy." She grabbed Gisele's shoulders. Her dark eyes blazed with anger, but her voice held more than a measure of fear. "Do you not realize what they could do with a mage as powerful as you? As well-trained as you?"

Gisele grabbed her hand. "Did you see Vale's face when she thought we weren't going to help her? Gods and devils, I've never *seen* someone's heart break before." The words poured out of her. After what they'd just been through, Roni deserved the truth, and Vale's large eyes shone in her mind, forcing her forward. "All she wants to do is help people. Just that and nothing else. Have you met anyone like that before? Because I haven't."

"No," Roni said with a sigh. "But we need all the help we can get. There is a reason you are out here with a *team*."

"They can track us. The Vox can lead them."

Roni shook her head. "The Vox can vaguely sense the Scourge, which means the opposite may also be true. They think they should be idle for a while."

Gisele nodded, but as soon as the Vox rested powerless in Roni's arms, she started after Vale's aura again. "I'm going to find her before she gets caught. You don't have to come. You can track me with the others." She only hoped the spike would continue to shield her no matter how close to the Scourge she came.

"Oh, to hell with that," Roni said, catching up. "I made Zara a promise I intend to keep, which is the only reason I'm not bashing you over the head right now."

Gisele rolled her eyes, but before she could retort, Roni said, "And by the way, you match each other in stubbornness. I can see why she's tempted to duel you on occasion."

Gisele snorted. Zara was tempted to *try*. But she held the words inside. She was grateful Roni had decided to come and wouldn't risk any hasty words that might drive her away. And Gisele was certain she could be much more stubborn than Zara when it counted. Not that Zara would ever find out most of what happened out here.

Clenching her fists, Gisele hurried after the aura, after Vale. Finding her was paramount. Any rescuing could come later.

After she destroyed the Scourge.

CHAPTER NINETEEN

Picking their way through the forest seemed to take hours, though Gisele kept her eyes on Vale's aura. It grew stronger until she looked up and saw it hovering in the air, a blue and gold nimbus surrounding a person-shaped void.

She sighed, happy but also frustrated, not to mention the fear, outrage, and sense of shame that persisted from her brush with the Scourge. "I can see you, Vale."

Vale blinked into sight. Both she and Roni made noises of surprise. "How?" Vale asked.

"I read your aura."

Vale stepped farther into Roni's light, lifting her own lantern, too. "My…" Her eyes burned with a thousand questions. Warrane must not have bothered to show her that spell.

"Later," Roni said. She glanced around at the dark forest. The various sounds of combat had faded, but she still seemed worried.

Gisele didn't blame her. She was nearly tapped magically and was physically exhausted on top of that. No doubt Vale felt the same. "Are you going to run again?" she asked before Roni could suggest returning to the beach.

Vale stiffened. "Are you going to try to keep me from helping?" She turned halfway away as if ready to bolt.

"No," Gisele and Roni said at the same time. Gisele advanced a step, hoping Vale listened. "I'm sorry we tried to convince you otherwise. We…I didn't realize how important it was to you to help your friends. I would feel the same way you do. No one's going to make you do anything you don't want to do." She glanced at Roni, hoping to cement that promise. Roni gave a tiny shrug as if saying she couldn't speak for everyone.

Then Vale unleashed that killer smile. Gisele shouldn't have worried about her listening. She seemed to take in every sensation with her entire being. Knowing how desperate she was to help her friends, Gisele wondered if Vale absorbed other people's pain the same way. But how could someone live like that? Empathy was one thing, but she didn't see the need to throw oneself on a pyre just for the sake of burning along with someone else.

"We should stay put," Roni said quietly. "Let the others come to us. If we try for the beach, we might pass each other in the dark."

Gisele didn't like the sound of that. Enemies lurked behind every tree out here. But Roni had a point. "You should check in with the Vox. See if the Scourge is nearby."

"You felt the Scourge?" Vale asked.

Gisele nodded as Roni powered the Vox again. "I had the pleasure of falling briefly under its spell, yes." She tried to keep her tone light, belying the leftover terror that reemerged as she spoke, shriveling her insides.

Vale's face fell. She clearly didn't believe any bravado. "Oh gods, Gisele, I'm so sorry." Tears sparkled in her eyes, and she rubbed Gisele's arm as if warming her. "I'm so—"

"It's all right," Gisele said, taking her hand. "You did nothing wrong."

"I ran."

"You didn't know the enemy was that close."

"Even so." She opened her arms a little, always the one to offer hugs, just like she'd said.

Gisele stepped in gladly, hoping Vale got as much from the quick embrace as she did. "It's all right," she murmured again. "No one is angry with you." Anyone who argued would have to deal with her.

They put together a rudimentary campsite with the backpack the Vox had delivered. They put out one lantern and turned the other way down before huddling together under a blanket at the base of a large tree. Gisele made sure to keep the anti-automaton spike close, hoping it could shield both of them should the need arise.

"You two should sleep. I'll take first watch," Roni said.

Gisele shook her head. "I need to learn more about the Scourge. And since the Vox was able to sense it…" She looked at where the Vox rested on Roni's wrist after confirming that the Scourge was no longer nearby.

Roni straightened as if to argue, then glanced at the Vox before nodding. "They agree. And I'll leave it to you two to explain this to Zara."

Gisele smiled at the Vox. At least the exhaustion helped her to not seem too excited. "Just so you know, I'm only a little bit victoriously happy. The rest is all necessity."

Their appearance didn't change, but the subtle head tilt spoke volumes.

Roni held them while Gisele took the glove and donned it slowly, with the reverence this moment deserved. She made herself breathe. Even if she didn't understand Zara's connection to an automaton, she knew the Vox was no simple machine.

Her mind seemed to expand when the chain glove was complete, the gem nestled against her wrist. Another intra velum opened in her mind, a different field of stars, and pain still pinged through her joints, but it was a whisper of its former self.

"So," the Vox said, their many stars winking as they spoke in a multitude of voices. "We finally say hello."

Gisele caught a hint of nervousness in their words. She sensed that they hadn't been connected like this to a mage in a long time. She could pick through their memories, these past operators, at will. If she wanted, she could erase them, overpower the Vox's invented personality until hers was the only voice.

"But I won't," she said in her mind, still within the Vox's stars. She could open her eyes to the real world, her mind only half in this place like when she cast magic, but… "I want to be here with you, get to know you."

"I can't tell how much of what you're saying is just flattery." And that seemed to bother them even more.

Gisele chuckled, imagining that they were usually the pro at this type of communication, used to unnerving new operators. "I get that you're feeling awkward, but humans have to interact without reading each other's minds, you know."

"It's damned inconvenient. Probably why I'm nervous to be in a mage's hands. Well, one of the reasons."

"You'll just have to trust me."

"I do," the Vox said with a sigh. "Because Zara does."

That was news. "Zara doesn't trust me with anything. Even choosing my own career path. Or with my own life."

A sense of amused aggravation traveled down the line. "Someday soon, the two of you are going to have to learn how to view each other without the lenses of childhood."

She would have rolled her eyes had they been open. "Well, we're not here to talk about Zara." She let her senses drift among these stars, but before she could fall too deeply into awe-stricken study, she paused. "Do I have your permission to…poke around seems a rude way to put it when talking about someone else's memories, but…"

The Vox chuckled. "If you tell me what you're looking for, I'll help."

"Early memories. Other automatons."

"I can't easily remember that far back." Their voices faded, distracted, even pained. "If I look too far, I can't remember being myself, so—"

"That's okay," Gisele said hurriedly. "I bet that's difficult as well as frightening. Let me." She glided through the star field, picking up echoes of experiences that had solidified into memory. It was astounding, a miracle. The Vox had formed themselves a mind, a freethinking being cobbled from thousands of operators, each leaving a mark. She kept drifting, and the feelings of the being now known as the Vox faded. She reassured them as if yelling back down a long tunnel before continuing forward. These early visions were hazy as any memory distorted by time. Centuries went past, even millennia, so much time that words for it became meaningless.

These stars emitted flashes, brief glimpses of a world with languages she didn't know and sights and sounds that seemed bizarre. Human faces were still recognizable beneath jewels, tattoos, and metal. Metal everywhere, dug into people's skin, whole limbs or clothes or eyes covered with it. Shiny black or pink or green or a multitude of colors she'd never seen metal take. Metal and glass structures reared as tall as mountains, metal birds flew through the air, far stiffer and clumsier than the Vox. Magic mixed with engineering and the natural world, combining with art and inventions completely molded by human hands.

Gods, no wonder automatons stumped all who tried to research them. This entire world was beyond anyone's reach. Even studying each of these flashes for years would only yield tantalizing clues, not answers.

Gisele paused, fighting curiosity and a burst of frustration. Perhaps if she focused on an idea or image, she could pull the memories to her instead of fumbling through them.

With a shiver, she imagined what the Scourge had done to her, trying to see it as an observer might so she didn't run from the terrified feelings. She combined that with what she imagined the Scourge looked like based on Vale's description.

After a few moments, a faded star drew closer. She saw into it as if through someone's eyes, whoever had operated the Vox at the time. Several other memories followed, all images of a dog-looking automaton that shone like the Vox, but it never changed shape. Unlike the Vox, it didn't feel sentient. It seemed more like a piece of furniture or a tool: not dead, simply never alive. Still, the sight of it sent tremors through her gut. If something was going to take over her body, the least it could be was sentient. Maybe she should focus her ire on the person sitting on the furniture and controlling it instead of on the tool itself.

She forced herself to study these images, even though she didn't want to see more mages being controlled. A flash of mages acting in unison made her flinch, but a small movement from one of them tugged at her. Smiling. One of them had been smiling.

Gisele steeled herself and looked again. The mages seemed to be steering a blast of water together, but they weren't moving completely in sync. Heads turned independently, hands moved, and one smiled. The Vox had registered the power of the Scourge, but it seemed to be merely unifying the mages' power, not controlling them.

Gisele hardly dared to breathe as she searched other images. Unified power again, not control. A smattering of language came from one mage as they looked at the Scourge, and one word stood out, oddly pronounced, but she caught it.

Conductor.

Like at the head of an orchestra, guiding, unifying, not manipulating. It let mages work together to create more powerful spells.

Gods, had these ancient people ever imagined that their Conductor could become the Scourge?

More importantly, if she got her hands on the Scourge's control gem, could it be turned back into the Conductor?

No, she couldn't get ahead of herself. The landscape behind every appearance of the Conductor was different, unique people surrounding it. Gods and devils, she hoped there wasn't more than one still somewhere in the world.

Stop. Had she not just warned herself about getting distracted?

Slowly, brimming with plans, she backed out of these memories, opening her mind to the Vox so they could see them.

"Utterly fascinating," the Vox said with tones of awe. "Can you show me the rest?"

Gisele laughed, happy to have dispelled the Vox's fears. "Maybe later. I hope we'll get to speak often now?"

"Perhaps." But their tone was teasing before they sighed. "I suppose I'll have to speak with Adella, too, or she'll feel left out."

"You won't find a kinder heart." Though she'd never say so to Adella's face. They couldn't have her getting a big ego.

CHAPTER TWENTY

Vale felt something tingling at the edge of her conscious mind as she watched Gisele and the Vox. Neither moved or spoke, but an invisible force surrounded them, making the air feel as heavy as it did before a storm.

"What's happening?" Roni asked.

Vale startled, putting a hand to her chest. She'd forgotten Roni was there. She exhaled slowly. Funny, she'd gone most of her life as a non-mage, but after the Scourge had found her and made her aware of her gift, non-mages felt a little...flat. Nothing hummed through the air around them, all their energy contained wholly within their bodies. Maybe if she found out more about this aura reading, she might feel differently.

"Are you okay?" Roni asked, concern in her voice.

Vale smiled, embarrassed by her thoughts. Roni might not be a mage, but she cared about others and deserved to be considered in the best light. "Sorry, yes. Just a little on edge."

"You were staring at them pretty hard." She nodded at Gisele and the Vox. "Getting anything?"

"Just a kind of...sense."

Roni snorted a laugh. "That's a very mage-y answer." Before Vale could try to elaborate, Roni held up a hand. "It's all right. I really only asked because it's been a few minutes, and if Gisele breaks the Vox..." Her look turned thoughtful. "Or vice versa, actually, Zara is going to be pissed."

Vale considered that for a moment, comparing it to the image she'd kept of Zara, the soldier who'd tried to save her, even though she would have been a burden. "She won't...hurt you?" The two visions didn't match, but the capacity for violence seemed to hide in so many people.

Roni drew back sharply, brows tightly drawn. "Of course not. What the fuck kind of question…" She rolled her lips under, and when Vale tried to apologize, Roni waved it away and took a deep breath before speaking softer. "No, I'm sorry, Vale. There was a time in my life where I would have asked the same thing, when everyone in the world and the gods themselves seemed like they wanted to give me a slap." She patted Vale's arm. "I'm sorry that your life seems like that thus far, but please believe me when I say there are many people out there who'd never raise a hand to you." She nodded toward Gisele and then touched her own chest. "Like us. And Gisele's sisters and Serrah Nunez, too."

Vale nodded slowly, though several voices inside her said it couldn't be true. Nastier ones said that it didn't matter because she had deserved a few slaps in the past and would no doubt deserve a few more.

She clenched her fists. No, she could believe, looking at Gisele now, she could believe. Gisele had pursued her into this forest to make sure she was safe. Even if Vale had no desire to be kept safe somewhere far away, the sentiment had to count for something.

And there were more people who would likely never hurt her, Cristobal and some of the other mages. Based on what they'd shared of their pasts, many of them had never been truly hurt until now and wouldn't know how to visit abuse on anyone else.

As incredible as that seemed.

She had to preserve it as much as possible. There might come a time when she could take the violence meant for them upon herself, save as much of that wonder as she could. That would truly be something.

And she'd do it beside people who cared at least a little, at least for now.

Roni was looking at her worriedly. "I mean it, Vale."

Vale tried to give her a placating smile. *I know you think you do.* But she couldn't repeat words from the lowest part of herself. "I know."

Roni didn't seem convinced, but her words said she was more than used to being the target of violence herself. She deserved as much compassion as the captive mages.

"I'm glad you're finally with people you can trust," Vale said.

Roni's expression said she suspected there was more not being said, but if they did share similar histories, she'd know not to pry without being invited. Indeed, she raised her hands in surrender. "I'm glad you're finally with people you can trust, too." She winked. "They'll prove themselves in time."

And what an incredible wonder that would be.

❖

Gisele opened her eyes with a sigh, the Vox still sitting on her hand. The pain came rushing back, just as she knew it would. Outside of the Vox's version of the intra velum, she had no place to hide. She stretched and rolled her head, trying to find some relief. When she looked around, even as dim as it was, she saw Vale's wide eyes and Roni's intense stare. She could almost feel them waiting for what she had to say. Quickly, she tried her best to describe it.

Vale sat open-mouthed through the whole tale, seemingly riveted. Roni looked at nothing, her brows drawn, one hand tapping her chin. "You think you could turn the Scourge back into the Conductor?" she asked when Gisele finished.

She wanted to say yes, to brim with confidence in front of Vale, but that felt too close to lying. She had to shrug. "I'd need the gem that controls the Scourge. Think you can steal it?" She said it jokingly, but Roni tilted her head back and forth, her expression thoughtful. She was rumored to be a very good thief, according to Zara. Listening to her bragging about such a thing had been strange, even with her assurances that those days were firmly in Roni's past.

Unless they were needed, of course.

"Did you sense the Scourge?" Vale asked.

"No," Gisele said at the same time that the Vox said, "No," in her mind. If it was nearby, maybe the Vox could help her resist it.

"Do you think I could cast through you?" Gisele asked them.

"I'm not sure," they replied slowly, and she felt them trying to access their older memories again. "I still can't quite see the memories you described to me. Try it now."

Even the thought strummed her joints with pain. "I'm tapped." She translated their conversation for Roni, who nodded.

"You two get some sleep," Roni said. "I'll keep watch."

Reluctantly, Gisele said good night to the Vox and powered them down, handing the glove back to Roni. If they were attacked, the Vox needed someone experienced powering them while Gisele and Vale used magic.

If they had recovered enough.

But by the gods, she'd gotten her wish. She didn't know if Zara would be proud or livid. Each would be entertaining for a different reason; both brought on childish glee.

Gisele slumped down the trunk of a tree, huddling on a pile of leaves under the blanket with Vale. She'd wondered how she was ever going to sleep outside, but now she could have passed out on a bed of nails. Roni moved a little farther away from the light and sat. If someone saw the lamp and came for Gisele and Vale, Roni no doubt intended to leap at them with the Vox. Gisele chuckled. Zara would have taken the lamp and made herself the target, but Gisele had to agree with Roni on this one.

Even if it did make her a bit nervous to close her eyes.

"I'm sorry again," Vale said softly, her breath tickling Gisele's ear. "For everything that's happened to you out here."

Gisele turned her head slightly. Vale's lovely face was only inches away, and Gisele had a sudden thought about kissing it all better, but something stopped her. Strange. She was attracted to Vale. Very much so. She'd never shied away from making the first move where romance was concerned, but something held her back, and she merely took Vale's hand under the blanket. "You're not responsible for all that's wrong in the world, Vale. None of this is your fault."

Vale took a breath, and Gisele imagined her lining up a recitation of her faults, so Gisele turned just enough to look her in the eye.

"I won't hear any argument," Gisele said in her best high-and-mighty voice.

It earned her a grin. "Well, anyway, whatever plan you come up with, I'll play any part. I mean it, no matter how dangerous."

"I think the idea is to find the least dangerous plan." Gisele frowned, but Vale didn't seem afraid at all. "Have you always been so quick to put yourself in harm's way?"

Vale looked away. "My life doesn't matter."

"Of course it matters." Gisele lowered her voice and tried not to be angry, even on Vale's behalf. Something told her that Vale would think it directed at her. Gisele turned, and as she thought, Vale had drawn away a bit, looking down as if meekly accepting a reprimand. "Vale," Gisele said softly, waiting for eye contact again. She didn't quite know how to begin, fumbling for words she'd never had to say. "You're not less important than everyone else. You deserve to live as much as anyone."

Vale twitched, so many emotions crossing her face that she looked like a flickering candle. "That's...no one's ever said something so nice." The words were softer than butterfly kisses on Gisele's cheeks.

She fought to hide her shock. What she'd said wasn't a revelation. It wasn't even eloquent. She bit back the urge to ask about Vale's life. How was it that someone as self-sacrificing, as lovely as her, had never been told that she deserved to live?

Gisele bit her lip against a surge of sadness. She clutched Vale's hand, overcome with the sudden need to say all the words Vale had probably never heard, to fill up any lonely spaces inside her with kindness. "You didn't deserve to be captured and hurt, Vale. None of this is your fault. None of what happened to the other mages is your fault. You deserve happiness. You seem...you are worthy of so much more. Kindness and softness and...love."

Love with someone else. Gisele didn't do that particular emotion. But she couldn't very well say that.

Tears swam in Vale's eyes, and she seemed almost frightened.

"We don't know each other well." Gisele brushed a lock of dark hair from Vale's pale cheek. "But I'm a pretty good judge of character, even with as short an acquaintance as ours. You have a beautiful, compassionate soul. Please don't be so quick to see that soul destroyed, for anyone's sake."

Vale had gone still. Gisele didn't even know if she was breathing. When she leaned forward minutely, Gisele closed her eyes without thinking, and Vale's lips met hers in a tentative kiss. Gisele raised a hand, ready to cup Vale's jaw and let her know the kiss was welcome, but Vale pulled back. "I'm sor—"

"Don't you dare apologize," Gisele whispered with a smile. "You can kiss me anytime."

Vale closed her eyes and sighed. The light was too dim to see if she blushed, but Gisele imagined it all the same. She closed her eyes and drew a little closer, letting sleep come for her while their fingers remained intertwined.

CHAPTER TWENTY-ONE

Vale opened her eyes to warmth beside her and covering her. She listened for the creak of the ship's hull until she slowly noticed that the ground beneath her wasn't rocking. And she couldn't still be alone and freezing on the banks of the river because someone lay next to her, and a blanket curled around them both.

She was with Gisele.

Perfect, splendid Gisele, who said things Vale had only heard about from others. The nastiest voices inside her said she would never live up to those words, not with a thousand lifetimes, and that was probably true, but right now, she held them as close as Gisele and wished she had the courage to kiss her again.

A kiss that had been welcome, if she'd read Gisele's expression correctly.

Her heart felt full enough to burst.

She wanted to close her eyes again. Sometime during the night, she'd pulled her head under the blanket but now saw gray light peeking around the edges. And something had woken her. Whatever it was, she had to keep Gisele safe. She lifted her head, blinking in the low light.

Gisele's mouth was open slightly. She lay on her side, one arm pressed along Vale's body. Strands of dark hair had come loose from her tidy updo, the pearl clasp askew where she'd lain on it. Even with a bit of dirt smudging her cheeks and a few leaves stuck to her hair, she looked heartbreakingly beautiful. Her words from last night still drifted through Vale's mind like a refrain, even if she couldn't agree with all of them. Gisele's life was worth more than hers. Nothing would ever convince her otherwise.

She glanced at where she'd last seen Roni the night before and found her dozing, the powered-down Vox in her lap. Vale had to smile.

So much for keeping watch. But as soon as Vale shifted out from under the blanket, Roni's eyes popped open, her hand going to where a truncheon rested by her side.

Vale smiled and put a finger to her lips, nodding to Gisele. Roni nodded back and stretched. If she'd been sleeping, she probably hadn't made any sort of noise. Birdsong fluttered from deeper in the forest. Perhaps that had awakened her, the first sounds of spring.

Nearer than that, a twig cracked, the sound eerily loud in the stillness.

Vale froze, glancing at Roni, who looked at the woods. She pulled the truncheon into her lap, and her eyes went unfocused while she wound the chain glove around her hand. The Vox stirred, and Vale breathed a little easier just knowing they were awake. It couldn't be the Scourge out there. It would have pulled at Vale and Gisele already, but it could be more Firellians.

Roni threw the Vox into the air, and they took wing, a gentle tinkling sound. Vale stooped, trying to make as little noise as possible as she touched Gisele's shoulder and shook her lightly. Gisele's eyes drifted open, but before she could make a sound, Vale pressed a fingertip to her lips.

Gisele frowned, slightly cross-eyed before she looked up. Her brows lifted, confusion giving way to alarm before she sat up, too, and Vale felt the intra velum descend over her like a cloak. She could almost see it fluttering around her shoulders. She should have done the same, shouldn't have had to wait to be shown what to do. She summoned the intra velum, her joints still creaky from all she'd done the night before, but she could manage some spells. Her field of sunflowers hovered over her vision as she stared into the forest.

When the Vox came gliding back through the trees, Vale couldn't help a jump, her heart flying into her throat. She took a deep breath and made herself let go of the flower of fire.

"It's all right," Roni said. "It's the rest of our merry band. Well, three of them, anyway."

Jean-Carlo, Marcella, and Cortez emerged from the woods not far behind the Vox. Vale stood back as everyone greeted one another and asked after their health. Serrah Nunez had returned to the boat, they said, and would meet them at a rendezvous point down the river. The four of them had camped on the beach after their skirmish with a few Firellian soldiers. They hadn't wanted to go looking for Gisele, Roni, and Vale in the dark, much as Roni had said.

"We're glad to find you all in one piece," Jean-Carlo said, but Vale sensed the frostiness in his tone. He stared at her and Gisele, his eyes like black daggers.

Gisele moved in front of Vale and crossed her arms. "You, too."

He drew himself up. "I trust I need not remind you again of the importance of staying together? Of informing everyone of your plans?"

"You don't," Gisele said smoothly, sounding bored. She quickly relayed what had happened to her and Roni, not moving from her protective stance. Vale wanted badly to take her hand but not with everyone staring. Luckily, the others came closer, listening to Gisele so intently when she spoke about communing with the Vox, they seemed to forget about Vale, and she could breathe again.

"The few Firellians we fought retreated at the sound of a whistle," Cortez said. "Maybe this Warrane called them back when you used the anti-magic spike to get away from the Scourge. They might have never encountered such a thing before."

Jean-Carlo nodded, though he still stared at nothing.

Marcella moved closer to Gisele. "It sounds terrifying," she said, but she still leaned forward as if intrigued. "I'm glad you're okay. All of you." She gave Vale a reassuring smile, another sympathetic soul. Vale wondered if mages in Sarras all lived together somewhere, looking out for one another. It sounded like a wonderful dream.

"Did you see where the Firellians went?" Roni asked.

Cortez shook his head. "We didn't want to pursue them without the whole team." He raised an eyebrow at Gisele.

She raised one back. Vale wished she could bottle that courage and hand it around.

"We did manage to get some information from our captive sailors," Jean-Carlo said. "And at least two Firellian soldiers won't be bothering us anymore."

Vale winced. He didn't have to be coy. She knew what that meant. "What did the sailors say?" she asked, fighting not to shrink when they all glanced her way.

"We don't know if it will help," Cortez said as he leaned against a tree and crossed his arms. "But they said that the Firellian government put out a bounty on automatons, a high one, apparently." He nodded to Roni. "That could be why the Newgate Syndicate was so anxious to get you to steal the Vox."

A sad look passed over Roni's face, and the Vox flew down to land upon her gloved hand. She gave them a warm smile. "They might have been looking for more Scourges or something similar that their mage-handlers could use."

Gisele held up the spike. "They must have found these in their hunt."

"I doubt they'd confirm or deny that no matter how politely we asked," Roni said dryly.

Jean-Carlo refocused on all of them and put his hands on his hips. "Unfortunately, their automaton search, if successful, could also mean more teams of captive mages are on their way toward Sarras. We need to"—he glanced at Vale—"round up this batch as quickly as possible."

Anger tingled along Vale's scalp at his obvious pause. No matter what else she was or how she acted, she was not a fool. "They shouldn't be harmed," she said, clenching her fists. Her fellow captives were depending on her, and Gisele believed in her, so she had to speak up. If she was worthy, she had to prove it. She borrowed some of Gisele's words. "They didn't deserve what's happened to them, and they don't deserve to die."

Gisele's proud smile made her insides melt.

Jean-Carlo's expression remained blank, and even the more sympathetic faces in their party seemed to be saying, "We'll try our best." But that wouldn't be good enough. Gods, she wanted to bolt again, to rescue the mages the right way, giving her own life if she had to, but the mages had to stay alive.

Gisele touched her arm and gave her a confident smile. Vale took a few deep breaths and forced her feet to remain where they were. She wondered if the captive sailors had survived the night, but she feared the answer too much.

The conversation broke up as Roni packed their meager campsite, the rest of the equipment was redistributed, and Cortez handed out a small breakfast.

Gisele put a hand on Vale's shoulder and leaned close. "Are you okay?"

Vale nodded, though her insides were in turmoil.

Gisele's touch became a caress. "You don't have to put on a brave face for me. You seem to wear your heart on more than just your sleeve."

With a sigh, Vale said, "My feelings aren't important."

"That's not true. You—"

Vale covered her hand. "Please don't say nice things about me right now. You're right. I am feeling a lot, and it won't take much more to make me burst into tears."

Gisele gave her a sad, affectionate smile. Marcella cleared her throat gently from behind them. Vale turned, cheeks burning. She hadn't realized anyone else was standing so close. "I'm the same way," Marcella whispered, and Vale was so grateful that both of them were here.

Even if it meant she had more people to worry about.

CHAPTER TWENTY-TWO

When everyone was packed and ready, there was still the question of where to go. To Gisele's surprise, Jean-Carlo led the way as if he had a destination in mind, but after a long walk, he stopped at a scrubby section of woods that looked like every other, save this one had a large pile of dead branches and leaves next to a huge fallen tree.

"This will be better for talking and planning," he said.

Gisele glanced around the space, wrinkling her nose at the strong earthy smell. "Why, because it's uglier? Do you think the Firellians wouldn't be caught dead somewhere like this?"

Cortez looked down as if hiding a smirk. Jean-Carlo moved to the pile of dead branches as if he hadn't heard. To Gisele's astonishment, one side of the pile lifted away, revealing a dark interior.

"This is a scout hide," he said. "Location courtesy of Zara, someone who knows her way around out here."

A reminder that Gisele didn't. She wondered how much trouble she'd be in if she lit the cuff of his trousers on fire just to prove that she had other important knowledge. Cortez seemed like he might find it amusing.

Jean-Carlo and Cortez went inside, and Gisele wondered how they were all going to fit until she followed and found a much longer space than expected, continuing into the hollowed-out tree. It was unadorned, without a speck of furniture, but it was clean and dry and clearly maintained. Jean-Carlo lit a lantern that hung from the ceiling, revealing several slick-looking bags hanging near the back, their tops tightly cinched. Gisele ran her fingers over one, and came away with a bit of moisture, as if someone had covered it in hand cream.

"Oilskins," Cortez said softly beside her. "For supplies. They're waterproof."

"Hmm." She supposed scouts had to think of everything. It was slightly embarrassing to find that this place existed after they'd slept outside the night before, but Gisele supposed they would have had a hard time finding it in the dark, even if Roni had known where it was. And Roni had said many times that though she'd been recruited into the scouts, she wasn't one. She hadn't completed the training and didn't want to.

Gisele wondered how Jean-Carlo had trained in some of his skills. Was there a school for nobles who wanted more of an education than general knowledge and which spoon to use at dinner? An interesting thought. She'd have to remember it when they returned to the city. She could stand expanding her knowledge a little.

As long as she didn't have to learn from Zara.

They sat in a rough circle and rested, sharing canteens.

"If I'm going to steal the Scourge's control gem," Roni said, "I need to scout their camp."

Everyone but Marcella nodded. "Shouldn't we focus on destroying it rather than repurposing it? I don't think it's wise to leave something intact that can be used to control mages." She shrugged. "Much as I would love the chance to study it."

"Taking the gem would cripple it," Jean-Carlo said. "We could decide at our leisure what to do with it after that." His tone seemed a little softer when he spoke to Marcella, and she smiled shyly, her cheeks red.

Gisele fought the urge to roll her eyes. Gods, what a sham. If he hurt Marcella with his manipulative shit, his trousers were destined for the flames, consequences be damned. And no matter what happened, she would make sure the Scourge didn't wind up in the hands of the intelligence agency.

Roni was staring into the middle distance, tapping her chin again. "I'll need some backup while I scout, but Gisele, Marcella, and Vale can't go. They'd be too close to the Scourge, and we don't know that one spike will shield all of them." She glanced at Gisele. "Is there a way they could look out for us magically? Like, some kind of magical sentinel?"

Gisele shook her head. "But there are alarms."

Roni winced. "Yeah, I remember those."

"They have to be hooked to something physical," Marcella added. "Something that has to be broken or disturbed for the alarm to function."

"Tripwires," Roni said. "I remember those, too."

"But you don't have to be a mage to spot them," Cortez said.

Gisele didn't like the idea of anyone going near the captive mages without magical help, but she also didn't want to risk getting too close to the Scourge, spike or not. "I could power the Vox and watch through their eyes as they go with you."

Marcella frowned. "We have no idea what could happen, though. Suppose the Scourge could reach you through the Vox somehow? Or their handler might sense the Vox."

Both chilling thoughts. "We'll do some experimenting to see if I can cast through the Vox. That might come in handy."

"If we can sneak in after dark, why not just kill Warrane?" Jean-Carlo said. "Then, even if we don't get the gem, none of the Firellian soldiers can power the Scourge." He looked at Vale. "Right?"

She frowned as if she might be sick. "That's murder."

Everyone quieted. Gisele put a soothing hand on Vale's arm. She was right, of course. Sneaking into someone's tent in the dead of night and slitting their throat could never be considered killing them in battle.

"I'm not an assassin, anyway," Roni said. Her eyes flicked to Jean-Carlo, then she looked away and rubbed her cheek as if trying to erase the glance. She might not be a killer-for-hire, but Jean-Carlo? Gisele doubted he'd kick up much of a fuss about such an assignment.

He pulled his bottom lip between his teeth before releasing it slowly. "Look, Vale, in war—"

"Are you going to say murder stops being murder?" Vale asked. Two bright spots bloomed on her cheeks, either a blush or in anger, but she didn't back down. "If I have to…" She looked at Gisele, then mashed her lips together into two bloodless lines.

"It's all right," Gisele said. "We already have a plan to steal the gem." She glared at Jean-Carlo, then at Cortez for good measure. The latter lifted his hands as if in surrender, but the former held her gaze, his face betraying nothing. Gods, she hoped like hell he wasn't going to push this, even though she'd been dreaming of a confrontation with him only moments ago. But she knew that if he pushed, Vale might bolt again, and Gisele didn't want to give her a reason.

Gods and devils, had she ever been this focused on someone's feelings before? She'd thought so. She'd been so certain that one-nighters like Henrietta felt as she did, that they were ships passing and nothing more, but she hadn't stayed to find out. And Henrietta's sad expression later that day had told her how wrong she might have been.

"If we try to carry out two different plans at once," Gisele said slowly, "we're bound to fail, yes?" She kept her eyes on Jean-Carlo for half a heartbeat before looking at everyone. "So we'll steal the gem, yeah? Roni goes in, maybe with Cortez and Jean-Carlo. Marcella, Vale, and I hang back, and I watch through the Vox." She patted Marcella's hand before she could bring up her former points. "After we do a little experimentation to find out what the Vox and I can do together. And if it does seem like the Scourge can get at me through the Vox, you can always take the glove off my hand. I can tell the Vox to start flying back if that happens or to hide themselves, and we'll get them later."

Marcella nodded, a satisfied smile in place, but Roni seemed a bit worried by the last part of her plan.

Gisele hurried on. "Everyone agreed?" she asked, looking to Vale first.

Vale nodded with a grateful smile. Roni, Cortez, and Jean-Carlo nodded as well, though what Jean-Carlo was thinking, she had no idea. It was enough to know that in his head, murder either wasn't always murder or was sometimes a necessity. It should have made her happy he was on her side, she supposed, but it still left her with a chill.

After everyone agreed, Marcella and Cortez went outside with Gisele and the Vox. Vale watched with her usual wide-eyed look from the doorway of the scout hide while Gisele donned the chain glove and felt the Vox stir in her thoughts again.

"Glad to see we're all still alive," they said in her mind, their chorus of voices only a little amused.

"What would you do if you woke up in enemy hands?" she asked as the question popped into her brain.

They were silent for a moment, but she sensed thoughtfulness rather than anger or anxiety. "I'd try to attack everyone I could before they gave me a command. Commands are hard to ignore. I suspect that's even truer if the person holding the gem is a mage."

Quite correct. Gisele had no doubt that she could force the Vox to do anything, including forgetting who they were, but she didn't mention it. Right now, she was the only person who had that information, and she saw no reason to share it, even with the Vox. It would only give everyone something else to worry about. "I feel the same way. About attacking, I mean."

And instead of dwelling on possible kidnappings, she asked the Vox to fly a little way into the trees. She put aside their intra velum to look through their eyes when they landed. Switching between her own sight and the Vox's was easy, though the feeling of movement in the brief overlay made her stomach wobble. She closed her own eyes and focused on the Vox's as they glanced about. Their vision as a hawk was far sharper than hers, homing in on the slightest movement. When they glided from one limb to another, she gasped, the feeling of brief weightlessness before the powerful wings lifted them filling her with joy. She couldn't contain a laugh, could barely contain the desire to flap her own arms.

The Vox chuckled. "Humans. You love flying."

"From a perspective where we can't fall? Who wouldn't?" She hadn't been with the Vox this fully when they'd first taken off, and now she didn't want to leave them. "No wonder Zara guards you so jealously."

"Flying is not the only reason we hold each other dear, thank you very much."

Gisele chuckled, making mollifying noises and not mentioning that Roni used that last phrase from time to time. What would the Vox adopt from her by the time all this was through?

For now, they had to get down to business.

Gisele tapped into her own intra velum, that familiar overlay of stars. Using so much magic the night before and sleeping on the ground made her body protest, but only with the aches she always had first thing in the morning. "Can you see the intra velum?"

"Not see," the Vox said slowly. "But I feel a sense of…readiness."

A good sign, Gisele supposed. She took a light hold on the star of wind but didn't want to open her own eyes and see where her body was pointed. "I'm going to cast a brief wind spell," she said aloud. "Turn me to face something small and insignificant."

"Jean-Carlo's sense of empathy isn't out here," Cortez said in her ear.

She snorted but didn't open her eyes, even as someone took her shoulders and shifted her slightly. "I notice you don't fire those bolts when he's around," she said.

"Oh, I do, trust me. Just not when the rest of you are around, too."

That would be some good dish for Serrah Nunez later, but for now, Gisele simply shook her head and focused on a clump of leaves clinging to the Vox's tree. "There," she said to them. "Keep that in sight."

They did so, and she released the small power she'd tapped. When the leaves fluttered wildly, she clenched a fist in victory. "Yes!"

"Did it work?" Marcella asked.

"You bet your boots it did." But something wasn't right. She'd only used a tiny amount of power, but the pain that flooded her was that of a larger spell. She pushed the Vox's sight to the side of her mind and opened her eyes to see Marcella leaning around her curiously.

"You stirred the breeze here, too," Marcella said, pointing to where a pile of leaves had been disturbed on the forest floor.

Damn. She hadn't considered that she might cast in both places at once. Marcella began scribbling in a notebook and asking questions, but Gisele wanted to curse the devils. She tried a few more small spells, trying to only cast through the Vox, but it felt like trying to flex a muscle she didn't have. She finally called them back. "If you need magical assistance," she said to Cortez, "I'm going to tap out quickly if I always cast two spells at once."

"Not to mention tearing up the forest around us," Marcella said. "You won't be able to use fire. You'll set the wilderness ablaze."

"No," a soft voice behind them said. Vale stood when they turned, her expression one of awe and happiness. "You're incredible." Her cheeks filled with pink. "I mean, it's…you're…" She shook her head and held her hands up as if stopping herself. "If you have to use fire, I can put it out."

Gisele nodded, smiling. "Like you did at the ship. Or Marcella can move it if we set up a campfire nearby, clear a space for it."

Marcella made another note in her book. Vale's expression turned a bit worried, and Gisele knew what she was thinking as if the words were written on her forehead.

"I'll only use it in defense," Gisele said. "Not to attack anyone." Vale's returning smile pulled at her insides again, and their brief kiss wandered through her mind. When she turned back around, Cortez was staring, his brows slightly up as if asking if she meant what she'd said or maybe if it was wise to make such a promise.

"Excuse us," Gisele said to Marcella and Vale. She took Cortez's elbow and led him a few steps away. The Vox hopped onto the chain glove, watching Cortez along with her. Good, two people looking for lies was better than one. "You have got to keep an eye on Jean-Carlo for this mission."

He didn't bother to ask why or for what. "You think he takes orders from me?"

"Does he take orders from anyone?"

"Only one person that I know of."

"Well, let's hope it's Roni because otherwise, you're going to have to intercede if he gets all…murder-y."

He crossed his arms. "Something tells me you wouldn't be so quick to throw that word around if not for a certain someone."

She took a deep breath. He had a point, but… "If you dissuade him hard enough, he'll listen to you, right? You've known each other a long time, haven't you?"

"We have. One of the reasons he doesn't take orders from me." He put up a hand before she could argue. "I will be as logical with him as I can. Vale is a powerful ally. It would be wise to keep her happy. Also, every mage we free is another possible addition to our ranks." He dropped his arms and took his own deep breath, staring upward for a moment. "But according to Vale, Warrane is a member of the Firellian military and a perfectly valid target."

Gods and devils, part of her agreed, but she shook her head. "Also based on what Vale said, he's capable of at least some sympathy. He might jump at the chance to change sides and go somewhere mages aren't reviled."

"If he comes face-to-face with Jean-Carlo, he better make that decision very fucking quickly."

She smiled, always happy to hear the more colorful swears when her sisters weren't around to fuss about it. "Is he going to follow Roni into the camp no matter what anyone says or does?"

"We both might, depending on how the camp is laid out." He nodded at the Vox. "With you two watching from the trees, ready to create a distraction if needed."

"Do you think he'll push past Roni into Warrane's tent and just kill him?"

Cortez considered for a moment, sighing. If he said yes, what could they do? Turn on one of their own? Truss him up like a chicken and leave him here? That would go down well with the higher-ups back in Sarras, sure.

"JC does what he thinks is best at the time," Cortez finally said with a shrug. "Just like when he dove into the water to climb aboard that ship. He sees a path, and he takes it, putting his skinny ass in harm's way more often than not." And the way he shook his head, his mouth an angry line, said that Cortez cared about Jean-Carlo's well-being, skinny ass and all.

"My thoughts exactly," the Vox said.

Gisele tried to hide her start. She hadn't realized she'd been thinking so loudly.

Cortez seemed not to have noticed, thank the gods. "But if there's a plan in place, he'll follow it. He wouldn't knock someone over trying to do his own thing unless he had to. If Roni is successful, and everything goes perfectly, he won't run around being all *murder-y*. At least, that's what my gut tells me. But if Warrane catches Roni or wanders out in front of JC mumbling about how he's going to kill every Sarrasian in the world..." He shrugged again.

Gisele copied him. That was the best they could hope for, she supposed. And as she turned back and met Vale's anxious gaze, she added another hope: if Warrane or any of the others died, Vale would forgive her.

CHAPTER TWENTY-THREE

Vale didn't know what to do with herself. Gisele had explained that the non-mages in their group were going to find the Firellian camp where the captive mages were, but they wouldn't try to sneak in until after nightfall. That left Gisele, Marcella, and Vale with nothing to do but wait. They'd play a part in the actual theft that evening, but right now, they couldn't go bumbling about the forest because of the Scourge.

Vale agreed with that part, even though she doubted Warrane was fully powering the Scourge at every moment. It would wear him out, just like using the Vox for too long seemed to tire Roni. The Scourge would likely be operating with only its base power: keeping mages from accessing the intra velum without Warrane's permission.

She'd said all this to the others, but they hadn't wanted to risk it. They valued one another, and they seemed to value her life, too. Gisele's caring words echoed inside her. She'd carry them in her heart until the day she died.

But how to best be useful right now? She couldn't remember the last time she'd had hours with nothing to do. Well, unless she counted being in the ship's hold, too exhausted to do anything but sleep. Gisele had told her to relax, but…how? Her shoulders kept hunching no matter how many times she made herself drop them and breathe. Every tiny sound of the forest made her jump. Why? The idea of facing Warrane or the Firellians again didn't scare her. At the thought of dealing with them, she felt only desperate determination. So what—

"Hey."

Vale whipped her head around at a light touch on her shoulder. She shrank back from Gisele's surprised expression, her heart thundering. It took quite a few beats before she convinced herself to breathe again.

"Whoa," Gisele said softly, her eyes wide. She held her hands up as if calming a frightened cat. "I'm sorry. I didn't mean to scare you. Are you all right?"

"Yes, yes. It's fine. I'm fine. I...overreacted. I'm—" She cut herself off. Gisele had told her to stop apologizing. But shouldn't she? She'd made Gisele worry for no reason, but now Gisele was sitting next to her, looking caring and concerned and as if she didn't need an apology. Vale wanted to lean into her arms and live there.

"You nervous about the mission?" She touched Vale's shoulder again, a tiny blanket of warmth. "I had a word with Cortez, and maybe he can convince Jean-Carlo that no one needs to die if we get that control gem. Even the Firellian soldiers will probably surrender if all their magical might turns against them."

That wouldn't stop Franka from killing a few Firellians, but as much as the idea of more violence sickened Vale, such thoughts weren't bothering her now. "You'll do your best, I know," she said. "There isn't anything you can't do."

Gisele's cheeks went a little pink, and Vale wanted to kiss her again. Marcella was there, scribbling in her notebook, but who knew how much attention she was really paying? And what if Gisele didn't want anyone to know that—

"Hey," Gisele said again. Her warm hand rested on Vale's knee this time, and Vale realized she'd been staring at Marcella and letting her worries spiral out of control. She forced her shoulders to relax once more, but the left one ached, and she imagined the muscles turning into knots. "If it's not the mission, what is it?"

Vale had to chuckle, though she felt far from amused. "I don't know. It's absurd, but I just can't...relax."

Gisele smiled crookedly. "Well, gods and devils, I can't imagine why. You've only been kidnapped from home, abused by Firellians, forced to use magic against your own people, thrown overboard, had to escape a raging river, and are now part of a tricky plan to free the other captives." She nudged Vale's knee and winked. "That's practically the same as cuddling up with a blanket and reading a book on a rainy afternoon."

Vale smiled. It was nice to hear her feelings justified, but none of that felt right for the way her nerves seemed too close to the edge of her skin. "That's a nice fantasy."

"You've never had a rainy day with nothing else to do?"

Vale shook her head. "And I don't know how to read."

Gisele went still, her easy smile dropping like a stone.

Vale stilled, too. Devils take her, she'd said the wrong thing. She'd surprised Gisele, disgusted her with stupidity, shamed herself—

But Gisele breathed out, and her next smile seemed embarrassed. "I'm sorry. I just assumed that…please forgive me."

"For what?"

"For assuming…anything."

Vale shrugged. "There are a lot of things we don't know about each other. It's okay. I accepted a long time ago that I'll never learn to read."

"Never? Why? I can teach you."

As glorious as that sounded, Vale shook her head. "I don't have the brains for it." They were words from her father's mouth, but that didn't make them any less true.

Gisele frowned, cheeks darkening again and not in a pleasant way. Vale thanked the gods that she directed this look into the woods before she took a few breaths, her shoulders rising and falling hard, then looked at Vale again, features neutral. "Who told you that?"

"My father."

Gisele's fists clenched. "I see. Was this after you tried to learn?"

"No, I've never tried." Vale couldn't stop her voice from getting smaller. Gisele was looking away again, and Vale sensed her trying to hold her temper back. If Vale had been home, and her father had been brewing such a storm, she'd have waved her siblings from the house.

"Vale," Gisele said after a few moments, a few more breaths. She looked a little calmer. "I don't want to argue with you about your own feelings or your past or…" She let out a shaky little laugh. "If you want, I can try to teach you. Despite what your father said, I think you *can* learn."

Vale took her hand, touched by the belief before anxiety seized her again. "I don't want to disappoint you. If I'm not smart enough—" Just when she thought to withdraw her hand, Gisele turned hers over and laced their fingers.

"Something tells me I'll never be disappointed in you."

Sweet, even if it did fill her chest with pressure. Gods, she couldn't let Gisele down now. She glanced at the notebook in Marcella's hands. What if she couldn't do it?

"*Hey.*" Gisele jiggling her hand made her turn back. She was smiling again, leaning forward slightly as if to better catch Vale's gaze. "I didn't mean to make you more nervous. Before I came over, you weren't sitting here worrying about reading, were you?"

"No," Vale said with a sigh. She forced thoughts of the future aside and focused on Gisele's warm hand again. Something else from their conversation nipped at her now. Never mind the reading; she'd never had an afternoon with nothing to do, rainy or otherwise. "It's doing nothing," she said softly. "I think that's why I'm nervous. Home always had something. Minding my siblings, tending to the chickens when we still had some, cleaning the house or everybody's clothes, cooking." Stealing the occasional bit of produce from neighbors when they had no other food to eat. She didn't say that one out loud, feeling more than a little guilty even though she'd left money whenever she'd had some.

"Sounds hard," Gisele said. "Never a moment for yourself."

"My father didn't like to see me sitting idle. If he caught me at it, he…" Reason bloomed in her mind, and all the tenseness, the need to look everywhere at once, made sense. She was waiting to feel the back of his hand, a limb so unlike Gisele's, they might as well have come from different creatures.

And she'd been enjoying the feel of Gisele's hand while her siblings only had his.

Guilt overwhelmed her. Which of her sibs had gotten his anger while she'd been away? She hadn't given them a moment's thought since this whole trouble had begun. Jaime had run away when he'd turned twelve a few months ago, but what of Karmen and Kai? Eight years old, too young to fend for themselves, too young to be battered about. She'd left them.

No, the new voice inside her said, the one that had only recently come to life. She hadn't left, would never have left. She *did not* abandon them.

Memories that she'd forced down came flooding over her. "A cart came through the village," she said softly, seeing it again, feeling the cold breeze go straight through her jacket, especially where she'd grasped an armload of wet laundry, the sharp scent of lye burning her nose. She'd seen the cart coming down the road and had stood on tiptoe, trying to see who it was, but when it had gotten closer, the laundry had fallen from her arms, and her feet had begun to move. "I didn't know it yet, but the Scourge was in the back under a blanket, Warrane riding beside it. They had a Sarrasian woman driving the cart, speaking for him. No one knew the Firellians were arranging everything."

Her father's angry voice had called her back, yelling about the laundry, yelling about having to do everything, yelling at Vale's dead mother, yelling, yelling, yelling, always. But she hadn't been able to stop. Her own body had betrayed her, consequences be damned. "They were traveling the countryside, using the Scourge to make possible mages come to them. I'd never even dreamed of being a mage." She wanted to think about the intra velum now, how she'd never be sorry she'd discovered magic, but she was still locked in that day. She saw the glee in the cart driver's piggy blue eyes, felt the weight of disdain when Warrane had spared her only one hooded glance.

"I was their first. Catch of the day, the cart driver said." Vale had never learned her name. She'd stayed behind once all the mages had been collected, and the ship had set sail. "She tried to tell my father they had a wonderful opportunity for me, that I could be a mage and make him proud." Her voice broke a little, but that day, she hadn't been able to cry or scream or do anything but stand like a stone as her father had looked from her to them, his fat cheeks flushed with anger, his nose marred by tiny red lines from drink.

"He didn't care until they gave him money." She'd heard it changing hands, had wondered how much he'd gotten for her, how little her life had been worth.

She hadn't gotten to say good-bye.

She'd abandoned *no one.*

But, gods, it still hurt.

Gisele's arms went around her when she sobbed. She'd held in her sadness for so long, but now, far from home—where tears hadn't been worth the price to shed them—all her worry and frustration and grief came pouring out of her. She turned her face into Gisele's shoulder to muffle her sobs. Appalled at herself for such a display, she still couldn't stop. The tears just kept coming until her own surprise at how many there were seemed to ease the flood.

Gisele was rocking her gently, and Marcella was rubbing her back, both of them mumbling sweet, soothing words she'd so often used at home and in the hold of the ship. "It's all right, it's okay, you're going to be fine."

Part of her wanted to argue, but it was so nice to hear. Was this what other people felt like when she muttered those words? Gods, she hoped so.

CHAPTER TWENTY-FOUR

Gisele tried to keep the rest of the conversation light. After Vale's revelations, she'd sputtered for a bit, not knowing how to comment on the life Vale had alluded to, her abusive ogre of a father who'd practically sold her to the Firellians, the siblings she'd spoken about in a tiny voice. It had seemed the most natural thing in the world to say, "We'll go back for them, I promise."

Marcella had given her a surprised look, but Vale had only clung to her harder, sobbing around grateful words. Gisele held her tighter. She'd never run from someone who needed her help, and she wondered if any of Adella's new charitable missions extended to small country villages. Or maybe the mages' guild could send more people out, looking for talent. Someone as powerful as Vale would have found her way to the guild in any of the cities, as such people were naturally drawn to other mages, but in the middle of nowhere? How much talent was left on the ground?

All issues to worry about later, never mind that they'd continue to scratch at a door in her mind like a cat wanting to get out.

After Vale wiped her tears, and the small talk grew painful, Marcella brightened. "Would you like to learn more spells, Vale?"

Vale glanced at Gisele as if for permission, and Gisele wanted to tell her it was a good idea, but after the stories about her life, Gisele felt desperate for her to make her own decisions, no matter how small. She smiled instead.

"I...I would, yes, please," Vale said. Her hesitancy bloomed into one of those fantastic smiles. "Maybe the auras?"

Gisele sat back against a log and watched. Marcella had a patient teaching style, so perfect for someone like Vale, and all her explanations were clear and concise. Gisele envied her. She always got a little frustrated when teaching, didn't know the best way to put things into words sometimes, and she worried her corrections sounded too much like "Just figure it out and do it." Marcella had once said it was because Gisele had never had to struggle with magic and seemed to understand it at a level that didn't require words. She just…did it. Luckily, she remembered being taught to read and was fairly certain she could teach that without sounding like an ass.

By the time the rest of their team returned, Marcella had walked Vale through quite a few spells, some of which would have no place in the fight to come, but a little knowledge couldn't ever be a bad thing. And Vale had looked so radiant while she'd learned. Gisele could have watched her all day.

But Roni smiled and nodded at Gisele, shifting her focus. "We found them."

Gisele breathed deep, anticipation coursing through her. "Fantastic."

Jean-Carlo laid out the plan again. They had some ways to walk. The distance between the scout hide and the mages' camp was too great for the Vox's operation, but they'd assured Roni that they knew just how far Gisele could be while powering them. Roni handed over the chain glove while she, Cortez, and Jean-Carlo took a short break to eat and rest their feet.

Gisele fought the urge to pace. She'd be walking soon enough so she sat again by her log, and the Vox perched next to her. "What did you see of the camp?" she asked.

"Minimal movement," the Vox said, their multitude of voices thoughtful. "Based on what Vale said, they'll likely rest most of the day, though they weren't bothering to make their camp invisible."

"The mages are probably worn out," Gisele said. Vale had told them that a few mages had made the ship invisible during the day while the rest of them were exhausted. Then, when those few passed out from the pain and the power, they were shoved in the hold while the rest of the mages woke. Warrane seemed able to pick which mages he used, though Vale had mostly seen him control all the mages within sight. Gisele wondered if he'd ever caught up the exhausted mages in his grip, if he could make their unconscious bodies march about like puppets.

She shivered. How could Vale value his life so much?

"Jean-Carlo thinks we should go in at dusk. They might not be awake yet, and visibility will be poor. Well," the Vox added smugly, "visibility will be poor for most."

Not for them. Gisele grinned. "We should have met long before this, you know. We'd make an unstoppable team."

"For the next few hours, we will." They were silent for a moment. "Zara's also the best at what she does, you know."

Gisele rolled her eyes, but the Vox laughed before she could ask if they were capable of having a single conversation that didn't include Zara.

"Just thought I'd mention it." The Vox went on to describe what they'd seen in the camp and what they'd interpreted based on their experience. They threw in any tidbits they'd gleaned from the others. Roni hadn't been on many missions in the country, but she'd asked a few questions of the others, and she seemed confident that they knew what they were talking about.

Gisele hoped so. She could only tell herself to be ready for anything.

She relayed all this to Vale and Marcella, and Vale seemed relieved that the mages appeared to be getting some rest, though the team hadn't seen inside any of the tents or lean-tos. They hadn't wanted to get that close until later. And after an hour or so crawled by, later finally arrived.

Gisele helped gather their supplies. Jean-Carlo wanted everything they had close by in case they had to run, though it would be up to Gisele, Vale, and Marcella to carry it in that case, as Cortez, Roni, and Jean-Carlo would be going in with only their weapons and their wits.

It was another slog through the forest, but this time, Gisele had the Vox giving her helpful tips along the way: when to go around undergrowth as opposed to through it, steering her around potential deadfalls, and generally taking her mind off how tedious a trek through the woods could be.

"When we get back," Gisele said, "make Zara take you on a pub crawl or something. Tell her that if she doesn't, I will."

"That could be interesting," the Vox said, eagerness in their voice. "Though we might have to fight any people desperate to get their hands on me."

True enough. Even without the Firellian bounty on automatons, the Vox was rare and beautiful enough to warrant all sorts of attention. "You'll only have to bite off one finger to get your message across to everyone."

"Ah, threat economy, I like it."

By the time they reached their destination, she was grateful for the Vox's chatter. She didn't feel as worn-out as Marcella and Vale looked. Luckily, they didn't have to proceed like the others.

"Good luck," Gisele said to all of them, including the Vox, who'd be going with Roni, Cortez, and Jean-Carlo while Gisele retained the glove, watching—and potentially casting spells—through them. She hugged Roni and offered Jean-Carlo a nod. When she nodded to Cortez, too, he stuck out his bottom lip.

"No hug?"

She chuckled, but before she could decide if she wanted to embrace him or not, Roni threw her arms around him and kissed him noisily on the cheek.

"Get off," he mumbled, but he was smiling, and the tiny push he gave her had no force at all.

Jean-Carlo sighed, the loudest note of exasperation Gisele had ever heard from him. His expression softened when Marcella offered him her hand and wished him good luck. He shook it briefly. After stepping away, she faced Cortez. She seemed as if she might go in for a hug, but he offered his hand, and they did an awkward little dance before settling on a handshake, shoulder-pat combo. Roni chuckled along with them before gripping Marcella's hands warmly.

Vale stayed back from everyone, shifting from foot to foot and biting her lip. Gisele moved to her side and took her hand so she wouldn't feel left out or obligated to do anything. She smiled shyly at the Vox when they landed on Gisele's wrist and said, "Be safe."

The Vox nodded before following Roni, Cortez, and Jean-Carlo into the trees.

"Get comfortable," Gisele said before sitting at the base of one tree, closing her eyes, and focusing all her attention through the Vox.

Flitting from branch to branch was as breathtaking as she remembered. She only wished they could fly higher, but no one wanted to take the chance of the Firellians spotting the Vox or even guessing they were in the area. Gisele still didn't know if the Scourge could sense the Vox, but it wasn't sentient. And if Warrane was resting with his charges, the Scourge might not be powered at all. Or he might be awake, and this might all be for naught.

Gisele fought to put such worries from her mind. They were committed now.

Night was coming on fast when the Vox reached a clearing in the trees. Gisele felt a tingle over her scalp as they shifted into an owl, and the campsite before them leaped into clarity. They turned at a small sound. Cortez lowered an unmoving sentry to the forest floor, and he and Roni sneaked quietly forward, bent double. Jean-Carlo was nowhere to be seen. Gisele could only hope that he'd stick to the plan.

The camp was larger than she'd imagined. In the center, two tents sat closely together as if making one large one. Five smaller tents were scattered around a patch of ground that had been swept clear of leaves and twigs. A couple lean-tos sat on the other side of the clearing, and a campfire smoldered near the large tent, its embers glowing dully. One man sat close to it, dozing into the hand resting on his bent knees. No one else stirred.

Twilight deepened, but the Vox's sight remained sharp. They caught a hint of movement near the lean-tos, something that might have been a startled bird taking wing or even another sentry shifting around. But a small, brief flash came from that direction, a signal, no doubt Jean-Carlo dispatching another sentry.

Gisele couldn't help wondering how Vale would feel about that, but she could waste no time worrying about it.

Roni crept from cover, keeping low in the gloom. She sneaked along the trees, staying behind the man snoozing before the fire. She paused at the back of one tent and tilted her head as if listening before she made a tiny hole. After looking through it, she proceeded to the next tent, then the next and repeated her pattern. At the tent closest to the large one, she paused for a long time, head cocked. The Vox leaned closer to get a better view. Roni worked quickly at a corner, dagger flashing. She paused so many times in her work that Gisele fought the urge to yell, "Just get on with it," knowing that Marcella and Vale wouldn't have a clue what she was doing.

"Patience," the Vox said, their tone amused.

Not her strongest suit, but she kept herself from holding her breath and continued to watch.

At last, Roni's head and torso disappeared into the hole she'd made. Dark had fully fallen. The camp would no doubt stir soon, but Roni still acted as if they had a million years to go.

"Just grab the damn thing and run," Gisele said, hoping she only said it in her head, or the others would be asking what she meant.

"Caution," the Vox said.

Great, patience and caution, traits she would only possess in some alternate life.

Cortez and Jean-Carlo seemed to agree. Cortez crept forward, following Roni's trail. Roni hadn't moved, the top half of her still within the tent. Cortez crept closer, his hand outstretched. Gods, if he caused her to jump and bring the tent down…

"That's far enough," a heavily accented voice said, ringing through the clearing. "One more move, and she dies."

CHAPTER TWENTY-FIVE

Gisele froze at the ultimatum even though her body wasn't anywhere near the camp. Dimly, she heard Marcella ask what was happening.

"I don't know. The Firellians are threatening Roni. I think she might be caught." Then Gisele tuned her out, focusing on the camp. The Vox hopped several branches to the side to get a better look. They stayed high in the tree, not daring to take wing. Gisele agreed. The longer they could remain hidden—

"And that includes your automaton," the accented voice said, a hint of amusement creeping in.

Shit.

Roni eased back from the tent, the gleam of a sword at her throat. A slight figure followed in a gray uniform. They pushed a few strands of short dark hair from their forehead with their free hand and kept the blade at Roni's throat as they stood behind her. Gisele had no clue about Firellian officer ranks, but the fact that this one had a few stripes and spoke with a very confident voice said it was probably Bijou, the lieutenant Vale had spoken of, the person in charge of this mission, though she wasn't happy about being burdened with a bunch of mages.

She looked pretty smug now as soldiers came from the other tents, lanterns held high.

Fuck, fuck, fuck. Even if Gisele sent a gust of wind to knock Bijou down, the spell would catch Roni, and they'd topple together. Roni no longer had her dagger in hand, so Bijou would have the advantage. But Gisele had to do something before the Firellians had a chance to grab Cortez and discover Jean-Carlo. They might have sensed the Vox's presence, but they might not know she could cast through them.

The Vox scanned the camp. The soldiers weren't moving toward where Jean-Carlo had signaled. Good, they might not find him. She searched for signs of the mages or the Scourge. She didn't want to set random fires without knowing where everyone was.

Someone called in Firellian, words she couldn't make out, but a couple of soldiers moved toward the Vox's tree.

Gisele gritted her teeth. "I won't let them take you, don't worry." If she had to issue apologies later, she'd do so, but she wouldn't give these assholes a chance to take the Vox apart.

"Fire," she said aloud, hoping Marcella and Vale were ready. She gripped that star, and the tent that had housed Bijou burst into flame.

Everyone cried out. "Their monsters are here," someone yelled.

Gisele would have loved to shout something sarcastic like "You should have surrendered while you had the chance," but her heart was too caught up to boast. Bijou kept her blade at Roni's neck for several moments, her expression shocked, but when the flames leaned in her direction, she fell back a step.

Roni leaped forward into a somersault, rolling toward Cortez, who drew his sword. He rushed to cover her and deflected a swing from Bijou. Several soldiers ran toward the fire. Gisele gave it another burst, driving them back, but the tent would be gone in seconds. She dragged some flames along the ground, trying to keep anyone from interfering in the fight between Bijou and Cortez. Roni was on her feet, watching Cortez's back. Gisele still couldn't see Jean-Carlo in the chaos, and the Firellian soldiers were moving around too much to pick out Warrane.

As the burning tent sagged, something came from within, padding slowly as if it was used to walking the corridors of hell. Gisele's breath caught as the fire licked around its body but couldn't seem to touch it, simply casting red and yellow reflections off its metal hide.

The Scourge.

And fire didn't seem to faze it.

If it was still moving, that meant Warrane was still alive.

And the mages were in this camp.

Gisele dared not burn anything more. Instead, she pushed some of the soldiers around with the star of wind, hoping to cause enough of a distraction that Roni and Cortez could slip away. But Bijou seemed like a skilled opponent, and one other Firellian had slipped through the fire barricade. They faced off with Roni, who'd admitted more than once that she wasn't very confident in her combat skills. Gisele searched for a way to help her with a spell, but everyone was so close together.

"Fly over there," Gisele said.

The Vox's voices sounded strained. "Can't move well while you're casting."

"Shit." She eased away from the intra velum, and the Vox took wing. She had no idea why casting would have that effect on them, but she hoped like hell that they'd get the chance for further experimentation.

Instead of stopping to let her cast, the Vox flew high, then dropped on Roni's opponent, clawing and pecking and slashing with their metal wings. Gisele half closed her eyes against the spray of blood and held in a cry of her own as the man screamed.

"Look out," Roni called. She stepped around as the Vox took wing again. Another soldier had been coming for them from behind. The Vox wheeled, but a figure in black stepped from the trees to engage this new soldier. Jean-Carlo.

Still, the Vox could dispatch this one, too, and maybe the others if they took a mythic form. They flew higher.

"If you become a roc, can you avoid killing the mages?" Gisele asked.

"Perhaps. I'll have to work quickly, and you'll pass out."

And the Vox would return to normal size and fall into the camp once she lost consciousness, but the others could retrieve them. The fire was going out. They might not have—

A tinny noise caught Gisele's attention. It had been building for several moments, she realized, but now it was getting difficult to ignore. Painful, almost.

And familiar.

"Vox, watch out," she cried, but it wouldn't do any good. The lightning was already streaking for them, compressed to look more like a comet than a jagged bolt. The blue-white glow filled Gisele's vision. "No!"

Pain blinded her. She screamed, grabbing her forehead and trying to remove the hammer that was no doubt sticking out of her skull. Someone was calling her name, grabbing her arms. She thrashed. She couldn't let the Firellians catch her, couldn't let them put her under the Scourge's control, couldn't—

"Gisele!"

Marcella's voice. The pain faded a little from her head, but gods, it was spiking through her body, her casting catching up with her now that the Vox—

"We have to go." Gisele opened her eyes and tried to stand. "We have to help."

Marcella helped her up, face pinched in concern. The forest around them was blackened and scorched in a few places, the air heavy with smoke and the scent of burning leaves. The campfire blazed. "What happened?" Marcella asked.

"Where's Vale?" Gisele turned in a circle, her panic feeding on the fact that Vale was nowhere to be seen.

"She ran that way when you said something about killing mages." Marcella pointed into the woods in the direction of the Firellian camp. "What happened?"

Gisele grabbed a lantern and started on Vale's trail. "I can tell you while—"

Marcella hauled her back by the arm. "She took the anti-automaton spike. We don't have another. Gisele, listen to me."

"I can't." Her heart was still pounding. That white glow stayed with her. The Vox had been hit. She couldn't feel them at all. The chain was a dead thing around her wrist. She began to cry and couldn't stop. How could everything have gone so wrong?

Marcella took her shoulders. "We have to wait. We have no protection from the Scourge. What happened to everyone else? Were they captured? Injured?" Her jaw tightened in a lump under her cheek. "Killed?"

"If you're too afraid to come, then don't." Gisele wrenched away. "Gods and devils, we have to help them."

Marcella yanked the lantern out of her hand.

Gisele whirled, her anger and fear focusing on Marcella's determined expression. "Give that back."

"No. You're not thinking clearly."

"Give it *back*."

Marcella shook her head.

Gisele sneered. "I could light the forest on fire instead."

"Do what you've got to do, you…" She looked over the ground as if an insult might be lying there, ready to use. "Person who's…bad at making decisions right now."

It was ridiculous. And she said it with a straight face, making it even sillier. Some of Gisele's panic faded in a wash of absurdity, but her laugh came out as a half sob. "You are really bad at insulting people."

Marcella drew herself up. "I take that as a compliment." She smiled a little.

"Gods." Gisele breathed out another laugh filled with tears and fell into Marcella's arms. "I'm sorry."

"Me too."

"But we have to do something." As much as she wanted to sink into the comfort of Marcella's embrace, Gisele pulled back. "I cannot just sit here, Chell, I can't. Everyone was alive when I last saw them, but the Vox…" She shook her head and clenched a fist against the tears. She would not fucking dissolve when her friends needed her. "They were struck by a ball of lightning, and now I can't feel them."

Marcella nodded and rubbed her chin, no doubt running the problems through her brilliant mind. A wave of shame washed over Gisele, but she kept silent, letting Marcella think.

"Remember what Zara said about the Vox getting hurt?" Marcella said at last. "And the little that Vale told us?" She pointed to the chain glove. "She sent a pulse through them, restarting them. See if you can reach them like that."

Gisele put a finger over the gem at her wrist. She didn't want to electrocute herself. She barely touched the wildly glowing lightning star and sent a tiny flicker into the gem, making her skin tingle.

A heartbeat passed. Another.

She swallowed. "Nothing."

"Try again."

She did, a little stronger this time, enough to hurt even through the joint pain and make her wince. Again, nothing. She shook her head.

"May I?" Marcella nodded to the chain and gem. Gisele nodded and held her hand out, breathing deep and trying not to see that white glow again, to feel that pain bouncing around her skull, but it was almost preferable to the worry.

Marcella put the chain and gem on the ground. She kneeled, hand hovering over them, and a tiny bolt went into the gem. Mages didn't often need their hands to cast, but for such fine control, it helped. Gisele sat next to her and reached for the gem, pressing it to her wrist without winding the chain around her hand. She reached for the Vox.

Nothing.

She restrained herself to a sigh when she wanted to scream. She put the gem back on the ground. Marcella bit her lip, and Gisele knew what she was thinking: how much could the gem take before they broke it? It wasn't really a gemstone but a creation like the Vox, its origins lost to history. But whatever it was made out of, it couldn't be struck by lightning indefinitely without breaking.

Then the Vox really would be lost to them forever.

Marcella gathered up the chain and gem and pressed them into Gisele's palm. "Keep trying." She glanced at the dark woods. "Maybe we can get a little closer." She stood and took a step into the trees. "We'll just have to—" She gasped, harsh as a whistle.

Gisele pushed to her feet, the pain from her knees threatening to take her down again. When Jean-Carlo stepped into the light, she let her knees have their way and sank to the ground. Roni and Cortez followed him, all of them looking haggard, their clothes dotted with blood. When Vale followed holding the Vox, Gisele launched upward, telling her knees they'd just have to wait until after she'd crushed Vale and the Vox in her arms.

CHAPTER TWENTY-SIX

Vale could have lived an eternity with Gisele in her arms. Knowing that someone like her—powerful, confident, beautiful, smart—still needed someone like Vale did something to her heart, melting her insides. If someone had tried to tear Gisele from her arms just then, she would have held on until her last breath.

"Thank the gods you're all right," Gisele said, shifting her gaze from Vale to the Vox and then all around. Her eyes widened, and Vale knew she'd caught sight of the newest member of their party over Vale's shoulder.

She stepped to the side. "This is Cristobal." And the fact that she'd been able to spirit him away made her chest feel almost as full as when she hugged Gisele.

He stepped past her into the light of the campfire, smiling shyly. His face and hair were both filthy, and tear tracks cut through the dirt from the dark circles under his sunken eyes to his sharply pointed chin. Like a lot of teenagers, he was all angles and bones, but a lack of food made him even thinner.

Vale clasped his bony hand. "He only speaks Firellian and a little Othlan."

Gisele stared at him in wonder. "How...what happened?"

"We need to move away from here first," Jean-Carlo said. His voice was flat, but anger wafted from him as strongly as any aura. He began to put out the campfire while the others shouldered their supplies.

Vale gently restarted the Vox as she had before. Something about touching them this way reminded her of the Scourge. Not its awful power, but the moment when she'd broken its hold. It made the same ache in her head, though nothing powerful enough to make her nose bleed. And when she awakened the Vox, Gisele gave her one of those grateful smiles and swallowed her in another embrace.

"You're brilliant," Gisele said in her ear. "I hope you know that. Absolutely brilliant."

The nasty voices inside made Vale want to stammer and deny and list all the stupid things she'd ever done, but Gisele seemed to mute them by her very proximity, and a little of the compliment sank in. No one had taught her how to connect with an automaton, how much energy to push into them. She'd felt her way through it the first time. When the nasty voices tried to argue, she stopped thinking so hard about the compliment and what it meant and just curled a mental hand around it, shielding it and saving it for later.

No, what she needed to think about now was what she'd seen after the plan to steal the Scourge's gem had gone wrong so she could tell Gisele. As they followed Jean-Carlo through the dark forest, she let her mind wander, lining up the events of that evening so they'd be useful:

As much as Vale abhorred violence and didn't wish to see it, having to listen to Gisele go through it without her was even worse. She and Marcella had been able to douse the fires Gisele had set or move them to the ready campfire, but now Gisele simply gasped or growled or muttered, her eyes tightly closed. Something had gone wrong with the plan. Gisele had been able to tell them that, at least.

It was too much to know and not enough at the same time.

Vale gripped the anti-automaton spike. Marcella thought it best to have it out and ready, a smart precaution, but Vale didn't feel the presence of the Scourge, not even a little. Gisele didn't seem like she was in the grip of it; they still didn't know if the Scourge could reach her through the Vox. The spike was useless here with them when it might be doing some good at the enemy camp.

Gisele sucked in a breath. "If you become a roc, can you avoid killing the mages?" she asked.

Marcella put a hand to her mouth and glanced at Vale with shock in her eyes.

Avoid killing the mages? Enough was enough.

Vale grabbed a lantern and ran, clutching the spike, ignoring Marcella's calls to come back. She heard another cry from Gisele and ran harder. It wasn't Gisele's body in trouble but her mind. And Gisele might have been worried about killing mages, but the others might not be, depending on what was happening to them, depending on what could be *avoided*. She needed to help, had to, her heart beating so wildly, it seemed to race in front of her.

She didn't slow as she spotted a glow in the trees and heard people shouting. After bursting into a clearing, she saw Bijou fighting Cortez beside a flaming tent. Jean-Carlo and Roni were facing off against Andre and one of the other soldiers. The fire spread throughout the camp, and others were trying to fight the flames or save things from the tents. Vale squinted past the brightness at where more people were huddled together near the middle of the clearing.

The mages stood idle, their expressions placid in the midst of all this chaos. Warrane stood at their head, the Scourge at his heels. He was yelling to someone and gesturing wildly.

Vale glanced at the spike in her fist. She felt nothing from the Scourge and had to fight down a cry of triumph. A layer of fear slipped away. Maybe she could get close enough to hurt it? Drive the spike into it?

Warrane waved, and the mages turned. The fire seemed to waver a bit, but he still looked panicked, digging his hands through his hair. Did he even know how to move the flames or put them out? She'd had to guess her way through it, and from what she recalled, he'd only ever created it. And with fear obvious in his features, he'd never figure out the right spell.

He yelled something again and shut his eyes. After a moment, the faces of the mages changed, matching his expression. He'd given the order for them to follow him, doing exactly as he did, the easiest way of controlling them all, as he'd once claimed. Vale hated to see his fear in their faces, but she didn't have long to look. He turned and hurried toward the opposite side of the camp, and the mages followed, moving exactly like him.

And most of the soldiers followed in his wake as if they were fine with abandoning their camp and supplies.

And three of their fellows, including their commander.

Vale forced herself away from that thought, from the combat, though the idea of anyone being left to die sent cramps through her stomach. She ran around the camp, trying to keep the mages in sight. Maybe she could follow them? But what could she do against the soldiers, against the magic? She could use her own magic, but would she be a match for any spells Warrane combined through the Scourge?

Several mages trailed at the end of the column, unwatched, unguarded, no doubt because they had to obey Warrane. The soldiers would probably gladly leave them behind, too, abandoning them to the flames.

Vale nearly stumbled to a halt. If no one was looking...

Maybe she didn't have to free everyone at once.

Cristobal walked near the very end, his wide frightened eyes the only sign of his true emotions. He came so close to one of the flaming tents that he had to close his eyes while sweat poured off his forehead.

Vale ran before she could think. She hit Cristobal as hard as she could, knocking him sideways. Her chest ached when she fell on top of him, and his breath came out in a *whoosh*. She banged her chin against his elbow but fought through that pain and felt her way down his arm as he struggled to rise. She curled his hand around the top half of the spike while she held the lower.

He went limp and gasped, then doubled over around a coughing fit. The air was thick with smoke and soot. "V...Vale?"

"Keep one hand on this and hold on to me." She dipped into the intra velum and used the flower of wind to clear the air around them, keeping them in a clean bubble just like the last time she'd been surrounded by flames. She fought down her fear just as she had then. Cristobal needed her to be brave.

She helped him to his feet. He kept one hand on the spike and put the other arm around her shoulders, his taller frame stooping over her. They scrambled awkwardly into the trees on the other side of the camp, feet knocking into one another like some awkward, newly born, four-legged creature.

She led him toward the back of the camp, and he seemed content to follow, his fingers digging into her shoulder. One fight still raged on the far side of the fire until Andre seemed to catch sight of Vale and Cristobal. He leaped over a pile of flaming leaves, abandoning his comrade, who called out in fear before a strike from Jean-Carlo put him down. Vale turned away from the sight, looking for Bijou but not seeing her. Roni stood off to the side, cradling the Vox's unmoving body. Cortez was on his knees, one hand over a streaming wound on his leg.

Vale grabbed the flower of fire and put out the blaze near him, her every joint filling with pain as she wrenched the flames into nothingness. Jean-Carlo strode over and lifted Cortez to his feet.

Roni hurried to them and pulled Cortez close to support him. He wrapped his arm around her shoulders, favoring his leg. "Vale, could you take the Vox?" Roni asked.

She and Cristobal shuffled forward, and Vale grabbed the Vox, holding them close. Worry arced through her at how still they were. She'd felled them once with a ball of lightning and sensed that the same thing had happened now. She could put them to rights as soon as everyone was safely away.

She hoped. Another thing to worry about later. Her future was rapidly filling with things to worry about later.

Jean-Carlo stared at the rest of the camp.

"The others ran," Vale said. "I can put the fire out."

"Let it burn." He wiped at a cut on his cheek, smearing the blood down his chin. It now looked like he'd been drinking it. "We can't fight all of them at once, and the fire should keep them moving away."

No doubt he was right, but Vale couldn't let this forest burn out of control. Who knew how many people would be affected? She curbed it some as they walked away, directing it all toward the middle of the clearing where it was running out of things to burn. She was limping along with the others from the effort, holding tightly to the Vox and Cristobal until they spotted Gisele and Marcella's campfire ahead, and it seemed safe enough to walk without clutching the spike. Vale left it in Cristobal's hand and hoped Gisele wouldn't be angry with her before she had a chance to heal the Vox.

CHAPTER TWENTY-SEVEN

They stopped for the night in a clearing that didn't seem far from where Gisele and Marcella had been waiting for the others to return. Or it might have been far; Gisele wasn't paying much attention. She reactivated the Vox even though fatigue lay over her like a heavy blanket. She didn't know exactly why, but she felt the need to apologize over and over to them. She only stopped when they threatened to quit speaking to her if she persisted.

"I know my own mind," they said. "And how to get myself into trouble all on my own." Then they kept lookout up in the branches while everyone set up camp.

Gisele helped as directed. She'd never handled a tent before and didn't see herself developing a passion for it now. Or camping as a whole, really. Beds were too wonderful an invention to be spurned. Roni sighed as she worked, too, as if she'd hoped never to see a tent again after her last adventure in the woods.

Cortez sat off to the side. His limp had gotten better as they'd walked, and Vale was tending to the wound in his leg. When she caught Gisele looking over, she smiled. "I used to see to all my family's injuries at home. An old couple who lived down the lane taught me."

Gisele bit back a remark about how the old couple should have saved her and her siblings from their father. Or they could have told the local constabulary. Gisele closed her eyes for a moment and made herself breathe. There'd be time to settle all that once everyone was safe. Gods, her list of things to do after she returned home was getting longer and longer. When would she have the time?

She almost heard Zara reply in her head. "If a thing is worth doing, you make time for it."

"That's one of my favorite Zara sayings," the Vox said in Gisele's mind.

Gisele snorted and muttered, "If she was here now and said that, I might take her up on that duel she's always promising."

The Vox *tsked*, but Gisele thanked the devils that they didn't suggest she'd lose. She would win against Zara for one simple reason: she'd cheat. She normally went out of her way to play fair, but she had no rules when it came to beating Zara. How could she? The challenge itself would irk Zara, but cheating would make her absolutely *livid*.

"Ah!" Gisele drew back her hand from the tent peg she'd been banging into the ground. She'd caught her fucking finger with the mallet and shook it to make the ache go away.

"Best pay attention," the Vox said softly, their tone amused and a *lot* of Zara in their voices.

Gisele summoned Jean-Carlo's stoic attitude and ignored them.

Once the tents were up, everyone sat around the lanterns to eat and tell their piece of the story from the Firellian camp. Cristobal went last, with Vale translating. She seemed to have a knack for languages, though almost everyone there spoke a little Firellian.

"We were in the dark," he said. "Kept in one of the tents. They usually let us rest during the day, our bodies under our own control, and only our magic subdued. But not today." He swallowed hard, his hands shaking. Vale put a comforting hand on his wrist, and he seemed to take strength from her. "Warrane had us all lying side by side inside the large tent. Some slept. I might have dozed. I hate sleeping on my back." He glanced up, his eyes fearful.

Did he think including personal tidbits was going to get him in trouble?

"Me too," Gisele said, offering an encouraging smile. It wasn't exactly true, but like Vale's touch, it seemed to give him courage.

"The Scourge wasn't with us," he said, "but Warrane looked in sometimes. I heard him speaking to Bijou about another construct like the Scourge, that he could sense it when it was nearby. They were afraid of it at first, afraid it might work against the Scourge's power." He shrugged, a hopeless gesture. Like Vale, he probably thought nothing worked against the Scourge, despite what had happened only a few hours ago.

Marcella bit her lip and leaned toward him, no doubt eager to ask about how the Scourge worked, but Cristobal wouldn't be able to tell them any more than Vale had. Gisele gave Marcella a wide-eyed look, hoping she got the idea to save her questions for later now that they'd gotten Cristobal talking at all.

"I guess they figured out that your construct couldn't affect the Scourge. There was some excitement after that," he said.

"Planning the trap," Cortez added.

Cristobal hung his head. "We would have warned you if we could."

"They know. We know," Vale said.

He smiled at her. "Warrane came to sit with us. He mumbled something about finding someone. I think he was looking for you," he said to Vale, then looked at everyone. "Or any mages among you. He kept doing it even after Bijou called out and threatened you." He shook his head and stared at nothing. "There was a lot of noise, then, yelling, a rush like flames. Someone cried out about a monster. That's what they call us." He frowned hard and seemed to ignore Vale's touch this time. "As if we're the bad ones when they…" He took another deep breath, and Gisele shared in his anger, his frustration. Of course, his had to be ten times the size of hers.

"Even in all the commotion," Cristobal said, "Warrane kept looking for mages instead of joining the fight. Several people called for him to do something, but he said, 'I know you're out there, I know it,' and things like that. Smoke was coming in, but we couldn't cough, had to just breathe it, though some were making choking sounds, gagging, their bodies rebelling."

Jean-Carlo passed him a canteen, seemingly as moved as everyone else. Good. Maybe he would finally listen when Vale said the mages deserved every effort to be saved instead of sacrificed.

Cristobal drank slowly while everyone else stayed silent, riveted. "Finally, someone ripped aside the tent flap and screamed at us to do something. Warrane jumped up as if he'd been sound asleep. He bade us come out. He called for the Scourge. The camp was on fire, and we had to just stand there while everything burned closer. I think the fire must have reached a cask of lamp oil or something because it seemed the very earth was in flames."

Gisele winced. She hadn't thought of casks of lamp oil when she'd been throwing fire around.

"Warrane had us throw a ball of lightning into the trees at your golden bird, your automaton. Then he tried to make us fight the fire, but I could tell he was scared. We only moved it around a bit. Franka was beside me, and she managed to call Warrane a son of a pig." He snorted a laugh, but the rest of his face looked ready to cry. "I think he heard her. He got even more scared and switched his command from 'do as I say' to 'follow me,' and we had to do whatever he did." He glanced at all of them. "That's how I think of the commands in my head. I don't know if he actually says that to the Scourge."

"It's all right," Vale said softly. She wiped away her tears and squeezed his arm. "None of us knows how the Scourge works. It's okay."

"And then you tackled me," he said, smiling at her. "You saved me, Vale. I knew you would." He gazed at her as if she was a god-touched hero from an old myth or maybe one of the gods themselves.

Everyone was silent for a few moments. Vale had a few more reassuring words for Cristobal, and she asked him at least three times if he'd had enough to eat. Gisele watched them, a warm feeling in her chest.

She could fall in love with Vale.

Oh gods. Gisele blinked back to reality. Where in all the hells had that come from? She didn't do love. None of her friends did, either. They were young and healthy and had all the world lying before them. Love was…an anchor. Like kids. Or a mortgage. Sure, she cared about Vale. How could she not? Vale was lovely and powerful and seemed to put her entire heart into everything she did. Gisele certainly wanted to know her better, wanted to keep all the promises she'd made, but that had just as much to do with helping fellow mages as it did with Vale.

Didn't it?

"You know the answer to that," the Vox said in her mind.

She jumped, then sighed. "I forgot you were there," she replied in her head.

"I've been listening. First to Cristobal, then to your noisy thoughts. When you first donned the glove, I didn't get a peep out of your head, but now…"

"Now what? You think we're bonding the longer I wear the glove?" Marcella might be interested in that, but to Gisele, it was just annoying. "Or maybe I'm tired." She had another thought and smiled. "Or maybe you should take it as a sign that you're trusting me more."

They snorted. "Maybe it's all three. I still can't quite see all your thoughts, but some people have more guarded minds than others. Zara could keep some of her thoughts back right from the start, though she never saw the need to. Roni is not only an open book, she's an annotated copy with footnotes and full appendices."

Gisele laughed. Everyone turned to stare. Her cheeks grew blazing hot. "Sorry, the, um, the Vox said something funny."

They all waited. "What did they say?" Roni asked, smiling back as if eager to share in the joke.

Gods and devils. "Oh, it was just…they…you had to be there," she finished lamely. She rushed to her feet and moved closer to the tree where the Vox perched. They chuckled in her head but had the decency to perch on a lower branch so she could see them as she spoke and wouldn't feel like such a fool.

"So now we know that Warrane can sense you through the Scourge," she said. "Too bad you can't sense them sensing you."

"Really? This is the conversation you want to have instead of talking about the possibility that you're falling in love with Vale?"

Gisele crossed her arms. "You're as bad as Serrah Nunez."

"I didn't have much time to observe them. Hmm. Maybe I should connect with more people. I wonder how Zara would feel about it."

"She'd hate it. You know that."

"But if they're people she knows and trusts—"

Gisele rubbed her temples, fighting down a wave of frustration. "Why the fuck are we talking about Zara again? Or how you'd spend hours gossiping with Serrah Nunez?"

"Or you falling in love with Vale?"

"By all the devils, I will rip this glove off, and you will spend the night in a sack."

"All right, all right, touchy." The Vox sighed. "What are we supposed to be talking about?" Before Gisele could remind them or carry out her threat or scream her head off, they spoke again. "Right, sensing the Scourge. Yes, I didn't feel anything except a sense that it was present. No sensing it sensing me, even when Warrane seemed to know exactly where I was for the lightning." A trill of fear came from them, as if they shuddered in her head.

Gisele ran a hand along their cold feathers. "I should have had you pull back from the fight. I'm sorry. I guess I thought that since the mages didn't make an appearance at the start of the fight, they weren't going to do anything."

"Not your fault. I could have thought of that as well."

"You're not as used to mages and what they can do."

"One of my former users said there's only one way to settle a case of 'who's to blame.'" They held out one clawed foot. "Arm wrestle for it."

Gisele laughed. "Not with those talons. How about we both stop trying to take the blame and just get on with life. Shake on it?" She held out a hand.

"Agreed." They curled their toes around two of her fingers, their grip cold, but the sentiment warmed her.

She drifted back to where the others had broken into small groups, talking quietly, but before she could sit with Vale and Cristobal, Jean-Carlo cleared his throat and stood, a subtle call for everyone's attention.

"Cristobal," he said, his tone soft, as if sensing that anything else might make Cristobal crumble into dust. "If you're up for it, we have a few more questions." He spoke in Sarrasian, letting Vale translate, though Gisele bet he spoke fluent Firellian. And she doubted he abstained now just for Roni's benefit. He no doubt wanted both Cristobal and Vale to think they could have a private conversation even while he was in the room.

"It's devious," the Vox said, "but I have to admire it."

Gisele sighed. She felt the same way.

CHAPTER TWENTY-EIGHT

Jean-Carlo asked Cristobal a few more gentle questions, keeping an open, friendly expression that seemed creepy to Gisele, or probably to anyone who'd actually spent time with him. But Cristobal seemed at ease while he answered, and Vale didn't leave anything out of her translations.

Not that she ever would.

Everyone was yawning by that point. Gisele stretched but waited to climb in a tent. With just two places to sleep, they'd be pretty squashed, but Gisele wouldn't mind if she was squashed with Vale. Cristobal would probably feel safest on Vale's other side, and Marcella might take the other side of Gisele, leaving all the mages in one tent.

When Marcella stopped to have a quick word with Jean-Carlo, her all eager smiles, and him exuding a near-parental aura of goodwill, Gisele rethought the sleeping arrangements. Maybe Marcella hoped to crowd into the other tent.

"Not so fast," the Vox said in her mind.

She started again, then sighed at herself. She needed to take the glove off before she became too tired and went to sleep with it on.

"Not yet," the Vox said excitedly. "Look, look."

With another sigh, Gisele closed her eyes and looked through theirs. Cortez was scowling at Marcella and Jean-Carlo. And when Marcella went to speak with Vale, Cortez took Jean-Carlo's arm and led him a few steps into the forest, away from everyone.

Except the Vox, who'd returned to a higher branch.

Gisele bit her lip. She could hear Adella in her mind telling her it wasn't polite to eavesdrop, but if the Vox was going to be listening anyway…

They chuckled but didn't object.

"Stop flirting with Marcella," Cortez said before Jean-Carlo could even ask what he wanted. "And if you accuse me of jealousy, I will find a way to leave you out here."

The brow Jean-Carlo had lifted eased down. "If you're not jealous, do you think her unsuitable for me or the other way around?"

"Oh, if I thought you were genuinely interested, I'd throw you both a party, but you're using her. You saw her early infatuation, and you're feeding into it in case someone in our happy party starts keeping secrets. Then, wooed by your charm, she'll come tattling to you as soon as she finds out those secrets, your own little spy."

"You still think I'm charming?" His voice was soft and different than before. More honest.

Cortez must have heard it, too, because he studied Jean-Carlo for a few moments. It must have been so frustrating to work with people who lied for a living. After a time, it would become difficult to tell even when they lied to themselves. "I didn't drag you out here to talk about my feelings. We're not together anymore."

"Because you decided we weren't."

"I *decided*?" Cortez took a deep breath, then another, maybe even counting to ten. "Just…leave Marcella alone, okay? If you want to be her friend, fine, but don't act like you're as taken with her as she is with you. She seems like a good person and doesn't deserve the future you have in mind for her." He took two steps back to camp before Jean-Carlo spoke again.

"And what future is that?" His tone was a bit defensive, a little snide, but to Gisele's amazement, it still sounded honest.

Cortez bit his lip so hard, it stayed white for a second after he let it go. He turned slowly, maybe counting to twenty this time. "The future where we all return to the city, and she eagerly awaits a continuance of your relationship, but you vanish." He closed the gap between them, and the Vox had to crane their neck to hear. "At first, she'll assume you're too busy. Then she'll worry that something happened to you. She'll check with friends, go to places you said that you frequent—but the people there will have never heard of you—and maybe end up checking hospitals to make sure you aren't lying wounded with no one knowing your name. By the time she figures out that you simply didn't care enough to say you weren't interested after all, she'll have wasted time and effort, and her heart will be that much more broken." Cortez stared Jean-Carlo down despite being an inch or two shorter. "And maybe you'll end up having to work together one day, but unlike me, she'll be able to kill you from across the room." He brightened. "I'd like to see that last part, but no, it won't be worth the price to her."

"Antonio—"

Cortez snorted a laugh and turned away. "Don't bother, JC."

"I'm sorry."

Cortez stopped and hung his head for a moment before turning back. "And I have no way of knowing if you really mean that."

"I do."

After staring at him for a long moment, Cortez shrugged. "It doesn't matter."

"It matters to me. And clearly, to you, too."

Cortez's face twitched, and Gisele recognized the look of someone trying to hold in their anger. If Cortez had been a mage, Jean-Carlo's trouser cuffs would have been hotter than burned toast. "Are you going to stop leading Marcella on?"

Jean-Carlo had the sense to hang his head. "I will."

"Then maybe I'll start to accept your apology."

This time, Jean-Carlo's smile seemed genuine, too. "Based on what Cristobal overheard in the Firellian camp, the mages are probably heading toward the city."

Cortez blinked a few seconds, no doubt from the change in topic, but he finally nodded. Maybe Jean-Carlo just wanted the chance to speak with him for a little longer. "Um, we figured that they might. Especially if they can keep up the invisibility while they're on the move."

"We'll never catch them in the forest. Well, you and I might, but the others?" Jean-Carlo shook his head.

"I don't relish the idea of tracking invisible mages through the forest and then being burned alive when we find them."

"Nor do I."

"Back to the ship, then," Cortez said. "We'll get to the city faster, then travel out to meet them. Maybe collect some more magical firepower before we go."

Gisele's face grew hot. It was one thing to throw around ideas about what they should do next without her, but if they were talking magic, she should have been in on the conversation. When they started weighing the pros and cons of having more mages, she opened her eyes and moved quietly toward where they were speaking, pretending she'd only overheard the last bits when she interrupted them.

"Without more anti-automaton spikes," she said, "we'd be putting other mages in danger and potentially supplying the Scourge with more prisoners."

They both stared for a moment.

"Oh?" she said, putting a hand to her chest. "Was I not supposed to overhear your casual discussion about mages and magic? The two subjects I'm an expert in? The reason that I'm on this mission?"

Cortez had the decency to look sheepish. Jean-Carlo looked like his usual inscrutable self. "We're just batting around ideas," Cortez said. "We would have asked you about it tomorrow."

"Yes," Jean-Carlo said, "we didn't want to risk waking you if you'd already gone to bed."

"Nice," Gisele said, nodding. "You play off each other well. Now, I am going to bed. If the two of you are going to keep watch, you'll need to be closer to the actual camp." She couldn't resist a last shot over her shoulder. "Unless you're going to stay out here and roll around in the leaves making out."

Even Jean-Carlo blushed a little. Cortez looked like he'd swallowed a live fish, eyes bulging, mouth desperately trying to shape words but only sputtering.

Gisele turned away and grinned.

The Vox chuckled along with her. "They're going to figure out you were listening through me now. And they'll watch for me in the future before they have a private conversation. No more eavesdropping on the dish-y ones."

"It was worth it," she said in her mind. "For those looks and because they've got to be wondering if I can read minds, no matter what I told them about that not being real."

The Vox flew from their perch and landed on the chain glove. "They won't think that for long."

"Long enough for them to learn not to underestimate me again." She gently kissed the Vox's metal beak. "Ready for sleep?"

"No, but I can feel how tired you are. Good night, O Scion of Espionage."

"Good night, O Paragon of Sarcasm." She held them close before slipping the chain and gem from her wrist.

❖

Vale didn't know if she'd ever been happier. Cristobal was free, relatively unharmed, and having eaten his fill, he was now lying next to her in a comfortable tent, each of them with their own blanket. And she could keep him close, keep him safe.

When Gisele crawled in next to her, tugging Marcella along, Vale's heart expanded even more. It was all she could do not to tuck her head into Gisele's shoulder or throw an arm around her waist. Gisele's sweet smile and wish of good night came just as Marcella put out the lamp, but Vale carried the sight and sound with her, taking comfort in the fact that Gisele was still right there. And everyone in their party had made it out alive today, and the remaining captive mages were still alive.

And she'd freed one! They were winning. Now, they just had to do it again. And again. And then some more.

The thought gave her hope instead of making her despair, and she drifted along with that feeling until she fell asleep. Even then, her dreams kept her uplifted.

When she opened her eyes again, light seeped past the edges of the tent flap, and the first thing she saw was Gisele's face, a beautiful sight to wake up to, one she would never tire of.

Guilt wormed through her; she shouldn't be thinking like that. She didn't deserve to conceive of a future where she'd be seeing Gisele on a regular basis, let alone waking up with her. Such fantasies belonged firmly in her dreams.

But sleep was barely done. Didn't she have a little more time? By the sounds from the others, she was the only one awake, so she couldn't stir. All she could do was dream.

She saw a little house in her mind's eye, a place she could live with her siblings in Gisele's city. Even Jaime would come once she'd found him. She'd join this guild for mages that Gisele and Marcella spoke of. She didn't know if they paid their members, but if not, she could get a job as a cleaner, maybe. She was a fair hand at cooking, too, and cities had plenty of restaurants. Surely, one would be short a cook or a server. If any of the mages freed from the Scourge didn't have homes to go to, they could come stay with her, and they'd learn magic together.

With Gisele.

Vale let her fantasy stretch a little further. To Gisele coming home to her or the other way around. Greeting each other at the door. Kissing hello. Eating together at a crowded table, the kitchen filled with happy voices. They'd sit by the fire after the children had been put to bed. Then they'd go to their own bed. Together, hand in hand. But they wouldn't sleep right away.

Vale's skin grew hot, and tingles passed through her belly and lower. She had to stop this fantasy in its tracks. She hadn't earned the right to consider Gisele in that way. And Gisele would never want her, the nasty voices said.

But she hadn't minded when Vale had kissed her. She'd even returned the kiss, and the look in her eyes had said…Vale wasn't sure, exactly, but it hadn't been an angry or insulted look. Encouraging, maybe.

Or that could have been her imagination. Or pity.

Vale winced. That thought stung more than the idea that Gisele could never want her at all. She'd rather have a future without kisses than one filled with gestures of pity.

The newest voice inside her said to wait. To see what Gisele did, to follow her lead. Maybe even ask how Gisele felt instead of trying to guess and read every gesture, every expression. Gisele would never erupt like Vale's father; she didn't have to stay one step ahead of every emotion to avoid a flood of scorching anger.

Wait. Be patient. Be useful. Focus on the task at hand. She'd lived by those words all her life. She could do it a bit longer. With careful fingers, she moved a lock of hair from Gisele's cheek. There was always the night for dreaming, and that was something.

CHAPTER TWENTY-NINE

Vale wasn't used to so much walking. At home, she was on her feet all day, but she'd never gone far from her village. Then she'd been riding on the ship, but walking anywhere, even while in pain, was preferable to standing around under someone else's control.

Her feet were aching and blistered from the sorry shoes the Firellians had given her, but she tried her best not to limp, not wanting to give Gisele something else to worry about as they trudged toward the river. She was already concerned that they were heading in the opposite direction of the mages, but Gisele had assured her it was just so they could get ahead of them since they knew the Firellians' destination.

Gods, Vale hoped she was right.

She checked on Cristobal again, tired of the fretting in her own head.

"I'm fine," he said softly, smiling a little. And he did look better. His skin wasn't as sallow, and though he still bore the marks of mistreatment and fatigue, he didn't have a continuous frown and didn't hunch when he walked. It was amazing what plenty of food and rest could do for a body. She felt the same way being in Gisele's care, though for her, that had a lot to do with Gisele herself, who didn't seem to be having the easiest time walking through the woods, either. At least they all slowed one another down.

Gisele was frowning at the undergrowth as if it had insulted her and muttering under her breath.

"How are you?" Vale asked, keeping her voice down in case Gisele was also embarrassed about having a difficult time.

"Miserable," Gisele said. "This forest is harder to walk through than a back alley in hell." She growled and didn't seem to care who heard her. "I thought forests were supposed to have paths and things."

"Only along major routes," Roni said. "Unless you can find a game trail, this is it."

"Leave it to the Firellians to find the most asinine route into Sarras. If they're having as much trouble as we are, it should have been easy to follow them." Gisele spoke up a bit, leveling a look back at where Cortez was shepherding them. Jean-Carlo led the way.

"They have a head start," Cortez said. "And they'll no doubt be watching for us to follow, stealthy as we are." He winked at Vale just as Marcella stepped on a rotten branch, the snapping sound echoing through the trees. She smiled back. The rest of them were just as noisy, even without speaking.

"Let's hope they really are heading for the city," Roni said.

Vale nodded. She'd overheard that part of the Firellians' plan, and Cristobal had said he'd heard it again in the forest. "But we don't know which part of the city," she added. "How big is it? The mages will probably be invisible, but someone might be able to see the marks of their passage. Can your people surround the city and watch?"

Most of them made little noises that might have been laughter, but they coughed or cleared their throats on top of it. Marcella was shaking her head. "The city's too big for that, I'm afraid. It's many miles across. To surround it with watchers, we'd need a sizeable chunk of the population."

Vale tried to picture it and failed. She was certain the Firellians had taken her to some kind of city or town when they'd boarded the ship, but she'd been unable to look around at the time.

"At least we have some idea of where they'd planned to go before they lost their ship," Roni said. "Somewhere along the river. If they scouted that area beforehand, and that's all the information they have, they might keep to it."

Cortez shook his head. "They're heading inland. They're not going to go all that way, then double back to the river just to attack that side of the city."

They fell to discussing and guessing and trying to disprove one another's guesses. They listed areas of their city, and each one sounded five times bigger than Vale's village. Her dream of a little house wavered. She wouldn't know where to look for one. Perhaps Gisele would help? If she was going to live there, too…

No, Vale couldn't entertain that thought out here, couldn't focus on walking without falling over if she lost herself in fantasy.

"What are they talking about?" Cristobal asked.

She told him in Firellian.

"And their city's called Sarras?" he asked. "Just like their country?"

She nodded. "I heard that from a peddler once. But everyone who lives there just says 'the city,' apparently."

He chuckled. "Maybe they all get confused, too. And you didn't come from there?"

"I came from Entrellas, a little village near the Firellian border, but I never knew we were so little and so close until…" She couldn't talk about it again, not without Gisele's arms around her.

Cristobal put a hand on her shoulder. "It's okay. You don't have to think about it. I'm from Ville-la-Riviere, the same town as Warrane."

Vale stumbled in surprise. "How do you know that?"

"I heard some of the soldiers bad-mouthing him as they walked past. They said something like, you can only get trash from a shithole town." She thought such a remark might have wounded him, but he rolled his eyes. "The only places in town that stink are the leather-tanning shacks. Everywhere else smells fine." He tilted his head back and forth. "Unless the wind is blowing from that direction."

Vale was still surprised that he and Warrane were from the same place. All she knew of Warrane was what he'd said about the building with the stained glass. She'd half expected him to come from an entire town of cruel people forced to work for even crueler ones. "Do you know the stained glass there? The one with the river of blood?"

He looked at her in surprise. "You mean the hospital? How do you know about that?"

She told him about Warrane's stained glass memory. "Did you know him when you lived there?"

"No, but it's a big place. Not as large as *the city* but still too big to know everyone."

Vale was burning to think of a way to use this information, maybe to convince Warrane that he was hurting his own people as well as Sarrasians, but…he no doubt already knew that and didn't care. She didn't know whether to sneer at him or weep for how low and ugly his life had become.

"Cristobal," Roni said, drawing their attention. "I've always been curious. Why do the Firellians hate mages so much?"

Vale translated. He shrugged. "The elders say that mages try to take over everything. Even governments and thrones. The magic makes them crave more power, and they turn into monsters." He snorted without humor.

Marcella frowned. "But can't the elders look at Sarras and see that it's not true?"

Another shrug. "Some elders say we shouldn't bother fighting with Sarras because the mons…mages will bring their country to ruin any day now. It's just the way things are."

"But now you have the chance to prove them wrong," Marcella said excitedly.

His jaw dropped. "I'm not going to tell them." When they all stared, Vale prompted him to explain a little more. "If I ever make it home, I'm not telling anyone I can use magic. The soldiers abducted me from the street with the aid of the Scourge. I'll just leave the Scourge out of it and make up something to happen after that, like I was put to work in a field or a mine." He shuddered. "I'm not going to live as an outcast, as a monster, until someone kills me in the night."

Everyone fell silent as if contemplating his words. Vale's heart ached for him. Finally, Gisele spoke up, her voice as tender as if she was exposing a raw nerve. "But how will you be able to not touch the intra velum? To never cast again?"

He shook his head firmly, with all the certainty of a teenager. "I just won't."

Vale gave Gisele a little wave, trying to signal her to drop it. She seemed to get the hint, but Vale had to agree with her. Now that she'd touched the intra velum and had glided through her sunflowers with power at her fingertips, she'd never go back to the person she'd been.

She thought of what Warrane had said about finding her father and reducing him to ash. She could. That was within her power now. Even as she thought it, she knew she wouldn't. Oh, she would see him again when she went to collect her siblings. And she would walk away from him. If he tried to hurt her or the children, she'd use her power, but only to blow him away like seed fluff in a high wind, roll him right out of their lives.

Another dream to covet, another brick in the road to a life of her own.

She touched Cristobal's hand. "If you ever change your mind," she said softly, "you're welcome to stay with me in Sarras."

He gave her a grateful smile that was somewhat pained, and she could almost see the thoughts whirling in his mind. Even after all he'd been through and seen, all the people he'd met, he couldn't leave the bias of his people behind. He didn't want to live surrounded by monsters, never mind that he already had, and most of them had no magic at all.

❖

Gisele nearly whooped when they broke out of the forest onto the banks of the Kingfish River. She wouldn't have cared if there'd been four boatloads of Firellians waiting for them as long as she didn't have to trip over another devils-cursed tree root.

And according to Jean-Carlo, their own boat was waiting not far down the river, as he'd led them through the forest at an angle, rather than going straight back. Gisele resisted the urge to push him into the water for that.

Now that they were out in the open, and she didn't have to watch her steps so much, she took Vale's hand as they walked, swinging their arms back and forth. "I know it's just the elation of being out of the trees, but I finally feel like we're getting somewhere."

Vale flashed an irresistible smile. "Cristobal and I may be getting somewhere new, but you're going back the way you came."

"True, but I see being on familiar ground as another bonus. We'll get to the city, prepare for the mages, then catch them unawares."

"It sounds easy when you say it."

She hoped it would be. If this attack was swiftly taken care of, it might deter others if the empire had any more Scourges or Conductors lying around. "Do you think the other Firellian mages will think like Cristobal and forsake magic?" The very idea made her shiver.

"I don't know. They might."

"But...how?"

"I don't know." Vale lowered her voice, even though Cristobal likely couldn't understand them. "I couldn't give up magic."

"Me neither."

"Just the feel of it...so free."

"Like flying."

"But feeling infinitely supported at the same time." Vale sighed and beamed. "It's the most wonderful thing I've ever felt."

Gisele squeezed her hand. "We're kindred spirits." Even Marcella hadn't seemed as upset by the idea as either of them. "You don't have to worry. Your future is full of wonderful things, especially if you stay in the city."

"I would love to." Her mouth opened as if she wanted to say something else before her gaze darted away, and emotions passed over her face too quickly to read.

Except one. Longing.

Heat flooded Gisele's insides, making her tingle from the toes up. "You know, there are ways to feel wonderful that have nothing to do with magic."

Vale licked her lips, and every muscle in Gisele's core tightened. "So I've heard."

As Gisele had guessed, Vale didn't have much experience, maybe none. That was okay. Gisele was more than happy to proceed at whatever pace Vale wanted. And by the look in her eyes, she wanted any sort of proceeding as badly as Gisele did.

Gisele wanted to say more, a few honeyed phrases, but nothing came to mind. All the seductive words she'd used on others fled her thoughts, and she lost herself in Vale's eyes, in her parted lips. She leaned forward slowly.

"Oh, thank the gods," Roni shouted.

Gisele leaned upright quickly, and Vale nearly leaped away before she looked forward, blinking rapidly as if to clear her thoughts. Gisele knew how she felt. She looked at where Roni was pointing downriver and grinning. Their boat waited just around a small bend.

"My feet will be singing Serrah Nunez's praises tonight," Roni said.

Gisele just kept herself from glaring. Vale put her hand to her mouth as if covering a laugh, and her cheeks had gone pink. Gisele sighed, her irritation fleeing. There was no way to stay angry when looking at someone as lovely as her.

CHAPTER THIRTY

The trip downriver was much faster than coming up. The boat didn't even need a helping gust of wind from Gisele or Marcella. Gisele wouldn't ask Vale to do such a thing without more training, and something told her Cristobal would refuse. He seemed determined to turn his back on magic forever.

Gisele barely managed to avoid asking him how he could give up something so special. She'd heard of mages retiring because they were afraid of the power, a scenario she could imagine. Magic dealt with elemental energy, and it could consume a person if they lost control, and their will wasn't strong enough. But a weak-willed person could still cast a few minor spells. Nothing useful, but they could still experience the rush of the intra velum. But to sneer at and avoid magic as a whole like Cristobal seemed to want? It made Gisele want to shout, "How dare you?" at the whole damn country. Her sinister side even wanted to show the Firellians the monster they were afraid of, but the rational part of her knew fear and respect weren't the same thing.

Even when some people deserved to be afraid.

Marcella sat with Cristobal near the mast and spoke with him in halting Firellian. Good. Her understanding nature would have a much better chance of swaying him than Gisele's badgering. If anything could change his mind, that was. Gisele tried to ignore them and enjoy the fact that she finally got to spend some time alone with Vale while not running for their lives or huddling under trees.

They sat together in the narrow prow of the boat. Every now and again, Vale would turn her face into the wind, her long dark hair streaming behind her. Gisele would have been content to watch her all day, but Vale's cheeks went red when she caught Gisele staring.

Gisele grinned but decided to spare her further embarrassment and not comment on her blushes. "Tell me about your siblings."

Vale spoke of them with a smile, and from there, they exchanged life stories hurriedly, volleying information back and forth, laying their lives bare in just a few hours. Gisele felt the same need for haste that she sensed from Vale. The last few days had taught her that she never knew when she might have to run. They had to use every moment, and Gisele soaked in Vale's details as she did the sun's rays.

Vale seemed to do the same, asking questions atop questions about Gisele's life, the city, her family history, everything. Gisele had worried that her noble status might be intimidating, but Vale seemed to know as little about nobles as she knew about cities. She seemed sympathetic as Gisele described how her family had once been wealthy, but her parents' deaths had cost them nearly everything. They'd scrimped and saved to keep their house in one piece ever since, until Adella's rich ambassador boss had died with Adella as her heir.

"Now you can fix your house," Vale said excitedly, patting Gisele's knee. "I often had to crawl up on our roof and put new tar paper over the holes."

Gisele fought the shock that wanted to take over her face. The differences in their classes didn't seem to embarrass Vale or anger her. Gisele wanted to feel as sanguine, but when she thought of the things she'd bought when people in the country were papering the holes in their roof, she felt a bit ashamed. She would definitely have to talk to Adella about increasing their charitable efforts. Maybe they could cash in on the craze Adella had introduced for embellished trousers, pair with designers to debut their newest creations at charity balls, and raise money for the poorer villages in Sarras.

So those villages could hire more constables who could arrest people like Vale's father.

As Vale asked more questions, Gisele had to put such thoughts away. Night was beginning to fall, the only night they'd spend on the river since they were moving so much faster. She and Vale had spent all day in their little spot at the bow, even eating there, moving only slightly to stay in or out of the sun.

And now they had to decide where to spend the night.

There weren't enough berths for everyone to have their own room. They'd all have to double up while two stayed on deck, taking turns steering the ship. Serrah Nunez and Jean-Carlo had already claimed that duty. And that left three beds waiting for occupants.

Gisele wouldn't let herself be pushy. She didn't even bring up the bunk situation. Roni did that for them, though she simply said they needed to decide who to bunk with. The big wink she offered behind Vale's back said the rest for her. Gisele fought the urge to glare and made herself smile placidly.

But when Vale's conversation became a series of blushing stammers, Gisele couldn't contain the fluttering in her stomach. To her horror, she lost all ability to speak, too. And she was the experienced one. Even if she didn't want to use any seduction techniques, she should say something kind or reassuring, or, or…

"So," she said. And then her brain deserted her.

"So," Vale answered. "I, um…"

Now they had a subject: "I." All they needed were verbs and objects and the rest of things that made sentences.

"If you want…" Gisele began just as Vale said, "We could always…" They apologized at the same time and indicated that the other should speak first. It was a rousing start, nearly an erotic novel all on its own.

Gisele took a deep breath and threw off this veil of sudden shyness as best she could. "I'd like to share with you. If you'd like to share with me, that is." Before Vale could respond, she hurried on. "Not that anything has to happen. I mean, certain things *have* to happen like breathing and sleeping, at some point. Or at every point," she added, feeling a yawning chasm opening underneath her, but she couldn't quit digging until she hit bottom. "No pressure on you. Or me, of course, not that you would." She clapped a hand over her mouth at last. "Gods and devils," she said behind it, the words muffled in her ears. "Please just push me off this boat right now."

When Vale unleashed her gorgeous smile, all the nerves in Gisele's stomach blew away as if riding the star of wind. "I'd like to share with you, too," she said softly. "Let's just see to that part first."

It left the future wide open, which was normally how Gisele liked her romances. No plans, no strings, just a shrug and a "Let's see where the road takes us." And where it usually took her was far away from whoever she'd just had sex with.

But as they made their way belowdeck, hand in hand, every road in her mind led to Vale. She realized with a start that this was the first time she'd ever gone to bed with anyone without having an escape plan. In the past, she'd told herself that the no-strings approach was what the other person wanted, too, that they understood each other, but she'd never really cared to find out beyond saying something in a bar like, "This is just a casual thing, right?" and then what could the other person say but yes? And that was if she even waited for a response or just slammed back whatever she was drinking, then accepted an invite back to their place.

She'd taken easy encounters and greedy kisses and had called it passion. Now, behind closed doors with someone as amazing as Vale, she didn't know what to do. Gods and devils, she was going to fuck this whole thing up.

In the forest, when she'd told herself to let Vale take the lead in anything physical, she hadn't envisioned standing paralyzed while Vale lit a candle and turned down the covers on the bed. She fought for something to say even as Vale approached her slowly, softly took her hands, and kissed her.

Who needed words? Gisele leaned into the kiss, and when they paused, she grinned back as that radiant smile appeared once more. They kissed again. And again. When Vale began undressing her, Gisele finally put her mind aside and let real passion take over.

❖

Vale had never wanted to freeze a moment in time until now. Resting in Gisele's arms while she could acutely recall every second of pleasure was a moment she could have happily lived in forever. The whole world, every responsibility, was locked outside the door, and Gisele's beautiful body was wrapped around hers, shielding her along with a beautiful heart and mind and magic. Vale let herself drift in the intra velum while she retained this bliss. She felt so complete, she nearly wept.

"Are you going to cast something?" Gisele asked sleepily. She'd said before that sensing another's connection to the intra velum wasn't common, another piece of evidence proving they were made for each other.

"No, just riding this high."

Gisele chuckled sleepily, one of the most satisfying sounds Vale had ever heard. She snuggled deeper into the embrace, sighing when Gisele helped by pulling her in tight. All that they still had to do, all the people who needed them, tried to catch her conscience again but couldn't quite reach her, a different kind of magic that Gisele possessed.

"No one has ever made me feel the way you do," Vale said.

"I feel the same way."

Another piece of evidence.

Vale almost said everything she'd been thinking, about the little house she'd imagined, about the crowded kitchen and the laughter of her siblings and coming home to Gisele every night or welcoming her at the door. But this moment was so perfect, she didn't want to clutter it, even with talk of dreams.

When the nasty voices tried to say that she only shied away from speaking because she knew Gisele would laugh at her or get angry or storm from the room, Vale turned her face into the soft pool of Gisele's hair lying across the pillow. Even the nastiest of thoughts couldn't get her in there, and sleep claimed her quickly.

When she awoke to find Gisele gone, those voices came streaming back in, pouncing while she was groggy and weak with sleep. She groaned and put her hands over her ears as if the voices were coming from outside. She slipped under the covers and squeezed her eyes shut hard, shouting inside until she drowned them out. They were just her own fears and concerns. They couldn't control her or hit her or make every bad thing in the world into her fault.

"We're still on the boat," she whispered. "Gisele couldn't have run away and left me, even if she wanted to. Which she doesn't. She likes me."

Everything that had happened between them wasn't a trick. None of it had been meant to hurt Vale or laugh at her. Gisele had no doubt left the room because she hadn't wanted to wake her.

"Wake me," Vale whispered. "I have to tell her to always wake me up." She forced herself not to dress in a hurry. She didn't have to stop Gisele from leaving or keep the rest of the crew from betraying her. No one was in immediate danger, and that included her heart. She made herself breathe deep and slowly walk upstairs. She was only a little embarrassed to find that almost everyone was up, but when Gisele smiled, Vale's darker feelings popped like soap bubbles. And when Gisele led her to the bow and showed her the city of Sarras in the distance, all feelings fled.

It was larger than her imagination could even hold.

"You can only get a good view of the docks from here," Gisele said, pointing ahead. "They're not the most picturesque sight in the city, I'm afraid."

There was more? Where? She turned her head and saw more buildings and walls and houses, the city stretching to the horizon in the early morning haze floating above the river. Except for some wild areas on the opposite side of the river, the city took up nearly every space she could see.

Any trees had thinned out long before. Now they disappeared entirely, except for a clump of them nearly on the horizon. Gisele pointed to the trees and said that was the army base. It looked like the other clumps of buildings, but it stuck out from the city like a finger. That would be their first port of call. Gisele had said they'd had a hard time getting out of the city before, and going straight to the army base seemed far safer.

Zara, tall and courageous and confident, would be there, which lightened Vale's heart, helping her shed some of the fear that this sprawl of city spawned inside her. Gisele's other sister, Adella, would be there, too, someone Gisele spoke of with a hint of reverence, the only mother she remembered.

Gods. Would there be time to change before meeting anyone? But what could she change into? This simple long shirt and linen trousers were all she had. Maybe she should ask to borrow something? But what about Cristobal? He was dressed the same as her, both in the rough clothing the Firellians had given them. She couldn't let him stand out on his own.

Gisele took her hand. "Are you all right? You don't need to be worried. Everyone's going to love you."

Sweet, but Vale couldn't help knotting her shirt in one fist.

Gisele glanced down, and realization seemed to pass over her face. "Oh. No one's going to judge what you're wearing, either. You did just escape imprisonment on a Firellian ship. My sisters aren't going to be wondering why you're not wearing diamonds."

Gods and devils, she hadn't even considered jewelry. The Firellians hadn't even let her keep her woven bracelet. And she'd never seen a diamond, though she knew it was a type of jewel. But which one? If she asked Gisele's sisters about their diamonds, they'd laugh if she pointed to the wrong one. She couldn't reveal how stupid she was during their first meeting.

"*Hey*," Gisele said, just as she'd said that same word at the scout hide, gentle but firmly reassuring. "Zara already knows you, so she won't be strange and uncomfortable, and Adella is the nicest person in the city."

Vale smiled, even though her stomach was cramping. "In that whole city?"

"If they had a contest for it, she would sweep all before her."

She sounded divine, but Vale's head was still full of nasty voices, and she jumped when Serrah Nunez laid a hand on her shoulder.

"Sorry, custard, didn't mean to startle you." He grinned. "And I know your predicament because I was eavesdropping on every word."

Gisele frowned slightly. "I'm not one of your gossip dishes, serrah."

"You're using that word wrong, cupcake, but I kind of like it." He patted Vale's shoulder. "I understand your plight, dear Vale, and I'm here to help." To Gisele, he added, "The right outfit can give one tremendous confidence." He straightened his immaculate coat. "I should know. Fashion is my life." Gisele opened her mouth as if to speak, but Serrah Nunez held up a hand. "Put yourself in my hands, Vale, my little sugar cube, and I'll have you ready for any room in Sarras."

Vale smiled as confidence already washed through her. "Oh, Serrah Nunez, would you?"

He put up a hand as if to shield his eyes. "Put that smile away before I lose my heart!"

She laughed, Gisele joining in. "Do you have something for Cristobal, too?"

Serrah Nunez put a hand to his chest as if grasping a wound. "Do I have something for Cristobal, she asks. My sweet, of course I do." He offered his arm, and Vale happily took it. "Let's scoop the boy up and go below. We're just lucky I went ahead and had two trunks of clothes put onboard when we decided on this ship as a backup plan."

"Two? How many trunks would you have if the boat had been the original plan?" Gisele asked, her tone teasing.

"Ignore her," he said, leaning down to Vale. "She's just jealous because she won't get to see you until you're ready."

"What?" Gisele hurried to catch up. "I want a fancy outfit, too. Please, serrah, you can't play in the clothes without me." She stuck out her lower lip, and Vale wanted to pull her in and kiss her, but Serrah Nunez was leading the way with a steady grip.

"Can't Gisele come?" Vale asked softly, wanting her there for every moment she could have her. "Please."

"All right," Serrah Nunez said with a sigh. "But only because you asked so sweetly, tartlet."

Gisele whooped and took Vale's other arm, kissing her on the cheek, and it was another perfect moment to hold forever.

CHAPTER THIRTY-ONE

Gisele hadn't thought Vale could look more beautiful, but Serrah Nunez seemed one to thumb his nose at the impossible.

The blousy, deep green tunic fell almost to Vale's knees, but Serrah Nunez tied a ribbon around her waist, nipping it in and leaving a bow on one hip. He did the same with the wrists so the sleeves wouldn't fall over Vale's hands, and she wore a pair of thick tights underneath. People could describe it as a very short dress or a modestly long shirt over tight trousers. It set off Vale's eyes, and the scooped neck accentuated her shoulders, especially after Serrah Nunez plaited her hair in a loose, almost fluffy braid, a gold ribbon running through it, and draped it over one shoulder. He added a dash of plum color to her lips and pronounced her ready.

Gisele couldn't help staring until Serrah Nunez whispered, "Don't you dare smudge her lippy with some hasty kisses, crumb cake."

Gisele chuckled. "Only if I get some lippy of my own."

He gestured to his cosmetics case. "Help yourself. I want to see the full mage look."

She nodded. She'd left her robe and headdress behind because she hadn't thought she'd need them, but she found a dark purple gown that would do. It was much too long, but Serrah Nunez kneeled with a needle and thread while Gisele stood in the middle of the small room. Vale held a mirror for her, and she painted her eyelids a smoky gray, wiping the edges with her thumb so the color spread to where her face began to curve. She added a bit of silver sparkle and chose a dark ruby color for her lips.

When she was finished, Vale stared as if Gisele had transformed into a goddess. Her cheeks went as pink as her lips, and Gisele felt heat in her face as well. "You look…" Vale said. She shook her head as if she couldn't think up the words.

"You, too."

But Vale's head kept shaking, and tears gathered in her eyes. "I don't think I deserve to go to the same place as you."

"Of course you do, Vale."

"You'd better believe it," Serrah Nunez said as he stood. "Everyone will take one look at you, sweetie, and think you belong anywhere you want to be."

Vale nodded, still looking a little worried but no longer on the edge of tears. Gisele hugged her, noting that the gown moved freely about her ankles now. Serrah Nunez had managed to tack the fabric up in the front and sides, leaving a bit of length in the back for a short train. The bodice had a crisscross of silver ribbon, startling against the dark purple, and was tight enough to expose a large swath of cleavage. "Maybe we should loosen this a bit," Gisele said, tugging at the ribbon.

"That's just for decoration." Serrah Nunez tapped his lips as he looked at her. "You're just more well-endowed than me, cookie. It doesn't look too low from this side, but if you'd rather, we could tuck in a scarf, give you a draping neckline."

Gisele shook her head. A scarf tucked into the square neck seemed like it would draw more attention. She shrugged, not minding. In fact, she kind of liked showing off a bit. And she wasn't going to a party with a lot of old-school nobility. The soldiers might not care at all. "Nah, I like it. It's a departure from the robe that comes all the way up to my chin." And Vale's gaze kept darting to her cleavage, too, which created a warm feeling in her tummy that she'd keep close until they had a chance to be alone again.

"Right," Serrah Nunez said, cracking his knuckles. "Let's do the hair."

By the time he'd pulled her hair up in a mass of curls and plaits that had thin gold chains crossing through it, they had almost reached the small dock that the military used. Gisele and Vale apologized for not leaving Serrah Nunez enough time to get ready, but he only shooed them out, saying, "All this, and you still don't believe I can work miracles?"

Vale and Gisele went up on deck. Roni whistled at them. She hadn't bothered to change out of the leather clothes she'd worn for scouting. Zara would probably approve. Marcella had changed into the mage's robe she'd been wearing when Cortez had fetched her and looked quite at home, though she mentioned how lovely they both looked. Jean-Carlo was back in his nobleman's dalmatica with his signet ring.

Cortez was...Cortez. His clothing was neat and serviceable and boring, but he seemed proud of his ability to blend into walls, so Gisele didn't comment. Cristobal had declined the offer to delve into Serrah Nunez's clothes and wore plain blue trousers, an unadorned white shirt, and an open gray jacket. Also boring. Probably on loan from Cortez.

They glided into the dock, pulled in by tying off ropes that wound around large winches onshore. Jean-Carlo went to have a word with the soldiers when Serrah Nunez appeared.

Gisele just barely kept from applauding at Serrah Nunez's transformation into something from a cotton-candy dream. The gown was a study in pink chiffon, with a matching swath of fabric wrapped into a short turban on her head, secured with the same diamond pins she'd worn in her cap and cravat earlier. She'd rouged and powdered and sparkled until her face seemed to have a different shape, softer, adding to the dreamlike quality of the gown.

Vale's jaw dropped nearly to the floor.

"I will take your stunned looks as marks of approval, marshmallows. I thought I'd go full fancy lady for an army base. Can't have anyone thinking I'm here to join up." She winked.

When they were all on the docks and headed for the base, Jean-Carlo offered Serrah Nunez his arm. She took it graciously, and they started for the base. Cortez *tsked* just as Gisele rolled her eyes, but she changed her mind about finding the gesture stuffy and offered her arm to Vale.

Vale took it, beaming, then looked back at where Cristobal was hesitating near the boat, looking lost and frightened.

"Go," Gisele said softly. "Be his escort. Even if I'll miss you terribly." She grinned so Vale would know she was teasing. Her large heart was one of the things Gisele lov...really liked about her, after all.

She was so shaken by almost using *that word*, even in her own mind, that she barely registered Vale guiding Cristobal forward. Roni and Cortez moved up on either side of Gisele, both offering an arm. She snorted a laugh and took them both. Marcella was already on Roni's other arm, though she cast a longing look ahead at Jean-Carlo.

"We're far too important to walk two-by-two," Cortez said in a snotty accent.

"Yes, we always go everywhere as a foursome, *dahling*," Roni said.

Gisele had to laugh, and they hurried a little to catch up.

The officer's building inside the base was a flurry of activity after they arrived. People were informed or sent for or sent away. Gisele didn't pay much attention as she lingered in the lobby, not until she was nearly bowled over by Adella. Zara seemed relieved to see her, too, but her one-armed hug was a lot less generous, maybe because of the sling holding her injured arm or because she had to hug around Adella, who wouldn't let go.

Gisele thought to squirm, but...*to hell with it*. She threw her arms around them, ignoring Zara's little squawk of protest and holding them both fiercely. She didn't even know why and couldn't bear to consider it at that moment. She just wanted to hold and be held.

When she finally released them, everyone was busy greeting everyone else. Gisele gave Bridget a hug, too, and then it was a chorus of "How are you?" and "What happened?" Questions flew around like bits of paper in a high wind.

Gisele held a hand out to Vale, who stood off to the side, whispering in Cristobal's ear. She motioned to him to stay where he was, then shyly stepped out and took Gisele's hand.

"Zara," Gisele said, "you remember Vale." She would have rolled her eyes at herself for sounding like she was at a damned garden party, but embarrassment had crept over her, much as affection had a moment ago.

Zara's eyes widened. "Of course." She took Vale's hand, holding it gently, as if it might come off and fall to the floor. "I'm happy to see you alive and well, Vale. Gods, Gisele, you did it."

Gisele wanted to bristle at the disbelief in her voice, but there was pride in there, too, and that shifted something inside her. As irksome as Zara could be, there was something about her being proud of Gisele that just—

She nodded, fighting the sudden choked-up feeling. Best not think too hard about any emotions right now. She introduced Vale to Adella, too, and told them that there was still work to be done, more mages to be rescued.

Adella looked from Gisele to Vale and back again, over and over. It was like watching someone observe a tennis match. And by the little quirk in Adella's lips and the sparkle in her eye, Gisele knew that she *knew*. She felt as if she was wearing a sign that said, "I really like this woman, and we had sex." She was certain her expression hadn't been that soppy, but Adella *knew* all the same.

Luckily, she was saved from Adella's impish looks by Jean-Carlo, who'd sneaked away at some point and now returned to say, "Everyone, let's move to the council chambers where General Garcia, Serrah Fabiola of the mages' guild, and Field Marshal Ortiz are waiting for us."

Gisele gawked. Why not throw in a couple of oligarchs as well? She'd be happy to see Serrah Fabiola again, and she'd already met the intimidating general, but Field Marshal Ortiz? He was a step above the general, had the oligarchs' ears, and was reported to be the head of the Sarrasian intelligence branch.

"Ooh," Cortez said in Gisele's ear as they all began to shift down the hall. "Bringing the family in." She gave him a curious look, and he lifted his eyebrows. "You didn't know? Field Marshal Ortiz is Jean-Carlo's cousin."

Well, well. Gisele couldn't decide if that made him more intimidating or less. "Is that why he wears the signet ring?" she asked softly. "So if anyone asks about it, he can brag about his connection to a field marshal?"

"Oh no." He took a deep breath and glanced around. "I'll tell you if you promise to keep it to yourself."

How delightful. She grinned, then mashed her lips together and locked them with a pretend key.

"He wears a signet ring because he's a direct descendent of the old kings and queens of Sarras. It's a house destroyed, but royalty still runs through his veins."

Gisele couldn't help gaping again. Oh, that explained so much. And that meant the field marshal had royal blood, too, unless he was a cousin by marriage. Well, well, and well again. Two potential monarchs in one room. Or did that make them princes? She wondered what the other noble houses of Sarras would think if they heard. Providing they didn't already know, of course.

And she'd just promised not to tell, devils curse it. The next time Serrah Nunez wanted to gossip, that little secret would be burning her lips.

She tried to put it out of her mind as everyone filed into a large room with a huge table polished to a mirror shine. She stood behind one of the well-cushioned chairs near the windows, Vale on one side of her and Roni on the other, and bowed to the head of the table where General Garcia, Serrah Fabiola, and Field Marshal Ortiz waited. After everyone bowed, they pulled out the chairs and sat.

Part of Gisele thought she should feel intimidated by the sheer power at the head of the table, the political and social and military clout, but gods and devils, they weren't the only ones with influence. Gisele reminded herself that she came from a noble house and was the most powerful mage in the city. She had a right to be here, especially since she'd brought someone who could share that last title with her. She held her head high and met any stares with one of her own.

Unfortunately, Vale looked like she wanted to curl into a ball under the table, and Cristobal clung to her arm as if he might faint. Field Marshal Ortiz's dark-eyed stare bored into them. He had the same high cheekbones and dark hair as Jean-Carlo, but a sharp widow's peak and a neat goatee added more intimidating gravitas to his expression. With the crisp, dark blue uniform, his entire look practically screamed *not to be trifled with.*

He leaned back in his chair, never taking his eyes off them, and gestured to Jean-Carlo, who strode to his side.

After a quick and quiet exchange, Jean-Carlo hurried around the table and kneeled beside Gisele. "Ortiz thinks Vale and Cristobal should wait in a different room."

"Why?" Vale whispered back, the sound high and panicked. "They're not going to forbid me from helping rescue the mages, are they? Because—"

He laid a hand on her arm. "You need to be debriefed by specialists who can ask the right questions. And we'll be telling our own tales in here."

And they were both fresh from being held by the enemy, not to mention the fact that Cristobal was Firellian. Much as Gisele wanted to keep Vale by her side, she understood that no one outside their group would know that Vale, at least, was trustworthy. And Cristobal probably needed her more than Gisele did.

"You should go," Gisele said softly. "Cristobal will be more at ease with less people around, and the person debriefing you will speak his language."

Vale nodded, always one to be swayed by another's plight.

Gisele squeezed her hand. "Don't worry. All the nobles and soldiers in Sarras won't be able to keep us apart for long."

That brought out a small smile.

"You can wait in the same room as Serrah Nunez," Jean-Carlo said.

Gisele took a quick glance around the room. She hadn't even

noticed that Serrah Nunez hadn't entered with the rest of them. She supposed just sailing the ship didn't guarantee one an invitation to this discussion. She shouldn't have been surprised.

But Vale seemed to brighten at this news, and she left the room with Cristobal, Jean-Carlo at their heels. Gisele smirked at the idea of a country girl like Vale being escorted through the corridors of power by a prince.

Gods, Cortez never should have told her. She was going to have to bite back that secret for the rest of her life.

CHAPTER THIRTY-TWO

To Gisele's surprise, everyone looked at her when it came time to explain what had happened on the river and in the woods. She took a deep breath, fighting down intimidation, telling herself that her sudden attack of nerves was only because she'd been certain Jean-Carlo would start the conversation.

And she *was* partly in charge of the mission. Time to act like it.

She spoke clearly, forcing herself to slow down instead of blurting everything. When she got to the part where she and Roni had pursued Vale on their own, she could feel Zara glowering and imagined Adella's fearful stare. Keeping herself from looking at them took almost all her will.

Jean-Carlo spoke the next time she paused, filling in the blanks for what the rest of their group had done: fighting a couple Firellian soldiers and searching for Gisele and Roni. Gisele still managed to keep her eyes on him instead of facing her sisters' expressions.

When she spoke about the Scourge, Serrah Fabiola interrupted with questions, most of which would have been covered if she'd simply waited. Gisele answered as best she could while Marcella chimed in with facts from her research on automatons.

Then it was time to talk about the Vox.

Gisele made herself look at Zara, feeling as if she owed her. She started with, "I had the privilege of powering the Vox and speaking to them about their time spent with other automatons."

Zara frowned, but it seemed a confused look rather than an angry one. She'd taken possession of the Vox when Gisele had first arrived, though she'd handed them over to the armorer rather than donning the chain glove immediately.

Before Zara had a chance to ask the questions no doubt racing through her mind, Gisele spoke of going through the Vox's memories to the earliest ones, when the Scourge had been the Conductor. Zara's expression transformed until she looked as fascinated as the Vox had been.

When Gisele said the Vox was able to detect the Scourge, and that she could cast magic through them, Serrah Fabiola had more questions. She shook her head when Gisele recounted taking the Vox into battle at the camp. "You should have guessed that this Scourge would be able to sense the Vox since the opposite is true."

Marcella looked sheepish, but Gisele barely managed to restrain her temper. "The Scourge doesn't appear to be sentient. Since the Vox had to tell me when the Scourge was near, we didn't know if its user would have access to that information."

"But what of the memories?" Serrah Fabiola asked. "You could have searched the memories for that same occurrence."

Ouch, that was true. She floundered for something to say.

"It's impossible to think through every scenario in the field," Zara said. "One has to make split-second decisions."

Gisele had to take a deep breath to keep her jaw from dropping. Zara didn't defend people simply because she liked them or even because she was related to them. She had to truly agree.

When it came to her and Gisele, that was rare indeed.

"And what's done is done," Adella said.

Her defense meant a great deal, too, but maybe a little less than Zara's. Adella was swayed by family ties, after all.

Gisele launched back into the story, and Jean-Carlo took it up again after the moment when the Vox had been struck. She couldn't help looking at Zara again, her eyes drawn like magnets to the polestar.

Zara's eyes widened, and she sat up a little straighter, her body going taut.

"Vale saved them," Gisele said. "Just like last time. They are completely healed. Their personality is intact. They had a little dent from falling, but they repaired themselves quickly."

Zara nodded, and Gisele hoped she'd spared herself a future tirade by pointing out that the Vox had suffered the exact same fate while in Zara's hands, *and* they'd even fallen from a greater height that time.

Jean-Carlo and Cortez outlined their ideas for what the Firellians might make the captive mages do next, adding that they were partly using information Vale and Cristobal had given them. Cortez added that Vale, at least, seemed determined to stop the mages and free them from captivity, pointing out that some of those captives were Sarrasian citizens. Gisele could have hugged him. Everyone in this room needed to know that Vale wasn't a threat and that they couldn't know which of the mages were their countrymen until they'd freed them all.

Field Marshal Ortiz leaned back, absorbing the information while idly tapping the arm of the chair with one hand. Serrah Fabiola was frowning at the table as if in thought, and General Garcia had her hands folded in front of her, her posture as rigid now as when she'd first sat down.

"We've had our share of magical troubles in the few days you've been gone," she said. "The constables have reported several attacks on mages, and most of the mages have been given quarters on the base for their own safety."

"Finally," Serrah Fabiola said flatly.

General Garcia didn't even look at her. "More worrying are the accounts of magical attacks in the city."

Gisele started back from where she'd been leaning on the table. "What?"

"Mages defending themselves?" Marcella asked.

"No, they appeared to be attacks from enemy mages."

"That doesn't make sense," Gisele said.

Marcella nodded. "The Firellians hate magic." She spoke quickly about what Cristobal had said.

General Garcia shrugged. "Nevertheless, the Firellians appear to have some mages working for them freely. There have been no sightings in the city of anything remotely resembling this Scourge."

Gisele slumped. How could anyone work for a country that despised them and enslaved those like them? It defied belief.

"Reports from within the empire are troubling," Field Marshal Ortiz said, and every eye in the room seemed drawn to him. Gisele wondered how many of them had forgotten he was there. "The Firellian government denies all knowledge of mages or magical attacks. They are reminding anyone who will listen that they have a long and honorable history of not using magic."

"Well, what else would they say?" Cortez asked.

The field marshal shrugged slowly and elegantly, just like Jean-Carlo. "It is unusual that they've tried none of their traditional invasion techniques. I think the Firellian government is scrambling to paint any mage under their direction as working for a splinter group of their military. After Commander del Amanecer uncovered the invisible ships and destroyed the base the Firellians were setting up on Sarrasian soil, the government knew their chances for a full-scale invasion were slim. We believe the magical attacks and this company of captive mages are meant to weaken Sarras as much as possible, destroying as much as they can, and then the Firellian government will reassess whether an invasion is possible."

It was almost insulting. As if people were dying just so someone could gain a better position in a political debate.

"I doubt an invasion is a popular idea among the Firellian people," Adella said. "When I was our ambassador, I thought that all their foot-dragging and arguing about the smallest details of trading was a way to waste time, but my research since then has indicated that their tactics might stem from financial troubles within the empire. They simply don't have enough coin to go to war."

Impressive. Gisele was happy to see that Sarras had reengaged Adella's diplomatic talents.

"That would fit with past patterns," Bridget said. "I wasn't that good of a student when it came to my old government, but Baxter, the old spymaster, grumbled about it enough that I got an idea of the government's ups and downs."

Field Marshal Ortiz nodded. "No doubt the tide of popular opinion in the empire would turn if Sarras was burning and ripe for picking."

Gisele shivered, noting a few winces or dark glances around the table. Everyone seemed to feel a chill from the field marshal's words. "These magical attacks inside the city?" she asked. "Were they… successful?"

No one seemed to want to answer. Finally, General Garcia sighed and said, "A significant section of the Haymarket was destroyed in a fire that we only managed to tame last night."

"Which parts?" Roni asked, her tanned face paling. She'd grown-up there, had friends there.

Field Marshal Ortiz named a few streets Gisele wasn't familiar with, probably parts closer to the Tides. The buildings in the Haymarket weren't the most up-to-date and couldn't be counted on to be in good repair. They were tightly packed and insufficiently patrolled, based on what Adella had told her. Gisele usually went past the Haymarket on mage business. She'd rarely gone down any of the narrower streets. It must have taken a while for the Sarrasian mages or even the fire brigade to make it in and fight the blaze.

"The oligarchs have implemented a curfew," General Garcia

said. "And added the sentinels to the ranks of constables patrolling the streets."

Serrah Fabiola frowned hard. "I've told them that a mage doesn't have to be roaming the streets to cast spells."

"But they might not be so quick to lean out a window and light the building next door on fire," General Garcia said. "They'd run the risk of getting caught in the flames."

Neither of their voices had much passion. This argument was no doubt a few days old. Gisele couldn't say which one she agreed with at the moment, though she'd be furious under a curfew. Adella had story after story of her sneaking out as a child.

"Stopping this group of mages headed for the city should remain our priority," General Garcia said. "Because of the damage they could do while united under this Scourge. You'll have whatever resources you need to fight them."

"Does that include Vale and Cristobal?" Gisele asked.

General Garcia traded glances with Field Marshal Ortiz. "I believe it would be in everyone's best interest if they remained…sequestered here on the base."

Gisele shook her head and tried to calm the nerves fluttering in her stomach. "That will probably work fine for Cristobal, but Vale is desperate to free those mages."

"She has been incredibly helpful thus far," Jean-Carlo added.

Gisele could have hugged him, too, as well as Marcella and Roni for nodding along.

"And every mage freed is one more who won't be fighting against us," Cortez said.

Gods, her list of people to hug was getting longer and longer. She could live with that. "Vale won't accept being left out," Gisele said. She didn't want to add that Vale would run if backed into a corner. Hopefully, she wouldn't need to.

"We'll make it clear that if she flees, she risks being labeled a fugitive," General Garcia said, clearly hearing the unspoken words.

"So she's under arrest?" Gisele asked, anger burning through her, though Garcia's gaze pinned her to the spot. "After everything she's done for us?"

Adella and several others made placating, shushing motions; others muttered over one another.

Gisele was having none of it. "Besides, she's a Sarrasian citizen. You can't just lock her up for no reason."

Serrah Fabiola looked sympathetic, but even she said, "Well, if it's in her own best interest—"

"She doesn't give a damn about her own interest. All she wants to do is help others." Gisele put her palms flat on the table but resisted the urge to push to her feet. "It's…the core of her nature. She'll never harm anyone if she can help it."

"Exactly," Field Marshal Ortiz said quietly. Everyone fell silent. "Based on what you've told us, she rushes in without considering the consequences, putting everyone around her in danger. And if it comes down to a choice between your lives or the mages' lives, or even between the mages' lives and the security of Sarras, she may choose the mages."

Gisele wanted to argue, a thousand rebuttals flying through her mind. Vale was gentle and loving and had a heart made of glass. She would always be on Gisele's side, and surely, that meant she would be on Sarras's side, too, since that was where Gisele lived.

But…

There was the way Vale spoke about the captive mages, the way she took care of Cristobal, the way she ran at even the idea that the captive mages might be hurt or killed.

Gisele cared about Vale. Maybe even loved her. Or could love her one day.

With this great unknown hovering between them?

Vale would gladly sacrifice herself, Gisele was certain. No matter how many times Gisele tried to convince her that her life mattered, too, she would give her life freely. But if she had a choice between saving one person or another, one group or another…

Gisele couldn't honestly say which she'd choose.

Field Marshal Ortiz gave her a gentle smile, but she had to hate someone in that moment, and he would do. Something in his expression said he knew that and accepted it.

"I'll tell her," Gisele said quietly. She was the only one qualified to walk into that other room like a devil and break the universe's most loving heart.

CHAPTER THIRTY-THREE

Vale tried to let herself sink into Serrah Nunez's comforting chatter in the little room where they waited with Cristobal. It wasn't an uncomfortable room, with padded chairs and a little table and a painting of horses grazing in a field.

It just wasn't next door, where she dearly wanted to be.

Not that Serrah Nunez wasn't a wonderful person to spend time with. She was remarkable and not just where fashion was concerned. She seemed to know a little about everything and even had a smattering of Firellian and could speak to Cristobal herself. At least about clothing and jewelry. But Vale couldn't have been happier when one of the Sarrasian guards opened the door, interrupting Cristobal as he tried to describe the latest fashions in the empire.

Then Gisele walked in, and Vale discovered she could be happier still.

That happiness wobbled in the face of Gisele's stricken expression, her somber eyes. She didn't even glance at Cristobal or Serrah Nunez, both of whom had fallen silent. With a sigh that sounded like a groan of pain, Gisele sat on the sofa next to Serrah Nunez, staring at Vale across a short table.

Gisele opened her mouth, paused. Finally, "I'm sorry" rushed out as if it couldn't wait for other words to go first.

"What happened?" Vale asked, putting aside her need to comfort until she knew what had gone wrong.

"They, um, that is, the general and the field marshal, they…"

Fear seized Vale's heart. "The mages? They're going to kill them?"

Gisele began to shake her head, then paused. "I…don't know." She breathed a laugh, a sound without humor before she closed her mouth and cleared her throat. "I will save them all if I can. You know that, don't you?"

"Of course." That had always been Gisele's promise, at least after they'd gotten to know each other, and Vale had already told herself that she wouldn't blame Gisele if some of the mages were hurt, not if Gisele had tried her best. So what was happening now?

Gisele was still staring as if waiting for something, still with that worried look. Vale wanted to prompt her to go on, but a memory rose in her mind. After she'd first met Gisele's friends, they'd said Vale had done enough to help, and they'd wanted her to stay on the boat.

"They won't let me come with you," Vale said quietly, praying that it wasn't true.

Gisele lowered her eyes, all the confirmation Vale needed.

The familiar sense of helplessness washed over her again along with fear and anger. She was rested now, so they couldn't be worried for her health. She was dressed up in pretty ribbons and cosmetics. They couldn't say she wasn't trying to fit in, even if she didn't have diamonds.

Gisele's expression said she agreed with the people in charge. If she wanted to fight their decision, she'd be angry rather than sad.

Vale swallowed all the hurt, fought down memories of all the sweet things Gisele had said, buried the precious night they'd spent together. Though she'd never felt as complete as she had in Gisele's arms.

Vale couldn't ask her why she'd come to this decision; it didn't matter. But because it was Gisele, Vale had to try one final time to convince her. "I have to help the mages," she said softly.

"I know you think that."

Vale curled her fingers into fists. "I have to."

"I can do it for you, Vale." Gisele pushed forward and covered Vale's fists with her warm hands. "I'll save them. You can trust me. I'll do all I can to get everyone out alive, safe and whole, and they can either return to their lives or stay in the city, and I'll help them however they need it. But you and Cristobal have to remain here on the base."

"I do trust you." And she did. Everything Gisele said rang true, but she didn't seem ready to sacrifice her own life. Not that she should. The world needed beautiful, shining souls like Gisele. That was why Vale had to go, in case a sacrifice was necessary. She flattered herself by knowing Gisele would miss her, but Gisele could still have many loves in her future.

Love? Yes, she was sure it was. She'd been lost since Gisele first emerged from the river like a water goddess, dazzling her into worship. And when Gisele had returned her interest, love had built a golden cage around her heart, linking her to Gisele forever.

Something within her had always known that it was her destiny to give her life for others, to save who she could, like Gisele said. And now the time had come, and though she didn't wish for death, exactly, she knew she could pay that price now that she had a goddess to mourn her. It was the only way someone like her could truly earn their place in the world.

"Please, Vale, say something," Gisele said.

What could she say? Even her anger had faded with her purpose being so clear. But she still felt a little hurt that Gisele couldn't acknowledge her purpose, too. "I have to go."

Gisele's grip tightened around her hands. "If you try to run, they'll arrest you."

"Aren't they arresting me now?"

Gisele sank her teeth into her lip. "That's what I asked, too."

"So you'll help me?" Hope ignited within her.

But Gisele paused too long. "If we both run and we're both arrested, there'll be no one fighting for the captive mages. Marcella and the others will try, but the mages don't mean as much to them."

Vale cocked her head, curious. "And they mean as much to you?"

"You do. You mean everything."

Such words were all she'd ever wanted. What future moments in her life could compare to what she was feeling now?

"Focus on the future," Serrah Nunez said.

Vale blinked at her. She'd forgotten anyone else in the world even existed. Cristobal hadn't said a word, watching everyone. "What do you mean?"

"This kerfuffle won't be the end of your life, Vale," Serrah Nunez said softly. "Or dear Gisele's. Think past it. Focus on what's to come, how happy you'll be when this is all over, and you can drink and dance and be free to let loose your passion." She opened her arms as if gesturing at all the world, someone who obviously never kept her passion restrained.

Vale thought of her little house, the happy kitchen. She wanted it, oh yes, but only if she survived the fight, only after she also did all she could. But the imaginary future would be one of the reasons she could die happy. Because of Gisele, she'd had a marvelous dream.

"I love you," Vale said. "For everything you've given me, for who you are."

Gisele trembled. Her arms twitched as if she wanted to move while being held back. "I...we'll..." She faltered.

Vale wanted to ask, to comfort her obvious distress. But something besides pain flickered in Gisele's expression. Doubt? Confusion?

"I..." Gisele breathed out. "Well, we'll drink and...and dance." She glanced at Serrah Nunez and Cristobal.

Embarrassment, perhaps? Vale could understand why she wouldn't want to speak openly about how marvelous it would be to spend another night in each other's arms, but she couldn't admit her love in this room? Cristobal wouldn't understand, and Serrah Nunez seemed like the sort of person who would always celebrate love.

Realization struck Vale like a fist. Gisele didn't love her. Or if Gisele did, she didn't see the little house in their future. Any house, perhaps. Vale's stomach went tight and cold. Did Gisele see any future for them? Or did she always love fully and passionately, then leave when the fire began to die? For all they'd shared about their lives, how well did they really know each other?

Gods and devils, she was stupid, just like her father had always said.

"Please, Vale," Gisele said again, and she looked near tears. "I do...I feel...I want to..."

Want to what? Feel love? Vale saw it in her eyes, shining like a beacon. Why couldn't she say it? They had only known each other a few days, some busy hours, but that was all it took sometimes. *When you meet the person your heart has been waiting for, how can you not know?*

Her breaking heart left her colder than expected. She didn't want to weep, made herself smile, and nodded.

Gisele's exhale sounded almost like a sob. She made a few more promises that Vale had to close her ears to. Vale tried to keep her face calm, easy when she felt dead inside. She translated for Cristobal and went meekly along with the guard who led them to a small building and an even smaller room that had six beds with trunks resting at the foot of each. They were told that they would have food and drink, that their possessions from the ship would be brought to them.

"You don't have to do that," she said, her voice sounding rusty to her ears, her throat tight and sore. "We don't want the clothes from when we were prisoners." Though they would fit this scenario, too.

She hugged Gisele and wished her success on the continuing mission and told her to be careful. She meant all of it. Nothing would ever make her wish Gisele harm. "Tell the others to be careful, too," she said.

Gisele nodded, swiped at her tears, and then she was gone as if she couldn't bear the sight of Vale anymore. Serrah Nunez said she would return and then departed as well, and Vale and Cristobal were left alone, though Vale knew there was a guard just outside the door.

Cristobal sat on one of the beds. "I'm glad they decided to keep us somewhere other than a boat." When she didn't answer, he raised his voice a little. "After they find the mages, do you think they'll let us go?"

"I'm sure they will." She sat on a bed across from him, marveling at the calmness inside her. As if all other emotions had fled. That was fine with her. If she couldn't feel good, she didn't want to feel bad, either.

"What's the matter, Vale? I know you want to free the others, but the Sarrasians can do it without us."

"I'm Sarrasian, too, you know."

He frowned. "Yes, but you're not like the rest of them. You're nice."

She chuckled, though nothing was funny. She stopped quickly. If she let any feelings in, she'd soon find herself a mess on the floor.

He sighed after a long pause. "You're going to escape, aren't you?"

She was too surprised to speak for a moment. If her plans were that obvious, had Gisele seen them, too? "How do you know?"

"I may have gotten to know you in the dark, but I know you. You cared about everyone in that hold. You brought me half a plum." While she was too shocked to speak, he stood and shrugged. "How can I help?"

The very words she'd wanted to hear from Gisele. She stood and threw her arms around him. As young as he was, he was still taller than her, and her head just reached his shoulder. He patted her back and kissed the top of her head.

"I can't let my big sister get into trouble," he said. When she hugged him tighter, he groaned. "Unless she breaks my ribs."

She pulled back, chuckling for real this time even as grateful tears dribbled down her cheeks. "Thank you, Cristobal."

He frowned a little and pointed at her. "I don't promise to use…

magic." He shuddered. "But I can do other things." He grinned darkly. "And I want to see Franka beat the shit out of Warrane."

She hugged him again. She'd always thought of her family as small, her father, a mother gone too soon, and three siblings. That wasn't true anymore, not with all the wonderful people she'd met. New family seemed as easy to gather as a handful of wildflowers.

CHAPTER THIRTY-FOUR

Gisele barely heard the conversation going on around her in the map room. After she'd left Vale in a guarded room on the base, everything seemed wrong in the world. Even the colors seemed muted, and she felt like she'd gone hard of hearing. She couldn't stop thinking about the look on Vale's face.

Well, *looks*, to be exact. In the space of a few moments, Vale had gone from happy to heartbroken, stopping occasionally on angry and worried. Her last expression lingered the most: resigned, bordering on empty, as if all the life and love had drained out of her.

And it was all Gisele's fucking fault.

She'd had a chance to say how much she loved Vale, and she'd missed it. Hadn't even been able to say what she *liked* about her. And why? Because Serrah Nunez and Cristobal had been sitting there? No, she didn't give a damn who knew how she felt. Because it hadn't seemed like the right time, stuck in a stuffy government building with a guard on the door? No, any life-or-death situation rated an "I love you." It didn't matter if it was in a country parlor or at the gates of hell.

Because she didn't love Vale?

Bullshit. She'd tried to argue with herself, to deny her feelings. She was too young; only old people who'd given up on dating fell in love. Gods, she wished she could sneer at love the way she used to when out drinking with friends.

But she was a coward.

And now love had flown out of her life as swiftly as it had flown in.

Vale had chosen her over everyone. She should have chosen Vale.

"Gisele," Zara said from where she bent over a map of the city and the surrounding area. "You're not paying attention."

No, she wasn't. And now everyone was staring at her. The general, field marshal, and Serrah Fabiola had gone to gather their forces or see to whatever it was that important people saw to. And everyone but Vale, Cristobal, and Serrah Nunez were left in a room filled with maps, asked to come up with a plan to present to the higher-ups in one hour.

Gisele tried to think of some sarcastic comeback, but all the wind had left her sails. "I'm sorry, Zara. I don't know anything about maps and strategy and where to deploy people. If you just tell me where I need to be and when, I'd appreciate it."

Everyone looked at one another in confusion. Adella stared at her sympathetically, and Zara's eyes were as wide as they would be in a pitch-black room. "Um, okay," Zara said. She straightened. "Do you need some food? Coffee? Or perhaps a, uh, hug…or something?"

That had to be Roni's influence. And now that Gisele pondered it, a lot of things about Zara had changed since Roni had entered her life. She was still the same Zara in many ways, but all their recent conversations played through Gisele's head, and she realized that Zara had been trying to understand instead of judging or being nosy.

"I'm sorry," Gisele said softly.

Zara frowned but now had a worried look. "No apology necessary."

"Excuse us," Adella said. She nodded for Zara to follow, then strode around the table and took Gisele's arm. "We need a moment."

Not even Jean-Carlo objected to her stern tone.

Gisele let herself be led into the hall. She didn't have enough energy to be irritated. Adella took them into the same small room where Vale had been, and Gisele had to make herself enter. Inside, she couldn't force herself to sit.

Adella took her hands, her skin warm, her expression open and ready to understand.

Gisele's lip wobbled, but she couldn't even feel horrified at that. "You were a great mother," fell from her lips. After failing to tell Vale how she felt, it seemed she couldn't keep any emotions inside. A sob burst out of her, and tears began pouring down her cheeks, but she welcomed them as a sign that she could still feel something.

"Oh, sweetheart." Adella's arms went around her, and Gisele clung to her as if to a raft in a stormy sea.

It wasn't enough. She flailed one arm until Zara caught it, and then Gisele drew her in, mindful of her injured arm. Even then, she needed something else, but she'd thrown all her other love away.

Adella squeezed her tightly. Zara's embrace was more hesitant, but her arm was stronger. Both of them were murmuring soothing nonsense in their own ways. When Gisele's sobs quieted to hiccups, Zara whispered, "What's wrong with her?"

It would have made Gisele angry before, or at least irritated, but that same hint of understanding that she'd finally uncovered stood out. She tried to say, "I hurt her," but didn't know how much of it came out clearly.

"What did she say?" Zara whispered.

"Something about hurting," Adella said.

Zara drew back and pulled Gisele around, holding her firmly by one shoulder. "Gisele, look at me." Her face was set, angry, and Gisele nearly sobbed again, dreading a lecture. "Tell me who hurt you."

It took a moment for realization to sink in. Zara wasn't angry with her. She was ready to kick someone's ass on her behalf. Gisele exhaled slowly, recalling with sudden clarity that whenever she'd been bullied as a child, she hadn't threatened to tell Adella—the closest thing she'd had to a parent—she'd named Zara as her savior.

And the bullies had always run away.

"I love you, Z."

Zara straightened, frowning confusedly again, her head tilted. "I love you, too, Gisele." She glanced at Adella. "Both of you, of course. You're my sisters."

Gisele took her hand and Adella's. She hated sappy scenes like this, nearly gagged at herself now, but she had to say, "I love you, too," to Adella and receive her love in return.

"Is that why you weren't paying attention in the map room?" Zara asked.

"Zara," Adella said.

"And what about the hurt? And why were you crying?"

Adella sighed. "*Zara*, give her a moment to speak."

"I should have chosen Vale," Gisele said. "She may be reckless but only when backed into a corner. She may not always choose the path that's best for Sarras as a country, but she will choose the path where the most people survive. And she'll always choose me. She loves me, and I couldn't say it back." She wiped her cheeks. "I should have told the general that if she makes Vale sit out the fight, then I'll do the same. Or I should have insisted or helped her escape or…or something! I should have spoken up, and now I've lost her."

"No, sweetheart," Adella said, rubbing her shoulders hurriedly. "You can fix it. We'll help you."

"With escaping?" Zara said. "I don't think…" She trailed off after a glance at Adella, and Gisele could only imagine the death glare. "I'm sure you could still stay out of the fight if you want, but taking a mage as powerful as you off the field would weaken our chances of success."

Even though her tone was matter-of-fact, Gisele could feel her pride. "If you had two good arms, you could probably beat the Firellian soldiers on your own."

Other sisters might have demurred or boasted. Zara merely shrugged. "As I do not currently have two good arms, we'll never know."

"At least you can bring the Vox to the field."

"Absolutely."

A spark of an idea bloomed in Gisele's mind. "The Scourge can sense the Vox when they're close to each other. We can lure them into a trap."

Zara's brows went up, her face thoughtful.

"Or maybe they'll try to trap us, and we turn it against them," Adella said.

Gisele traded a glance with Zara and knew they were thinking the same thing. "You can't go into the field," Zara said just as Gisele muttered, "You can't fight, Del."

Adella put her hands on her hips, but she didn't succeed at looking fierce in her embroidered trousers, silk jacket, and hair done up with jewels. "I may not be a mage or a soldier, but I can…do other things." She pointed at the door. "I was helping with the planning."

"As long as you're not thinking of running into combat," Gisele said.

Adella pointed at Zara. "You can't run into combat, either, not with a broken arm."

"I can guide the Vox from farther back."

"Then I can wait with you."

"And if the enemy does find me, I still have one arm to fight with." She waggled her fingers.

Adella sputtered for a moment before rolling her eyes, and Gisele realized just where she'd picked up that habit from herself. Gods and devils, all the times she'd tried to distance herself from her sisters, and she would always be partly their creation.

"I know how you can help," Gisele said, another idea looming large. "You can help me prove to Vale that I do love her."

Adella's face lit up, but she didn't wink or mock or tease like a devil. "Yes, yes, happy to help. What would you like me to do?"

"Help her escape, of course."

❖

Vale had to stand on tiptoe to look out the window at the back of the room. Thankfully, Cristobal could see out clearly. It was small, without glass, and shutters lay folded back against the outside wall. No doubt those would be locked after dark. A soldier in a brown uniform walked back and forth out there, patrolling a narrow alley that led behind their prison and several other small buildings.

The even smaller window at the front revealed another soldier standing guard at the door. Vale was confident she could slip through either window, and Cristobal was thin enough to follow. But what to do about the guards?

"It doesn't take him long to reach the end of the alley and turn," Cristobal whispered. "Only a few minutes."

She could make herself invisible, but climbing out and taking a few steps down the alley before she could sneak around another building would make noise. And the alley was a gravel path, even noisier. The guard's crunching steps echoed between the buildings. He was sure to hear, and no doubt he'd been told that he was guarding mages, as well as whatever else he was keeping an eye on. It would be even more difficult to pass the stationary guard on the door from the front window.

"I'm afraid he'll hear us even if we use invisibility," she said.

Cristobal frowned hard, his dislike of magic seeping out of every pore. "We could wait until dark. Then we wouldn't need it."

"We'd still be noisy. And they might lock the shutters after dark or put on more guards." She bit her lip. "And the fight might be over by then. Plus, how will we find our way around once we do get out?" It wasn't like they'd taken the time to explore when they'd first arrived.

Cristobal *tsked*. "So negative. That's not the Vale I know." He smiled softly.

She took a deep breath. Right. When she'd sneaked up the ladder in the ship's hold to eavesdrop on Warrane and the others, she hadn't let herself think of everything that might go wrong.

Still, she doubted the guards here would be even as sympathetic as Warrane.

"I know," Cristobal said. "I'll make a bunch of noise at one window, like I'm climbing out. If one guard calls the other away, you can sneak out."

A hard knot formed in her stomach. "What if they hurt you?" He shrugged, but she couldn't let it go so easily. "I can't let that happen."

"You wouldn't be letting me. I volunteer."

"No, Cristobal. I can't let…you shouldn't get hurt."

"It's my choice."

"No."

"Vale." He walked a few steps away, lifted his arms, then dropped them, frustration roiling off him. After a deep breath, he kept his voice low. "You're not responsible for me."

She wanted to shout, "Yes, I am," but he'd ask her why, and she'd say his life meant more than hers, and like Gisele, he would probably argue, and they couldn't afford the time right now. "Please, Cristobal. I…couldn't bear it if you got hurt."

His face twisted in pity. "You're going to have to. You'll just have to be strong."

She shrank back from him. "What do you mean?"

"People are going to get hurt. People have been hurt already." He gestured vaguely at the wall. "And someone you care about may die." A thousand rebuttals rushed to her mouth, but he spoke again before they could get out. "And you only have one life to give."

The words punched her in the gut. She had to sit, staggered. Gods and devils, he was right. She couldn't fling herself in front of everyone at once. What if she gave her life, but someone else needed her later? What if she saved one person when she could have saved ten?

No, she just had to be smart, had to find the way to save the most people if she couldn't save them all. But gods, how?

Cristobal sat across from her. "They won't kill me. Maybe if I act like I'm just in trouble or sick or something, they won't even hit me. Lucky for us, the Sarrasians don't seem to hate mages on sight, the fools. No doubt it will be their undoing, but we can take advantage right now." He put a hand on her arm. "If they do hurt me, it won't be badly. I can take it." He sat up proudly.

Vale didn't know what to say. Everything he said rang true. Well, except for the part about the Sarrasians being fools for not hating mages.

The guards that escorted them here didn't seem cruel. They were Zara's people, and they knew Cristobal was young. Anyone who looked at him could see that.

Still, cramps wandered through her belly at the thought of leaving him here. The feelings weren't just for him. Outside these walls, she'd be alone again, with no Gisele waiting to fill the empty places inside her.

"So?" Cristobal asked. "Do we have a plan?"

She breathed deep, told herself she couldn't ignore the earnestness in his face, that she had to let him make his own choices. "Yes."

He smiled proudly. "Good. Should we wait for dark?"

She gnawed her lip. In daylight, she could make herself invisible, but more people would be around to hear her. No one knew her here. She wouldn't be recognized if she walked around openly, but she didn't exactly fit in. Maybe she should have asked for her Firellian clothing back. The blue color wouldn't match the brown Sarrasian uniforms, but it would be less eye-catching than her silk shirt and ribbons. Maybe she could say she'd changed her mind and ask to have those clothes back? Would that be too suspicious?

A knock on the door sent her to her feet, her heart leaping about in her chest. Cristobal stood, too, his eyes wide in fear. Vale licked her lips and had to swallow twice before she managed, "Come in?"

The guard opened the door, and she was certain he was about to accuse her of planning an escape, but he simply stood to the side, and Serrah Nunez sailed into the room.

Vale breathed again. "Serrah, I forgot you were coming back."

Serrah Nunez grinned and nodded to the guard, who shut the door, leaving the three of them alone. "That just shows I can pass unnoticed when I want, cream cake, even in this fabulous creation." She held the dress out to one side, then glanced at both windows before stepping closer. "And it does more than just look good."

Vale smiled. She wouldn't have been surprised to see the dress transform into a hundred different objects, but she had to ask. "Like what?"

"Like this." She hiked her skirt up to the knee and bent over, fussing with the material on the inside. "Damn. Hang on a sec."

Cristobal's eyes went even wider. "What is she doing?"

Vale could only shake her head.

Serrah Nunez drew two small bundles of cloth from beneath her skirt before she straightened. "I ruined my big reveal, but oh well, let's try again." She cleared her throat. "And it does more than just look good." She looked at Vale expectantly.

After a moment, Vale said, "Like what?" again, hoping that was the right response.

"Like this," Serrah Nunez said triumphantly, letting the bundles unroll to reveal two brown Sarrasian uniforms. "It's also a handy escape tool."

CHAPTER THIRTY-FIVE

To Gisele's experienced eye, Zara seemed one step away from careening off "the well-worn path," Adella's saying for when Zara froze, unable to act because events were too unsettling.

Helping someone escape from army custody certainly qualified.

Gisele resisted the urge to point out that Zara wouldn't have to actively participate, letting Adella take the lead.

"Go back in the map room," Adella said. "Tell them Gisele and I need a few more minutes alone. It's not a lie."

Zara frowned. "Don't patronize me."

Shit, maybe Roni was teaching her too much. "Fine," Gisele said. "It will be a lie of omission, sure. But think on this: Vale is a Sarrasian citizen who's being held unlawfully. She committed no crime, never went before a magistrate, and had no opportunity to hire a solicitor."

Zara nodded slowly. "In that case, we should pursue her release through the proper channels."

"Like whom?" Adella said. "All the proper channels eventually lead to the very people who locked her up."

"If she represents a threat to Sarras—"

Gisele stamped a foot like Adella always did when she wanted their attention. "They're only holding her because they won't take the time to speak to her and find out she's not a double agent or whatever. I have spoken to her. I know her. I...I love her, Z."

Zara stared for several seconds, her frown remaining, but her dark eyes looked stricken, wavering. She couldn't scoff at love anymore, not after meeting Roni.

Gisele held her tongue. She had more ammunition: Zara had helped Adella escape from house arrest once. And she'd helped Bridget flee the city, though Bridget had gotten back into Zara's good graces by returning to face questioning. Well, if Zara did it once, she could do it again.

Strangely enough, Gisele didn't want to win this argument that way. She wanted love to win on its own. And like Zara, Gisele had never loved anyone before, never mind the colossally separate paths their lives had taken.

"You trust her?" Zara asked quietly.

Gisele drew herself up. "I swear, on our parents' names, that Vale means no harm to Sarras or her people."

Zara nodded once. She drew a small notebook out of her uniform jacket, and Adella held it for her while she wrote clumsily with her uninjured hand. "Give this to the armorer, and he'll give you access to the Vox." She tore the paper out and handed it over, then wrote another. "Go to the main barracks and ask for Sergeants Jaq or Finn Aquino. They'll get you past any guards and off the base."

Adella *tsked*. "Not much of an escape if we're going with an escort."

Zara gave her a flat look, and Gisele copied her. "This isn't supposed to be exciting, Del," Gisele said.

"Maybe not for you." Adella took the last note. "Come on. Back to the map room with you, Zara. I'll get the sergeants. Gilly, you get the Vox."

Gisele ground her teeth. "Don't call me that baby name, Del, you know I hate it."

Adella gave her a perfect smile before dashing from the room.

Gisele exchanged another look with Zara. It seemed like they'd never convince their office-bound sister that danger wasn't fun. "Good luck, Z," Gisele said.

"And you. Please catch her before she does anything rash. Once you're clear of the base, send someone back to tell me where you are."

"Will do."

They parted, Gisele walking on air. Even breathing was easier now that she was doing the right thing. She collected the Vox, told them the plan thus far, and they seemed happy to help free Vale and even happier that Zara understood why it needed to happen.

"I'm so proud of her," the Vox said.

Gisele chuckled. "Me too." And it was a strange feeling, indeed. The whole day seemed beyond strange, the future like a wide-open book. All Gisele knew was that she wanted Vale in it.

Which made her that much more frustrated when they found

the prison door wide open and the guard inside on one of the beds, unconscious, with the imprint of Serrah Nunez's largest ring on his jaw.

❖

Since Vale had been kidnapped, so many events had qualified for the most frightening thing she'd ever done. Walking boldly through an army base in an ill-fitting uniform didn't quite beat fighting to free herself from the river, but it tied with eavesdropping on the Firellians on the ship, maybe even with running off by herself in the forest.

Serrah Nunez seemed perfectly at home, exclaiming over every detail of the base as if she was being given a tour. "Try not to look so petrified, sweetie," she said out of the side of her mouth. "Take a cue from Cristobal and look bored."

She was right. He managed to look as if he'd rather be anywhere else, but she saw beads of sweat at his hairline. "I can't help it," Vale said. "Everyone looks when you talk."

"It's called hiding in plain sight. Or evading attention by drawing a different sort of attention. Or something like that." She smiled brightly.

Vale returned the smile and hoped it didn't seem too sickly. She would so much rather be sneaking or invisible, but the army base was like a maze, and she didn't know if she could have found her way out alone. Serrah Nunez seemed to have memorized some of it when she'd taken the uniforms from the laundry, "A place no one ever thinks to guard," she'd said.

They didn't seem to be traveling toward the main gate or the dock. "Where are we going?" Vale asked.

"Somewhere we can slip out and be unnoticed." Someone passed between two buildings ahead, and Serrah Nunez slowed. "Now that's very interesting. What year was it built?" she asked loudly.

The passing soldier gave them a disinterested look before going on their way. Serrah Nunez might have been right about no one caring about a tour, but each time she attracted attention, Vale felt as if her heart might burst. She only hoped nothing on her uniform indicated that she was in charge. She would never be able to bluff her way through giving orders.

They came out from between two tall buildings that looked like houses and reached a fence that stretched far in the distance, maybe circling most of the base. Serrah Nunez muttered and looked around, though her expression stayed interested.

"Are you lost?" Vale asked, her innards threatening to give out.

"Not a bit. Just a little…" She glanced around again.

Vale clenched her fists to keep from trembling. Soldiers patrolled along the fence in the distance, some of them with dogs. And Serrah Nunez stuck out too much in the open with her pink gown. Vale couldn't take it. "This way," she tried to say brightly, but it came out a whisper. She walked back between two buildings. "We can't plot an escape route in the open."

"We can't whisper while hiding, either," Serrah Nunez said smoothly. "I saw another gate before, seemed less guarded than the river gate or the main entrance. Could have sworn it was over here." She moved into a narrow gravel lane as she spoke, but she couldn't walk quickly, not if they were going to stick with their charade.

And she shouldn't be leading the way if she was being given a tour. Vale had a quick word with Cristobal, and he moved in front of Serrah Nunez, though she steered him with a hand on his back. Gods, this couldn't last. They'd get—

"Excuse me," someone called, right on cue.

Vale was almost relieved. At least the waiting to be caught was over. She turned and saw a tall thin man holding a sheaf of papers. His uniform was brown but seemed different than hers. Oh devils, was he a higher rank? Should she salute? She didn't know how.

The tall man frowned from behind wire spectacles. "Are you supposed to be in this area?"

"They're just giving me a tour, dumpling," Serrah Nunez said, fluttering her lashes and flashing a smile.

"Not in this area." He didn't seem moved by her charms, probably wasn't moved by anyone's. "Who's your commanding officer?"

"Zara del Amanecer," Vale said quickly. She nearly put a hand over her mouth after it escaped. Gods, she was going to get Zara in trouble, too.

"And who's yours," Serrah Nunez asked sweetly.

The tall man's frown seemed confused this time. "Commander? You're scouts, and you're giving tours?" He mashed his lips into a thin line. "Goofing off, more like. Look here, I'm Colonel Hoffman's clerk, and I don't think—"

A ray of golden light flashed between them, and the clerk staggered back, gawking. Vale nearly cried out in relief when the Vox settled on a nearby railing. She held out her hands, and they flew to her, perching carefully on her fingers in one of their smaller forms.

"Oh," the clerk said. He licked his lips. "If you have…then you must be…oh." He pointed to the Vox, then back to Vale and Cristobal. "Um, my apologies." He backed up a few steps. "Please, continue your tour." He made as if to turn, then hesitated. "But a little bit that way, if you don't mind, away from the officers' quarters."

Vale nodded, though how she was supposed to tell the officers' quarters from every other area, she had no idea. "Thank you," she said to the Vox when the clerk was gone.

They inclined their head, and she wished she could hear what they were saying. But if the Vox was here, that meant…

"We are well and truly nicked," Serrah Nunez said.

"Not quite," a new voice said, a beloved voice, *her* voice.

Vale turned, and Gisele stood there, smiling, coming to the rescue again. Vale nearly leaped for her, the Vox taking wing before Gisele caught her. They exchanged apologies in a rush, and Vale couldn't recall why she'd been upset with Gisele, but a heaviness in her chest said that what was forgotten could be remembered. They were off-balance somehow, and all the kisses in the world wouldn't put them right.

Gisele caught her face. "I love you," she whispered. "I should have said it sooner, should have said it when you did, but I was afraid. I don't know what our future looks like, hell, even what Sarras's future looks like, but I know I want you to be in mine."

The world began to tilt back into place, and Vale's heart lightened. But… "I can't go back to that room, can't avoid this battle." Though what she would do in a fight, she still had no idea. She couldn't even clear her tight throat or stop her tears at the moment.

But she had to be there for the other mages, and that was something.

Gisele kissed her cheeks, her lips, her eyelids. "You'll never be a prisoner again if I can stop it. I've come to help you escape." She glanced around. "Well, escape more."

Someone snorted, and Vale realized there were more people here. Adella stood beside Serrah Nunez, both of them smiling through a few tears. Another soldier stood close by, a frown on her face. Her skin was dark with light patches, and the name sewn high on her chest was F. Aquino. "This is the worst escape attempt I've ever seen," she said.

Gisele sighed. "Vale, this is Sergeant Finn Aquino, one of Zara's scouts. Sergeant, this is Vale." Her tone turned harder. "Who does not deserve your bullshit."

The sergeant snorted again, seeming almost amused as she shrugged. "Well, if your noble selves would care to follow me, I will see you through the side gate before the alarm is raised. My brother Jaq won't be able to cover for you for long." She looked Vale and Cristobal up and down. "You got your own clothes on under there?" When Vale nodded, so did she. "Good. Take off those uniforms. Wearing them actually means something to us."

As Vale and Cristobal stepped out of the lane and hurriedly stripped before someone else came along, Serrah Nunez bowed to Sergeant Aquino. "No disrespect intended, Sergeant. As you can see, my plan didn't go entirely as…planned."

"So I do see, yeah." She gave Serrah Nunez a slower once-over. "You might have done better if they'd dressed like you, serrah. Of course, only someone as willowy and graceful as you could pull that look off."

Serrah Nunez gave her a slow wink, and Sergeant Aquino laughed, leading them down the path at a brisk clip.

"How do you know her?" Vale asked. She'd wiped away her tears and hoped her face wasn't conspicuously puffy.

"I don't," Serrah Nunez whispered back. "But believe me, cupcake, I will." With an impish grin, she hurried ahead to walk by the sergeant's side.

"Love seems to be in the air," Adella said. She took Vale's other arm, grinning at her and Gisele. "If we don't all get caught and imprisoned, this is going to be a good day."

CHAPTER THIRTY-SIX

Gisele thought her days of sitting under trees had ended with the mission to the middle of nowhere. But Sergeant Aquino had led them into the patch of forest near the base, and now Gisele was sitting on the cool ground under another damned tree.

But at least this time, Vale cuddled close, her head resting on Gisele's shoulder, and no one was exhausted or in pain. It made all the difference.

If Gisele didn't look at Adella, Zara, and Cristobal, she could pretend that this was a normal day. She'd taken the perfect woman on a picnic to the forest, and they were relaxing in the shade with the leaves gently whispering above.

"I'd freeze this moment if I could," Vale said softly. "Live in it forever."

Gisele kissed her hair. "Why this one?"

"Because I feel calm and unhurt, and no one needs me." She tilted her head back. "And I have you."

Gisele nearly said, "I need you," but she knew what Vale meant and didn't want to spoil the mood with any disagreement. But she felt compelled to kiss her and say, "I think I'd pick last night on the boat."

Vale's cheeks turned a delicate pink and set off the smile that Gisele would never tire of. "We can freeze more than one moment." She kissed Gisele, the movement turning almost fierce, a reminder that their lives wouldn't stay peaceful for long.

"If you've finished canoodling," Zara said from a nearby tree. Sergeant Aquino had gone to inform her of their whereabouts, but Zara had come out to meet them, insisting on powering the Vox, too, and generally being annoying.

With every word Zara spoke, she got harder to love, never mind

Gisele's earlier epiphany. "What, Z? We already have a plan. You said it yourself, the mages will probably avoid the road, and most of the ground around the city is open, so they'll no doubt stick to areas that have cover." She gestured around. "This forest is their best bet and the place we're most likely to catch them."

Zara scowled as if she'd eaten a lemon. "Your idea is just to sit around and wait for them?"

"Would you rather I stood around tensely, instead?"

"We should make tripwires and position fallen branches to make a path of our choice appear more passable."

"No one's stopping you."

Zara put her hand on her hip. "If we all work together—"

"Children, enough," Adella said.

Gisele bit back a reply, wondering when Adella's power over her was going to fade. If it ever would.

"Zara, make your tripwires and things. Gisele needs to save all her strength for casting magic," Adella said.

Gisele had the strongest urge to stick out her tongue but didn't. She should have gotten some kind of credit for that.

But Adella pointed at her. "Don't antagonize your sister."

"I didn't!"

"I saw you thinking it."

"Condemned without a trial," Gisele muttered.

Vale chuckled. "I like your family. Even when you're fighting, I can feel your connection."

"That's good," Gisele said with a snort. "Most people probably think we hate each other." But most people weren't as in tune with others as Vale was. It was sickening that she was so astute because she'd grown up with an ogre for a father. Gisele held her closer. If the Firellians wanted to find monsters, they should have taken that man.

"Someone's coming," Zara said quietly.

Vale stood swiftly, pulling Gisele up, too. She kept the intra velum close until Zara relaxed.

"The Vox says it's Serrah Nunez." She paused. "And some more familiar faces."

Gisele exchanged a glance with Adella. Serrah Nunez had gone back to the base with Sergeant Aquino. She'd muttered something about keeping up the pretense that she'd done nothing wrong, but Gisele thought it had more to do with the flirty looks she and the sergeant had exchanged.

When Serrah Nunez came into view with Bridget, Roni, Cortez, and Jean-Carlo, Gisele wasn't even that surprised.

"Let me guess," Adella said, "they twisted your arm, serrah?"

"No," Cortez said. "We're just not as stupid as you seem to think."

"What about the plan you were creating for the general?" Zara asked. "We shouldn't be the only ones out here waiting for the mages."

Jean-Carlo lifted a hand as if signaling for silence. "We're not. Marcella took our plan to Field Marshal Ortiz, General Garcia, and Serrah Fabiola. They'll send out the occasional patrol and distribute soldiers, mages, and agents around the city and also at several weak points inside. We told them our team would make a stand in the forest." Before Gisele could point out that he'd given away where Vale and Cristobal had gone, he pinned her with a look. "A different part of the forest than the one we're currently in." He crossed his arms, looking far more perturbed than Gisele had ever seen. "Really, you couldn't let me in on what you were going to do? I'm getting a little tired of cleaning up after all of you."

Everyone was silent for a moment. When Cortez snorted a laugh, it seemed to set everyone off. Several people made little *oohing* noises, the only response to someone being so touchy. Zara added, "You've never cleaned anything up for me."

Serrah Nunez said, "And playing the part of the grumpy uncle…" just as Roni slung an arm around Jean-Carlo's shoulders, saying, "You love it, JC."

He glowered at everyone. The tension in Gisele's shoulders eased as Vale laughed into her hand. Gisele laughed until she coughed, but the noise died down quickly. They were out here to do a job, after all, one that called for at least a little decorum.

For now.

❖

With the future so uncertain, Vale should have been frightened, but all the what-ifs made her energized. It didn't make sense. Their group might even be waiting in the wrong spot, for the gods' sake. She should have been gnawing her lip off in worry.

But with Gisele, it felt like she could carry the world. If she had to give her life for any of the people surrounding her, it would be worth it.

She kept that to herself, knowing they would argue. They didn't understand, and she didn't care to convince them. The stars were aligning as they seemed destined to. And if the happy little house would only ever exist in her dreams, well, that would be more than just something. That would be enough.

Gisele twirled the anti-automaton spike in her fingers. She seemed tenser after the others had arrived. She cast the occasional glance at Zara, and Vale could practically read her mind. She wanted to be the one in communication with the Vox, but Zara had taken back the glove as soon as she'd arrived. The Vox would serve as a scout and a lure because Warrane could sense them through the Scourge. But Gisele had admitted that she didn't know if the same held true while the Vox slept, so Zara kept them awake. Warrane and Bijou might lead the mages right to Gisele and the others if they thought their team was still as small as it had been.

"What if I need to cast magic through the Vox again?" Gisele asked for the second time.

Zara shrugged. "Then I'll give the glove back." But the tension in her face betrayed her fear. Vale didn't blame her. The Vox had been felled by magic twice in a short span of time. "I'm more familiar with this terrain than you are. I can suggest better places to hide."

Gisele put her hands on her hips. "It's not like they'll be safer with you. If the Vox comes close enough to sense the Scourge, Warrane will also know where they are and be able to target them."

"Knowing where something is and seeing it are two different things," Zara said. "Warrane might know the Vox is behind a certain tree, but if he can't see them, he can't hit them with a ball of lightning."

True enough. Gisele grumbled an assent. And the Vox couldn't move around much while Gisele was casting through them. Better that they were in Zara's hands, and she could relay any helpful information.

Not that Vale would say that to Gisele. Better to let her mumble.

Still, she put an arm around Gisele and rubbed her back softly. "You're going to wear yourself out with worry."

Gisele sighed and rolled her head back and forth. "I know you're right, but I can't help it." She smiled, a loving look that Vale also wanted to freeze. "How are you so calm?"

She shrugged. "If things go wrong…they go wrong."

"That's not helpful, love." Gisele kissed her temple. "Wouldn't it be better to say you feel optimistic? Or are you the sort of person who always thinks the worst so they won't be disappointed?"

That seemed a sound plan, but she shrugged and took Gisele's hand. She leaned in for a kiss just as a rumble came from nearby, followed by harsh screams.

Zara drew her saber. "Damn. One of the other patrols must've found the mages before the Vox. Let's move." She sprinted away, her injured arm not seeming to slow her. Gisele put an arm around Vale and ushered her forward, but they both had to keep hold of the spike as they ran.

And that wouldn't help all the mages who were present.

"Cristobal?" Vale called over one shoulder.

"Don't worry," he said. "I'll be well behind you."

Good. He'd be safe that way. At least someone would. Vale braced herself; the nerves would overwhelm her now. But, no, that strange sense of calm remained. Live or die, stand or fall, she was finally in motion, taking the fight to the Scourge, and the captive mages would be freed.

Cortez caught up with Zara and slowed her down. They were supposed to be going cautiously, giving Gisele and Vale space to use their magic while staying far enough away from the captive mages that any spells could be defeated or redirected. Still, they had to reach the mages before the mages reached the city. No one knew exactly what Bijou planned to do. Destroy buildings on the outskirts? Target the people? Vale wouldn't have been surprised if Bijou just wanted to light as many fires as she could, damaging the city and its walls and creating a path more Firellian troops could use to invade.

Chilling. And another reason to free the mages that no one could argue with.

Zara pulled away from Cortez, gesturing angrily, and as Vale came around a bend in a narrow path through the woods, her breath caught.

A large patch of the forest was now a smoldering ruin. Charred, twisted lumps lay scattered across the ground. Bodies. Humans or maybe horses, one charred lump looked too much like another. Vale gasped, breathed them in, and choked on the acrid smell. She looked for the captive mages, but there was nothing. Warrane had to have two or three maintaining invisibility while the others threw offensive spells. She ground her teeth and hoped he was in agony from his toenails to his hair.

Gisele turned in the direction of the city, but there was nothing other than trees, a small clearing, and the outbuildings of the city in the distance. "Stand clear," she yelled.

Cortez and Zara fell back and to the side. Everyone else scattered. Vale felt Gisele enter the intra velum. She held it close, too, but couldn't tell what spell Gisele was going to use until a massive gust of wind flowed from her, whipping the new leaves off the trees and blowing branches and twigs about like a hurricane while the undergrowth and grass were pressed flat.

Three people blinked into existence as they rolled across the ground.

Vale's heart leaped. Aha! If any mage went too far from those maintaining the invisibility spell, they'd reappear. She seized the flower of wind and repeated the spell from a slightly different angle. Two more mages appeared, but the three Gisele had uncovered were turning, faces impassive, staring toward Gisele and Vale.

"Get ready," Gisele said.

Vale nodded. When a barrage of wind came toward them, Vale countered it with another, throwing her strength against theirs. The field between them became a maelstrom, and pain reverberated through her body, but she kept up the barrage. Time was more on her side than theirs. Reinforcements would be coming from the city. Thankfully, any mages among them would still be well away from the Scourge.

Fire blossomed toward them, but Vale left that to Gisele, and the column of flame turned up and away, scorching the treetops, then rumbling uselessly into the air. When Vale's opponents cast fire spells, too, Vale copied Gisele. The mages were strong, especially when working together, but they only had one person thinking and reacting for them, and he couldn't keep track of everything at once. Between a gap in the flames, Vale bowled her opponents over again.

Cortez and Jean-Carlo ran toward the fallen mages, no doubt seeking to disable them before they rose again. Vale's chest ached. She cried, "Don't kill them." Damn. Now she'd have to keep an eye on the mages and her allies.

And where was the Scourge? And Warrane? If they could just knock him out…

She couldn't take her hand off the anti-automaton spike and find out. She felt like she was forgetting something, too, something important.

"Shit," Roni cried, and Vale heard the ring of metal on metal.

Adella moved to Gisele's side and shouted, "Cortez! Jean-Carlo!"

They looked over their shoulders before they reached the mages, then turned and sprinted back toward Adella.

"Focus," Gisele said. "And don't panic."

Vale breathed deep and nodded, trying to ignore the commotion behind her, guessing at what she'd forgotten: the captive mages had an escort of Firellian soldiers, and they'd timed their attack very well.

CHAPTER THIRTY-SEVEN

It took all of Gisele's will not to turn around. A breeze ruffled her hair, surely the wake of someone's movement, but she gritted her teeth and kept her connection to the intra velum. A crackle of lightning came her way. She seized the right star and created her own bolt, shooting it through the enemy's and into the ground. The enemy lightning followed, always attracted to the path of least resistance.

She only hoped a similar path didn't lead to her back at the moment.

No, Adella stood beside her, eyes on the physical fight. She'd yank Gisele and Vale away from any strikes. Gisele would always trust her sister. But it was still damned hard not to look.

Vale dispensed with a ball of fire, grunting with the effort and throwing one arm up as if opening a window. It seemed as if the entire force of captive mages had turned their attention on her and Gisele. Even those who were still invisible.

And there was no sign of Warrane or the Scourge, but the mechanical movements of the mages said the thing was close. Maybe it was invisible, too, but Gisele didn't have time to launch another gust of wind. She fended off one coming her way, pitting her strength against two or three mages at once, maybe more. None of them seemed as strong as her or Vale. And based on what Vale had told her, some of them were no doubt struggling against the Scourge's influence. That might weaken their power.

Shame it did nothing to weaken the pulsing pain in her joints. With any luck, the captive mages would spell themselves unconscious before they hurt anyone. It didn't matter how much control the Scourge had over them; if their bodies gave out, their connection to the intra velum would slip free like a rope from a damaged pulley.

"Lightning," Vale cried.

Gisele cursed. She kept her grasp on the wind star while fumbling for her own lightning, managing a quick bolt to stab the other and ground it as well. Vale dealt with two more bouts of flame. "You have to steer lightning…into the ground."

"I…" Vale grunted and managed her own burst of wind, scattering the enemy mages farther. One on the very edge shook their head and crawled a few feet away. "I don't know how."

"Leave it to me." Gisele glanced at the mage who was inching away from the group. They seemed free of the Scourge but could do little more than crawl, apparently. "We're wearing them out. I'll do the offense…you keep rolling them around. And if you see Warrane…" She didn't finish the thought, hoping that Vale wouldn't need her to. She'd try to knock Warrane out rather than kill him, for Vale's sake, but if they found where he was hiding among the invisible mages, they had to hit him with everything they had. If he went down, any magical firepower went with him.

Leaving the wind spells to Vale, Gisele retreated further into the intra velum, letting her eyes go half-closed, feeling with her senses as much as looking for attacks. She shifted from spell to spell, countering the enemy mages as quickly as she could. Pain was building inside her, the simplest spells costing more with each casting, no matter how economical she tried to be with her efforts. Warrane was probably shifting his focus as quickly as she shifted hers and commanding the captive mages to fire spell after spell.

Gisele's vision flickered. She could feel herself coming closer to her limit, could nearly see it like the finish line in a race. Still, she held back her fear, keeping control, careful to direct flame and lightning and wind outward. If she tapped out in the middle of a spell, she might cast it where she stood and hit herself and Vale and Adella and all the others.

No, by the gods, she would not.

She tried to push that finish line further away, using the smallest of spells to deflect, once letting the fire so close that her face tingled. Too close. She couldn't let Vale get distracted from looking for openings. If they could reveal Warrane and attack him, this would all be over.

And he had to be getting weaker, too. The captive mages' spells had slowed a bit, but there was still strength among them. Gisele wouldn't fall, couldn't. She slipped a little further into the intra velum, recalling in bursts the tall tales of mages who had given themselves over to it completely and had been consumed by the magic.

All nonsense, at least until now. Deep in the intra velum, with spells still flying from her, she glimpsed another star hiding in her periphery as if shy. But it pulsed, its energy unlike any elemental force. It felt a bit like the other field of stars she'd glimpsed in the Vox. Instead of guiding magic, letting the elements loose at her command, this star exuded a sense of…becoming the magic, becoming an…

"Archon," the star seemed to whisper. The pinnacle of magic, an apex caster, one with the elements, and terrifyingly powerful.

Cold as a ball of ice. Emotion had no part in magic.

An archon would be ephemeral, too, she sensed. The power might last long enough to blow a hole in the world, but it would burn out quickly. Humans weren't meant to be made of the same stuff as stars.

Just a few short days ago, she might have chosen that path despite the cost, before she'd let herself realize how much she loved her family and friends. And before she'd met Vale, before she'd known she could feel this way about someone.

Love pulled her back, Vale's hand on her wrist. She was still casting as automatically as if under the Scourge's influence herself. The pain came rushing back, filling her joints with broken glass, but she pushed through, made herself listen to Vale's voice, feel the touch on her arm.

Vale's hand was as red and swollen as Gisele's, but she was still on her feet, still casting. Brave and beautiful and powerful.

"Look," Vale said, a strained whisper, no doubt all she could manage.

The Scourge had appeared in the middle of the mages. Several of them were on the ground, unmoving, no doubt spelled into unconsciousness. One more on the side appeared to be loose but in no state to flee. The mages who'd probably been keeping up the invisibility spell were now firing others, but they were still tired, and Warrane had to be…

Where?

The mages around the Scourge didn't fit his description. Gisele couldn't see anything on their wrists. But Zara didn't have to be right next to the Vox in order to power them. The bastard could be anywhere. And they couldn't fully break his hold until they took the devils-cursed control gem away from him.

"We'll have…to keep them casting," Gisele managed. She had to put one hand on her knee to keep upright. Vale was holding on to her with her free hand. "Make them all…fall asleep."

"I don't know…if I can," Vale said, sounding as tired as Gisele felt. "Did you feel it?"

Gisele shook her head, even though Vale wasn't looking at her. It took so much effort to talk, and pain pounded through her head from her sore jaw, all her joints rebelling, her body warning her that it would not stand for much more of this. Literally.

"The archon," Vale said.

Gisele gasped, her heart pounding. "How?"

"I saw it…you were in deep…followed you."

How in the world? They weren't casting in sync like those tied through the Scourge or the Conductor, but Vale had somehow sensed Gisele's place in the intra velum? No wonder that feeling of love had drawn her back. But why bring it up now?

Unless.

"No," Gisele said, forcing all she felt into the words. "Vale, you can't!"

"To destroy the Scourge. For them…for you." Her touch became a caress. "I will. I love you." She let go of the anti-automaton spike.

"No!" Gisele felt the power of the Scourge flow over Vale. She would need to be tied directly to it in order to destroy it, a conduit between it and the might of an archon. Vale's mind hurtled into the intra velum, searching, giving herself over to the magic.

Like hell. They'd just found each other, and Gisele wouldn't let her slip away that easily. But she couldn't reach Vale while running along a safer path. She released the anti-automaton spike and gave herself over wholly to the intra velum.

❖

Vale prepared herself for the will of the Scourge, of Warrane. Her limbs locked in place, and she knew the spells he wanted her to touch. She threw all her anger at him, willing her field of sunflowers to stay where they were. She'd seen beyond them to a flower on a hill, to the archon, and she pushed through the field, moving in fits and starts, her will versus that of the Scourge. She threw every ounce of anger, everything she'd felt since she'd been taken from her home, every ounce she couldn't express under her father's roof. She hadn't been allowed to express many feelings there, but they'd been hiding just beneath her skin.

For Gisele, for everyone, she let them free.

Blood rushed from her nose, covering her lips, but she wouldn't need that body for much longer. To give herself for others was her destiny. She'd never really doubted it, even when envisioning her little house and a life with Gisele. This was the moment she'd been made for, the ultimate gift.

The only one she had to give.

She accepted that. But the anger hadn't left her. Indeed, it seemed to be gaining on her as she reached toward becoming an archon. She supposed she needed her rage to keep from falling under the Scourge's grasp, but now that she'd spotted that pinnacle of magic, the way toward it seemed much easier, and the Scourge had less of a hold. So why should she be angry?

Because it wasn't her anger.

Wonder filled Vale's mind as Gisele's presence flowed around her. She was mad, too, at the Scourge and Warrane but also at Vale herself. How was she doing this, putting her feelings in Vale's mind?

Not putting, sharing. Gisele's presence was quite clear on that. She offered love without judgment, whole and complete, and argued that Vale did not have to give her life. Another way could be found.

No, Vale wanted to say. She'd always known it would come to this.

Unless that was just her insecurity talking. Her father had called her worthless so many times, she'd begun to believe it.

No, no, no. Putting herself in harm's way was the one thing she could always do. No matter how many times she'd been hit, she could suffer being hit again.

Not anymore. She was surrounded by people who cared about her, people who could hit back on her behalf. And if she didn't want that, the people she loved could at least pull her out of the way. For however long she wanted, she had someone who would stand by her side, and she would never have to suffer at anyone's hands, not ever again.

But…she tried to argue, to bring back what she'd always known at her core.

Love surrounded her, Gisele's love, her strong presence. They could push through the Scourge, could overcome everything, together. But not if Vale touched that flower and became an archon of magic. She'd leave everything behind, then.

But if she was brave enough to stay…

Vale looked into the core of herself again, that dark and lonely place, but instead of spying what she'd always known about sacrificing herself, she saw her father staring back at her.

You are so much more than that.

Gisele's words, Gisele's feelings, offering all the love.

Vale sighed and let herself receive it.

CHAPTER THIRTY-EIGHT

Gisele cried out in joy when she felt Vale turn from the path of the archon. They'd been able to join emotions because of the Scourge, she was certain of that.

Or was she? That felt more like the power of the Conductor.

But the Scourge still pulled at them. It felt much weaker than it had in the forest. It wasn't sentient, but maybe somehow, it wanted to return to what it had been?

Gisele kept her anger and turned her own will on the Scourge, seeking to remind it of who it had been, who it could be again, if it could even understand such things. She clutched Vale's hand. "Hold on."

"Always." Vale's iron will blended with hers, matching it. People might underestimate Vale, but they'd be turning their backs on a lion.

Gisele pushed at the force trying to control her limbs, her magic. Something scrabbled at her mind, but it didn't feel like the metal paw of the Scourge. This felt desperate, scared. Warrane? Gisele clenched her jaw. Vale might want to offer him compassion, but at this moment, he would bend, or they would break him.

The captive mages had ceased to cast, those still under the Scourge's control sagging like marionettes held by invisible strings. Warrane seemed to be putting all his effort into trying to bring Gisele and Vale under the Scourge's power. He hadn't been casting his own magic, but the effort of powering the Scourge still had to be draining him somehow. Gisele didn't know his limit, but for all her joy at having helped Vale see the value in herself, she was fast approaching the end of her strength.

No, he would bend, bend, *bend.* "Don't make me break you, you bastard," she whispered. "Don't make *her* do it, the one person who's been nice to you this entire trip, who's been kinder than you fucking deserved."

She could taste his desperation, joined with him through the Scourge just as she was with Vale, only fighting for control, her will and Vale's versus his and the gem.

"Please, Warrane," Vale said.

Gisele felt his power surge, then waver. In time, Vale could talk him down.

Time they didn't have.

Gisele only hoped Vale's infinite compassion didn't extend to all automatons.

She seized the moment and the star of lightning, letting her attention divide, giving Warrane an opening, but before he could bring the entirety of his will to bear again, she compressed the bolt of lightning into a ball and hurled it, the effort bringing her to her knees.

A flash of white blinded her, but she heard the Scourge collapse with a metallic *clang*.

The power flying about the battlefield died.

Gisele let out a harsh breath and pulled Vale down into an embrace. Her nose was bloody, and Gisele felt as if hers might be the same, but she was too amazed to care.

Adella was yelling at them, asking if they were out of their minds and trying to press the spike back into their hands. If Gisele ever needed to borrow some anger, she could get plenty more from her sister. "We're all right, Del."

Better than all right. Sharing the intra velum with someone, with Vale, whom she loved and adored more than anyone after they'd been able to peek into each other's minds, had been the most sublime experience of her life.

Gods, she'd never felt so close to anyone before.

"Are you sure?" Adella asked.

Gisele managed to open her eyes again, still holding Vale. The captive mages seemed to be moving a little. The Scourge was a heap in the grass, never to rise again. If the mages in Sarras ever repaired it, it would stand as the Conductor.

Vale looked in her eyes, tired but not broken, so much more than anyone's sacrifice. "I love you," she whispered.

"I love you, too."

"Thank you."

"For what?"

"Showing me what I look like through your eyes."

Gisele hugged her again. "I'll do it every day. I promise."

"With the Conductor, I can show you all my love, too," Vale said in her ear.

Gisele chuckled, her heart full. "Don't let my ego get too big." She finally took a moment to look behind her, not feeling a sense of urgency anymore. The Firellian soldiers were down, though she saw with surprise that most of them appeared to have been taken prisoner, their arms tied behind their backs. Their wounds even had bandages, some of them pink. Serrah Nunez was missing a few layers from her skirt. She had a wound on her arm, too, and a bruise on her shoulder where her dress was torn.

But she also had blood smeared across her rings.

When she met Gisele's eye, she stepped forward and offered a folded square of pink fabric, offering another to Vale.

"Is everyone okay?" Vale asked.

Heads nodded all around, though they weren't without wounds. Cortez had a bandage tied around his thigh; either his old wound had reopened, or he'd managed to get a new one. He rested against Jean-Carlo, who had a swath of pink peeking from where his dalmatica was torn across his chest, and a trickle of blood ran near his temple. Cortez held a bandage to it, and they leaned toward one another, both looking exhausted. Roni had a gash in her side that Bridget tended to while Zara kneeled beside them, the Vox on her shoulder. A few spots of blood decorated the sling on Zara's arm, but Gisele couldn't tell if it was hers or someone else's.

"Has it stopped?" Adella asked.

Gisele couldn't turn her head to look. It was too much effort. "Huh?"

"Your nose?" Adella kneeled, her eyes concerned, and Gisele wanted to be annoyed that Adella seemed more concerned about her bloody nose than anyone's actual wounds.

But she was just too damn tired.

Besides, it didn't seem worth it, not anymore.

Adella took the cloth and helped Gisele and Vale clean their faces. Vale thanked her, then frowned at the captives. "Where is Warrane?"

Everyone glanced around as if Warrane might appear out of thin air. Someone asked the obvious question, "He's not one of these?" but Vale didn't seem to have the energy to say that was why she'd asked.

Jean-Carlo pointed to where the city sat in the distance. A group of cavalry and infantry were headed this way. "They'll find him," Gisele said. "He's on foot, and even if he ran like hell as soon as the tide turned, he can't have gotten far."

Vale bit her lip as if she wasn't sure of that.

Or as if she was worried he might be killed.

"Vale." Gisele shook her head, too tired to say that they couldn't go looking for him to make sure he surrendered peacefully, but she'd seen inside Vale's mind and knew how much it hurt her to do nothing while someone else suffered.

"Come on," Gisele said, pushing to her feet. "We'll help look for him." She looked at Adella. "Would you mind terribly if I leaned on you, Del?"

Adella had the sense to keep her smile small. "Not at all. You're welcome anytime."

Gisele nodded, promising herself that she'd do something nice for Adella when everything was sorted out. Nothing that would go to Adella's head, nothing that would say that Gisele would welcome her help whenever she offered. Just something that said Gisele would try to be slightly less annoyed by her in the future.

Perfect.

❖

Vale wanted to tell Gisele to stay behind, to take the rest they both needed, but more than rest, Vale needed Gisele with her. She needed her love and courage and support, needed her presence.

And after what they'd shared, she wasn't afraid to ask, knew that call would always be answered.

They limped through the sparse woods together. Adella supported Gisele, and Bridget offered her arm to Vale. Zara had apologized for not offering to help, but she wanted to report to her superiors. And the looks she'd cast at Roni said she didn't want to leave her injured love behind, either.

Vale certainly understood that. She would have walked hand in hand with Gisele, but they might have fallen over if one tried to lean on the other. And Bridget seemed strong and supportive and happy to be anywhere Adella was. Vale couldn't feel more comforted by love than if she'd had a blanket woven from it.

And she did feel a little stronger away from the downed mages and the wounded. She'd warned Zara that Franka and a few of the others might be spitting mad when they awoke. Zara had promised to find someone who spoke Othlan to calm her down. Vale could only wish them luck. Hopefully, the Sarrasian soldiers would put them together, so they could see one another when they opened their eyes. Cristobal had marched out to see them, and he could tell the Firellians among them that they had nothing to fear. She wondered idly how many Firellians among them would choose to stay somewhere magic wasn't hated. The others might be invited to stay as guests of the Sarrasians until the current conflict was over.

She'd do her best to convince them to go along with it.

When it came to the Firellian soldiers, Vale didn't know what to think. Bijou had spit at her feet as she'd walked by. She didn't care; it couldn't hurt her. Gisele had muttered darkly, though. Vale tried to resign herself to the fact that she had no say in how the Sarrasians treated their prisoners, but just the fact that they'd been taken prisoner instead of killed gave her hope.

As for Warrane, he would be wise to surrender to the first Sarrasian who found him. Who knew what the other soldiers would do to someone in a Firellian uniform if he didn't halt when ordered?

"Let's take a rest," Gisele called. She leaned against a tree, giving Adella a rest, too.

"Good idea," Bridget said.

Vale stared at her, about to apologize for being a burden, but Bridget didn't seem worn out. Her concerned gaze lingered on Vale. "Thank you," Vale said, leaning against her own tree not far from Gisele. Bridget moved away slightly, joining hands with Adella. Vale closed her eyes and breathed deeply of the crisp spring air and the earthy scent of the forest.

And freedom.

And...sour alcohol?

She swallowed her sigh. She knew that smell, Warrane's smell. She turned her head from side to side, getting a stronger scent from her left, the stench of fear and sweat mingling with the drink.

He was nearby. And afraid.

"I'm going into those bushes," Vale said loudly, pointing behind her tree. "To relieve myself."

The others nodded, Adella adding, "Don't go far."

Gisele rolled her eyes behind Adella's back, but she didn't bother to say something like, "She can take care of herself." Maybe she was finally seeing how nice it felt to have someone care about her.

Vale took a deep breath, pushed off the tree, and walked slowly to a clump of bushes. The scent got stronger, but she wasn't afraid. He might attack her, with magic or his bare hands. She still didn't fear him, remembering how he'd weakened during the fight. He had to want this nightmare to end, too.

And Gisele might have resisted the urge to say that Vale could defend herself, but that didn't make it less true.

Warrane had no power over her now.

When she came around the clump of bushes, he didn't seem surprised. He was sitting, hugging his knees and shaking. He'd gone pale, sweat pouring off him. He was spinning the gold bangle around and around on his wrist and chewing his lip all the way down to the whiskers covering his chin. Tear tracks ran from his bloodshot eyes into his sparse beard, and his fingernails were filthy, as if he'd been clawing at the dirt.

He mouthed her name, barely making a squeak.

How could she have ever found him fearsome?

Vale kneeled in front of him, and he shrank back like a dog with a brutal owner. "It's all right," she said softly. "It's going to be okay." They were the words she'd used with his captives, the Firellian captives, people he'd mocked or kicked or shoved. She'd sensed a distracted air to his brutality, then, thought it showed a lack of caring about the captive mages, about everyone. But after everything, the fruit, the hope that she'd get revenge on her father, even throwing her overboard, she hadn't been able to believe that.

Now, seeing him sitting here crying and powerless and scared, she wondered if he'd treated the captive mages the way he'd been treating himself inside, thinking that all mages were worth the hatred the Firellians heaped on top of them.

"It's all right," she said again, holding out her arms. "It's going to be okay." She had to keep repeating it, had to sit as still as a stone and call back to Gisele and the others and say she was fine and didn't need help. She could have asked them to come. Bridget could probably tackle Warrane and carry him kicking and screaming to justice, but Vale wanted him to cross this line himself, to see if she was right. To her surprise, she didn't want to save him, just wanted to give him a little courage to carry with him.

It felt like a gift to her, too, something she could do for herself and no one else.

After a war of emotions crossed his face, he collapsed into her arms and wept like his very soul was breaking. She held him for his own sake and for hers and for every person who'd ever been a vessel for someone's cruelty.

CHAPTER THIRTY-NINE

Gisele had never felt so relaxed while in the midst of a whirlwind. People seemed to blow in and out of her sight, delivering news or requesting help or just spending time with one another. At least it was a happy whirlwind.

As soon as they handed off Warrane to the military and turned the Conductor over to Serrah Fabiola with its control gem, Gisele and Vale were carried home in a coach that Gisele barely remembered. She only woke up slightly when arriving home. Someone carried her upstairs and put her to bed. She was too tired to say she could climb on her own, even if it wasn't true.

When they put Vale in bed beside her, she didn't care to object to anything.

They next woke up just long enough to bathe, eat, and hear that everyone they cared about was okay, all the prisoners were still being held by the sentinels, and the captive mages were on the mend, even those who were mad as hell.

Like Franka. Cortez reported that she hadn't agreed to calm down until she'd seen Warrane in chains. The sentinels had complied but hadn't been able to catch her before she'd broken his nose.

Vale gasped, compassion personified, but Cortez assured her that Franka had walked away calmly after that and now seemed content to relax in the accommodation the military had provided. Cristobal had apparently asked for her to tell the story more than ten times already.

Gisele would have liked to hear it herself but not as much as she wanted more rest. Luckily, Adella insisted Gisele and Vale take a bit of Gisele's pain tincture, slip back into clean sheets, and sleep.

A day later, Gisele opened her eyes to find Vale smiling at her.

When Vale gave her a passionate kiss, Gisele left the bed only to lock the door.

Later, after they were both curled around each other and breathing hard, coming down from ecstasy, Gisele said, "Well, that's my new favorite way to wake up."

Vale laughed and kissed her, and all seemed right with the world. She and Vale dressed and descended from their room to sit in the warm kitchen, crowding around the table. People came and went, but Gisele felt calm through it all, as if nothing could hurt them while they were under this roof that she and her sisters had worked so hard to keep. Everyone who set foot in it seemed right at home, making it worth every penny.

Zara baked up a storm, setting out new pastries and nibbles along with endless cups of coffee or cocoa or water. Her energy felt a little exhausting, but Gisele couldn't mock anyone who kept putting goodies in front of her.

Serrah Nunez dropped by just after noon dressed in a gown of shimmering peach silk and armed with a bottle of expensive gin. "I've received a note from a certain sergeant," she said. "Inviting me for a real tour of the army base."

"I can give you a tour," Zara said with a frown. "Why—" Roni cut her off, whispering in her ear. "Oh." She frowned. "A sex tour?"

"No," Roni yelped. Her tanned cheeks went a little red. "Not a sex *tour*." She leaned back in to whisper again.

Serrah Nunez threw her head back and laughed. "We live in hope, cupcake." She leaned toward Gisele, her eyes twinkling. "Speaking of romance, guess who's rented my attic room for a few steamy days?"

"Who?" Gisele said, feeling as if she was back in Serrah Nunez's bedroom, gossiping in her pajamas.

"Our nondescript spy and the grumpy uncle."

Gisele's jaw dropped. "I knew it!"

"Who?" Zara asked, her brows drawn in confusion.

"Cortez and Jean-Carlo," Roni explained, looking equally delighted to be in on the secret. "How do you know it was steamy, serrah?" She winked. "Were you listening at the door?"

"Certainly not, treacle, shame on you." Serrah Nunez shrugged one shoulder. "But some noise may have drifted down the hall."

Gisele cackled and clapped. Oh, that was going to make some fine ammunition for later. She'd only seen Jean-Carlo blush once, and she desperately wanted to see it again. And to see Cortez's embarrassed, swallowed-a-live-fish look. There was nothing better.

Roni mashed her hands together as if she might swoon. "Oh gods, I'm going to give Cortez and JC so much shit." She put a hand to her forehead. "I have so many jokes in mind, I'm getting lightheaded." When Zara looked concerned and guided Roni to a seat, Gisele laughed harder.

Only, she hoped Jean-Carlo had let Marcella down easy and had apologized. Otherwise, she was going to give him a Franka fist, as everyone now referred to it. To her satisfaction, Marcella did stop by and confirmed that Jean-Carlo had done the decent thing, no Franka fist needed.

Once Serrah Nunez departed, the sunlight was starting to fade from the kitchen windows. The evening saw only Gisele and Vale, Adella and Bridget, and Zara and Roni in the house, all piling around the kitchen table again.

Zara laid a plate of sticky buns on the table and sank into a chair next to Roni, who kissed her temple. "You're paroled from the oven, babe," Roni said. "I don't think anyone else is coming over tonight."

"And if they are, they can go hungry," Adella said, patting Zara's hand.

Zara nodded and stretched. Gisele couldn't resist saying, "Thank the gods. My arm is getting really tired of dipping sweets into my mug." Even Zara chuckled a little. Maybe Roni's presence was enough for her to understand a joke or two.

"What's the word from the Bastión?" Bridget asked.

Adella chewed while looking up, as if she was lining up the facts in her mind. Ever since the mission to stop the mages had been a success, the Sarrasian government had invited Adella into their halls on a daily basis to get her opinion on what the Firellian Empire might do next. They'd finally seen how important an ex-ambassador's knowledge was, at least acknowledging that she was as good a source of information as Bridget the ex-spy.

"The Firellian government is really pushing this whole 'splinter group' excuse for the incursions and attacks. Apparently, a few rogue military leaders were behind it and will be swiftly dealt with."

Gisele sighed. That seemed like typical government bullshit. "What's Sarras going to do to respond?"

Adella shrugged. "Not much we can do. Demand that the scapegoats be handed over? That might appease those in the Bastión and the citizens calling for war."

"The people in the Haymarket suffered a lot," Roni said. "Even though there haven't been any new mage attacks in a few days, the grief-stricken want payback."

"Sure, but they don't want to march on the empire themselves," Bridget said. "We have to hope they'll be happy that the government has promised to rebuild."

"And with the money our charity can raise," Adella said, "we might be able to do some real good, see actual change."

Roni still frowned. "Haymarket folk are good at making a little go a long way, but unless the government wants riots on their hands, I suggest they work quickly." She looked at Zara. "You don't think the higher-ups will do something stupid like bring the army in to keep the peace, do you?"

"Gods, I hope not," Zara said. "The army should only be used against an enemy."

Gisele agreed. Heads nodded all around the table. Adella pulled out a journal and a pencil that never seemed far from her grasp anymore. "We'll recruit some more medical staff and step up food distribution."

"Um," Vale said quietly.

Everyone went silent. Gisele blinked, too. Vale was a comforting presence that she never forgot, but she hadn't spoken much all day, seemed as content to let everything flow around her as Gisele was. "What is it?" Gisele asked softly, smiling to let her know her opinion was welcome.

"The mages can help," Vale said. She still went a little pink under everyone's stare. "When Marcella stopped by earlier, she said that Serrah Fabiola has made great strides with the Conductor. Mages united in power can clear away rubble quickly or create water by drawing the moisture from the air."

Gisele grinned. Creating water was a devilishly hard task, but if mages could support one another's work through the Conductor, they could halve the time and effort.

"Wonderful," Adella said. "You two can go ask her tomorrow." She lifted her brows at the end as if giving them the option of refusing.

Gisele rolled her eyes. "Of course we will." She wouldn't even complain about being volunteered, one of her new gifts to her sister.

"And there's one more bit of news," Adella said. "There's a rumor going around that I will be reinstated as the ambassador to the Firellian Empire." She smiled and nodded amidst the chorus of congratulations. "And even more astonishing, the Firellians have agreed to let the new ambassador set foot on Firellian soil."

Gisele gawked. The empire was famous for sending ambassadors out to other countries to do their negotiating. They didn't let people in. "You're going to Montagne Noire?" she asked, imagining the capital city, the astounding architecture she'd only read about, the open-air markets and columned promenades. The beauty of the Imperial Gardens was said to bring people to their knees. "Oh, you're so lucky."

Adella popped another bite of pastry into her mouth. "And for the inaugural visit, I can bring an entourage." Her eyes moved slowly around the table. "Let me see, I'll need someone well-versed in Firellian etiquette and espionage." She nodded at Bridget. "Someone from the military as my personal bodyguard." Another nod for Zara. "A member of the Sarrasian intelligence community." One nod for Roni.

Gisele fought the urge to fidget. She knew it was coming, but she could hardly wait.

"And I suppose a couple of mages would be nice."

Gisele whooped and hugged Vale tightly. When she drew back, Vale was smiling, though her eyes were wide as saucers. "I never dreamed I'd get to see it." Gisele had shared a few passages from a book about the empire earlier in the day, a precursor to their reading lessons, which Vale seemed as if she might take to like a fish to water. Seeing her as delighted with herself as Gisele was felt like the rarest of gifts.

Gisele hugged her again, holding her close enough to whisper in her ear. "And on the way, we can collect your siblings."

Vale squeezed her tighter.

"What of your father?" Gisele asked, not wanting to ruin the happiness of the moment, but she had to ask.

Vale snuggled into her neck. "If he hasn't changed, I'll leave him there. He can't hurt me now, not my body or my heart."

Gisele kissed her cheek. "There's always the Franka fist if you change your mind."

Covering her laugh, Vale leaned her head on Gisele's shoulder.

The others were still chatting about the trip to the empire. "I don't know if I'll be welcome there," Bridget said.

"I don't know about that," Adella said, "given that one of the officials we'll be meeting with is Baxter."

Bridget's jaw dropped. "The old spymaster's coming out of the shadows?"

Adella shrugged. "Taking a larger part in the government, perhaps? Who knows, maybe he even designed parts of this invasion plan to fail."

"Gods," Bridget whispered, letting out a long breath. "Well, he'll either hug me or order my arrest."

Zara waved off-handedly. "Don't worry. They'll have to get through all of us to get to you." She said it matter-of-factly, but Bridget ducked her head and smiled all the same. Zara shifted her gaze to Gisele. "Or you. They do still hate mages, after all."

Gisele's ire rose just a tad, but before she could speak, Vale took her hand. "Don't worry. We can take care of ourselves."

Gisele had to kiss her after that, Adella's cry of "Aw," be damned.

"They only have to call me monster one time," Gisele said.

"And you'll show them what a real one is like?" Roni asked.

Gisele touched her forehead to Vale's. "I'll prove them wrong by ignoring them." Vale's answering smile almost knocked her back with its brilliance. "But if they get violent, I might have to singe a few trouser cuffs."

"I'll help you," Vale said. "If that's what it takes to make sure everyone is safe, there won't be an unburned pair in town."

It seemed like Adella didn't even try to contain a squeal of joy. She linked an arm through Bridget's and set her other hand in the middle of the table as if they were all about to take the field in a sporting contest. Zara followed, then Gisele, until everyone at the table had one arm connected to their beloved, and one hand resting atop everyone else's.

A family.

Gisele thought of it as a different kind of magic, one that no pain, or worry, or challenge in the world could break.

About the Author

Barbara Ann Wright writes fantasy and science fiction novels when not hoarding glitter. She has won a Golden Crown Literary Award and has been a finalist in the Foreword Review Book of the Year Awards and the Lambda Literary Awards. Her first novel, *The Pyramid Waltz*, was one of Tor.com's Reviewer's Choice books of 2012 and made BookRiot's 100 Must-Read Sci-Fi Fantasy Novels by Female Authors. *Lady of Stone*, the prequel to *The Pyramid Waltz*, was recommended on Syfy.com. Her work has also won five Rainbow Awards.

Books Available From Bold Strokes Books

A Cutting Deceit by Cathy Dunnell. Undercover cop Athena takes a job at Valeria's hair salon to gather evidence to prove her husband's connections to organized crime. What starts as a tentative friendship quickly turns into a dangerous affair. (978-1-63679-208-8)

As Seen on TV! by CF Frizzell. Despite their objections, TV hosts Ronnie Sharp, a laid-back chef, and paranormal investigator Peyton Stanford have to work together. The public is watching. But joining forces is risky, contemptuous, unnerving, provocative—and ridiculously perfect. (978-1-63679-272-9)

Blood Memory by Sandra Barret. Can vampire Jade Murphy protect her friend from a human stalker and keep her dates with the gorgeous Beth Jenssen without revealing her secrets? (978-1-63679-307-8)

Foolproof by Leigh Hays. For Martine Roberts and Elliot Tillman, friends with benefits isn't a foolproof way to hide from the truth at the heart of an affair. (978-1-63679-184-5)

Glass and Stone by Renee Roman. Jordan must accept that she can't control everything that happens in life, and that includes her wayward heart. (978-1-63679-162-3)

Hard Pressed by Aurora Rey. When rivals Mira Lavigne and Dylan Miller are tapped to co-chair Finger Lakes Cider Week, competition gives way to compromise. But will their sexual chemistry lead to love? (978-1-63679-210-1)

The Laws of Magic by M. Ullrich. Nothing is ever what it seems, especially not in the small town of Bender, Massachusetts, where a witch lives to save lives and avoid love. (978-1-63679-222-4)

The Lonely Hearts Rescue by Morgan Lee Miller, Nell Stark & Missouri Vaun. In this novella collection, a hurricane hits the Gulf Coast, and the animals at the Lonely Hearts Rescue Shelter need love—and so do the humans who adopt them. (978-1-63679-231-6)

The Mage and the Monster by Barbara Ann Wright. Two powerful mages, one committed to magic and one controlled by it, strive to free each other and be together while the countries they serve descend into war. (978-1-63679-190-6)

Truly Wanted by J.J. Hale. Sam must decide if she's willing to risk losing her found family to find her happily ever after. (978-1-63679-333-7)

A Good Chance by Ali Vali. Harry, Desi, and Desi's sister Rachel are so close to getting everything they've ever wanted, but Desi's ex-husband is coming back to get his revenge and rip apart their chance at happiness. (978-1-63679-023-7)

A Perfect Fifth by Jaycie Morrison. Streetwise pianist Zara Keller and Lady Jillian Stansfield couldn't be more different, yet their connection brings a new awareness of who they are and what they truly want in their lives—including each other. (978-1-63679-132-6)

Catching Feelings by Ana Hartnett Reichardt. Andrea Foster expected to catch a lot of pitches from the Alder Lions' star pitcher, Maya, but she didn't expect to catch feelings. (978-1-63679-227-9)

Defiant Hearts by Lee Lynch. In these stories, you'll find your lovers, friends, and lesbians you wish you knew—maybe even yourself. (978-1-63679-237-8)

Love and Duty by Catherine Young. All Princess Roseli wants is to marry her three lovers, but with war looming, she must instead marry Princess Lucia to establish a military alliance between their planets. (978-1-63679-256-9)

Serendipity by Kris Bryant. Serendipity brings jingle writer Annie Foster and celebrity pop star Bristol Baines together, and their undeniable attraction keeps them close, but will their different paths drive them apart? (978-1-63679-224-8)

The Haunted Heart by Jane Kolven. A ghost, a ring, and a quest to find a missing psychic—it's a spell for love. (978-1-63679-245-3)

The Rules of Forever by Nan Campbell. After reconnecting at their high school reunion, Cara and Lauren agree to embark on a textbook definition friends-with-benefits relationship, but trying to keep it uncomplicated is harder than it seems. (978-1-63679-248-4)

Vision of Virtue by Brey Willows. When virtue and desire come together, be prepared for sparks in this next installment of the Memory's Muses series. (978-1-63679-118-0)

The Artist by Sheri Lewis Wohl. Detective Casey Wilson and reclusive artist Tula Crane are drawn together in a web of passion, intrigue, and art that might just hold the key to stopping a killer. (978-1-63679-150-0)

Cherry on Top by Georgia Beers. A chance meeting leaves Cherry and Ellis longing for a different life, but when Ellis's search for truth crashes into Cherry's insta-filter world, do they have any hope at all of a happily ever after? (978-1-63679-158-6)

Love and Other Rare Birds by Angie Williams. Ornithologist Dr. Jamie Martin and park ranger Rowan Fleming are searching the Alaskan wilderness for a bird thought to be extinct, and they're about to discover opposites really do attract. (978-1-63679-108-1)

Parallel Paradise by Mayapee Chowdhury. When their love affair is put to the test by the homophobia of their family, community, and culture, Bindi and Rimli will need to fight for a chance at love. (978-1-63679-203-3)

Perfectly Matched by Toni Logan. A beautiful Cupid named Hannah, a runaway arrow, and just seventy-two hours to fix a mishap that could be the best mistake she has ever made. (978-1-63679-120-3)

Slow Burn by Missouri Vaun. A wounded wildland firefighter from California and a struggling artist find solace and love in a small southern town. (978-1-63679-098-5)

The Inconvenient Heiress by Jane Walsh. An unlikely heiress and a spinster evade the Marriage Mart only to discover true love together. (978-1-63679-173-9)